Praise fo

"Fans of Dan Simmons and Wilbur Sm
his standing within the ring of historical
the sheer brutality of the First World W
becomes only a backdrop to a greater mystery, one of ancient gods and harrowing deeds. One that seizes the reader by the throat and hauls them forward through the pages in a rabid, wild-eyed fervor until either dashing them on the rocks of despair or raising them high in triumph and glory. I won't tell you which, but know that if I could, I would read it fresh a hundred times over."

–William Bolyard, author of *Demons in the Taillights* and *Sober Man's Thoughts*

"Hoover moves at a break-neck pace with the skill of a speed climber. He manages to weave terrifyingly realistic flashes of combat that read like an Ernst Jünger story with a tale of survival among Alpine horrors that rival anything by Dan Simmons or Michelle Paver. *The Sarvàn* cements Hoover as a master of Horror."

–Mac Caltrider, award winning journalist and author of *Double Knot*

"In gritty prose that is both ethereal and raw, Douglass Hoover once again proves why his is a voice to be heard. *The Sarvàn* is a stark and haunting novel that forges myth in the shadow of the Great War. With echoes of the great war writers that came before him, Hoover distills a tincture of horrific realism and surreal violence into a mythic narrative built upon the scaffolding of history. What Hoover has crafted is a window to the old world—where legend and truth intersect to form the archetypes that guide us in bearing witness to man's oldest and most indifferent god: war."

–Kacy Tellessen, Eugene Sledge Award winning author of *Freaks of a Feather: A Marine Grunt's Memoir*

"Hoover is one of the best writers I know… *The Sarvàn* is brilliantly written and meticulously researched and has everything I love: cold mountains, hot frauleins, ancient horror. My only complaint about this book is that it ended (but what an ending)."

–Ben Timberlake, author of *High Risk*

"A multifaceted, genre-blending adventure that dances between genuine history and profoundly satisfying fiction. A new peak for the folk-horror genre."

–Joseph Donnelly

"Hoover once again blurs the line between the snarling beasts of imagination and the savage horrors of reality. *The Sarvàn* stands as an expertly woven tapestry rich with history, excitement, and raw emotion — all of which collide in a brutal and ultimately fulfilling climax that will leave you reeling long after you close the cover."

–Nick Orton, author of *Tales From The Gridsquare* and *The Transcript*

Also by Douglass Hoover:

The North Woods

The Accursed Huntsman

The Homestead

the Sarvàn

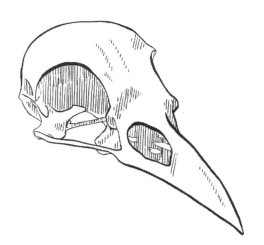

Douglass Hoover

www.douglasshoover.com

This book is a work of fiction. All names, characters, places, and incidents are the product of the author's imagination and/or are used fictitiously. Any resemblance to actual events, locations, or persons, living or dead, are purely coincidental.

If you purchase this book without a cover, you should be aware that this book may have been stolen property and reported as "unsold and destroyed" to the publisher. In such case neither the author nor the publisher has received any payment for this "stripped book."

The copyrighted portions of this book may not be reproduced or transmitted in any form or by any means, electrical or mechanical, including photocopying, recording, or by any information storage and retrieval system, without permission in writing from the publisher.

Published by
BlackPit Publishing
www.blackpitpublishing.com

Copyright © 2025 Douglass Hoover
All rights reserved

ISBN 978-0-9994074-3-1
Printed in the USA

www.douglasshoover.com

For Ella

"Only the dead have seen the end of war."

– George Santayana, 1922

Prologue

France, Spring 1916

THE NIGHT was silent.
Dead silent, Edward Blackwood thought with a defeated smirk. The irony was not lost on him. While he wasn't dead, at least not yet, in that moment he must have seemed it — laying out there in a sea of rotten wood, torn steel, and upturned muck. His breath came shallow and his body remained motionless even as the rats scrambled down the ridge of his spine and tickled his face with their long whiskers. Even as they began to nibble at his flesh with their jagged little teeth.

The world around him was an inky black. This was *true night*, as his grandfather used to call it. The moon was absent and the stars were shrouded by roiling thunderheads that threatened to douse the soggy trenches below at any moment. Aside from the sporadic beams of spotlights that knifed out from the German lines ahead, this was as dark as the world under the open skies could get.

There was a sour knot deep down in Blackwood's belly. It had been there for hours, growing steadily through his painstaking slop across No Man's Land. As he had slithered through the briny muck, the knot had similarly slithered its way through his intestines, wrapping itself around his nerves and squeezing ever tighter, vying desperately to steal his attention from the critical task at hand. It was not fear. He knew fear well enough by now. Fear was something he could control. Something he could suppress. This was something else entirely. Something stronger. Something he was, until now, unfamiliar with.

It was the undeniable certainty of his impending death.

There would be no return for him this time. If he were to see the sunrise, it would only be at the behest of whatever cruel devil governed these European wastelands — a true miracle born from the bloody chaos and violence he'd been crawling toward since nightfall. But there were no miracles in this war. There was only cold, merciless death.

A nagging voice spoke up from the back of his mind. It whispered to turn back. To live to fight another day. To lie to his commanders and say that he had been spotted by a sniper or machinegun nest and had barely escaped with his life. He smothered the craven thought in its cradle. He had *volunteered* for this mission, he reminded himself. And they had never lied to him about what it was: a suicide mission, through and through. Even the officers had admitted it with burnt-out eyes and solemn brows. Someone had to do it, he'd told them with a straight face, why not him? What was so precious that he had to lose?

The answer was nothing.

If he were to turn back now, retreat through the sea of festering bodies and splintered stumps, it would make him a coward. A coward whose weakness would come at the cost of countless lives — the lives of brothers and sons, fathers and uncles. Of the men he'd fought shoulder-to-shoulder with for over a year now. Men he'd come to see as family, despite his own callous inability to express it.

In short time, the call would go up along the Canadian lines. His brethren would rise to the call, sprinting headfirst across that vast expanse of No Man's Land. If the German machinegun emplacements were still operating at that point, those men would be cut down like wheat to the scythe.

The machineguns *had* to be destroyed.

That was his mission. That's why there was only forward for him now, into the lion's den. And as for what waited for him there… perhaps glory, he thought ruefully. Perhaps salvation. Perhaps only blood and horror. He knew his odds leaned drastically toward the latter, but still, those were the dice he'd chosen to roll.

Blackwood closed his eyes to the darkness, inhaling the stench of fetid death and churned earth. He let his worries fade, centering himself and focusing on the one thought that had carried him this far through the hellfire that burned along the front lines of the Great War. It was the one great epiphany that had allowed him to keep going for so long, to keep volunteering, pushing, slaughtering, surviving…

It's all nothing, he repeated to himself silently. *There is no God. There is no judgement. The only thing to fear is death. And when death takes you, you won't even be around anymore to give a damn.*

From the German lines to the north came a distant pop. The insides of Blackwood's crimped eyelids lit up with the dullest of orange hues. One of his two companions, both of whom huddled in the mud behind him, let out a whimper. Blackwood ignored it, keeping his eyes cinched shut — he would not allow the flare to blind him to the night. Its phosphorus load hissed somewhere far down the stretch of No Man's Land. Then the distant *rat-at-at* of a machinegun rang out as it arched its rounds over the muddy wasteland.

As the orange hue faded another flare came, this one just overhead. He shoved his face down, pressing into the mud as he prayed that their concealment was adequate. Seven long seconds passed before the flare above burned out with a sizzle. The darkness returned. No machinegun fire followed.

Good.

They had not been seen.

He opened his eyes once more to the blackness. In one hand he clenched the rough wood of a trench club — a discarded wagon spindle fashioned at the tip with a jagged strapping of steel. With the other hand he clawed at the mud ahead, worming his fingers through the slime and hauling himself forward ever so slowly.

Inch by inch they slithered onward as time seemed to lose shape in the vacuum of war. Behind him, his two companions trailed silently.

"*Ich habe letzte Nacht von meiner Frau geträumt,*" a voice came from ahead. "*Sie war traurig, ich glaube, ich wurde getötet.*"

Blackwood stilled. He didn't look up, gauging their distance solely by ear. A second voice responded, and together the two Germans laughed.

Blackwood was fluent in the language of his enemy. He'd learned it from his grandfather after being dumped on the old man's doorstep in Montana as a child. He knew these soldiers were jabbering about their lives back home, as men tend to do during the boring lulls. But it wasn't their words that mattered to Blackwood. It was their tone. Their voices were steady with the subtle highs and lows that relayed the relaxed, almost giddy demeanor of unseasoned soldiers.

He tilted his head, letting one side of his face sink against the earth. Keeping one eye shut, he directed the men behind him toward the voices. Then he lay still, listening and waiting patiently for the next flare.

"*I dreamt last night of Hilde, of her carrot stew,*" one of the German soldiers said. His voice carried a boyish lilt.

The other soldier stifled a laugh. He sounded older, maybe even old. "*You miss other things about her too, I imagine. A pair of them, ya?*"

The first soldier's retort was cut off by the hiss of a flare. The night lit up, and through his one open eye Blackwood took in the scene before him. Twenty meters ahead, maybe less, was a short break in the rows of crossed beams and barbed wire. A pair of spiked helmets gave away the two sentries hunched behind a low sandbag parapet.

One helmet tilted toward the flare above. "*You know, it's odd,*" the younger voice mused. "*I never thought I would find beauty in a place like this. But the way they dance up there in the sky, like spirits looking down on us…*"

The helmet jolted from a light smack. "*Do not look at it, you fool. How do you expect to see the damn enemy coming if you're blind to the darkness?*"

The flare gazer slouched lower, his helmet dropping below sight. He muttered a bashful apology as the flare sizzled out and sheer darkness reigned once again.

"Now," Blackwood breathed. His heart had begun to pound, and he embraced the electric surge of adrenaline as it dumped into his veins. Opening the eye that still favored the darkness, he rose from the muck into a low crouch. His feet moved in fluid kicks to avoid the distinct suctioning of mud under his boots as he glided forward and, with his free hand, he drew the curved knife that hung from his belt.

"*Bah, she's too good for you—*" the older German joked. His next words were cut off by a dumbfounded gasp as Blackwood slipped over the parapet and dropped between them. Before he could gather the breath to scream, the club had dented his helmet and caved in the side of his skull with a horrible *thwack*.

Blackwood released the club to fall alongside the sentry's body. He spun and drove forward into the younger man, the flare gazer. The boy was slight, and the force of Blackwood's violent body check pinned him against the duckboards and drove the breath from his lungs. Blackwood clamped a rough palm over the German's jaw, stifling his gasping mouth. He thrust upward with the knife. The blade slid through the thick wool of the German's coat and into the soft flesh of his belly. Blackwood buried the blade to the hilt and wrenched it upward in search of lungs and heart as the boy convulsed in his grip.

The sky erupted into light as another flare sizzled to life overhead. The boy gawked, a look of sheer horror playing out across his gentle features. He was young, far younger than Blackwood's own thirty years. His cheeks were smooth beneath Blackwood's rough fingers. Smooth enough to have not yet felt the cold touch of a razor. Soft brown eyes bulged from his skull, and his tears cut lines in the filth that coated Blackwood's hand. Hot blood soaked through the wool and spilled over the knife's hilt, bathing Blackwood's wrist.

Together they stood there, locked in the deadly embrace for the entirety of the flare's short lifespan. As the light above petered away, so did the life from the boy's eyes. Blackwood forced himself to watch as they glassed over and rolled back. A profound feeling of revulsion filled his belly — not for the poor boy dying in his grip, but for himself. He swallowed the bile that was suddenly in his throat, sending the feeling down with it — burying it deep in the uncharted depths of his soul.

As the darkness returned the boy sucked in a final, wet gasp against Blackwood's palm. His legs gave out and he slid down the uneven wooden planks of the trench wall, dropping away from the wicked knife like discarded meat. Blackwood wiped the blade clean on his pants as he watched the cadaver convulse in the darkness. It was a dirty business, he reminded himself. A dirty, rotten business for dirty, rotten men.

Men like himself.

Two shadows slipped over the parapet and into the sentry post beside him.

"Give me his rifle." Blackwood's voice was barely more than a whisper. One of the men nodded, seizing the dead German's Gewehr and passing it to him. He weighed the weapon in his hand before testing the edge of the bayonet that stretched out from its barrel.

His subordinates huddled close, awaiting his go-ahead. Cold sweat had begun to dislodge the mud caked on his brow. He swiped it away. "You know what to do. Be silent. If the alarm is raised, launch your flares."

The men nodded in unison. He did not wish them good luck. It would be a useless gesture at this point. Luck would not dictate their success, only ferocity.

He sent the others right, to the south. After a turkey peek around the corner, they were off. Blackwood watched them go. He checked that the rifle was chambered before peeling out northward along the opposite path of the winding trench.

The German earthworks were wide, at least wider than the meager Allied trenches Blackwood had come to call home. The Germans had proven themselves to be the superior engineers in this sick new style of warfare. While the Allied trenches were often little more than poorly reinforced ditches, the Germans had a knack for burrowing like badgers. In this way they had created a maze of death — it was not rare for a small alcove to open up to a deep bunker filled with the bloodthirsty bastards.

In the darkness he could only make out the vaguest of shadows between the two high earthen walls. He skulked around the crates and munitions, listening and pausing at any hint of movement. A flare went up down the line, and in its flitting light he spotted an inlet. Just as he saw it, a pair of voices came from around the bend ahead. He darted forward, slipping into the alcove and almost stumbling over the form of a German soldier reclined against a crate. Blackwood brought the bayonet to bear, but the soldier was still. Gentle snores emanated from his lips.

To kill a man in his sleep was wicked. A sin. One of the few sins of the battlefield that Blackwood had yet to indulge. Even despite the urgency of his mission, he had no plans to break that streak now. He pressed into the darkest corner of the alcove and lowered the rifle.

The roaming duo approached, meandering along and muttering to each other in German. Blackwood slowed his breath and shut his eyes, listening to their movements and waiting for a pause in their speech or a hitch in their step.

There is no God. There is no judgement. The only thing to fear is death. And when death takes you, you won't even be around anymore to give a damn.

The soldiers passed without incident, paying no heed to their companion snoring in his inlet. What little relief he felt was short-lived. They would continue on and no doubt find the slain bodies of the other sentries in short time. He had much work to do and little time to do it. Inching out of the alcove, he watched as they disappeared around the next bend.

The machinegun bunkers were constructed much like the sentry post: a solid platform elevated two steps above the rest of the trench. This allowed the two-man gun team that manned it to stand with their heads at ground level. Sandbags lined the outer edges, opening up just a few inches to allow the gun's barrel to freely scan the stretch of No Man's Land before it. Neither of the men manning the first gun heard Blackwood approach. They weren't aware of his presence as he slipped up the steps behind them. The man behind the gun didn't even notice as Blackwood rammed the curved knife through the base of his companion's skull. If Blackwood had disappeared in that moment and that gunner had lived, he would likely have told the story of the midnight phantom that had killed his friend. But he didn't live, as Blackwood slipped a garrot over his helmet and yanked it tight around his throat. The thin wire burrowed into flesh before biting through. Blood sprayed out over the machinegun in rhythm with his slowing heart. Like the others, he died silently.

Blackwood lowered the body gently to the ground. He wasted no time pulling one of the half dozen mines from the satchel slung across his back and kicking a shallow impression in the mud. He emplaced the mine just beneath the gun, covering it lightly and pulling the pin to arm it.

Their mission was simple: mine the machinegun emplacements — as many as possible, at least. If they were to blow the guns immediately, it would draw the sleeping Germans to bear. Such an action would be supremely foolish. If — really *when* — they were caught, their last action would be to signal the Allied attack with a red flare from the pistol clipped to his side. In theory, the mad rush of rising Germans would detonate their own gun nests, giving the Canadian Regiment the chance to break their lines without the insurmountable obstacle of machinegun volleys to stop them. It wasn't the strongest plan, but the brass had insisted that desperate times called for desperate measures.

The next machinegun nest was close, and by the time he had emplaced the mine between two more corpses, Blackwood found himself in shock that neither he nor his companions had yet raised the alarm. Whatever company of Germans it was that held this section of the trench was clearly inexperienced to the utmost degree. Those he'd already killed were a mix of the oddly old and far too young. Fresh recruits, he imagined. Or even some reserve element pulled in by the desperate German command, men bound to die before they'd ever fired a shot. *Poor bastards*, Blackwood couldn't help but think with a grimace as he kicked dirt over the mine.

Had he not been caught in his own musings he might have noticed the creak of a hinge behind him.

"*Alarm...*" came a quavering voice.

Blackwood spun. A doorway hung open on the opposite side of the trench. In its blackened threshold stood an old man. A streak of white ran through the black of his hair, and his uniform was disheveled, clearly just donned. Blackwood might have charged, but the German was just out of reach of the bayonet. He'd known going in that a single shot might not raise the alarm, but he'd hoped to avoid gunplay at all costs. With no other options, he raised the rifle. As the sights leveled over the old man, the darkness behind him ignited in the pale-yellow radiance of a bulb, illuminating dozens of wooden racks packed thick with slumbering soldiers.

It was a barracks bunker.

"*Alarm!*" The old man found his voice, his stuttering call becoming a shout. "*Alarm! To arms—*"

The rifle bucked and the old man gasped and crumpled. It was too late. Inside, the soldiers awoke with a start. They yanked free of their sheets and dove from their racks, shouting and scrambling for their weapons.

There was no conscious thought that went into what happened next. Blackwood, fueled purely by instinct, seized the machinegun from its emplacement. Despite its immense weight, it felt light in that panic-fueled moment. Water sloshed in its barrel as he turned on the stunned and groggy young faces that stared back at him in disbelief. He yanked the trigger.

Blinding bursts of flame and deafening thunder erupted from the barrel. Wooden racks exploded to splinters and half-dressed men staggered and screamed as bullets ripped through them. The bulb exploded into sparks. In the sudden darkness, all that illuminated the carnage was the strobe-like flash of the machinegun as it cast the doomed men inside in a spastic dance of death. Those still in their racks thrashed, and white sheets erupted red as Blackwood wrestled the bucking gun. The water-cooled barrel began to burn in his hand as the belt of ammunition slithered ever more into the roaring weapon.

By the time the machinegun clicked empty, only ringing remained in Blackwood's ears. The last of the screams had died alongside the men who had issued them.

Somewhere down the line a German shouted. The glow of electric torches appeared as men roused and rushed to understand the sounds of chaos. The machinegun clattered to the duckboards at Blackwood's feet, its barrel pouring a heavy cloud of steam. He struggled to rip free the flare pistol at his side. Pointing it toward the heavens, he pulled the trigger. It snapped backwards in his hand, then the flare popped above, casting the scene before him in a gloomy red hue.

The old man's body lay at the mouth of the darkness. He was still alive, his hand weakly grasping at the air and his teeth bared in anguish. An impossibly thick torrent of blood cascaded out over the threshold beneath him as he let out a weak cry. It was a scene fit only for hell.

Blackwood collapsed back against the crates of ammo. *They're coming!* the voice of reason screamed in the back of his brain. *They're coming to slaughter you! Run, idiot! Run!*

Yet somehow he felt no urgency at all. He'd done things before, horrible things in the name of war. But this was somehow different. It was as if he had broken past some barrier of wickedness that had finally damned him beyond all else. His body was heavy, and even the thought of his own demise seemed inconsequential in that moment.

From somewhere deep inside the bunker, another man — another victim of his merciless rage — cried out weakly for his mother. Blackwood felt the hot tears begin to flow from his eyes.

From the Allied lines to the west came a series of hollow booms. He barely comprehended them. In that moment, they mattered just as little to him as the Germans rushing down the trench to kill him. Nothing mattered. Not the war, the men, the medals. It was as if the growing void in his chest had swallowed up every reason he had to keep going on.

It wasn't until the shrill cacophony of whistles sounded down the German line that he realized what was happening.

"What?" he muttered, the daze beginning to break. He stood and stared back out over the span between the trenches. "You were supposed to charge. What the hell are you—"

His voice was cut off by the shriek of artillery overhead. A thunderous crash echoed down the line and the earth shook. Then came another, and another. Blackwood stumbled backwards as the blinding explosions vomited waves of churned earth and dazzling sparks.

He didn't register the impact as a shell struck just beside the machinegun nest he occupied, nor did he feel the heat or even the violent shockwave that launched his body hard against the duckboards. The only thing he felt was the searing pain of shrapnel ripping through the flesh above his left eye. Then there was blackness.

PART ONE

Excerpt from *World at War: One Canadian Soldier's Journey from Damnation to Redemption* by Charlie Tremble, 1963

Heraclitus once said about soldiers in war: 'Out of every one-hundred men, ten shouldn't even be there, eighty are just targets, nine are the real fighters, and we're lucky for them, for they make the battle. But the one, one is a warrior, and he will bring the others back.'

For our unit, this one was an American of all people. I'll probably get walloped for admitting such a thing, but it's the truth. I didn't know him too well — don't know if any of us did. He was a quiet fella, the type that liked to keep to himself. He seemed regular enough when he first came to us. At least until Ypres. That's when he earned his nickname from the French: Le Bête. The Beast, they called him. I'll tell you, he earned that moniker the rough way. There's plenty of graves been filled by that fella's hands over there in that horrid place.

After Ypres he was always on the front lines, volunteering again and again for the worst of the worst. It was like he wanted to die but no one had the stones to kill him. After a certain point, the rumor started that God himself had some stake in this fella's survival. Or maybe even the devil.

'Course we were all proven wrong. In the end, the Germans got him. He went off one night on a raid that went sideways. None of us ever saw him again after that. To be honest, after all I'd seen, I was shocked by it. I was one of the ones who didn't think he could be killed, the way he'd carried on. In the end, I suppose it just goes to show the one universal truth of war — death doesn't discriminate, no matter who you are.

1

December, 1916

A LONE honeybee floated through the rural forests of northern Bavaria. She wove deftly between bristling pine boughs and jagged birch branches, soaking in the dappled sunlight that leaked through the canopy above.

If someone were to have spotted that bee out there alone on that cold day in early December, they might have imagined her mad. They might have thought her hive had been toppled by a bear, or that she had been cast out of her colony due to some unknown malady. By all rights she shouldn't have been there. She should have been tucked away tight alongside the teeming horde of her family, slumbering peacefully as she awaited winter's end.

But there had been no bear, and there had been no malady. Early that morning, this bee had abandoned the safety and comfort of her home and flown for miles through the frigid air, drawn away by the irresistible beckon of some invisible trail.

Her path led her down a road that ran like a scar through the heart of the forest. When her wings grew weary, she stopped to rest on one of the emaciated corpses that dangled from the branches. The corpse she chose hung naked and half frozen. It had been a man once, and despite the way his withered skin clung to his ribs, his stomach had begun to bloat. This gave him the ironic façade of a fullness that he hadn't actually felt in months, perhaps even years before his recent death. The bee crawled over his sunken cheeks and broken nose, searching for a ridge to rest her weary body upon. She settled on the bottom lid of a half open eye. The shriveled cornea watched her with an empty stare, but she didn't seem to mind as she set to work cleaning herself in the warmth of the sun.

A bitter wind blew in from the east. It carried with it the sour stench of sweat and blood, of cordite and burnt oil. Beneath the bouquet of misery was another scent, far more subtle than the rest. It was the very thing that had drawn the bee so far from her natural cycle — a faint, nearly indecipherable sweetness that tinged the air.

 The branch above creaked in the wind and the bee set off once more, buzzing a quick circle around the swaying body before leaving it behind. She continued down the road, passing through the alley of dead men that swayed on either side. She didn't notice them, focused solely on that subtle, sweet odor. It spoke to a part of her being that had never before been engaged. Something unfathomably compulsive that hummed with urgency.

 Soon she came to a tall stone wall crowned in an intertwining mesh of dead vines and barbed wire. She flew low over the shallow moat of mud that ran along its perimeter, flitting her tiny antennae as the scent grew stronger. Ahead was a gate. She slipped through the rust-spackled bars and between the handful of grey uniformed men that idled just inside. The air reverberated with sounds of pain and toil. Keeping to the shadows of loosely stitched tents, she passed over sunken planks and haggard prisoners. Once more she wanted to rest, if only for a moment. The cold stung and her wings felt numb. But the sweet scent was strong now, strong enough to drive her into a fervor.

 The scent was intense as she emerged over a hard-packed work yard. So intense that it was dizzying. Euphoric, even. She reveled in it, weaving a pattern above the sorry looking men who kicked up motes of dust as they labored under the winter sun.

 Whatever she was looking for, it was here.

∽

 Edward Blackwood didn't notice as the bee darted closer and closer. Tedium and exhaustion had beaten his mind numb to such trivial things. All he could take in was the din of work and the shouts of the guards perched high in their watch towers. Their words were mocking and cruel, harsh insults hurled with impunity at the slowly dying men below.

 He should have been used to it by now, should have grown thick enough skin to disregard their degrading harassment. After seven months in this hellhole most men would have accepted just about anything with apathy — especially death. But not Blackwood. The endless taunts served only to fuel the fire that burned deep in his belly. He would not allow Rothenspring to break him.

Most German prisoner of war camps dotted the lands just beyond the trenches. Not Rothenspring. Rothenspring was a great distance from the Western Front — closer to Austria-Hungary than it was to France. There was good reason for this: Rothenspring was a camp that did not exist. At least, not officially. It was a place where the rules of war did not apply and where the Red Cross was not welcome. Despite the German Empire's attempts to conceal this disgraceful cesspool of torture and death, Rothenspring's reputation had woven its way through the whispers of both Allied forces and the Germans alike. To the Germans, it was *Der Zorn des Kaisers,* or *The Kaiser's Wrath.* A befitting title considering that it had been erected as a place of punishment for the Empire's most despised enemies. The Allies had come up with their own, more blunt name for it: *The Bleak Death.* It was a place of desperation and horror for those unfortunate enough to be condemned to it. Spies, night raiders, the Allied elite, even a few intelligence officers who preferred not to share their secrets. Rothenspring was home to all types — the final destination for those who were deemed to have earned their place amongst the walking dead. What happened behind those old stone walls wasn't about war, it was about vengeance.

Blackwood wiped the sweat from his brow, his fingers brushing against the raised flesh of the X-shaped scar that hung over his left eye — a reminder of the night of his capture. Across the yard a guard barked. Blackwood heaved the sledgehammer in response, bringing it down hard. The resulting impact sent a shudder through his arms. He ignored the vibrating pain, repeating the motion again, and again. The hulking stone before him chipped away bit by bit. He knew it didn't matter — even if he were to shatter it into a thousand tiny pieces, there would be another stone, and another, until the end of time.

The men around him were ragged. Many had been there far longer than he had, and most had broken far sooner. The nearest of them, a frail looking man with the scant scrub of a beard, had begun to slow. His boulder looked much like it had at dawn and only a few small chips littered the earth at his feet. He was younger than Blackwood, though by how many years was impossible to know. After enough time in Rothenspring, even the most youthful of men appeared ancient. His face was weathered and arms thin, his filth-mottled skin clinging tight to his bones. Each strike of his hammer came steadily weaker and more erratic. A grimace showed with each heft, and after only a few more, the hammer slipped from his grasp and he collapsed with a weak moan.

"*Stand up!*" a passing guard commanded in German.

The prisoner tried to obey, but he couldn't find his legs.

"*What is it, another one?*" a rasping voice came from across the yard. It was a voice that Blackwood had come to know well, one that belonged to a particularly nasty Unteroffizier named Klaus. He was one of the camp's lower-level overseers, a rabid pack leader amongst the gang of sharp-toothed curs. His stubby form emerged from the throng of laboring prisoners, a cruel grin spread across his face. The winter sun glinted off his bald head, accentuating a jagged scar that ran ear-to-ear across the back of his skill. His foul smile squished his already podgy features, somehow making his moonlike face appear even rounder. "*Stand up, swine!*"

Blackwood lowered his hammer and tried to help the man to his feet.

"*Get back!*" Klaus jabbed his rifle toward Blackwood as he approached. Blackwood obeyed, stepping back to resume his work.

Klaus approached slowly. His head tilted as he regarded his prey. "*You do not want to work, is that it, swine?*"

The prisoner stared at the dirt between his hands. He was still, his breath weak. Even if he could have understood the German's language, he was too far gone to respond.

"*If you cannot work, you have no use. Do you understand?*" Klaus's fingers brushed absently along the bolt of his rifle as if it was the strings of a mandolin. "*Are you too lazy to live?*"

Still, the prisoner did not respond. Blackwood hefted his sledgehammer, imagining its rough iron head pulverizing the brutish guard's skull. It was as fruitless a fantasy as taking a swig of cold beer. He knew he couldn't make it more than two of the ten steps that separated him from the stumpy bastard before the horde of snickering guards would cut him down.

"*Very well.*" Klaus shook his head, walking in a slow circle around the downed prisoner. "*Maybe you just need a break. Let him have his break, he clearly needs it!*" the German goaded, drawing a symphony of sniggers from his underlings.

He passed closer to Blackwood. Close enough for Blackwood to once more consider the hammer.

The prisoner muttered something. It was in French, a language that Blackwood could not understand even if he had heard it clearly.

"*You sound like a frog with shit caught in its throat. Are those your last words, swine? Some weak croaks?*"

The man began to sob, heavy, gasping sobs that raked his body and filled the air with his misery. Klaus's deep chuckle nearly drowned him out.

A gunshot split the air, echoing across the yard.

Blackwood shut his eyes. For a brief moment, Rothenspring was dead silent. Then, slowly, the sounds of work began again. Soon it was as if nothing had happened. When Blackwood glanced back, the man's bone-thin body lay prostrate. A gelatinous hunk of his brain hung from a gaping hole in his skull. One of his legs still twitched.

"*I'd say we grind him and toss him in with their dinner,*" Klaus called over the ruckus of work. "*But they don't deserve the meat!*"

The other guards laughed, some with light snickers, others uproariously enjoying their leader's antics. Blackwood's eyes bored into the shiny cap of his skull. His grip tightened around the thick wooden handle and he felt himself giving in to the urge.

Just as he began to turn, a jolt of pain came from the back of his neck. The hammer slid out of his hands as he slapped instinctively at its source. Something small and fuzzy crunched between his fingers.

Klaus's head snapped toward him at the sudden movement. His meaty hands fumbled to recycle the rifle's bolt. "*Is it your day to die too?*" he spat, raising the barrel.

Blackwood said nothing. Slowly, he held out his hand, exhibiting the dead bee for Klaus to see. He didn't bother with words. As far as anyone here knew he only spoke English, a language they couldn't understand. Klaus approached, his hackles raised and rifle leveled. He glanced to the bee for only a second before slapping it away. Blackwood didn't look away, instead glaring back at him.

Above the yard a door clacked open. The camp's commander, Captain Schneider, stepped out onto the second story balcony of the camp's logistical office. He was a sloppy-looking man. His uniform maintained a permanently disheveled state that barely contained his drooping gut, giving him the appearance of an unevenly burnt candle. He searched the yard for the source of the commotion. When his eyes found the still twitching body, he gave a disinterested sniffle. Blackwood might not have paid this interruption any heed had it not been for the man who emerged beside the Captain. It was another officer. From the look of his pressed trench coat he was a newcomer to the quagmire of Rothenspring. In contrast to the commander, this man was well built and his features sharp. While Captain Schnieder returned to the comforts of his office, this new officer remained on the balcony, eyes locked on the fresh corpse.

"*Back to work, swine!*" Klaus roared, his face close enough for Blackwood to smell the stink of his breath and feel the droplets of flying spittle.

Blackwood nursed the sore lump on his neck as he retrieved his hammer from the dirt. Klaus trudged away, leaving the body where it would likely lie until he grew sick of its stench. Blackwood gave the dead bee on the ground one final glance before resuming his toiling. He found himself caught in the irony — might Klaus have been more respectful of the little creature had he known that it had just saved his worthless life?

It was nearly dark when the work whistle sounded. Blackwood's shoulders ached as he tossed his hammer in a cart alongside the others. Many of the boulders were gone now, including his own. At dawn he knew he would return here, only with a shovel instead of a hammer to load the endless heaps of crushed rock onto trucks to be transported to the Front. Or maybe it would just be dumped outside of the gate. He didn't know. He didn't care.

In between the work yard and the series of ragged two-hundred-man barracks tents stood the cafeteria shack. It was little more than a three-sided hovel of rough wooden walls standing over a table laden with their evening rations. Blackwood fell into the rows of slumped shoulders and haggard faces.

A man caked in mud covertly maneuvered his way back through the line until he stood in front of Blackwood. "It's there. Same one as you said it would be," he said without looking back. His name was Dickie, and he was Blackwood's only friend in this wicked place.

"Be quiet," Blackwood breathed. "Not here."

None of the prisoners immediately surrounding them showed any sign of interest in their mutterings. They each maintained a dead-eyed stare through the man before them, lost in their own pain. Even so, it wasn't worth the risk to speak in the open.

When Blackwood made it to the serving table, he took one of the dirty tin mugs from a pile and held it out. The prisoner doling out rations didn't bother to look up as he slopped a paltry ladleful of sauerkraut inside. On top of it he plopped a ration of mildewy black bread only half the size of a man's palm. Blackwood took his food — the only food he would have to sustain him until the next evening — without a word. He made for the outer edge of the crowd of men seated in the dirt. Dickie followed him. Only once Blackwood had found a spot away from the others did they sit.

"You were right," Dickie began. "It's a culvert. They took me out for lumber duty today. I f-faked a trip, fell into the ditch outside the gate like we talked about. Managed to get good eyes on it." Dickie's eager grin showed off a metal cap. He was an American, like Blackwood. Only while Blackwood had gone north to sign on with the Canadians, Dickie had sailed east to enlist with the British. At this point it didn't much matter who they'd fought for. They were both considered outsiders among the Europeans — prisoners and guards alike.

"Good," Blackwood muttered, shoving down the acrid sauerkraut. It tasted like it had turned, but he swallowed it all the same.

"There was light coming through the other side, m-must be that drain grate behind the shitters — has to be. We've looked this place up and down, where else do you see a s-spot that culvert could end?"

Blackwood nodded, his eyes trailing the guards as they milled about.

"We're r-ready then, eh?" Dickie was trying to sound calm, but his stutter betrayed his anxiety.

Again, Blackwood nodded. "Tonight. There won't be much moon. With any luck we'll get some cloud cover too."

Dickie flashed a nervous glance toward the line of latrines across camp. It was a long distance from the barracks tents, a lot of open ground. Blackwood could sense the flurry of mental calculations in his friend's head.

"You sure we can g-get all that way without being caught?"

Blackwood chewed the black bread and shrugged. "Only one way to find out."

2

IT WAS black inside the barracks tent. A cold breeze leaked through a tear in the canvas just above Blackwood's head. He nestled further into the damp straw that served as his bedding. Waiting. Listening.

A bell rang in the distance signaling the guards' shift change. Silently, he began to count down from one thousand. The changeover would take less time than that, but he didn't want to be caught by some guard who was meandering off to take a piss before bed. The new shift would be groggy after having just been woken, less alert and more eager to slack off on their patrols.

Finally, his countdown ended. The guards would be settled into their posts by now, bleary-eyed and cursing the cold. He tried his best to mute his buzzing nerves as he thought over what was to come next. Their plan was solid. At least as solid as a plan as stupid as this could be. There was no other choice — risk death tonight or roll the dice between starvation and murder over the coming winter. He reached out and gently shook Dickie awake.

"It's time."

Dickie didn't respond. Blackwood could feel his friend's shoulder trembling in his grasp. Whether it was from anxiety, fear, the cold, or a combination of all three, it didn't matter. The time had come.

Blackwood snaked his hand underneath the wet canvas and through the mud until it closed with a squelch around a tent stake outside. It pulled free easily enough — he'd been loosening its grip in the earth every night for a week. Free of its tether, the canvas loosened just enough for him to slither underneath.

A frigid rain dappled Blackwood's shoulders as he emerged into the night. He waited for Dickie, hauling him free as he birthed from the mud. Together they set off. Their first stop was a burnt-out fire pit just to the fore of the barracks tents. They crouched low and moved with as much stealth as the soggy earth would allow. The rain had turned the ashes into a thick charcoal paste. They rubbed it over their exposed skin until their faces and hands matched the dark grime of their uniforms. Each of them had torn away the light brown arm bands that had been stitched on their upper sleeves — identifiers sewn there by the Germans. Without them, their filthy black pants and coats left them as little more than shadows in the dark.

By day they had mapped out the path to the latrines. Now, creeping cover to cover in the darkness, their path was far less certain. Blackwood carried the narrow steel tent stake at his side. He would need it to pry open the grate, but he also knew he could use it to take a man's life in a pinch.

When they made it to the edge of the final barracks tent, they found themselves staring out over the wide-open work yard.

"They're lazy," Blackwood had told Dickie days before. "They won't patrol as regularly as they should. One good opening, and we're there."

Now he prayed that his words had been true.

Minutes passed. The only guards visible stood in a tower overlooking the front gate. Their searchlight creaked in its bracket as they scanned the woods beyond the wall.

"I'll go first," Blackwood breathed. He eyed a lone cart that sat thirty yards away. It was their sole cover in the sprawling work yard, and it was barely big enough to crawl underneath. Even so, it was better than nothing.

"Now," he whispered, more to himself than to Dickie. He took off in a stooped sprint. His heart hammered in his chest as he barreled forward, lifting his feet high and rolling them heel-to-toe as they slapped in the muck. His focus went to his peripheries, searching for any sign of movement in the darkness.

Something shifted to his right. He barely had time to slide under the cart before a guard emerged from the shadows of the tower. Blackwood finagled between the cart's wheels, yanking his legs into a tight embrace.

"*Are you good up there?*" the guard called up to the tower.

"*Ya,*" an annoyed voice answered. "*Did you bring coffee?*"

"*No. We're out.*"

The guard in the tower gave a disappointed grunt. "*What good are you anyways?*"

Blackwood grimaced as his thigh began to cramp. He bore the pain in silence.

"*Hey, Hanz!*" a second guard in the tower called out.

"*Ya?*" the patrolling guard called back.

"*Fuck you.*"

The guard below, Hanz, didn't respond. His boots *schlopped* in the mud as he meandered away. Blackwood waited, counting to thirty before emerging from under the small cart and massaging away the cramp.

That last stretch was the most nerve-racking, but it was only forward now. Broken stones littered the ground and crunched under his feet. He had underestimated how loud they would be, and at least twice he was sure he was done for. Somehow no alarm sounded, and no spotlight shone over him. Through some miracle he managed to reach the outhouses and squeeze between them. On the other side he searched the ground for the drain grate that would lead to their freedom. When he found it, he let out a sigh of relief. Though it was heavy iron, the edges were loose. He jabbed the tent stake into one of the gaps. With a single mighty heave, the grate lifted and he managed to wrestle it free of the opening.

Had he not been so focused on the grate, he might have heard Dickie stumble on the rocks. But he didn't. He didn't hear Dickie slam into the ground or his quiet yowl as his ankle torqued out of place. Blackwood didn't hear it, but the guards did.

A shout went up from the tower. The searchlight squealed against its bracket, and the blinding white beam fell over Dickie's prostrate form. He scrambled to regain his feet but it was too late. A siren blared and the night jolted awake with electric torches and stomping boots.

Blackwood could only watch from his position in the shadow of the latrines. Dickie's features were skewed in terror. He staggered forward, his ankle unable to propel him with any speed. A horde of guards bore down on him. The first caught him with a butt-stroke that sent him spinning to the earth. Together they beat him mercilessly as he pleaded between gasping screams. Blackwood held his breath, gripping the stake tight. His mind raced as fast as his heart. The grate was open, he could slip through now and slide the grate shut over him. He would be halfway to the Front before they even realized he was gone.

Dickie cried out as a boot caught him in the spine. He was done for. They would hang him up in the trees that surrounded the camp. That was how they dealt with their problems here. Attempted escapees, those driven mad, those who refused to work, all of them graced the branches outside the gate. The forest was a graveyard that swayed in the breeze, and Dickie had earned his admittance. There was nothing Blackwood could do for him now.

Blackwood's feet were already dangling over the edge of the hole when he heard Klaus's shout above the others. *"Hold now! Don't kill him. Not yet."*

Blackwood froze. It was Klaus's voice alone that stirred the deep realization of the horrors Dickie was bound to endure. The floggings, the torture, the gleeful look in those piggish black eyes as the Unteroffizier administered his pathetic wrath.

Blackwood didn't have a choice in what happened next. It wasn't reason or compassion or even loyalty that drove his actions. It was a pure and murderous rage.

The guards, huddled around their catch like wild dogs yipping at a lame rabbit, didn't see him coming until he was already amongst them. He struck the first one upside the head. The stake clacked loudly off a boiled leather helmet and the man fell back, stunned. Blackwood drove forward, staggering several others and managing to bury the jagged tip of steel into soft flesh. A fist caught his ear, and another. He struck twice more before he was tossed to the ground. Swift kicks pummeled his ribs but he did not cower, instead biting and grasping and ripping until a jarring strike to his head left him dazed.

When they finished he was barely conscious. They flopped him over onto his back. Klaus emerged from the huddle to stand over him. He was clad in stained long johns. He glared down at Blackwood and spat. "*Chain them up.*"

"*We should shoot this one now,*" one of the Germans demanded, clicking the safety off his rifle. "*He gored Fritz!*"

Klaus shook his head slowly. "*No. No, no, no…*" He trailed off with a twisted grin. "*That's too quick for this swine. I like to watch them hang.*"

3

BLACKWOOD AWOKE to the freezing cold.

He hung from the rafters by tight steel manacles. They dug into his wrists, drawing blood. The Germans were clever in their cruelty; the chain above was just long enough that he could *almost* sit, but to do so would likely pull his shoulders from their sockets. Thus he'd been forced to kneel all night long on the dusty wooden floor. His arms rang with a numb tingle as he struggled to stand.

The holding cell — if that's what one could call the cramped stall of the supply barn he now found himself in — had been shrouded in darkness for what felt like an eternity. Now scant rays of morning light cut lines through the edges of the ill-fitting door. Blackwood could barely make out Dickie hanging beside him. Unlike Blackwood, Dickie hung limp. He'd never gathered the consciousness to get his legs underneath him. Instead, he draped there, buttocks suspended just inches off the floor and legs splayed out uselessly before him. His head lolled to the side. Despite the lack of light, Blackwood could make out the swollen welts that bubbled up over his friend's face — a score of hornets couldn't have made such a violent mess of lumps and blood-smeared scabs.

"Dickie…" Blackwood breathed.

Dickie didn't respond. Blackwood tried again, a fraction louder. Dickie let out a wheezing cough but gave no sign of comprehension.

Boots clomped outside, and the door swung open. The guard that entered was stone-faced and silent. He made straight for Blackwood, unlocking the manacles as several more grey-clad Germans appeared in the brightness of the doorway. The chains went slack and Blackwood's arms flopped uselessly to his sides. They began to ache as blood rushed back into them.

"*Move*," the guard ordered, prodding him toward the door.

The morning air carried a bitter cold as they marched him across the waking camp. Blackwood struggled to keep pace, stumbling as often as not, but the not-so-occasional jab of a rifle barrel kept him upright. A horde of fellow prisoners huddled near the cafeteria, chewing their meager rations and making an avid point not to look his way.

To the trees, then, he thought, almost aloud. Ever since the day he'd first marched through Rothenspring's gates and seen the rows of corpses that flanked the road, he figured he'd one day end up amongst them. Now, slogging along on the brink of his own demise, Blackwood felt oddly detached. It made sense to him. After all, there was only so much killing a man could do before the tables finally turned.

But the guards did not make for the gate leading outside of camp. Instead, they turned right by the labor pool and led him to a one-room shack in the corner of the compound. This was a building he knew only by reputation: the interrogation shed. At least, that was what his fellow prisoners called it. Any new prisoner who was imagined to have information critical to the Germans was brought to the rickety building upon their arrival. No one spoke of what happened in that shack, but they had all heard the screams emanating from within.

The lead guard knocked once on the door.

"*Enter,*" a firm voice called from within.

Blackwood was shoved inside. It was a small shack, poorly built and ugly. Its weathered clapboards gapped with rotten seams that whistled with the cold winter breeze. His eyes caught on the umber stain of stale blood on the floorboards.

A single modest wooden desk outfitted the room. The flat light of a reading lamp illuminated a man sitting casually behind it. Blackwood recognized him from the day before — it was the officer who had stood on the balcony beside the camp commander. He was tall, his face evenly balanced and handsome in a sharp, gentlemanly type of way. His collar was pressed, and his uniform was so starched that it could probably stand at attention on its own. He was comically out of place in this shitheap, clean and crisp where even the highest officers were coated in soot stains and grime. The insignia on his collar was that of a Major. He didn't look up from his notebook as Blackwood stepped before him.

"*You can leave,*" the Major said offhand to the guard. The guard hesitated, glancing between the officer and the prisoner, then snapped a curt salute and departed. The door smacked shut in his wake like a gavel.

Blackwood let the pregnant air settle. Inside, his nerves were frayed, though he wouldn't let it show on his face. Seconds passed. Then minutes. Still, the Major's attention remained rapt on the notebook. Perhaps he was the camp's new commander, Blackwood figured. Being a Major, he did outrank the current commander. Or maybe he was some sick tourist — a bored administrative officer who wanted to know the feeling of plunging a knife into living flesh. Blackwood had met enough rear-locked bluebloods to know it wasn't impossible. Hell, it wasn't even unlikely. As long minutes came and went, he decided that this was the case. He was to be fodder for some demented coward's fantasy. A meat-dummy. A plaything.

Only, when the Major shifted, Blackwood spotted a piece of steel hanging from the man's chest: an Iron Cross. He knew this device, a rare award for gallantry among the German ranks.

This was no tourist.

The Major did not look up when he finally spoke. "Edward Blackwood is it?" the Major asked in flawless English.

Blackwood didn't bother to respond. He had no intention of validating this charade. Perhaps one last moment of defiance would satisfy just a bit of the hatred that boiled inside of him.

"I'll take your silence as a yes." The Major scanned the page before him. "An American caught fighting alongside the Canadians? At least, that's according to what I've heard from the commander here. He says you were captured performing a night raid on the Front. It's rare to see raiders taken prisoner — especially those from the Canadian ranks. A savage reputation your lot have. Why was it that they took you alive?"

Blackwood smirked. "I reasoned with them."

"Mmm… plucky. You tried to escape last night, *ya*?"

Once again, Blackwood didn't answer.

The Major glanced at him over the thin pair of reading glasses. "I'm giving you the dignity of a conversation. Those animals out there wished to hang you at sunrise. I stopped them. Well, stalled them at least. In return I would ask of you the respect of answering my questions." The Major's face held no malice. If anything, his manner of approach was coldly businesslike.

"I had to use the latrines," Blackwood lied. "I'm not one to shit in my own bed."

"And this is not allowed here, to use the latrines at night?"

"Not unless you want to be strung up with the others."

"That's quite inhumane. I apologize for your treatment by my countrymen, Herr Blackwood. They do not represent us all."

Blackwood's eyes narrowed. "What the hell is someone like you doing here?"

The Major placed his notebook down and leaned back. "My name is Anselm Wulfson. I am a Major with the *Abteilung III B*, and have been sent here on a mission crucial to the Kaiser himself. I am not one of your guards, and I am not cruel. However, even despite your unfortunate situation, as a man in uniform I will ask that you refer to me with appropriate respect paid to my rank."

"*Abteilung III B*? You're German intelligence then?" Blackwood paused before he added, "...Major."

"Yes." Major Wulfson looked Blackwood up and down before continuing. "It wasn't always this way. I was in the infantry myself for some time. Perhaps someday we shall swap stories of our times on the front lines — two combatants caught in this travesty of a war. However, today is not that day. I am here on behalf of the Empire to right one of the longstanding wrongs of our time. Rothenspring has become an increasingly purple bruise on the Kaiser's face. No such camps exist beyond our enemy's lines, at least not that we are aware of. Rumors of the atrocities committed here appear to have bled over the Front and into our enemies' ears. It would not bode well for our own captured soldiers to have the French and the British follow in the example we are setting, would it?"

Blackwood couldn't help but smirk. He'd never bothered with the politics of war — it didn't do to dwell on things you couldn't change when you're up to your haunches in the muck of a trench. Now he held an immense amount of doubt that politics, of all things, would save him from a bad death.

"I do not find it amusing," Wulfson continued. "Ironic, perhaps, that what is good for a man fighting alongside the Canadians might be good for a German soldier... but not amusing. Are you aware of the conventions set in Geneva in 1906?"

"No," Blackwood lied again. He was well aware of the so-called *rules of war*. He, alongside his Canadian regiment, had viewed them more as loose suggestions.

"What's happening here at Rothenspring is a crime on an international scale. I've been sent here to facilitate the end of that crime. My mission, to put it simply, is to exfiltrate the sick and wounded from this camp and ensure their safe transport to Switzerland. The Swiss, being a neutral nation, have a longstanding arrangement with both sides. They will house and feed and properly care for prisoners of war delivered to them at the expense of their home nations. I imagine this is something you'd be interested in, Herr Blackwood, *ya*? Spending the rest of the war in a Swiss chateau enjoying proper treatment and lodgings?"

"I've heard the Swiss exchange only takes the cripples and the sick. I don't think I would qualify, Major, unless you plan on hacking off one of my limbs."

"Well therein lies your predicament. My requests for use of the railways have been rejected — the trains must focus their payloads on the war effort. Our path is… different. Unique in a way that has not been accomplished before." Wulfson leaned in, scanning the bruises that littered Blackwood's face. "Can you hike? Carry weight?"

"Yes."

"Even after that beating you endured last night? They seemed… aggressive."

"If a German knew how to use his fists, I'd've been dead a long time ago."

Wulfson's eyebrow raised the slightest bit.

"…Major," Blackwood finished.

The corners of the Major's mouth twitched ever so slightly before returning to their standard straight line. "Very well. I will be gathering those in the greatest need here today and rummaging what supplies I might. With a cohort of these broken prisoners, we will traverse the mountain roads of the neighboring Alps. Our journey will be long and on foot, but the successful establishment of this new route to Switzerland will likely come as a relief to all those involved, as, in time, Rothenspring will be no more. In order to accomplish this undertaking, I need men capable of carrying the weight of the supplies. Men who have honor. Men with the capacity for *obedience*, especially knowing the preferred outcome of such an operation. Would you be such a man?"

Blackwood looked for a marker of jest. There was none. "I don't have much of a choice, do I?"

"I'll admit that you've made this part of my job easy. On one path, you regain your freedom and your life. On the other, these men would have you swinging from a tree before my breakfast is served. So, I will ask you this only once more: are you or are you not willing to fulfill this role?"

"Sure, Major. I'll be your pack mule."

"Good. That will be all."

"What about Dickie? The other man they took last night. He's a friend of mine, he deserves this more than me," Blackwood said quickly.

Wulfson paused, staring at the desk for a moment. He called for the guard before he looked back up. When he did, Blackwood swore he saw a hint of sadness in the man's eyes. "As I said, that will be all, Herr Blackwood."

4

FOR OVER a week the convoy of 150 prisoners snaked down worn roads toward the distant shadows of the Alps. They were the broken and the ill. Men with gnarled stumps for limbs and scarred craters left by shrapnel. Many hacked at the cold air, their lungs infested with tuberculosis or pneumonia. Those who might appear to a passerby as relatively healthy suffered from the most terrible condition of all: shellshock, the mental rot of a war-torn mind. These were the men whose psyches had been shredded to pieces by constant barrages of artillery and the savage violence of the Front. They darted in and out of their own ranks like a swarm of flies, some vying for the openness of the edges while others sought the security of the mass of bodies. At the head of it all, riding atop a black colt, was Major Wulfson, though he had come to be known by a different name by those he led — *the Savior of Rothenspring*.

On the tenth day of their journey they passed out of the foothills and entered a tight pass between two rising slopes. The winding road took them deeper between the mountains until dusk, when the order to make camp was given. As the working party began staking tents and building fires, a distant boom echoed from the peak to the west. Every man froze in place as the sound grew to a rising thunder. It rumbled and crashed and shook the tent poles. Shrieks of terror went up from among the shellshocked and chaos broke loose as they began to scatter like madmen. The pop of rifles joined the fray as the guards opened up. Their slaughter was stayed only when Wulfson charged down the line atop his great black steed, roaring for them to cease fire and threatening their lives. Then, all at once, the great thunderous noise was gone. A thin haze of snow hung in a cloud over the road ahead.

∽

Major Anselm Wulfson savored the last acrid puff of his cigarette before crushing it under his boot. The nighttime air had a frigid bite to it. He didn't mind. The cold was something he'd known most of his life.

"*Major Wulfson, will you join us?*" a voice called from inside the command tent.

He paused for a moment, taking in the neat rows of campfires that stretched down the road before him. Freezing men huddled about them, their thin frames cutting harsh silhouettes against the flames.

"*Poor bastards,*" he muttered to himself before pushing through the canvas flap. A portable stove burned in the corner, filling the room with the distinct scent of woodsmoke. Behind a folding desk sat Felix Neff. He was a sharp-faced young Oberleutnant who had been an administrative overseer at Rothenspring. His feet were kicked up on the desk and his mouth was stuck in its usual grimace — he had at no point bothered to hide his displeasure of leaving the comforts of the camp to travel the mountain roads. It had been the camp commander's order that he accompany the convoy, much to Wulfson's chagrin, in the hopes that the inexperienced young officer might earn some seasoning. The fact that Neff was the commander's nephew likely had something to do with his insistence.

At the tent's center, discreetly eyeing the stove with envy, stood a young private. His skin was still red from the cold and his coat was wet with melted snow.

Oberleutnant Neff motioned to the private. "*This scout reports that the road ahead is entirely impassable. From what he's told me, I would agree with his assessment.*"

Wulfson regarded the rosy-cheeked young man. "*How far does the debris go?*"

"*The avalanche took out a decent stretch, Major. The slide of the debris stretches a few hundred meters,*" the private began, then shifted uncomfortably. "*However…*"

"*What is it?*" Wulfson prodded.

"*There are many pockets, voids in the snow. I almost lost myself in one, at least three meters deep. Had it collapsed it likely would have been my grave.*"

"*I don't think you need to lecture Major Wulfson here on the dangers of an avalanche, Private.*" Neff smirked from the corner.

The scout's eyes darted to the Iron Cross hanging from the Major's chest. "*I… I apologize, Major, I would not presume—*"

Wulfson stopped him. "*It is not necessary. The maps showed a river that intersects the road ahead. Did you manage to find if the bridge was still intact?*"

"*I did not see a bridge, Major. I did see the river, but it disappeared under the snow that came down the mountain.*"

Wulfson nodded. "*You've done well, Private. Fill your belly, warm yourself and rest.*"

The private clicked his heels and gave a rigid salute before departing the tent.

Neff sighed and waved a flippant hand after him. "*Do you think this could have been intentional? Enemies hindering our way?*"

"What enemies?"

"*I don't know. It sounded to me as if an explosion was set off. Perhaps the Italians, or the French—*"

"*We are in Bavaria.*" Wulfson spoke over his subordinate. "*There are no Italian forces here. Furthermore, why attack a prisoner convoy enroute to Switzerland? Men to be freed. No, there are no enemies lying in wait. This was simply the mountain shedding her skin.*"

"*I suppose it doesn't matter,*" Neff said. "*The trek back will be short. I would be lying if I didn't admit I was feeling some semblance of relief.*"

"*The trek back?*"

The Oberleutnant's brow knitted. "*Major Wulfson, you cannot—*"

"*I cannot? I cannot what, Herr Neff?*" Wulfson purposely left out the junior officer's rank, a scathing reminder of his station. The Oberleutnant's feet fell away from the desk and he straightened in his chair. Wulfson did not like Neff. From his understanding, the man was neither a veteran of combat nor a particularly efficient overseer. Beyond that, his attitude had grown a bit too casual during their short journey together.

"*I simply mean…*" the Oberleutnant started, his voice faltering as he tried to mask his own frustration. "*I mean that with the bridge likely destroyed and most of these men invalid, we cannot possibly hope to continue on our current route. Would you not agree?*"

"*Not on our current route, no.*" Wulfson pulled a coiled map from one of the crates. He unfurled it on the desk before Neff. "*Less than a kilometer back — toward the mouth of the mountain pass — there was another road. Smaller, for certain. But a feasible choice to circumnavigate this new obstacle.*" He pointed to the scant black line on the map, so thin it was barely visible. "*This route, it will take us in a wide arc through the heart of the mountains. If the path is still viable in winter, then it should deliver us back to our original route within only a week's time. A week and a half, at most.*"

Neff's face sank. He watched Wulfson's finger trace the thin line through a series of mountains, ending finally in Switzerland. "*This is… forgive me,*

Major, but surely you cannot expect a cohort as pathetic as ours to traverse mountain passes when even the road itself has proven too dangerous. This seems to me an unnecessary risk."

"*Risk?*" Wulfson's voice turned to derision. "You speak of risks, but what do you know of them? Have you even been to the trenches, Herr Neff?"

The Oberleutnant bristled but said nothing.

"*I have,*" Wulfson went on with growing ire. "It has been mere months since I have choked on the gas in France. Before that I had a hand in slaughtering the Italians on the other side of these very mountains. I have watched men die horrible deaths with honor for the glory of the German Empire. Even now, hundreds of thousands stand bleary-eyed and bleeding in ruts that run thick with disease and blood. What risks do you imagine us taking — here — that surmount the same orders that force those men to charge over the top and into certain death? The machine that runs this war is not a negotiable beast. When commands are given, the cogs move and they are followed. Our mission is to forge a new route to deliver these sorry prisoners for the sake of our own captured men. Men who've actually bled in this conflict, Herr Neff. We will complete this mission, whatever the cost to ourselves or our comfort. To turn back now is to reject the command of the Kaiser out of cowardice. You know the punishment for such an act of defiance, I assume."

"That is not what I meant, Major Wulfson. I am simply saying—"

"I hear what you are saying." Wulfson held Neff's eyes until the Oberleutnant looked away. When he went on, he forced the anger out of his voice. "Your concerns are not without reason. But you yourself have seen the orders that I brought with me to Rothenspring, given to me by the Generaloberst himself. Turning back now would be a failure. And we will not fail. We cannot fail. Our only option is to pivot to this new route… I will not, however, take this action without due diligence. I will scout it out myself. In the meantime, you are to make camp here. Do you understand?"

"Yes, Major."

"You will await my return for seven days. In that time, traveling light, I should be capable of ascertaining whether this detour will be a viable option. If I have not returned on the eighth day, assume me dead. At that point, and only then, you may abandon this mission at your leisure."

"You plan to go alone, then? Into the wilds of these mountains?"

"No. I will take six of your men," Wulfson said. "…and five prisoners."

Neff burst out in a laugh. When Wulfson did not mirror his mirth, he grew solemn. "*Surely you are joking?*"

"I am not. A squad of a dozen is what this mission calls for, especially if we encounter additional obstacles along the way. I do not have faith that you will be able to keep this convoy in check if I were to take all twelve from the ranks of the guards. The prisoners I will take are bound for freedom. They have no reason not to follow orders, especially when their lives are at stake. I chose the working party myself. They are men who I believe are at low risk of attempted escape. Men who have something to lose if this all goes awry. I will choose the best five among them, and they will have to earn their passage to Switzerland the hard way."

Neff remained silent. Under the desk, Wulfson could see he was wringing his hands.

"What is it? You do not approve?"

Neff spoke slowly, picking his words carefully as they came. "*I mean no offense, Major. I… I worry that this mission we have found ourselves on, it seems oddly desperate. One would think that with the Kaiser's sudden desire to see these men arrive at Switzerland unharmed, he might have freed space for them on the trains.*"

"*It is not wise for an officer to doubt the Kaiser,*" Wulfson said.

Neff nodded in understanding, but his eyes told a different story.

Wulfson sighed, eager to be finished with this conversation. "*I understand your predicament, Oberleutnant. Truly, I do. It must seem odd to a man as young as you, so new to the ways of war, for a Major such as I to arrive unannounced with a satchel of orders and throw your whole life into chaos. But this is the way of war. You must learn to adapt quickly, or I'm afraid you will not keep your rank for long. You will await my return for seven days, starting tomorrow. These are your orders. Do you accept them?*"

Neff bowed his head in submission. "*Yes, Major. I will await your return.*"

Wulfson pulled the cigarette case from his pocket and offered one to Neff, who politely declined.

As Wulfson made for the tent door, the Oberleutnant spoke up quietly. "*Major, is it true what they say about you? About what happened in the White War?*"

Wulfson stopped just inside the doorway. He lit the cigarette hanging from his lips and, without looking back, asked, "*What do they say?*"

"*What was in the papers, I mean.*"

Wulfson spoke over his shoulder as he left. "*I wouldn't know. I never read them.*"

5

FIVE PRISONERS stood in a loose formation outside of the mobile command tent. A harsh wind swept down the road, whipping up snow and stinging the prisoners' cheeks. The glow of dawn outlined the great mountains that surrounded them.

Blackwood stood at the end of the formation. To his right stood a haggard Scotsman named McCulloch. He was wide shouldered and burly, and his skin hung loose with age. Blackwood put him at a hard-lived fifty, not a day younger. Beneath the bristling grey-and-red beard, his face twisted into a knowing scowl. Beside McCulloch slouched a gangly, hatchet-faced British man named Fletcher. Blackwood had seen the Brit around camp where he had always given off the paranoid, almost spastic impression of a rodent caught in a pantry. Next in line was a newcomer to the prison camp, a young Italian with boyish features named Enzo. He was unweathered, his eyes unbroken, and Blackwood knew at first glance that this teen had never seen the darkness of war beyond Rothenspring. Last in the row came a short, middle-aged Frenchman with round features and soft eyes named Dubois.

If just a few years prior someone had managed to track down Blackwood as he rustled cattle in the shadows of the Rockies and told him that he would soon find himself amongst such a hodgepodge group on the steppe of a mountain range thousands of miles away from home, he would have laughed in their face. Yet here he was, staving off the cold as he stood at rigid attention, awaiting the commands of an enemy officer.

Enzo shivered ceaselessly. He was thin and appeared perpetually on the verge of hypothermia. His eyes darted toward Klaus and a group of five other guards huddled just out of earshot. He whispered something in Italian. Down the line, the Frenchman Dubois responded quietly, also in Italian. Blackwood shot him a look, and the small man shrugged. "He asked what the Germans were saying."

"You speak Italian?" Blackwood asked out of the corner of his mouth.

"Italian, German, English, French, some Portuguese…"

"Oi, what are the Krauts saying?" Fletcher hissed, his voice thick with a Cockney accent.

"They are complaining. Something about an expedition," Dubois said.

Klaus broke from the huddle and jabbed a menacing finger toward them. "*Silence, swine!*"

Major Wulfson's voice came in German as he swept out of the command tent. "*It is fine. Silence is no longer necessary for these few.*" He was dressed in thick layers and bore a pack strapped heavy with mountaineering equipment. Moving to stand before the formation, he addressed the prisoners in English. "You are no doubt wondering why you are here. More so, I imagine you're wondering if I will deliver good news or bad." He paused to light a thin cigarette. He had to shield the flame from the wind, and when he exhaled the smoke danced wildly before his face. "It is both, I suppose. I have chosen you five for a crucial task. Yesterday's avalanche has blocked our path forward. I would think that all of you are eager to complete this journey — especially considering that failure to do so would result in your return to Rothenspring. In order for us to reach our destination, the forging of an alternate route has become an unfortunate necessity. There is one such option: a secondary path through these mountains. It appears rough, to say the least, and its viability for the convoy is in question. I have chosen you five to assist us in its scouting. Together, our small company will forge ahead in order to assess its accessibility. Your tasks are simple: you are to carry supplies, set tents, and gather wood as needed. You have all exhibited ability and strength thus far in our journey. That is why you were chosen. I expect you to show me more, still, in this new endeavor."

Blackwood bristled at the idea of being trapped on some remote mountain road with Klaus and only a handful of other prisoners. In his months spent in the Germans' grip, he'd learned that being singled out for anything always proved to be a dangerous evolution. When corralled with sheep, it was best to stay hidden amongst the flock. Now, with Klaus no doubt still ripe with the disappointment of not stringing Blackwood up next to Dickie, the Major's news felt more like a death sentence than an opportunity.

Wulfson went on. "As I have told all of you before, the Swiss internment camps are a far stretch from the cruel furnishings of Rothenspring. You lot will be treated with kindness and generosity there. The lodgings, from what I have heard, are among fine mountain resorts. Thus, I imagine it should be your top priority to make it across these mountains. God and the Kaiser both have granted you this opportunity for freedom. Both have sent me to ensure that this task is seen through to completion. In order for me to do this, I need your pledge, on your honor, that you will obey my commands. In return I offer my own pledge that by the end of this, every one of you will find yourselves released from the Kaiser's grasp. Is this agreeable?"

He looked at the prisoners one by one. Each gave an affirmative response until he came to Enzo. The boy was obviously lost. Dubois piped up, rehashing the officer's speech in a burst of Italian. Enzo nodded vigorously. "*Si*, erm… yes. Yes, is good."

Wulfson, appearing content, turned toward the guards. He paused and looked back at Blackwood. "I will tell you this only once. If any of you still harbor the dream of escape, know that to realize it will mean a most painful death. By bullet in failure, or by the elements in success."

The crew of a dozen set off by mid-morning — five prisoners, six guards, and the Major. Each prisoner had been outfitted with new boots and thick German army coats that had been stripped of rank and insignia. The guards had complained at this, but Wulfson quickly silenced them. They looked on with vehemence as their captives pulled on the dull grey uniforms that matched their own. Each of the prisoners was then issued a heavy pack full of an assortment of camp supplies, food, and tents. The guards, on the other hand, packed light, making sure that the bulk of the burden fell on the prisoners' backs. Of the Germans, Wulfson alone carried his fair share.

They retraced their route from the previous day. In less than an hour they discovered the thin path that diverged to the north. A fresh crust of snow covered the slender trail, and soon they found themselves on a gentle incline up the mountainside. Wulfson led the party and maintained an aggressive pace. The bleak tones of withered winter grass that peeked from the snow grew sparse as their elevation increased. Ahead, the endless peaks faded beyond each other, melding with the white clouds above. As far as the eye could tell, the mountains looked to go on forever. Higher and higher they climbed. By noon the convoy below them had become little more than a swarming blip in the still sunny valley. By midafternoon it was gone, disappeared completely around the bend of the mountain.

Blackwood's legs ached and sweat had soaked through his cotton undershirt by the time Wulfson finally commanded the party to halt beside a rocky outcropping. With dusk approaching, the prisoners were ordered to assemble the canvas tents lashed to their packs. Little more than dark splotches of rock and scraggly dead bushes stood out around them against the stark white. They used the waning light to gather wood from a few sparse pines and assembled a trio of small cooking fires. Highest on the mountainside was the Major's, who camped separately from the others. A short distance down from him came the guards'. Lastly, at the lowest point, the prisoners made their own. It was dark by the time they settled around the flames. They could see Wulfson's solitary fire above, but no sign of the brooding Major in the darkness. The guards bickered loudly as they swapped glorious stories of their time on the Front. Klaus's cackle swept down the mountainside. Every so often, they would pause and whisper quietly, casting dark looks toward the prisoners. After some time, it became evident they were zeroing in on Dubois.

"They know that I speak their language," Dubois said. "I think they'd like to shoot me now and be done with it."

"I think they'd like to shoot us all," Blackwood muttered, then, as an afterthought, "Why is it you know so many languages?"

"It was my job," Dubois said. "I was a teacher before the war. Language was one of my specialties."

"I'm more worried about these mountains than them Germans," Fletcher piped up. He clutched his knobby knees close to his chest and leaned toward the fire. The way he curled into himself made him appear more as an awkward jumble of sticks and triangles than a man.

"*Oui*," Dubois agreed. "I imagine an avalanche to be one of God's most terrifying punishments. We are indeed lucky that—"

"I ain't talkin' about no damn avalanche," Fletcher cut in.

"Then what are you so afraid of, *mon ami*?"

"This ain't God's country. Look out there." Fletcher waved a wide arc over the surrounding mountains. "You see any lights? Not a single one, not even a fire. Even the bloody Germans don't want to live out 'ere. I ain't saying I'd rather be in Rothenspring, but somethin's wrong with this place. I can feel it deep, deep down in me bones."

The Scot named McCulloch let out a barking laugh. "City folk, all you sassenachs. Turn off the lights and yer wee cock shoots right up into yer belly."

"Aye. I'm from the city. But I seen things. Things that'd make you tremble, you bloody *sawney*."

McCulloch's eyelid twitched. "I dinnae think I heard you right, little lass…"

"I said—" Fletcher started loudly, beginning to rise.

Dubois seized the Brit's sleeve and yanked him back down. "Enough!" the Frenchman hissed, glancing back at the guards. They'd gone silent at Fletcher's movement. Now, they watched the prisoners closely, rifles resting handily on their laps. "Do not give them an excuse."

Fletcher didn't resist being pulled back to his seat. He returned the Scot's glare with a tight sneer. The bad blood between the Scots and the English was not news to Blackwood, but he still found himself caught off guard by the rapid escalation of their loathing.

A tense silence reigned over the encampment. Only after the guards had returned to their chatting did Enzo tug on Dubois's sleeve. "*Ci spareranno, vero?*"

Dubois nodded with a burst of Italian. The boy looked worried.

"What did he say?" Blackwood asked.

"He asked if the guards will kill us."

"And?" Fletcher pushed.

"I told him the truth. Probably, yes."

Fletcher blew out through his nose. "Yeah, that's not bleak at all."

Dubois shrugged. "I have good ears. I have been listening to them when their Major is not around. They already whine of this charge. If it were up to these men, we would be shot, all of us, and they would return to their warm cots. This Major, they do not like him. They say he brings nothing but trouble. This is unfortunate, as he appears to be the only reason we are not put to death here and now." He dared a quick glance over his shoulder, to the guards' fire. His face was solemn in the firelight when he turned back. "If we hope to make it to our destination, then it is not the mountain we should fear, my English friend. We best pray that the Major does not stumble on the slope. Or, even worse, find himself laying down at night in a bed of German knives."

6

EMIL HANZ emerged from his tent into the bitter cold of the alpine air. The rising sun glared off the surrounding sea of white as he gave in to a deep shiver. He couldn't be sure if the temperature had plummeted overnight, or if the warmth of his tent and tight blanket bag had spoiled him. Shielding his eyes, he tried not to let the misery faze him.

At least he was not at Rothenspring, he thought. Though a guard, he often found himself comparing his own suffering in that dank shithole to that of the prisoners. He knew well enough that this was an exaggeration — he couldn't imagine being on the receiving end of the heinous violence that his peers inflicted upon their captives. Just witnessing it was bad enough to turn his stomach. He didn't belong there any more than a fish belonged in the sky. Guard duty at Rothenspring was reserved for the worst of the worst. The delinquents, the savage, the psychotic. Men too unruly or mean or cowardly to be trusted in a trench.

No, there was no place in Rothenspring for a young, idealistic dreamer like Hanz. That's how he saw himself, at least. He'd been small as a boy. Short and frail in a culture that valued strength over all else. Despite this, he wasn't one to let those things that he couldn't change get him down. As a child he'd lain awake at night imagining himself the hero of fantastical myths and great battles. He'd been so unabashedly eager to prove his worth that on his seventeenth birthday he'd beaten the sun to the enlistment station.

After a failed attempt to enlist in the infantry — where the recruiting NCO laughed in his face and proclaimed that he wouldn't even be able to see over the edge of the trench — he ended up in the artillery. While it wasn't infantry, it was a fine enough duty for him, one where he could maybe, just *maybe*, see some real action. In training they had promised that his role would be of dire consequence. He believed them. He worked hard and did well. When he finally made it to his unit, he spent three glorious weeks manning a cannon just behind the lines. They were the best three weeks of his life.

It was a single loaf of stale bread that had destroyed his future. It was early spring, and the frost still coated the grass at dawn. Their supply train was overburdened and understaffed, and the more seasoned men were growing thin with hunger. Hanz was small and quick and sneaky enough when he needed to be. They told him how the old farm over the hill was brimming with food and that it would not hurt anyone to help the farmer "share" his plentiful bounty. Only, when Hanz managed to scale the gate and surpass the lock on the storeroom door, he found nothing more than a few loose bags of grain and one stale loaf of rye bread. He'd taken it for his new friends, as well as a buttcheek full of birdshot in his mad scramble to escape the ornery farmer.

Their Leutnant was a grizzled, battered old goat. When he became aware of Hanz's crime, he'd gone into a red-faced rage. None of the other soldiers stepped up in Hanz's defense. Hanz, ass still smarting, was made an example of and a new rule was set among the company — if you steal from Germans, you get a choice: duty at Rothenspring or a bullet. In hindsight, Hanz imagined he might have been better off choosing the bullet.

When he first trudged through the gates of Rothenspring, Hanz still clung to the belief that he might matter in some small way. It had taken less than a month for that belief to be gagged, slaughtered, and ground into a fine paste under the boots of his new peers.

He glanced around the mountainside at the other guards. There was Johan, a smarmy man with a cleft chin and a rumored penchant for rape. From what Hanz had heard, he'd left more than one poor French girl beaten and bloodied before being banished to Rothenspring.

Breaking down the tent beside him was Victor. Victor had the build of an ogre from the fairytales. He had the intellect and mean spirit of one too.

Next was Dietmar, the swarthy and ever silent watchman who was known to trap live rats around the prison camp. He'd kill them slowly in all manner of ways, then lace their bodies with poison and lay them out for the cats and birds. Hanz had once watched a hawk drop from the sky midflight — he'd imagined the poor creature had come across one of Dietmar's "gifts."

Lastly was Frederick. He was young and fresh faced, and the closest thing Hanz had to a friend. Like Hanz, he had been made an example of by his command over a small slight. Sadly, after four months spent amongst the rowdy gang of bullies, the kindness behind Fredrick's eyes had begun to fade. It made Hanz wonder just how long he had before his own soul began to seep away.

A hard slap to the back of his head sent Hanz stumbling forward.

"What are you standing around for?"

"*I'm sorry, Unteroffizier,*" Hanz yelped, darting to disassemble his tent without daring to look back.

Unteroffizier Klaus didn't bother to acknowledge him again. He was the worst of them. Klaus was barely taller than Hanz, a fellow *shortstack*, as some men would say — though they'd never say it to Klaus's face. He was a mean son of a bitch. No one knew exactly what he had done to earn his way into the ranks of the damned. There were rumors, of course. Some whispered that he had been caught torturing men as they surrendered, or that he shot his own commanding officer. One rumor even had it that he had been caught eating a fellow soldier in the heart of winter. Whatever he had done, they had allowed him to keep his rank. This fact alone had led Hanz to the horrible realization that Klaus may not have been sent to Rothenspring as a punishment at all — that he may have done the unspeakable and *requested* this duty. Hanz could not imagine a more terrible type of person than one who would voluntarily take on such a task.

None of it mattered, he reminded himself as he shoved the tent in a sack and tossed it in the pile for the prisoners to pick up. He was here now, countless miles from civilization, surrounded by a gang of gruff, mean psychopaths that got their rocks off dominating others — regardless of what uniform they wore. When Hanz had been chosen for this mission, he had hoped it was his way out. He thought that if he could prove himself to this Major, then maybe he could earn his way free of this deranged unit. He even held the scant hope that afterward he might be able to scrap together enough medals and rank that he could return home after the war with his head held high and name scrubbed clean. But Klaus had already taken to mutinous mutterings in the dark of night. None of the others wanted to be here any more than their NCO, and they'd lapped up the Unteroffizier's sentiments eagerly. A German Major who wished to secure the freedom of their enemies did not sit well with this group. Hanz worried that should this expedition take a dark turn, he would have to choose a side. And it wouldn't take a keen strategist to understand that the side with the most rifles would win.

He could only hope with all his heart that it would not come to that.

It wasn't long before the encampment was packed and they were once again on the move up the mountainside. Their path had been clear in the lowlands, but now, as they traversed the wide-open slopes marked only by a scattering of scraggly pines, Hanz couldn't help but wonder how the Major was so sure of the way.

Throughout the morning their pace remained fast, much faster than Hanz would have preferred. For every step the taller men took, he found himself forced to scramble one and a half. Despite this, what Hanz lacked in height and fitness he believed he could make up for with sheer willpower. The pace slowed by midday but the exhaustion had already set in. He chugged on like an old truck, clouds of exhaust pouring out of his face as his engine sputtered. The column had spread thin and through happenstance he found himself trudging at the rear of the line alongside the French prisoner, who similarly struggled to keep up.

"*You must keep pace,*" Hanz warned him in German, as it was the only language he spoke. He knew from the paranoid mutterings of the other guards that the Frenchman spoke it as well.

"Yes, sir."

The other guards marched far ahead, unburdened by the weight of their lightened packs. Satisfied by their privacy, Hanz said quietly, "*When we're not around the others, you can call me Hanz.*"

Despite his exhaustion, the Frenchman stiffened. He surveyed Hanz's face, clearly looking for some insight into his motivations. Hanz offered a weak smile in return.

"*I am Dubois,*" the Frenchman said.

"*You cannot fall back, Dubois. The others do not like that you speak German. They would enjoy getting rid of you if you were to become a burden.*"

Dubois nodded between wheezing breaths. "*Thank you, Hanz. I… I appreciate your honesty.*"

This Dubois had an odd air about him. Perhaps that of a banker or a doctor, but not that of a soldier. Hanz couldn't quite tell what it was about the Frenchman that made him think this, but the impression stuck. "*You were not a soldier, were you?*"

"*Why do you say that?*"

Hanz shrugged, though the motion was difficult under the weight of his pack.

"*I… I was a teacher.*" Dubois seemed to pick his words carefully. "*Duty called, and I answered. Just like you, I imagine.*"

Hanz grimaced. The duty he'd been stuck with felt nothing like his calling.

Dubois looked ahead to the others. "*If you are as friendly as you seem, then you should be wary. They will likely punish you if you are caught speaking with me like this.*"

"*Not if they cannot hear. If they see my lips moving, I suppose I could just say I was chastising you. I think they would like that.*"

"*Why risk it at all?*"

Hanz couldn't tell him the truth: that he felt horribly alone amongst these monsters. That Dubois seemed, at least in that moment, a soothing presence he might latch onto. Instead, he said, "*You know, these mountains, they have all sorts of stories about them. Where I come from, people are afraid of this place.*"

"*And where is it you come from?*"

Hanz flicked his chin east. "*That way.*"

"*Ah, Germany.*" Dubois's voice carried a cautious hint of sarcasm, as if testing the waters.

Hanz chuckled. "*Yes. Germany. Where I come from, they say that these mountains have all sorts of creatures not seen anywhere else. Wolpertingers and tatzelwurms, even great hairy men that live like apes in the snow. I keep looking to the ridges, hoping I might spot one.*"

"*Wolpertingers?*"

"*Ya, Wolpertingers.*" Hanz felt the tiniest brushstroke of excitement. He'd always loved the folklore his father had shared with him by the hearth, but as a man he'd been urged to leave such childishness by the wayside. Outwardly, he had. But many a night had been spent recounting the old tales silently in his bunk. "*They look like rabbits, but with the antlers of a deer and the wings of a bird. They say to see one is good luck.*"

"*Then I hope we see one.*"

"*Ya, to see one is good luck, but to kill one…*" Hanz felt his words growing faster in his excitement. He didn't notice that Dubois had broken eye contact to stare at the ground ahead. "*To kill one is to bestow a terrible curse on yourself, and all of your fam—*"

"*Private!*" The shout ripped through the air. Hanz's eyes snapped up to find Klaus standing on the ridge ahead, glaring back at him furiously.

"*Yes, Unteroffizier!*" Hanz's pulse skyrocketed in fear. He ran forward to the waiting brute.

"*Why the hell were you speaking with that swine?*" Klaus demanded.

Hanz searched for an excuse in the suddenly swirling panic of his mind. "*I was telling him to move faster, that I would shoot him and—*"

"*Don't lie to me, boy. You like them? You want to be friends with the pigs?*" Klaus's eyes burned into him. When the Unteroffizier spoke, long strings of spittle drew lines between his teeth. Klaus looked over his shoulder, no doubt making sure Wulfson had disappeared over the hill ahead. Satisfied, he reached into his coat to where his belly folded over his belt and withdrew a wooden-handled grenade. The green painted steel of the grenade's potato masher head was chipped and the white lettering had worn away — it was not something a guard should have, and Hanz had no doubt that the Unteroffizier had kept it hidden on him for quite some time. Klaus brandished the explosive menacingly inches from Hanz's face. *"If you enjoy the company of our prisoners so much, perhaps I should treat you as one. Would you like that? Would you like it if I shoved this grenade up your ass and kicked you down the slope? How far do you think you would roll down the mountain before you popped like a greasy little pimple?"*

"No, *Unteroffizier*, please," Hanz stuttered. "*I was doing nothing wrong, I told him he was swine, he was scum — there! Ask him!*" He jabbed a hand to Dubois, who passed silently, his gaze still averted.

"*I ask* nothing *of these swine. They are less than the shit on my heel.*" Klaus shoved the grenade back into his coat. He spit in the snow. "*You would do best to remember what they are, boy. If you cozy up to them, they will slit your throat in the night. And if you forget that again, I will do it myself.*"

"Yes, *Unteroffizier*." Hanz nodded adamantly. "*I will not forget. I will not.*"

Klaus raised a fist to strike. Hanz cowered, but the punch never came. When he looked back up, Klaus was already trudging away in the wake of the others. Hanz's bottom lip quivered, but he managed to hold back the tears as he once more fell in line.

7

FOR TWO more days they hiked on as the horizon was swallowed on all sides by jagged white peaks. The temperature continued to drop with each rough mile covered, and the nights found them shivering violently in their tents. The veil over the guards' vehemence grew ever thinner with each passing day, while the prisoners' concern over the Major's tenuous control grew ever stronger. Blackwood watched it all unfold from a distance — the guards began to travel in a cloistered pack, muttering and glaring and holding their rifles tight to their sides. Klaus's rebellious attitude, initially buried beneath the expectation of rank, now simmered close to the surface. The aura of impending violence impregnated the air. The prisoners could almost taste it, but if the Major noticed it, he showed no sign.

On the fourth night they camped in the depths of an alpine forest. The wind was strong and they barely bothered with the fires, taking to their tents early in hopes of a solid night's rest. That goal would elude them, as it was still the dead of night when they awoke to the Major's hurried shouts. When Blackwood slipped out of his tent, he found the air thick with falling snow.

Not wanting to be overwhelmed by the ever-quickening snowfall, they geared up in a mad rush. The storm exploded into a tempest so fast that the winds threatened to tear the half-folded tents from their grasp. Wulfson did not mince words in expressing that to sit stagnant for long meant that they would likely be buried alive. In the darkness he had them line up single file behind him. He lit a lantern and burned the wick bright. When he gave the order for each man to seize hold of the pack to his front, the guards refused, not wanting the prisoners to have their backs. Wulfson tore into them, ordering them to the back of the line. In this order, with the guards taking up the rear, each man did as he was bid, grabbing hold of the pack to his front as Wulfson led them into the storm.

The roiling clouds hid the moon, and the whirlwind of white transformed the bright lantern into little more than a vague, glowing orb as it bobbed ahead. They tromped blindly through the forest until dawn. As the glow of morning spilled out from beyond the crown of peaks, they broke free from the trees and into an open expanse of mountainside. Here they faced a steep upward climb. The snow raged on, plummeting from the sky in a heavy blanket that caked their shoulders and grew in piles atop their packs. It grew so thick in the air that it swallowed the mountains around them in a dense haze. A bitter wind howled and threw sheets of ice against their frozen faces. The light of day, which in the darkness Blackwood had imagined would be their ally, only worked to further blind them in the endless sea of swirling white. His eyes stayed crimped shut against the searing brightness, his only source of navigation being his frozen grasp on McCulloch's pack to his front.

As the day dragged by, the burning in Blackwood's legs gave way to a terrifying numbness. The trough of snow he waded through grew from his shins to his knees, and his breath was hard to come by. Still, the train of bodies did not slow. His body screamed out to stop — to release his death grip on the straps of the Scot's canvas pack and collapse into the snow. He battled against this impulse with every fiber of his being, and as his thoughts became fewer and more scattered, he held onto one crucial fact: if he were to let go, to lose the train ahead, he would be damning both himself and those men behind him to the mercy of the nasty gaggle of Germans that took up their rear. He tried to let this image alone live in his head, using it as fuel to drive him forward as all other thoughts succumbed to fatigue.

Behind him, Dubois stumbled. The Frenchmen nearly went down, yanking hard on Blackwood's pack in order to keep upright. Blackwood almost lost his own grip as a result. He shouted out to McCulloch, but the Scot couldn't hear him over the wind. Or perhaps he chose not to. It didn't matter. The train didn't so much as pause.

Perhaps the guards were right, a silent voice weaseled its way through the fog of exhaustion. *Perhaps this Major Wulfson is the madman they claim he is. Perhaps he truly is leading us blindly to our deaths.*

The day seemed endless, and the very concept of time had devolved into a fragmented illusion when a rasping shout echoed from ahead. Ice crystals cracked apart in his lashes as Blackwood opened his eyes. Ahead of McCulloch's burly form was a vague shadow — a tall break in the wall of white. As they moved toward it, something cackled in the air overhead. It must have been a mirage, but Blackwood swore that for half a second, he could make out something dark gliding in the wind above. A bird, long-winged and black.

It was a mad thought, the idea of such an animal braving this tempest, one that he likely would have dismissed even if he were of sound mind at that moment. But his mind was broken, and as the crevasse ahead grew closer he forgot he'd even seen it.

The thin gash in the mountainside was twenty feet tall and only the width of three or four men. The howling wind and blinding snow came to a merciful stop as they trudged inside, the ravine's jagged stone walls shielding them from the storm's onslaught. Only after the last in line had entered into the sanctuary did the train come to a halt.

"*Sit!*" Wulfson shouted, turning back and motioning to the stone façade. "*Sit! Rest!*"

Blackwood struggled to unclench his frozen digits from the Scot's pack and collapsed in the snow. Enzo fell next to him. Blackwood did what he could to right him, but the boy was nearly limp in his grasp. Around him the other prisoners panted in unison, red and haggard faces gasping at the oxygen-starved air.

The guards pushed past them, kicking their feet as they shuffled deeper into the safety of the crevasse. Blackwood didn't notice that there were only four of them until a shout rang out.

"*Where is Frederick?*" Klaus demanded, his words halting between deep heaves.

The last guard in line, the small one named Hanz, looked back in astonishment. "*He was just here…*"

"*Where is he?*" Wulfson shoved through their gaggle, passing the prisoners and looking back out into the swirling tempest beyond the crag. "*Who held him?*"

"*He was behind me, the last in line,*" Hanz called back. His chittering teeth and forlorn expression betrayed that he was barely conscious of his own words. "*He's here, he must be! He was just here!*"

"*Idiot! Did you not feel him let go?*" Wulfson demanded. He alone appeared fully alive amongst the ranks of half dead. His face was a mask of fury as he bore down on the violently shivering Hanz.

"*I… He's here. He must be! He… he…*" Hanz's words came in sputters, dying off as he blinked rapidly in confusion.

"*Damn you!*" Wulfson roared, glaring down at the quivering private.

Klaus stared dumbly at the exchange. His eyes were open wide and his sagging cheeks glowed red with the cold. "*Where is he?*" he demanded, too exhausted or maybe too stupid to comprehend.

"*The mountain took him,*" Wulfson said coldly as he pushed past the guards and moved farther into the ravine.

A series of exaggerated expressions played out over Klaus's brow. It began with the crinkled flesh of confusion, then slowly his eyebrows lifted in realization. Finally they burrowed into a deep V, and his gaze followed Wulfson's back with eyes steeped in loathing. "*What the hell are we doing out here, Major? You would have us all freeze to death! Now a man is dead! A good German man! How many more of us must die here for the sake of this worthless mission? For the sake of these damned swine?*"

"*Enough!*" Wulfson barked back, wheeling on his subordinate.

Klaus bristled. His hand had migrated to the strap of the rifle that hung over his shoulder. His fingers twitched.

Wulfson's own hand glided over the pistol at his side. The two Germans faced off as Blackwood watched, the cold and exhaustion sapping so much of his concentration that he was only half aware of his own stakes in the confrontation unfolding before him. Wulfson stood straight, eyes locked with Klaus's as his hand came to rest on the stippled grip of his Luger.

Klaus's rage ebbed, and his hand fell to his side. He leaned back against the ravine wall as the fight drained from his face.

"*You will stay here and rest,*" Wulfson commanded. "*No one is to test the storm. I will scout ahead alone. There must be better shelter down the slope. Eat, rest, recover. We will begin again shortly.*" He didn't bother to translate his words for the prisoners.

No one responded. As the Major turned, a blast of wind shot through the ravine, swirling snow in every direction and blinding them all. Blackwood buried his face in his arms, breathing heavily through the ice-crusted sleeves of his coat. When the wind died and the snow dissipated, Wulfson was gone.

"Com'ere." McCulloch's monosyllabic grunt was accompanied by a meaty hand seizing Blackwood's arm and hauling him in close. On his other side, Dubois was similarly held tight. "Grab the others. Your sweat'll chill now we're nae moving. We'll need the body heat."

Blackwood complied, grabbing ahold of Fletcher and issuing him a command to do the same with Enzo. The men shifted, forming a tight seated circle. Their faces drew to within inches of each other's as they huddled close. Blackwood looked over to the Germans. They stared back hatefully, then proceeded to form a similar huddle themselves.

Above the chattering of teeth and howl of the wind, Dubois was muttering something. Though it was in French, Blackwood recognized the cadence of the words — it was the Lord's Prayer.

"God won't help you here." The bitterness of Blackwood's tone surprised himself.

"Aye," McCulloch agreed. He stared at the Germans over the mass of heads. His face was wind burnt and withered with fatigue, the deep creases around his eyes appearing more as spiderwebbed glass than flesh. His wild beard hung thick with snow and frozen snot. "Be sharp, lads. This is it. If they're ever gonna shoot us, it'll be now. You can see it in their eyes. Any minute here and they'll get it in their heads that they're better off without that damned Major. They'll cull us, then clip him when he comes back." He wiped the snow from his brow. "This is the end of the road, lads."

Fletcher shook violently. His words were weak. "We're proper screwed then, aren't we?"

"No." McCulloch reached a hand under his shirt. He withdrew a jagged rock the size of a baseball. "It's them or us. They're as cold as we are, in better shape too maybe, as they've nae been haulin' the weight we have. But it doesnae matter. With one of theirs gone, our numbers match up. That said, we only get one shot while the Major's gone. With any luck, the bolts of them rifles'll stick in the cold. It's now or never."

Blackwood looked into the old Scotsman's eyes. They burned with a savage fierceness that ignited a fire in his own. He nodded once.

"You're a bloody fool," Fletcher got out, then he bent low and groaned. "But I'm with you. God help us."

Dubois didn't respond. His head was down, his prayer barely slipping from his lips. Blackwood shook him. "Tell Enzo."

The Frenchman didn't look up. Blackwood knew in that moment that he was lost to them.

"*Capisco*," Enzo said weakly, motioning toward the rock in McCulloch's hand. It seemed he understood well enough.

"Alright." McCulloch took a deep breath. "The next time the wind brings the snow through here, we go. They'll be blind to us as we close the gap. Go for the knives on their belts, it's quicker than the rifles up close."

One at a time, the men repositioned themselves with their feet under them, ready to spring. Blackwood crouched, listening closely and waiting for the telltale howl of the wind. He flexed his numb hands inside the leather gloves, willing feeling back into his frozen fingers as the seconds dragged on and his heart galloped harder and harder.

Outside, the wind picked up. It whooshed past the mouth of the ravine, growing stronger as the gusts mounted.

"It's coming," Blackwood whispered.

A distant gunshot shattered the tense air. Then came another and another in rapid succession. Every one of the prisoners flinched hard, jerking to face the huddle of guards. But they too seemed caught unaware, wheeling to look further down the ravine toward the source of the barking reports. McCulloch made to seize the opportunity and stood, but Blackwood caught the sound of the Major's voice in the distance and hauled him back down.

"*Come on!*" Wulfson's voice echoed down the ravine. "*There's a village!*"

PART TWO

Excerpt of a letter from Colonel Alexandre Barbier to his wife, Gwyneth. 1813

There is only one stretch in these endless mountains to which my men will not so much as entertain the notion of going. Five scouts we lost there in a week, another two the following. The locals of the foothills speak of legends and curses, of whole armies swallowed up by whatever evil lives between those peaks. I will not test it, even if Napoleon himself were to command me. Let the executioner take me rather than the devil himself, I say.

MONTANA, 1894

A rickety postal cart rattled along in the shadows of the Rockies. Two figures perched atop its plank seat. One of them was the postman, the other was a boy of eight.

The forests and foothills were a thing of beauty to the boy. Where he'd come from, such places existed only in fairy tales and on postcards his mother could never afford. His life had been one of dull greys and the burnt red of brick. As he stared out over the rich green meadows brimming with buttercups and the great dome of blue above, he felt the magic of the wilderness inside his chest. A deer bounded across the road ahead. He let out a gasp and pointed.

The postman did not seem to care. He was nervous, as evident from the sheen of sweat on his brow and the way he gripped the reigns so tight that his hands had grown red.

"Are you frightened?" the boy asked.

The postman scowled at him. "How old are you, boy?"

"Nearly nine."

The postman sighed. "Yeah. Yeah, I'm frightened. You would be too, if you knew what was out there."

The boy's spirits were sullied, not just by the man's words, but by the sincerity with which they were delivered. "What's out there?"

"Indians, wolves, bears worse of all. Great big ones that'll swallow you up in one gulp. I shouldn't've taken this damn job. Fuck the money, not worth it. I should take you back to the train station. You'd be better off wherever you came from."

The boy hadn't liked the train. It stank of stale cigarettes and musty fabric. A week aboard it had been enough for him for a lifetime. "Mama said bears are more afraid of us than we are of them."

The postman shook his head. "Not out here."

"Why not?"

"If your mother's such an expert, then why ain't she the one carting you around?" the postman snapped.

The boy's shoulders sank. "She's dead."

The postman's features softened. "Eh, it's alright, kid. The horses'll keep 'em bears at bay." Under his breath, he added, "I hope."

They spoke little more as their route took them over the hills and through the valleys. A mountain loomed high above when the boy finally caught sight of a small cabin through the trees.

"This the place?" the postman asked.

"I don't know."

The postman's brow raised. He pulled out the envelope that the boy had given to him at the train station and read the writing on the back. "That's it, best I figure."

The sun was already past its peak when they reached the cabin. The postman dismounted first, making for the door. Meanwhile the boy, now for the first time doubting the veracity of his mother's claim regarding bears, kept close to the horses.

The postman knocked at the door. There was no answer. He banged with a closed fist. Still, nothing.

"Dammit," he swore quietly. He waved the boy to join him. "Alright, up. C'mon."

The boy joined him outside the door and took the envelope when the postman offered it. "Where are you going?" he asked as the postman made back for the cart.

"Back to town."

"But—"

"Just… just stay here. Whoever it is that you're here for, I'm sure they'll be back."

The boy tried to protest, but the postman wasn't interested in conversation. With a sharp lash of the reigns, the horses spun the cart around. It lurched away in a plume of dust.

Lacking a more rational option, the boy took a seat atop a bench by the door. There he waited as the sun sank lower and lower.

The night came with rain, killing any hope of sleep. When the moon rose, wolves began to howl in the distance. He cowered deeper into his thin coat and thought of his mother. By dawn his stomach had soured with hunger and his skin trembled with a wet chill.

He'd only just drifted off when a crunching came from the underbrush. In the depths of the forest ahead, he saw a great mass of umber fur ambling toward him. His eyes blurred with tears as he recognized the lumbering beast for what it was. A bear. He stuffed himself underneath the bench, praying silently that it would not find him. Closer and closer it came, its soggy footsteps in rhythm with its guttural panting.

When it touched him, he cried out. The rough paw recoiled as a man's voice came sharp in a language he could not understand. The boy opened his eyes to see a gruff face above cowled in a great fur coat. The weathered features bore a familiar likeness.

Cautiously, the boy emerged from his hiding spot. The old man scowled at him as he presented the letter. It was wet with rain and tears. The old man peeled the paper apart, his lips moving as he read the blotched words. His eyes grew sad, and he regarded the boy, who looked away. "Your *mutter*, she is Eleanor?" he asked in broken English.

The boy nodded.

"And she *ist gestorben*? She *ist* passed?"

The boy nodded once more.

The old man dropped stiffly to a knee. He took the boy's shoulder in a firm grip and struggled to find the right words in English. "I did not know I have grandson. I am Erich," he said, poking a finger to his chest.

"Edward," the boy said quietly. His eyes remained locked on his own dirty boots. "Edward Blackwood."

The old man lifted the boy's chin with a calloused finger until their eyes met. The boy stared into them, two grey orbs hidden in a thicket of earth brown and pale grey hair. They were kind and hung over a sorrowful smile. "You like honey, Herr Blackwood?"

The boy nodded.

The old man stood with a pained groan. He pulled the bearskin coat from his shoulders and wrapped it around the boy, then led him into the cabin.

8

THE PARTY from Rothenspring lumbered through the snow with purpose now, a chain of bodies once more bound to each other by frozen hands. The prisoners shared a silent prayer for Wulfson's claim of a village to be true. None of them had seen it for themselves — only a wall of billowing snow had met them as they emerged from the far side of the crevasse. If Blackwood had been capable of stringing together coherent thoughts, he would have worried that this supposed village might have only been a means for Wulfson to avoid the impending mutiny. But this idea was buried far too deep in his frost-scalded mind to actively comprehend.

In time, a shadowy rectangle materialized out of the blinding whiteout. Even through the whipping snow Blackwood could make out the distinct texture and crisp edges of stone walls. It was a house. They trudged by as another building appeared, then another, their features becoming clearer as the world darkened with dusk and the glaring white gave way to grey. The buildings were dilapidated and looked abandoned. Jutting, broken beams speared skyward from collapsed roofs and windows hung shattered by weather and neglect.

"No one lives here!" McCulloch barked. "It's dead!"

The gravity of this realization sucked Blackwood's heart down into his guts.

"*Hello!*" Wulfson's shout was barely audible over the wind. The hazy glow of his lantern shook as he called out again in German. "*We need shelter!*"

From the whirlwind of elements another light appeared. What began as a faded blip grew brighter with each step as if it were an angel emerging through the clouds. It was a torch, Blackwood realized as the wind whipped its flames higher. Beneath it a figure braced against the storm. The shaggy fur of a bearskin coat encompassed them. The dead creature's stout ears and pale yellow fangs shone from their cowl. When the figure reached Wulfson, they exchanged words Blackwood could not hear, then waved the line of men forward with the torch.

Wulfson kept his pace, slogging a path behind the stranger through the knee-high snow when Blackwood felt a heavy tug at his pack. Turning, he found Enzo panting violently. The boy's eyes were crimped shut and his face was beet red. He began to slump forward against Blackwood's pack.

"Buck up!" Blackwood grabbed the Italian's arm and hauled him forward. "We're almost there!"

They passed more houses, most broken, though a few appeared as if they might be habitable. As the buildings became more frequent, the orange glow of life began to shine through ice-encrusted windows. Blackwood realized they were on a street. The stranger trudged ahead, leading them out of the cover of the buildings and into an open expanse. Ahead of them loomed another structure, longer than the others and two stories tall. The stranger hauled open the door and disappeared inside. Wulfson leaned against the door frame, slapping each of the men on the shoulder as they entered, counting them off through chattering teeth.

Passing over the threshold felt like stumbling into a hot oven. Blackwood recoiled as the stagnant heat struck his face and filled his lungs. Twin fieldstone hearths roared on either side of a large dining room filled with a dozen rough-hewn tables. The warm hue of flames radiated over well-oiled beams and floorboards polished by time. In the back, beyond the neat rows of tables, stood a spartan bar. Scores of bottles glimmered from the shelves above.

"Aye, been a long bloody time since I seen a good tavern." McCulloch's voice shook with cold as the gaggle of prisoners crossed to one of the fireplaces. He seemed the only one among them to have maintained his wits through the last leg of the trek, and when Enzo stabbed his frozen fingers too close to the flames to warm them it was the old Scotsman who delivered a rough cuff upside his head. "Dinnae want to do that, lad. Heat 'em too fast and you'll lose em."

The guards took to the opposite hearth in much the same manner, for once not bothering to keep their eyes on the prisoners. Blackwood barely noticed them, enraptured instead by the scent that filled his thawing nostrils — fresh baked honey bread and the hoppy tang of beer.

"*Stay here.*" Wulfson delivered the curt order in German before repeating it in English. He strode to the rear of the bar where Blackwood saw their mysterious rescuer waiting for him beside a door to a dimly lit kitchen. The duo disappeared and the door creaked shut, then there was silence.

"*I didn't think we'd make it,*" Johan muttered loud enough for Blackwood to hear from across the room.

Another guard grunted in agreement, then Klaus spit into the flames. "*Not all of us fucking did.*"

"*Cosa stanno dicendo?*" Enzo whispered to Dubois, who was still glassy-eyed and expressionless.

"*Shut your fucking mouths!*" Klaus snapped over his shoulder. Enzo, harried and still disoriented, cringed at the harsh command. Klaus grumbled something, then wheeled on the prisoners and barked a German order they all recognized. "*Stand at attention, swine!*"

All five of them spun in place and stood rigidly at attention. Even Dubois's crystal gaze broke as the command brought him crashing back to reality.

"*I don't give a damn if you can understand me.*" Klaus's voice was sharp. "*A German soldier is now dead because of you. You will pay the price for that, you understand? You will pay for all of thi—*"

The door behind the bar creaked open and a man strode out, stealing Klaus's attention. In his hands, the man cradled a wide bronze tray piled high with bread and thinly sliced meat. Blackwood, still locked at attention, only dared a quick sideward glance as the man made his way to one of the longer tables and set the tray down. He was older, and his clothes were patchy and well worn. The bright white scruff of a beard tangled out from equally ghostly features, and a crown of thin, stringy white hair ran around his head. Even his eyebrows and lashes were so white that they looked crusted with hoarfrost, though he clearly had not just come in from outside. His eyes, so dark a red that they were almost black if not for the orange glow of firelight, gave away a condition that Blackwood had only heard of in stories — the man was an albino.

"*Welcome, my friends,*" the man proclaimed in German. His voice was crackly and cheerful. "*My name is Sovilo. You are welcome guests in my humble establishment. Please, come eat!*"

The guards didn't require a second invitation. Even Klaus seemed to lose his train of thought, darting to take the seat closest to the tray and shoveling a wad of meat between his blistered lips.

Sovilo looked to the prisoners, who remained at attention. "*Come, friends. Fill your bellies.*"

"*No,*" Klaus managed between harried mouthfuls.

Sovilo regarded him with one pale caterpillar of an eyebrow raised. He cleared his throat, then raised a single finger and spun it in a slow circle around the room. "*Herr Soldier, this is my place. In my place, all are welcome, and all will eat. It is not up for you to decide.*"

The table shuddered as Klaus slammed his fist down. The room itself seemed to flinch, only the tavernkeeper did not.

"*I don't give a damn who you are or what you think is yours, barkeep. We are the Kaiser's soldiers, and these are our prisoners. They will do as I tell them, and so will you. Now fetch us beer, and be fast about it.*"

Sovilo considered Klaus and the other men before him. His pale lips curled into a tight smile that did not reach his eyes. "*You sit before me, an army of five, and threaten me in my own home? Herr Soldier, just how many of us do you think there are, here, in this village?*"

The warm air chilled over as every chewing mouth froze in place. Klaus's wind-burnt face screwed up, but he kept his tongue behind his teeth as he realized the implication set out before him.

"*Is there a problem?*" Wulfson demanded as he reentered the room.

Klaus picked at the crusted edge of his mouth and glared at Sovilo. "*No, Major. No problems here,*" he finally said.

"*Good.*" Wulfson lorded over him, as if challenging him to change his answer. Only once Klaus's beady eyes averted did Wulfson turn to the prisoners and speak in English. "You, Dubois, are you too frozen to translate?"

Dubois shook his head. "No, no, Major. I can translate."

"*Good,*" Wulfson resumed in German and regarded the room as a whole. "*I only wish to say this once. This is the village of Melvilla. I have spoken with these people's leader, and they have very graciously agreed to grant us refuge from the storm. The prisoners will take the top floor of this boarding house. There is only one entry and exit.*" He pointed to a thin stairwell that led up to the second story. "*The stairs will remain guarded. You guards will sleep in the side room there.*" He pointed to a door opposite the staircase before his eyes landed on Klaus. "*I should not need to say this, but you will treat our hosts with absolute respect. If you do not, you will find yourself huddled in the snow for the night. Is this understood?*"

The guards grunted in affirmation, and when Dubois had finished translating — in full for the English speakers and with a brief burst of Italian for Enzo — they all nodded.

"*Good. We are all tired. You, Victor.*" Wulfson motioned to the hulking guard. "*Take the prisoners upstairs. All of you, get some rest.*"

Victor stood and ambled toward the staircase. Wulfson caught him by the arm. "*Bring the tray for them.*"

A look of betrayal crossed the oafish guard's face. After a half-second of hesitation, he obeyed, taking the tray out from beneath the greedy fingers of his compatriots before leading the prisoners upward.

The door at the top of the stairwell opened into a central sitting area. A handful of spindle-backed chairs and end tables were scattered about the room, and four doorways branched off into bedrooms. One of the twin chimneys that rose through the floor opened into its own hearth. It blazed hot and cast the room in a cozy orange. Victor tossed the tray down on a table with a clatter, causing the bread to tumble off onto the floor. He glanced around for only a moment. Satisfied at their containment, he shook his head and muttered a curse before departing.

Once again the prisoners congregated around the fireplace, this time stripping away their wet layers before basking in the dry warmth. They split the food up evenly without a word. The bread steamed as Blackwood broke its crust apart. It was fresh and doughy, and what remained of the meat was tender and rare and dripped with blood. No words were exchanged as they ate. Even when their bellies were full and their bones had finally begun to thaw, an exhausted silence remained.

Fletcher was the first to break away and pick out a room. Through the closed door, the others could hear his exaggerated groan as he collapsed into bed. McCulloch went next, then Blackwood, who chose the room closest to the stairs.

They were humble accommodations: a pair of beds and dressers skirted the walls, and a single glass-paned window hung on the far side. The blankets were thick wool and warm to the touch. Blackwood crawled underneath them and resisted the urge to moan in pleasure.

As soon as his head hit the pillow, there was a knock at the door.

"Yeah?" he answered cautiously.

The door opened. Enzo stood there sheepishly. The boy glanced over to the empty bed on the opposite side of the room. Blackwood sighed. Chance had paired them in the smaller of the two tents during their trek through the mountains. Now, it would appear, the tradition was to continue. He nodded to the spare bed. "Go ahead."

Enzo smiled. "*Grazie*."

Blackwood cocooned himself in the blankets as the snow battered the windowpanes. It had been a lifetime since he'd felt the comfort of a real bed, and though he fought to stay awake long enough to enjoy it, he quickly fell into a deep, dreamless sleep.

9

WITH THE suddenness of plunging into a frozen lake, Blackwood was awake. He sat up and oriented himself. The room around him was bathed in the cool tones of morning. Crisp beams of light reflected through the warped glass of the window, highlighting the lazy motes of dust that hung in the air. Enzo lay in the bed across the small room, his baby smooth face at peace. The Italian looked horribly young in that moment. Too young for all of the hell they'd been through.

Despite the seemingly serene moment, something felt wrong. Blackwood could not recall the last time he'd awoken naturally. Every awakening he'd experienced since hitting the Front had been either the sudden nosedive into the chaos of war or the misery of Rothenspring. Now, in this hovel nestled away in the mountains, the wrath of the guards was — for the first time — eerily absent.

It was too good to be true.

Their bloodthirsty tormentors were still here, just a floor below them. A great shadow under black waters, unseen, unheard, yet hungrily aware of their prey floating helplessly above.

Blackwood didn't know what was coming next, but he felt in his gut that it would be bad.

When he left the room, he found McCulloch sitting before the hearth. His head hung forward, amber-and-grey-spackled beard splayed out over his bare chest while his raucous snores filled the second story sitting room. Blackwood eased the bedroom door shut behind him, careful not to wake the slumbering Scotsman.

Dubois stood alone by a row of windows that faced the rising sun. Fletcher was absent, no doubt still sleeping. Or perhaps cowering in some dark corner, as seemed to be his nature.

Dubois offered only a curt nod as Blackwood retrieved his clothes from the pile before the fireplace. The thin cotton shirt was warm and dry, but the German army-issued woolen pants still held an unpleasant dampness.

"Good to see you back amongst the living," Blackwood said as he joined the Frenchman.

Dubois grunted in return. He stared out of the windows, his brow furrowed in concern.

"What's wrong?" Blackwood asked.

"The guards are out there. They are… working."

From their vantage and with the storm passed, it was apparent that the village was located in a small valley directly against the side of a mountain. Before the tavern stretched a circular plaza. Three sides of the expanse were bordered by humbly constructed buildings, much like the one they now stood in. On the other side, exactly opposite the tavern, the smooth white blanket of snow broke against a jagged cliff that ran high up the side of the mountain. Blackwood followed its craggy face upward. High above, jutting from the peak of the cliff, a stone-walled tower stood out against the bold blue of the sky.

At least two score of workers milled about in the plaza. Most of them carried shovels, while a few hauled carts laden with snow. Working amongst them, Blackwood counted four distinct grey uniforms. Only Klaus and Wulfson were missing.

"This isn't right," Blackwood muttered, more to himself than to his companion.

"*Non*," Dubois agreed. "It is not. I fear that every drop of sweat they shed will come back to drown us."

Blackwood shifted focus from the laboring guards to the village itself. The buildings were not traditionally German, at least not in the wattle-and-daub fashion that Blackwood had seen during the war. Many of them were stone-built and capped with heavy thatched roofs. The few built from wood, like the tavern, bore great, ancient looking beams polished to a glint by the elements. There were at least thirty buildings, as best Blackwood could see from his position, with more expanding outward beyond the limits of the windows. While those in the forefront were in good condition, the most distant of them appeared dilapidated and abandoned. Their caved-in roofs reminded him of their evening slog the night before and the heart wrenching despair of the mountain. An inadvertent shiver ran down his spine. The village felt archaic, as if the mountains had swallowed the small party up and spit them out an eon before their own time.

"I must admit, I have never seen anything like it," Dubois said, breaking the silence.

"Doesn't look that special to me."

"Not the village." Dubois pointed to a dark splotch at the base of the cliff face.

With the blinding light of the sun just cresting the mountain ahead, the jagged stones were still shrouded in shadow. As the bleariness of sleep dissolved, Blackwood realized that the swath of darkness opposite them was not just some trick of the light as he had first thought. Centered at the base of the rocky façade was an inlet that was about half the breadth and height of the tavern, if not a tad smaller. Three steep steps led up into the darkness, where he could barely make out the distinct shape of stone columns built in an even row.

"What the hell is that?" he asked.

"I've been wondering the same thing," Dubois said. "I have only ever seen anything like it once before."

"Where?"

"In a place called Petra many, many years ago." Dubois waved a delicate finger toward the shadowy inlet. "Do you see the grooves in the columns, the intricacy of the volute?"

Blackwood squinted to see the details of the pillars, but the sun reflected off the glass and stung his eyes. "What are you talking about?"

"The volute — where the pillars meet the arch. If the clouds return, you can see them better. The stone is shaped into an ornate spiral. This is a classical style. Roman, maybe Greek. It is not something one would expect to find in a place like this."

Blackwood gave Dubois a sideways glance. He had concluded long before that the man who stood before him was no soldier. Now, as the Frenchman stared off at the scenery outside, lost in deep thought, Blackwood gave in to his curiosity. "What exactly did you do before the war?"

"Hmm?" Dubois snapped back to the moment at hand. "Oh, as I have said before, I was a teacher."

"Yeah. Sure. If you're a schoolmarm, then I'm a midwife."

Dubois gave a light chuckle. "Well, perhaps teacher is the wrong word. I suppose in English the correct term would be an academic. A professor maybe is the better word. I, erm… I specialized in language and antiquities."

"I didn't think the French conscripted academics."

"*Non*, they don't. My imprisonment was an unfortunate misunderstanding, I'm afraid. As you say, I am as much a warrior as you are a midwife."

"Great. Lucky us." Blackwood realized the sarcastic bite in his voice a second too late. He gave Dubois a friendly slap on the shoulder to make up for it. "So, professor, what do you make of this dump?"

"Ahhh… I do not know. An eclectic time capsule perhaps. A Roman ruin populated by the descendants of the barbarians who sacked it. Or, perhaps, these people were wanderers come only recently to settle in this broken old villa." He hunched his shoulders candidly. "Or perhaps we're still on the mountainside, and this is simply a shared delusion as we drift into the long dark night."

In truth, it was a thought that had crossed Blackwood's mind as well.

"Something else I noticed." Dubois nodded down to the plaza. "Look at the villagers. Do you see anything odd about them?"

Beneath the thick coats and layered furs Blackwood focused on their individual features. All of the villagers were slight with thin shoulders and long hair that spilled from beneath their hats and cowls. It suddenly hit him. "They're all women."

Dubois nodded. "I have been watching them since dawn. I have counted seventy-three. The only man I can be certain that I have seen so far is the tavernkeeper."

McCulloch shuttered awake with a gasping snort. His head jerked left and right, frantically taking in the room. Finally his gaze landed on the two men and he gave a stout grunt. "I figured they'd have us standing in line by now."

"No." Dubois looked back out the window. "The guards are quite busy, at least for the time being."

McCulloch coughed and rubbed his eyes. "Eh?"

"Don't worry. I'm sure we'll pay for our reprieve soon enough." Dubois said before fading away into his thoughts once more.

10

THREE FEET of snow had fallen overnight. Under the layers of his uniform, Hanz's long johns had grown damp with sweat despite the cold. His shoulders ached under the toll of the spade, and his legs were still sore from the mountain trek. Around him, the other guards looked to be hurting as well.

They had been awoken that morning alongside the rising sun. The room that the five enlisted men shared was cramped and windowless — a small offshoot to the side of the bar with stale air and lumpy mattresses. They had jostled in the dim lanternlight, elbowing each other as they struggled to pull on their clothes in the overcrowded confines. Wulfson, who had his own quarters nearby, had pulled Klaus aside and issued a quiet set of orders. The *Unteroffizier* had begrudgingly saluted, then the group of them had been armed with dull wooden spades and sent out into the cold. Too tired and confused to make a fuss, the four privates set to work shoveling snow alongside the growing horde of villagers. Klaus had not joined them. Instead, he sat glumly on a bench by the tavern's door, smoking a cigarette and glaring off into the distance.

"*This is horse shit, you know that?*" Johan grumbled nearby.

Hanz pretended not to hear. Over the hours spent shoveling, the other guards had bantered with each other regarding the prisoners' absence, mostly in the form of dramatic threats and vile insults. Now, as they began to grow weary, the threats had grown less hollow.

"*How is it that we are the ones out here breaking our backs while they lounge?*" Johan went on. "*It is a disgusting violation of our pride. I swear, I'm going to beat them to death one at a time with this godforsaken shovel.*"

Victor shrugged. The hulking, low-browed oaf had proven himself to be a man of few words, but even he had begun to complain. "*It's Wulfson's doing. That bastard loves his little pets more than his own countrymen.*"

"*Fucking Wulfson. Traitor. Bastard. Cunt piece of shit,*" Johan hissed quietly. When his tantrum finally waned, he leaned against his spade and scanned the villagers. "*Any of you seen a single man among them yet?*"

Dietmar and Victor both grunted negative responses. Hanz tried to ignore the question, but when Johan fixed his glare on him, he shook his head.

"*All broads.*" Johan gave a nasty smirk, his mood visibly shifting. "*Who knows… maybe this won't be so bad, ya?*"

Hanz mustered his courage. Johan had beaten him before, once at Rothenspring and once while making camp on the mountain. The man was thin and sinewy but had a certain gift for inflicting pain. Still, the knowledge of Johan's sick inclination for rape spurred him on. "*Johan, these are our countrymen.*"

Johan scowled. "*What are you implying, pipsqueak?*"

"*I…*" Hanz started, then thought better of it. "*I just mean that we should be polite.*"

Johan waved him off and resumed his observations. None of the villagers were particularly close, and when he called out, he had to raise his voice to just below a shout. "*You there, sweetheart, where is your man?*"

The woman he'd targeted was short and middle-aged with long dusky hair that spilled from beneath her wool cap. She ignored him.

"*Can you hear me?*" he called again, slower as if she was an idiot. "*Do you lot even speak German up here?*"

"*He is gone,*" she answered coldly.

Johan gave a pandering look of compassion. "*Oh, my dear. How lonely you must be…*"

Without a word, she lifted her spade to her shoulder and strode away, angling across the plaza to continue her work outside of earshot.

Johan spit in the snow and scowled. "*Uppity bitch.*"

The morning continued much the same. Johan made a game of reorienting himself to harass whichever unfortunate woman was nearest. While Dietmar appeared disinterested in the game, Victor seemed to take pleasure in it, tailing Johan and guffawing at each of his failed attempts at seduction. The two of them migrated about the slowly clearing plaza, Johan a hungry mutt and Victor his big, dumb puppy. Again and again the women dispersed before them, avoiding the curs like sheep trapped in a pen.

Not for the first time, Hanz felt a great embarrassment to be clad in the same uniform as these men. He decided he must do what he could to distance himself from the pair of shameless buffoons. He shifted his work southward, eventually migrating into one of the narrow streets that led out of the plaza and cut between the houses. One spade-full at a time, he worked his way farther down the street. The buildings on either side of the lane were two stories tall. They hung over the tight street, shrouding him in a canal of stacked stone and long shadows. Here he found himself alone for the first time in recent memory.

Somewhere along the way he began to hum. The song was one he loved — a building orchestral piece from an opera his father had taken him to as a boy. *Salome*, it was called. Though he could not recall the story itself, he could still picture the actress's dramatic flourish as she spun across the stage, still feel his father clasping his shoulder as he gasped at the magnificence of it all.

His mind wandered to the old man. What would he think of Hanz now? His father was a gentle soul but with the ability to draw upon some deep well of fierceness when needed. A man of kind words and strong deeds. A man that a boy could look up to. Despite having never approved of the war or of Hanz's desire to join in the fighting, he had been there at the station when Hanz left, smiling sadly with one final hug.

Would he be ashamed of where his son ended up?

Would he be revolted by his boy's cowardly silence in the face of wrongdoing?

Hanz already knew the answer to these questions; there was no doubt his father's disgust would mirror his own self-loathing.

A crackling wheeze broke through the wall of shameful thoughts. He startled, glancing all around but not finding its source. The sound came again — a long gasp, hollow and raspy, followed by a sickly wet exhale. Some animal sense deep inside of him quivered to life. It was the noise of illness and death. He looked upward. The building beside him blotted out the morning sun. Its timber was dark and rich, and what had once been roughhewn logs had been worn smooth by the wind. A single window hung at the center of the second story. A figure stood beyond it, obscured in darkness.

Hanz tensed. The figure stared back, its breath fogging the glass. Hanz felt his sphincter clench, and his hands cramped from their bone-tight grip on the spade.

In a languid motion, the figure raised a hand to the window. The fingers that pressed against it were thin and bony and tipped with long yellowed nails. The palm itself was spackled with thick callouses and ruddy with wear. It moved like a starved spider trapped in a jar. When it finally drew away, the nails squealed against the glass. A tingle went up Hanz's spine.

As fast as he had realized it was there, the figure was gone, disappearing further into the darkened room.

Hanz swallowed stiffly. When he spoke, it was just to make sure he still could. "*It's just some old timer,*" he said, then again in a voice that held no certainty.

An angry shout rang out from across the plaza. Hanz tore his eyes away from the window to look back. In the distance, an enraged Johan clasped his face while one of the village women stalked away from him. Johan furiously made to step after her, but Victor caught his arm. Johan struggled for a moment before finally ripping free. The woman was already gone, and all he could do was return angrily to his work.

"*It's just an old timer,*" Hanz repeated one last time, struggling to find confidence in his own words. His feet were already moving under him, carrying him back out to the plaza. Despite his own disgust with his companions, Hanz didn't hesitate for a moment to return to their side.

11

KLAUS SHIFTED in his seat. His heel bounced off the icy cobblestones with nervous energy. The stone bench was unforgiving on his tailbone, and the cold had seeped through his coat. He was tired of smoking. He'd burned through half a dozen of his cigarettes while watching the others work, and the stash in his pack was already running dangerously low.

Wulfson had ordered him and his men to assist the villagers in clearing the snow, but such a chore was well beneath an NCO such as himself. Instead, he sat all morning in the cold, his resentment building to a point where he wished the pompous officer would dare to chastise him for his laziness. Wulfson, however, had not left the building to join or even oversee the working party. He was no doubt cozied up by the fire, probably drinking a pint and laughing with the albino freak who claimed ownership of this backcountry tavern.

Klaus worked the blood back into his numbing fingers with a flurry of strumming movement. What the hell was he doing out here anyway? Freezing his balls off while the swine rested upstairs? It was a joke. And not a funny one.

"*Fuck this*," he muttered, standing and shoving his way through the door.

The tavern was warm, burgeoning on hot. It felt almost unpleasant against his frozen cheeks. Wulfson stood by the bar. Beside him, speaking in quiet tones, was the albino. The Major looked up at the intrusion. "*What is it, Unteroffizier?*"

Klaus wanted to spout something nasty back, but all that came to mind was, "*it's cold.*"

Wulfson scrutinized him. Klaus drew in a breath to speak again, but the Major held up a single, jutting finger and returned to his hushed conversation. Klaus imagined one of his bullets nicking off the degrading digit on its way to spray the Major's brains out over the bottles that lined the shelves beyond. The albino spoke quietly and at length, his eyes occasionally darting over to where Klaus hunched, thawing.

Klaus didn't like the tavernkeeper. Truth be told, he didn't like most of the rural bumpkins he'd encountered since joining the army. He was a city dweller himself, raised on the hard streets of Berlin. His life had been one of scraping and survival, and he'd been raised to see the farm folk as little more than haughty, entitled savages. This one in particular seemed especially vile. The tavernkeeper's nearly opaque flesh blended with the starch white of his collar, and his horseshoe of slicked back, stark white hair might as well have been an extension of his glistening dome. The albino fit right in out here in this snowy hellscape, the odd malformity masking him like a tiger's stripes in the jungle. Klaus wondered how many generations of these wild people had inbred with siblings and parents to produce such a foul abomination.

"*Very well,*" Wulfson said with a curt nod to Sovilo. He spun on his heel and made for the door. "*Unteroffizier, fall in.*"

Wulfson had already brushed by him before Klaus had a chance to gather his thoughts. He followed his superior back into the cold, sputtering to find his words. "*Major, what is going on?*"

"*Men! Fall in!*" Wulfson barked across the plaza. The four privates jolted at his voice and scurried to comply.

"*We cannot leave the prisoners unguarded!*" Klaus protested, stumbling over the ice to keep up.

"*You, Victor!*" Wulfson called to the closest guard. "*Go to the tavern and watch the stairs. No one in or out, do you understand?*"

"*Yes, Major,*" Victor responded with a salute.

Wulfson seized him roughly by the arm as he passed. "*Need I make it clear: if a hair on any captive's head is harmed, I will have yours.*"

Victor appeared caught off guard by the threat. "*Yes, Major.*"

"*Major!*" Klaus tried, but Wulfson once more ignored him, continuing onward across the plaza as the remaining three guards scrambled to catch up and fall in line. They made for a long structure that stood close to the cliff face. When they reached the doors, Wulfson spun on them and spoke sternly. "*When we are inside, you will not speak unless spoken to. Is this understood?*"

Every one of them acknowledged, Klaus last of all.

The doors were heavy oak and squealed as Wulfson pushed through them. The building was only a single room. It stretched a good fifty feet long and half as wide. The air was dank, and the only light came from a single flickering hearth. The windows, what few there were, were covered in thick hides that doused out the sunlight. Klaus blinked at the sudden darkness as the door creaked shut behind them.

"*Come, stand before us,*" a woman's voice called from the far end of the hall. Her accent was thick and had the distinct rolled *r* of the Bavarian dialect.

Klaus could just barely make out her silhouette. She was seated at a table atop a raised platform that denoted her status. On her right another figure hunched, and to her left were the bare spindles of an empty chair.

"*Come.*" Wulfson waved the guards forward. Klaus squinted to make out the details of the room as they passed through it. It reminded him of some pathetic excuse for a church. Two rows of characterless benches stood on either side of a center aisle. The walls were decorated with an eclectic array of items; animal skulls glinted white in the firelight alongside tattered tapestries depicting brutal scenes of violence between men and beasts. A loose raven cackled from the rafters, drawing an uncomfortable glance from his men. The whole place felt backwards and primitive. Pagan, even. Though Klaus was no man of God, he still hated the pagans and the gypsies with a passion. Despite the hall's warm trappings, the aura that filled the air was not a friendly one. It reminded Klaus of his father's nightly beatings as a child. He could almost smell the musty leather stench of the old man's belt. When they reached the head of the room, Wulfson waved them in line before the seated figures.

"*You are guests here,*" the woman at the center of the table said. Her voice was cold and domineering. It cut through the muffled silence of the room like a knife. As his eyes adjusted, Klaus managed to make out the golden blonde hue of her hair and the sharp cut of her cheekbones. She was young, perhaps still in her twenties. And not bad to look at either. Beside him, Johan gave an unsavory grin.

"*We are,*" Wulfson responded, his voice lighter than usual, as if addressing an equal. "*I understand that you wished to speak with me and my men.*"

"*Your men. Yes…*" the second figure muttered. Unlike the first, her voice was haggard and cracked between syllables. Her extreme age was even further exemplified in her deep hunch. She waggled a bony finger toward the row of men. "*You lot, tell us your names.*"

Klaus winced at the command. He was not one to take orders from some old hillwalker hag. Wulfson shot him a warning glance, and he complied. "*I am Unteroffizier Matteo Klaus.*" He motioned down the line. "*These are Privates Dietmar, Johan—*"

"*From their own mouths,*" the old woman cut him off.

Klaus fell silent with a scowl.

Dietmar began, stating his name and rank in full. Next came Johan. Before Hanz could speak, the old woman held up a hand. "*Johan, ya?*"

Johan nodded.

"*You are the one that harasses the women?*"

Johan's face dropped. "*I…*" he stammered. "*I… No, I—*"

"*What is she talking about, Private?*" Wulfson demanded.

"*It was just innocent conversation,*" Johan insisted. "*If I knew these gashes would be so damn prissy about it—*"

The younger woman snorted. "*You would insult us now? After we rescued you from the mountain's rage? After we've fed you? Housed you? Given you warmth?*"

Even in the dim light, Klaus could see that Johan's face had grown red. Klaus felt his own temper rising. Wulfson be damned — these were *his* men, and he would not have them scolded by some fatherless wenches. "*What is this about? Why have you asked us here?*" he demanded.

"*I have* asked *nothing.*" The young woman leaned forward. "*I had ordered you to come here. You are in my village, soldier. This is Germany, not some conquered state. There is no war within our boundaries to justify your man's rotten behavior. I do not know how it is where you come from, but here, people answer for their actions.*"

Klaus balked. "*We don't answer to you, woman. The day I take an order from a—*"

"*Stand at attention!*" Wulfson snapped.

Klaus stiffened. Slowly, he adjusted his posture and steeled his jaw. The raven above cackled as if mocking him. He decided then and there that — should this whole thing go sideways — he would roast the damned thing for dinner.

Wulfson addressed the women once again. "*Fraulein, if my men have offended you, I apologize. As you well know, we owe you and your people our lives.*"

The younger woman sat back, taking her time in observing them one by one. She had an essence of false regality to her, right down to the way she returned Klaus's loathing glare with a look of sullen superiority — the look one might give a temperamental child during a scolding. It was the look a woman would only dare to give Klaus if she was foolish enough to imagine herself immune to the back of his hand.

"*Major Wulfson,*" she said. "*As we have already discussed, eleven extra mouths will put a burden on our food stores. You promised us work in repayment. Unfortunately, these men of yours have proven themselves poorly fitted for the task. If you expect us to house and feed you through the winter—*"

"*Through the winter?*" Klaus blurted out. "*Major, what is she—*"

Wulfson let out an audible growl. "*If you speak again, I will take not only your rank, Unteroffizier, but your dignity at the lashing post as well. Do you understand me?*"

Klaus's teeth ground together so hard they might break. His rifle hung heavy on his shoulder, and his fingers began to twitch.

"*You have not told them?*" The young woman sighed and angled to address the guards. "*The storm has cut off the mountain passes. It is only the first of many this winter. We are alone out here, and there is nothing for a great many miles in any direction. To leave now would be to face certain death.*"

Klaus could feel the hot flush of his face. How could Wulfson be so stupid? What sort of officer would be so foolhardy as to trap them on this godforsaken mountain, marooned in the snow like some mincing sailors at sea? And what was to keep them there? The bald-faced lies of some uppity bitch? He wanted to scream, to shout in Wulfson's face what a fucking moron he was, how these pathetic hillwalkers were so obviously taking advantage of them for their labor. Instead, he remained silent, trying to breathe past the growing lump in his throat.

"*As I was saying before,*" the young woman resumed, returning her gaze to Wulfson. "*You owe us work in exchange for your lodging and food. This was the bargain we struck, and I must insist that you make good on your end. It is apparent that these soldiers…*" The word slipped through her lips like an insult, and she let it hang accusingly in the air before she went on. "*…cannot compose themselves with the dignity becoming of a German. To put it simply, I do not trust them. Especially this one.*" She nodded toward Johan, who now hunched, staring at his feet like a cowering dog.

Wulfson cleared his throat. "*Fraulein, I assure you—*"

The old woman cut him off. "*You have prisoners with you. How many?*"

Wulfson paused. "*Five.*"

"*Are they able to work?*"

Wulfson paused again, this time even longer as he sized her up across the dark room. "*Yes.*"

"*Good.*" The younger woman slapped the table. "*Then it is settled. Your prisoners will work for us. These soldiers of yours, consider them on thin ice. I want them to keep their distance from my people.*"

Klaus had begun to visibly shake. The vein in his temple throbbed so hard he imagined it might burst. There was no way that Wulfson would agree to such a thing, not at the command of this… this… little *strumpet*. The Major would tell her to fuck off. To eat shit and die. Hell, he'd set the whole pack of them loose on these arrogant hillwalkers and show them the true meaning of German rage.

Instead, Wulfson simply sighed. "*You must understand, my charge is to keep these prisoners in captivity. What you are suggesting leaves them far too open to escape.*"

Even in the dim light, Klaus could see the cat's smile on the old woman's lips. She chortled, a sickening rattle of a sound. "*I assure you, the only escape they will find from here is a cold death, Herr Wulfson.*"

12

BLACKWOOD HAD just drifted off into a light afternoon nap when he was roused to the clamber of boots on the stairwell. He was already on his feet by the time the door to his room banged open.

"*Outside!*" Klaus snapped in German, jabbing a stubby thumb over his shoulder.

The main floor of the tavern was empty besides the gaggle of guards meandering through the dining area. They muttered curses as the prisoners passed by on their way out the door. In the cold of the plaza, Klaus lined them up on the slippery cobblestones and called them to attention. A snow-muffled silence filled the air as he lit a cigarette and took a long drag.

"*Frenchman, tell them my words. All of you, find yourselves some spades. You are to finish clearing the snow,*" Klaus spat. "*Keep to the plaza, or I will cut your...*" His voice trailed off, his eyes drifting to the tavern windows. "*Just— just do it, damn it!*"

Dubois translated the orders dutifully. The prisoners fell out of formation, fanning out and setting to work.

Blackwood had watched the guards work all morning, even witnessing Johan's slap with a bit of glee. He had seen the way the women avoided the guards and now found himself expecting the same treatment. To his surprise, however, the villagers seemed far more at ease with the new company. They did not shy away as the prisoners slowly integrated amongst their ranks.

After the first hour, Klaus disappeared back inside, leaving one of his underlings, Dietmar, to sit alone on the tavern's bench. He watched the prisoners silently, toying with a short knife he'd pulled from his boot.

As the prisoners worked their way to the rear of the plaza, Blackwood noticed Dubois not-so-casually migrating toward the carved stone edifice in the cliff face. He looked fascinated by the masonry and seemed to be carrying on some sort of quiet conversation with himself.

Blackwood had found that, of all the prisoners, he enjoyed the Frenchman's company the most. Enzo seemed little more than a boy lost in his own world while Fletcher was spastic and paranoid. McCulloch stood out as a beacon of strength, but his gruffness and callous nature did not make for the most pleasant of company. Dubois at least had an air of calmness about him which was complemented by a quick wit.

The alcove that held the Frenchman's attention was smaller than it had seemed from the vantage of their lodgings. With the sun finally at their backs, its shallow depths were illuminated. It sank a mere twenty feet into the cliffside. The stone steps were worn smooth, and four precisely measured pillars rose up to support a wide pediment. Beyond the pillars there was a single darkened archway sealed by an ancient-looking wooden door.

Blackwood ignored the distracted Dubois and continued to work in comfortable silence. The afternoon slowly melted into evening, and as the shadows grew long, Blackwood found himself working alone in a corner of the plaza.

A soft voice came from close over his shoulder. "*Sprechen sie Deutsch?*"

Startled, he spun on instinct and nearly knocked the woman over. She was young — perhaps just a few years younger than he was — and stood bundled tight in a heavy coat. Long blonde braids escaped a woolen cap and draped over her shoulders. She grinned at Blackwood's surprise, revealing a row of pearly teeth.

It had been some time since he'd seen a woman up close, and even then, it had only been while passing by the brothels the French Army ran in the rear. There he'd grown accustomed to the tobacco-stained smirks and weathered grimaces of the working girls. Now, as he took in the forest green eyes and cold-flushed cheeks of the woman before him, he found himself smitten.

"Do you speak German?" she asked again in her native tongue.

Blackwood shook his head, then added quickly in English. "I don't understand you."

She sighed, then muttered in German. "*I only ask because your trousers are torn. Though, I suppose it is not such a shame. Old Bethilda has been enjoying the view of your backside.*"

Without thinking, Blackwood slipped a hand behind him to feel for the tear. There was none.

The woman snickered. "*I thought you couldn't speak German…*"

"*How did you know?*" he hissed, eyes darting back to the guard who still lazed by the tavern.

"*Sovilo, the tavernkeeper, told me. He noticed last night when he spoke to your captors. He said the Frenchman translated, but that the handsome one with the scar on his face did not react when the Frenchman spoke, only when the Germans did. If you are trying to conceal this skill of yours, you must try harder.*"

Blackwood cursed under his breath. The previous evening was a blur. He'd been bone weary and frozen, and looking back now he realized he must have been easy to read. He only hoped that the guards hadn't picked up on his lapse as well.

"*You are German?*" she asked.

"*American,*" he said, then quickly, "*the guards cannot know I speak your language.*"

She shrugged. "*I will not tell them.*"

"*Please, don't,*" he reiterated, his tone darkly serious.

"*I said I won't,*" she snipped, then paused and cocked her head, considering. "*Unless you upset me. Then I might.*" A devilish smile played on her lips. Blackwood wasn't amused. She continued to work, tossing a heavy shovelful of snow into the cart beside them with a grunt. "*Tell me, why are you in my village, American?*"

Blackwood glanced around, once again making sure they would not be overheard. "*Your leader didn't tell you?*"

She chuckled but did not respond.

"*We're headed for Switzerland. At least that's what they say.*"

"*I've heard it's nice there. Perhaps I too should go some day. Have you been before?*"

Blackwood clenched his jaw. "*You know, you're putting my life in danger speaking to me like this.*"

She waved him off. "*No one can hear us. Not your guards, at least.*"

"*Please, just leave me be.*"

"*You seem very afraid of them.*"

Her disappointed tone irked him. "*I've seen them murder more people in one week than you have living in this entire village. If you knew what was good for you, you'd have your men make an appearance soon. Otherwise…*" he trailed off, leaving the implication hanging in the air.

The woman faltered in her motion and the snow slid from her shovel. She recovered quickly. "*Our men are not here.*"

"*Where are they?*"

"*At war. Where else?*"

"*All of them? The whelps? The elders?*"

She stood straight, stabbing her shovel into the snow and looking at him resolutely. "*Yes. All of them.*"

Blackwood shook his head. "*Your Kaiser must be desperate.*"

"*What is your name, American?*"

"Blackwood."

Her smile returned, but behind her eyes there was a shadow of sadness. "*Well, welcome to my village, Herr Blackwood. I do hope you find your stay comfortable.*"

She was gone before Blackwood could respond, retreating across the plaza toward a group of women. He watched the sway of her body through the long coat and tried to dismiss the lurid thoughts that suddenly consumed his mind.

This place was not as he had expected. Then again, he thought, none of this journey had been.

13

THE SKY outside was black and the fire in the tavern's upstairs sitting room glowed orange. The prisoners were huddled together, having pulled a handful of chairs into a close circle so that their words would not be heard through the floor.

"It feels almost too good to be true," Dubois mused. "A warm bed and hot food, and the company of so many women to boot."

"Aye. Dinnae get any ideas, Frenchman. They're still Germans." McCulloch snickered.

Dubois winked. "I assure you I am very happily married, but a man can still browse through the shop window, can he not?"

Blackwood ignored their squabbling. Beside him on one side, Enzo stared off into space while on the other Fletcher's beady eyes darted about and his fingers drummed with nervous energy.

McCulloch eyed the Brit. "What's your problem, sassenach?"

Fletcher scowled at the term. "I don't like 'em."

"What, women?" McCulloch gave a hearty guffaw.

"No, you bloody ape. These mountain folk. There's something wicked here. I can feel it."

McCulloch threw himself back with an exaggerated sigh. "Again with this. Is there anything you're not afraid of, boy?"

Dubois took a more gentle approach, leaning forward and asking, "I am curious, what do you find to be so wrong with this place?"

Fletcher glanced around the circle. "None of you feel it? It's like a cloud in the air. Something… something nefarious and immoral. I mean, you seen what's downstairs?"

"The guards?" Dubois ventured.

"No, mate, not the bloody guards. That damnable freak behind the bar."

Dubois winced. "Come now, *mon ami*, the color of a man's skin is no way to judge him. We are not Americans."

"Don't lump me in with him," Blackwood muttered.

Dubois chuckled. "I am only teasing, cowboy. Fletcher, what is it that bothers you so about that poor man's malady?"

"That ain't no poor man," Fletcher spat. "Them folk, them whiteys, they're born rotten. Children of Satan, some say. I seen one once, just before I was captured. I was running a message along the Front. That's what I did, I was a messenger. No one quicker. No one better. I got a medal from the General his'self for how good I was. Then one bloody day I get orders to warn another regiment about a German charge. Run halfway across the damn Front before I end up at this burnt-out little shack. Stop there to get some cover and catch me breath, and right there in the shadows I end up seein' this little girl. All blank faced, she was, like a ghost, but with them demon red eyes. Looked right at me and shrieked so loud I thought I might jump out of me damn skin. Got me running again, she sure did. Running straight into a bloody kraut patrol."

"Huh." McCulloch smirked. "Hell of a messenger you must have been, stumbling into a whole wad of krauts."

"I was a *fantastic* messenger," Fletcher spat. "Them Germans shouldn't've been there. No way. Don't know how it happened. Wicked brat must've scrambled me head. Put a curse on me or such. I tell you, they're a spawn of the devil."

Enzo piped up to Dubois, who answered in Italian.

"What'd you tell him?" Fletcher demanded.

"That you are a very odd man."

"Call me odd all you like, but I'm telling ya that there's something wicked happening here. This place, these people… a hundred broads with only one man, and him one of them pale folk?" Fletcher's face reddened as his words came faster, fueled by a spastic energy. "I've heard tell of places like this. Places where the devil walks free. I'm tellin' you right now, we're never leaving this village. It's got a curse to it. Don't believe me? What about you, Scotsman? You can't say it doesn't happen. You know exactly what kind of wickedness I'm talking about!"

McCulloch picked at his fingernails lazily. "I never know what the hell you're talking about."

"I'm talking about your wicked countryman, *Sawney Bean*."

It was like a light went out behind McCulloch's eyes. His face sank into a grimace that he turned on Fletcher. "Watch yer mouth, you long-faced imp."

Blackwood caught the sudden change in demeanor. "What's he talking about?"

Fletcher, suddenly avoidant of the Scot's glare, went on. "A whole wicked family from up in the Highlands, in a place just like this, they—"

"*Enough!*" McCulloch snapped with enough power to quiet the Brit.

A tense silence reigned. Blackwood's gaze shifted from man to man as he waited for the argument to reignite. It seemed that Fletcher had found the sense to let it go.

Dubois was the one to break the ice. "It is quite cruel for one to dangle such a tantalizing thread and not deliver, you know? Will one of you not enlighten the rest of us as to what this is all about?"

"Well," Fletcher ventured with a nervous glance to McCulloch, who now stared angrily into the flames. "Up in the Highlands, there was this fella—"

"Oh, damn you!" McCulloch hissed. "Shut your minge. If anyone's gonna tell that villain's tale, I willnae let it be a bloody sassenach."

The others waited as McCulloch gathered himself. He leaned forward, his glowering eyes returning to the flames. When he spoke again, his voice was low and his words halting and steeped in disdain. "It were a few hundred years back. And it *weren't* the bloody Highlands he was hiding out in, ya cunt. Sawney Bean come from Haddingtonshire. According to legend, he was the son of a grave digger. That's where they say he first went wrong — too much time spent wallowing among the dead.

"Some say he was a normal enough lad. Others say he was a slow type, thoughts droolin' from his lips and what not. Didnae have much a way at life, at least not till he met a woman called Black Agnes. Wicked one she was. A witch. A real one, not one of them cunning folk mashin' herbs in a shack. No, she'd pledged her soul to the devil, and when she got her hands on that boy, she brought him right in line with her. These two, they took to each other like curs. No wedding, no vows, nothing like that. They were poor as the dirt his father dug. But unlike his pa, he wasnae the workin' type. No, digging graves didnae suit the life they wanted after."

McCulloch rose to throw a log on the fire. When he settled back in his seat to continue, Blackwood noticed the ire in his voice; it was clear the old man didn't want to tell this story. It was also clear that he believed his own words.

"Sawney Bean and Black Agnes… ugh. They took to the forest, highwaymen at first. They'd catch poor folks on the road late at night, slaughter 'em and steal everything down to the clothes on their backs. Only took a handful of killings before the locals caught on, though. A party of men managed to root 'em out, drive 'em deeper into the wilderness and away from the well-traveled routes. That's where they began to starve. He weren't no woodsman, and she, being a witch, had no affinity for trappin' or hunting beasts either. But they was good at one thing: killing folk. People say it was starvation that led 'em to their first taste of human flesh."

An overly dramatic "*Mon Dieu!*" escaped Dubois's lips.

McCulloch's grim stare silenced him. "It's no joke, Frenchman. They solidified their pact with the devil in those woods by eating of their own kind. And the devil took 'em deep under his wing, and he used 'em well."

"Aye!" Fletcher cut in, his passion reignited with a sense of validation. "Brought 'em right up into the Highlands—

"Keep your forked tongue in yer geggie!" McCulloch snapped. "It wasnae the Highlands they hunted, dammit! 'Twere the Lowlands, down at Bennane Head. They found a cave on the shore. It weren't a normal cave though. It was like the devil knew of their coming back when the stones were formed, made it special for 'em. The mouth of it flooded with the high tide, keepin' 'em hidden in there, washing away their tracks every morning and eve. It was from there that they'd range out, always in the dark. They'd take to the roads, hunting weary travelers under the moon. 'Course by then they'd lost all taste for the finer foods — all they had a hunger for was human flesh. Some they'd slit their throats and drag 'em back to their cave to feast on by day. Others they'd wrangle as playthings, and not *just* the women. Bring 'em back and rape 'em, eat 'em slow just a piece at a time, pickle their own parts in front of 'em while they hanged in cages in the dark of the cave. They say Sawney's brood took over a thousand lives in Ayrshire over the next score of years…" McCulloch trailed off with a shudder.

"Brood?" Blackwood asked.

"Eh?"

"You said brood."

"Aye… their brood. There were only the two of 'em to start. But like all evil things, they bred. Old Black Agnes bore sons and daughters to him. Wicked little things caught in the devil's snare from birth, suckling human bones soon as the tit ran dry. The sons they ate while they were still tender. The daughters they kept. In time, those daughters bled, and Sawney bred them too. It kept this way until wicked old Black Agnes had the coven the devil'd promised her, the brute Sawney at its head. By the end there were said to be more than two score of the wicked broads that sprung from his loins."

"*Quoi?*" Dubois ejected. The mirth had melted from his face, replaced with horrified disbelief. "*C'est dégoûtant.*"

McCulloch shrugged and ignored the interruption. "I weren't there. Don't know the whole truth to it, only what folks say. From what I hear, by the time the king's men found that cave and put the blade to those cunts, what they found had 'em falling on their own swords. Bodies, scores of 'em. Fingers and peckers pickled in barrels, tongues hung from wires to dry to jerky in the sun. A thousand bones cast out in the shallows. A whole beach of death, rotting and filth. They say there were still some alive in them cages, defiled and missing bits, begging for death. I suppose the soldiers gave them their wish, because they say no one came out of that place alive…"

A heavy silence settled over the room broken only by the snapping flames.

"Now you get it." Fletcher stared from one man to the next. "Now you understand what we're dealing with. Scores of women and one crusty old whitey — this ain't some bloody fairy tale. Witch folk, covens that bleed men dry of their seed and their blood. Been around since before Christ, they have. Now you look around here and tell me this ain't exactly the place a wicked thing like Black Agnes would be. Take it from me, if we ain't careful, these bitches'll boil us and wear our bones for jewelry."

"How have you not been strangled yet?" McCulloch muttered.

"Is it true?" Blackwood asked the Scot, ignoring Fletcher.

McCulloch waggled his head for a moment in thought, then clicked his tongue. "Aye. At least a part of it."

"*Incroyable…*" Dubois muttered. "Well, we must post a watch by the window then, yes? Set a schedule with sentries and a system of alarms. We must all be on the lookout for a wicked woman riding a broom through the night."

The others shared in a chuckle, only Fletcher was unimpressed. "Oi, laugh it up. You'll see. You'll all bloody see… You still don't feel it, do you? You'll feel it. The devil's here on this mountain with us, and by the time you fools wise up, it'll be too late."

Blackwood had felt his weariness catching up with him all evening. He stood and cleared his throat, having had his fill of the beady-eyed Brit. "The only devil I'm worried about is downstairs wearing a German uniform. I'd say it's a good idea for you to remember that, Fletcher, because *that* devil might actually get you."

With that, Blackwood retreated to his room. Enzo followed shortly after, and both men took to their beds. Blackwood purged his mind of the Scotsman's silly tale but had a more difficult time ignoring the thoughts of the woman from the plaza. Those deep green eyes and that sly smile stared back at him from the back of his eyelids as sleep slowly overtook him.

⁓

It was dark when Blackwood awoke to a gentle shake. He seized the outstretched hand that rocked him. Enzo yelped and drew back. The pale glow of moonlight from the window illuminated the boy's hands held up in submission.

"What?" Blackwood demanded.

"You… you hear?" Enzo sputtered the broken English words, miming toward his own ears.

Blackwood sat up. Outside, a light wind hummed against the shutters. In the deep quiet of night, he heard it: a muffled howl. It was long and morose — almost doglike, but not quite. It leaked through the window and permeated the small room.

He crawled from the bed and crossed to the snow-caked glass panes, easing one open. An icy breeze stung his cheeks as he stared out into the night. A few windows still glowed with the warm light of embering fires, but besides that, the village appeared dead.

The call came again, emanating from somewhere down the rows of houses. It sent a primal shiver up his spine. Enzo cowered as Blackwood steeled himself against a mounting discomfort.

"*Che cos'è?*" Enzo whispered, edging closer.

Blackwood shook his head, dismissing the eerie feeling in his gut. "It doesn't matter," he said, latching the window and crawling back beneath the covers. "Go to sleep. We've got enough shit to worry about."

14

THE NEXT morning as they ate a breakfast of fried eggs and potatoes, Wulfson explained the evolving situation to the prisoners as well as their new role in it. They were to be split up amongst the villagers, working largely without oversight from the guards. The news was a bit shocking, as none of these men had experienced such freedom of movement in a very long time. Before he doled them out, Wulfson was sure to warn the prisoners of the futility of a bid for escape as well as the dire consequences for any sort of attempt to take up arms.

Just as he finished, the tavern door eased open and a group of women funneled inside. Wulfson addressed them in German. He motioned to McCulloch first, then pointed him toward a frumpy woman whose leather apron bore dark stains. "McCulloch, you will accompany Frieda to the butchery. You are there to assist in reorganizing the stores. You are not to lay hands on any blade. If caught doing so, you will be shot. Is this understood?"

McCulloch stood and nodded. "Aye, Major. I can do that."

"Enzo," the Major said next, nodding to Dubois to translate. "You will work the mill with Hilde."

A young, particularly busty woman stepped forward. Enzo's eyes widened for a moment as Dubois translated, and the Frenchman could hardly hide his smirk.

"Blackwood, Dubois, you are to assist in the splitting and delivery of firewood from the woodshed. You will be guided by Gertrude and Maria." Wulfson motioned to two women who cast warm smiles at their new charges. "And Fletcher, you were a dispatch rider, *ya*? I assume you have experience with horses and livestock."

Fletcher coughed to clear the eggs from his throat. "I suppose so, Major."

"Good. You will go with Irma to the barns."

The woman that Wulfson pointed to was middle-aged and gave him a disinterested nod.

"There is a bell outside the door. Its ringing will be considered a direct command to return here. Do not dilly dally. Stay on task. I need not repeat what will happen should you fail to do so."

⌇

The barns were located on the far edge of the village. Their stalls were sparsely inhabited by pigs and goats and a handful of cows. Several score of chickens wandered about, many roosting in the rafters of the hay loft above. Three horses were penned side-by-side with a mule and an emaciated bull that had an oddly reddish coat. In the corner napped a mangey looking mutt that didn't bother to look up as Fletcher entered.

Irma stayed with Fletcher only long enough to point out the well pump and guide him to the ladder that led to the hay loft. She mimed the actions of feeding animals and refilling water troughs while jabbering in incoherent German, then she departed, stalking back toward the village center.

Fletcher didn't like the way she'd looked at him. The village folk seemed to have taken a shine to the other prisoners, some even going so far as to smile and wave as they had shoveled the day before. Fletcher, on the other hand, had found that his own scowl was more often than not returned to him. It was because he alone saw past their pleasant charade, he'd decided. It was always that way with the cunning folk. They feigned goodness and a humble life when in reality they were little more than godless pawns of the horned man downstairs.

He stifled a yawn as he climbed to the loft. He had been on guard in his small bedroom until the wee hours of the morning, waiting on some inevitable horror to be unleashed upon his sleeping companions. It wasn't the guards he feared — well, he did fear them, but he'd found a new sense of dread over the horde of women that now ushered them about, drawing them further from the safety of numbers and no doubt working to cast spells on his compatriots. All night he'd sat there on the edge of the bed, clutching a short plank he'd managed to pry from the floor behind the bedstand. Nothing had come in the darkness besides the hellish moan that had punctuated the midnight hour. Now, as he rubbed his swollen eyes and tried to clear the fog from his mind, he wished he'd managed just a bit more shuteye.

He pitched bundles of hay to the ground floor before descending the ladder. Scanning the rows of livestock, the thought struck him that they themselves could be involved in the wickedness. Did witches not have familiars? He observed the creatures closely one by one. They seemed normal enough — but that was the Devil's way. At least according to his mother.

She had been a righteous Protestant and had taught him everything he knew about the devil. Her knowledge went far beyond the typical superstitions too. It wasn't just that one should avoid black cats or passing under ladders. She had taught him of the voices that whisper in the darkness. By ten years old, he'd memorized the names of the demons that prowled the lonely streets of London's East End. By twelve he'd become convinced that his neighbor, the old man Thompson, was possessed by none other than Beelzebub himself.

Of course, as Fletcher came into adulthood, he'd begun to reject these ideas. His mother passed from the pox and slowly her lessons slipped away into the haze of memory. It wasn't until the war that the old beliefs came barreling back to seize his mind once more. On the battlefield he'd found that a heavy respect for the forces of evil served him well. Prayer and sacrifice suddenly yielded real world consequences. After one particularly close brush with death — where he swore the Lord himself intervened to save him — he'd decided to once and for all devote himself to the smiting of the Wicked One.

One of the horses tossed its head as he passed by. He stopped, eyeing the beast. She was a thin nag with a shaggy coat. He tried his best to gauge her big brown eyes for the spark of intelligence. She looked back at him dumbly. Only partially convinced, he tore free a handful of hay from the bundle and held it out. Her thick lips grasped at his fingers greedily. The sensation brought an inadvertent smile as his mind went to his own mare from before the war, a beautiful Welsh Cob named Aggie.

In the next stall a black colt reared and slammed its hooves against the door. Fletcher flinched and staggered back. The colt stilled again, eyeing the remaining hay still clutched in his hand with jealousy. Fletcher's gaze drifted down to the rippling muscles of its haunches. It was a formidable animal. Strong. Perhaps even strong enough to drive through the several feet of snow that covered the mountain paths.

The thought quickly snowballed into a loose plan. He would need supplies for such a flight. Supplies that would be difficult to gather in his current predicament. Food, layers, a lighter or even flint. A weapon would be good as well, if he could get his hands on one. Even with a full kit, he knew his odds were slim. Slim, but not impossible. Plus, he thought to himself, death on the frozen mountainside would be preferable to whatever eternal damnation a thrall of witches might inflict.

A sharp tap echoed down the row of stalls. The incessant bleating of the goats cut to cold silence. Fletcher turned too quickly to face the source of the noise, nearly tripping over his own feet.

In the aisle ahead loomed the figure of an old woman. She was stooped, her head bent so deeply with age that it sat level with her rounded shoulders. Only her face and gnarled fingers emerged from the thick layers of wool that covered her. In one hand, she clutched a rough-hewn cane.

One of the goats dared a quiet *baa*. She used the cane to deliver another sharp tap against the beam beside her, silencing it.

Fletcher sucked in a deep breath. He ignored the impulse to flee, instead venturing a tentative step forward to peer at her face in the dim light. Her skin was blemished with age and shattered in all directions with wrinkles. Thin lips folded against each other over a toothless mouth, and her jowls hung loose. More than anything, it was her eyes that caught his attention. They looked right past him. Milky, dead orbs, as if a thick haze of winter mist had settled over the woman's mind. He reached up and slowly waved his hand in a wide arc, watching the dead pupils for movement.

She chortled. It was a wet, gasping noise, and despite the perceived levity, her creased lips didn't lift into a smile. "I see you well enough, *kleiner rabe*."

Fletcher felt a chill run up his spine. "You speak English…"

"Yes. A man taught me, long ago," she muttered absently. "Long, long, long ago…"

Fletcher, already convinced this was some brood queen of the witch hive, felt his heart pump faster with her answer. The way she delivered the words implied eons, not decades. He'd heard of witches living well beyond the lifespan of normal, God-fearing folk, subsiding off the blood of innocents and children. The horrible image of Black Agnes manifested in his mind, and he grew even more certain that the old Scottish tale was more fact than fiction. Straightening his posture, he cleared his throat and spoke with as much authority as he could muster. "It's said that the Devil must make himself known to those who spot 'im. So I ask you this once, coffin-dodger, are you in league with Satan?"

She didn't give her odd little laugh this time. Her lips pursed, and her brow somehow furrowed deeper. "No, *rabe*, your Satan does not live here."

"He ain't *my* Satan," Fletcher came back.

The old woman looked through him. "You're the one who speaks of him."

In that moment, Fletcher wished for nothing more than to be rid of this haggard wench, but he wouldn't be doing the Lord service in letting her slink away without an admission of what she was. "Don't you go twisting my words," he hissed, then added hatefully, "…*witch*."

In a motion that Fletcher imagined might haunt his nightmares forever, her tongue darted out and dragged across her lips — a ripe slug emerging from its cave to moisten the cracked earth beyond.

"A shame…" she muttered. She looked as if she might say something else, but instead she slowly turned and began shuffling away.

Fletcher ran a hand through his greasy mop of hair and realized he was trembling. He'd been through hell on earth in his day. He'd run messages through gunfire and choked on both German and Allied gas alike. He'd even taken a bullet once from a kraut sniper, though it had just been a grazing wound. Now, watching the old hag shamble away, he yearned to be anywhere but here — including the Front. "You know I've got God on my side. Who've you got?" he called out, more for his own benefit than hers.

"*Du kennst Gott nicht*," she muttered in German. Though he had no idea what it meant, it still gave him a chill. She halted in her slow shamble for only a moment, not bothering to turn. "The snow is too deep for these horses. In case you were wondering."

"Get out of my head, witch," Fletcher said under his breath once she had disappeared through the door and into the bright sheen of snow. He shook his head, and when that didn't clear his mind, he slapped himself. The colt stomped its feet, and he realized that the goats had resumed their bleating. He turned to the colt and considered the old woman's parting words.

"Bollocks, all of it," he muttered. "Never trust a witch."

Though somehow he knew she was telling the truth.

They were well and truly trapped.

15

BLACKWOOD BROUGHT the axe down in a heaving arc, splintering the log before him. It was midafternoon and his shoulders had begun to burn from the repetitive motion. Dubois moseyed before him to emplace another hunk of wood on the splitting block.

The Frenchman sang quietly as they worked. His voice was too flat for the tune, but the melody was nice enough. Blackwood hummed along, timing his strikes in rhythm with the lyrics. They had worked this way for hours. Now, the heap of split logs had grown to encompass their quadrant of the open-sided woodshed. When they finally ran out of space, they transitioned to tossing the firewood into a nearby oxcart.

Blackwood hadn't seen the guards since that morning. They had been hovering outside the tavern, glowering as the prisoners migrated away to their various working stations. He figured they were most likely still there — they did not seem the type to willingly give up the comforts of their lodgings to patrol the cold streets. As odd as it was, their absence set him more on edge than their presence. They could be anywhere, stalking just out of view or crouching in the shadows, watching him over iron sights. All it would take was one small move in the wrong direction, one slip-up caught in the wrong light, and he might be gunned down like a dog where he stood. Blackwood was the type who preferred to see it coming.

With the cart full, Dubois called out in German to the two women. They sat nearby bundling thin branches into faggots of kindling. Maria, the younger of the two, finished tying a knot then pointed north up the road that led into the plaza. "*Bring it to the meetinghouse, if you would. It is the long building beside the cliff. Lucia should be there. She can show you where to stack it.*"

"*We shall return shortly then,*" Dubois said with a short bow. He translated for Blackwood, who simply nodded in return. Apparently, Blackwood's oafish slip-up in front of Sovilo had at least escaped the Frenchman's eye.

There were no oxen in the town, at least as far as Blackwood had seen, so the two men positioned themselves under each side of the yoke. Together they raised the ox cart onto its single axle and set off. It was heavy, and Blackwood had to stoop to make up for Dubois's short stature. They had only traveled a few hundred feet along the icy road when Dubois called for a break. They lowered the long wooden arms to the earth. Dubois straddled one and sat.

"*Coucou*, cowboy," Dubois said once he'd caught his breath. "Have I ever told you the story of Jean Bernard?"

"You've never told me any stories."

"Haven't I?" Dubois massaged his thighs. "Jean Bernard was a soldier from my town. He fought in the trenches, an infantryman, I believe. One night the sky lit up with the thunder of artillery and he… he lost all of his *amies*, his friends, to a bombardment. As it went on, he just… Well, I suppose he gave up. Ran as fast as he could toward the rear lines, his mind lost to fear. He passed right by the other soldiers and kept on, passing the officers, then our own artillery. He kept running in this way, running and running and running, until he was so far away that the grass was once again green and the air was quiet." Dubois wiped the cold snot from his nose and raised his brows, looking for some reaction from Blackwood.

"What the fuck are you talking about?"

Dubois readjusted and went on. "He reached a point where he'd run so far that he could not go any further. There he collapsed in the road. The next thing he knew, someone was kicking his boot and demanding to know who he was. He startled." Dubois began to act his words out. "'Who am I?' Jean demanded. 'Who are you?' The man standing over him, obscured by the sun, puffed out his chest. 'I am the General in charge of this Regiment,' the man proclaimed. '*Mon Dieu!*' Jean exclaimed. 'The damn General! I did not realize I had gone *that* far!'" Dubois smiled mischievously and waited, as if for applause.

Blackwood stared back deadpan. After a short silence, Dubois sucked his teeth. "You see, the joke is that the general is so far from the—"

"No, I get it," Blackwood interrupted. "Are you ready to get back to work?"

Dubois sighed. He straightened his coat and shook the blood back into his legs as he stood. "Sometimes you are too serious, cowboy. What is life without some fun?"

Before Blackwood could respond, Dubois lost his balance on the ice. His stubby legs kicked out before him as he toppled to the ground with a loud thump.

Blackwood snorted, then erupted in a belly laugh as the Frenchman sat up with a groan.

"I take it back," Dubois muttered. "You're not too serious. You're just an ass."

This only made Blackwood laugh harder. He hauled the Frenchman to his feet and Dubois's frown quickly melted. He himself began to laugh as they lifted the heavy yoke and resumed their trek toward the plaza.

The meetinghouse wasn't difficult to find. Blackwood leaned against the cart as Dubois knocked cordially at the door. Across the plaza, Blackwood spotted Hanz sitting on the bench outside of the tavern rubbing his hands together and shivering in the cold. For a brief moment they locked eyes. Blackwood forced himself to break away first. A silent fury rose in him at the act — to avoid the cretin's gaze was as against his nature as a thing could be. He knew from overhearing the guards' mutterings that the sniveling rat had never so much as smelled the stench of the trenches or glimpsed the scene of open combat. Yet here, he was a superior. Blackwood spit in the snow to clear the bad taste from his mouth.

Dubois knocked again, louder this time, and a woman finally answered. Blackwood recognized her. She was the same woman he'd spoken to the day before.

"*Lucia?*" Dubois asked.

"*Yes?*" She looked confused, then spotted the cart behind Dubois. "*Ah, yes. The firewood. Come in.*"

She led them into the hall. It was primitive and oddly ornate. Blackwood took in the countless bleached skulls that spotted the walls alongside a score of violent tapestries. It reminded him more of an ancient hunting lodge than a meetinghouse.

"*The wood goes here.*" She pointed them to an inlet beside the stone chimney.

The two men set about unloading the cart. The woman, Lucia, followed them outside and gathered a load of wood in her arms.

"*No, no,*" Dubois protested. "*Please, let us.*"

"*Nonsense. You think I would let our guests toil alone? Don't forget whose village this is, Frenchman.*" She winked.

Dubois smiled and raised his hands in submission.

Together the trio unloaded the wood in silence. Lucia carried her own weight easily, hauling heavy armloads back and forth more efficiently than Dubois. The hall was warm, and she had abandoned the thick wool coat she had been wearing the previous day. She now wore a loose cotton blouse tucked into a long skirt that was cinched tight around her waist, revealing the feminine curves of her figure. Blackwood struggled to conceal his glances.

With the last of the wood stacked, she swung the door shut behind her before they could depart.

"*Fraulein, we must—*" Dubois began.

She cut him off with a dismissive wave. "*Come, you must take a break.*" When both men exchanged a glance, she went on. "*Those nasty guards are not here. You are allowed to relax. Come, warm yourselves by the fire.*"

They did as she insisted, taking their seats on a bench while she took her own on a chair by the flames.

"*I am Louis Dubois,*" the Frenchman began politely, then motioned to the man beside him. "*And this is... erm.*" He turned to Blackwood, switching to English. "I'm terribly sorry, but I am afraid I do not know your first name."

"Edward," Blackwood said, though his eyes were locked with Lucia's. There was a sparkle of intrigue in them — she must have assumed the other prisoners already knew about his secret linguistic proficiency.

"Ah." Dubois cleared his throat. "*This is Edward Blackwood.*"

"*Oh, we have met already. It is a pleasure to see you once more, Herr Blackwood. I was hoping we would speak again.*" Her lips formed a thin smile.

He stifled a groan. So much for keeping his secret. "*The pleasure is mine, fraulein.*" He muttered in German.

"*Je n'en reviens pas!*" Dubois looked shocked. "*You speak German?*"

"*A bit.*"

"*My sincerest apologies, Herr Blackwood. I imagined your compatriots would have known.*" Despite her words, Lucia's face showed no sign of regret.

Dubois looked at Blackwood with both newfound respect — and maybe a hint of distrust.

She went on. "*Thank you for the firewood. I'm sorry if I appeared caught off guard. I was not expecting you so soon. You two work quickly.*"

"*Nonsense,*" Dubois insisted. "*It is we who must apologize for interrupting.*"

She regarded him kindly. "*You're too polite, monsieur Dubois. I can always tell a gentlemen when I meet one.*"

Dubois grinned back, resuming the charming — if not a bit clownish — air that had slowly emerged over the last two days. He gave a dramatic seated bow finished with a flourish of his hand.

Her laughter tinkled lightly in the air, oddly resonant in the long hall. Blackwood was unwillingly captivated by the sound.

She took a loaf of bread from a nearby table. After tearing a hunk off for herself, she handed the loaf to the men. "*How are you finding our little village?*"

"*Oh, my dear, it is absolutely wonderful!*" Dubois's dramatic stylings grew as he flourished his hands about. "*The air is crisp and clean, the water purer than the driven snow. And the food, oh, the food...*" He tore a shred off the loaf and held it up like a piece of found treasure. "*Your baker has skills beyond that of the finest French cuisine. I must steal him once this wretched war is over. He will be the toast of Paris.*"

Once again, the hall filled with her infectious laughter. "*Her,*" she corrected. "She *will be the toast of Paris.*"

He bowed deferentially in his seat once again. "*Of course.*"

"*You are quite the character, monsieur Dubois. I think you could charm a viper.*" She turned her smile on Blackwood. "*And what about you?*"

"*What about me?*" Blackwood shifted in his seat, eyeing the door. "*We should get back.*"

"*No.*" Her smile ebbed and her tone shifted to take on a domineering edge. "*Maria and Gertrude can handle the work at the woodshed. I need you two to help me with another task.*" She stood and hauled a small crate from one of the nearby benches. "*I hope you both have good knees.*"

Blackwood was hesitant, but truth be told he had no idea who he was supposed to be answering to — Wulfson was oddly absent, as was his wont lately, and the guards didn't seem to care, so long as they were warm in the tavern. This woman seemed as good a boss as any.

He took the crate and Dubois took another. Whatever was inside gave off an unpleasant smell, not quite foul but a bit sour. Lucia donned her coat and retrieved a carafe of steaming water from the hearth. She led them outside into the plaza and toward the recess in the cliffside.

Up close, the structure was even more impressive than Blackwood had previously thought. The pillars stood a dozen feet high and just beyond them a wide wooden door led through the stone wall.

"*This is magnificent craftsmanship,*" Dubois marveled as they passed underneath. "*I must admit, I have been admiring it from afar.*"

"*If you think this is impressive,*" Lucia said, "*just wait.*"

She hauled the door open and they entered into a great void. Ahead of them stretched a long aisle between two rows of pillars, each bearing a sconced torch. The flickering firelight evaporated into the blackened emptiness of the cavern. The air was stale and damp, and the hollow echo of their footsteps betrayed its immense size.

"*Try to be quiet here.*" She gestured into the darkness. "*We do not want to wake the bees.*"

"*The bees?*" Blackwood whispered. He cast a wary glance at Dubois, who was too enthralled with his surroundings to be bothered.

Lucia led them down the aisle to where the pillars ended. She disappeared into the dark for only a moment, then returned wielding a large lantern. In the sudden light, Blackwood could make out an ornate door directly ahead. Carved into the rockface above it was a massive relief — at least ten yards across and equally as tall. The figures depicted in it were eerily lifelike. It showed a man kneeling over a sprawled bull, the bull's head thrust high in the air, its eyes bulging and terrified. Across its throat, the man drew a long dagger. Both sun and moon hung above as a scorpion, a dog, and a coiled snake looked on. He nudged Dubois, who still stared at the pillars, but by the time the Frenchman looked, Lucia had strode away, and the shadows had already consumed the relief.

"*This way,*" she called, heading for the back corner of the cavern. "*As I said, I hope you have good knees.*"

They crossed through an archway carved into rough stone and the ceiling opened up to a thin shaft. A timeworn wooden staircase led upward in a tight spiral. When she put her weight on the first step, it creaked. The darkness above swallowed the sound. Blackwood imagined that this must be what it was like at the bottom of a capped well — a place he would never have ventured willingly. He eyed the worn stairs with unease. While they appeared stable enough at first glance, the sound that the dried lumber made as she continued upward made him hesitate. "*Where are you taking us?*"

"*Did you see the tower atop the cliff?*"

"*Yes.*"

"*This is the way up.*"

"*And what's up there?*"

"*The ravenry,*" she said. "*Try to keep up.*"

Together they began their ascent. Her lantern shined bright as the stone floor below disappeared into shadows. Blackwood followed behind her, picking his steps carefully. Behind him, Dubois's breath quickly devolved into haggard gasps. Even Blackwood began to pant. Lucia, however, did not seem to break a sweat. After some time, she paused and looked back. "*Do you need a break?*"

"*Yes, please,*" Dubois said graciously, setting his crate down and plopping to a seat on the stairs.

"*What is a ravenry?*" Blackwood panted.

"*It's just what it sounds like, Herr Blackwood,*" she said. "*You should both save your breath now; we are only halfway there.*"

Dubois whimpered.

They rested for several minutes before Dubois regained enough of his composure to resume their climb. This time the Frenchman gassed out early and they were forced to slow their pace lest they lose him in the darkness below. When they finally reached the top, they were met with a wooden door. Lucia finagled the latch, and Blackwood followed her through into the blinding daylight. As he erupted into the cold, he found himself in a wide cylindrical room. The walls, or rather the wooden parapets that stood between the stone columns that supported the conical ceiling above, were only chest high. Spindly cages stood piled atop old crates and broken perches, and nest boxes hung from shelves mounted to the columns. At least a dozen ravens scampered across the rafters and quorked at their arrival. Lucia shushed them, hanging the lantern before filling a small trough with the warm water from the carafe.

She motioned for Blackwood to bring her the crate. From within she pulled handfuls of kitchen scraps — mostly meat trim and stringy fascia — which she doled out in a second trough. The birds cackled and swarmed before her, snipping at each other as they feasted greedily. Blackwood stepped back, uneasy with the ravenous creatures' proximity. Long discarded eggshells crackled beneath his feet.

"*C'est beau,*" Dubois muttered once he'd caught his breath. He stood at the ramparts, staring out over the breathtaking view. An endless sea of snowcapped mountains stretched before them in every direction. Blackwood followed the Frenchman's eyes as they fell downward to the edge of the cliff below. "*It is high enough here for a man to get sick.*"

"*Ya,*" Lucia said, shooing a particularly aggressive raven back so that the smaller ones could feed.

Blackwood leaned over the edge of the wooden planks and stared down. They were indeed atop the tower. Forty feet below them, the base of the tower disappeared into the snow less than an arm's length from the cliff's edge. Far below that, the village appeared tiny — the people milling about the streets little more than insects scurrying back and forth.

"*This village of yours… it truly is remarkable,*" Dubois said.

"*Is it?*" Lucia shrugged. "*I suppose it is easy to get used to when you have spent your whole life here.*"

"Ah, but you are blessed to have done so, my dear. There are many people who would give a great deal of money just to visit a place like this."

"If you say so."

Dubious began to say something else but held back.

Finished feeding the crows, Lucia placed the lid back onto the crate and sat casually atop it. "*What is it?*"

"*I am afraid I do not know where to start,*" Dubois admitted. "*I don't mean to offend, but what on earth is this place?*"

"*This is Melvilla. Surely someone has already told you that.*"

"*No, I mean…*" Dubois's hand floated erratically through the air as he stammered to find the right phrasing.

"*I know what you mean, monsieur Dubois.*" She smiled gently.

"*Then you know that this… this tower of yours, the cavern below, the stonework… It is… it is extremely unorthodox to see such a thing so far from civilization.*"

"*I do.*"

Blackwood found himself annoyed by the Frenchman's drawn-out politeness. "*He's trying to ask you who built it.*"

Dubois scowled but Lucia chuckled. "*I figured. You seem like a learned man, monsieur Dubois.*" She flashed a wry grin at Blackwood. "*You, maybe not so much. What do you two know of the Roman Empire?*"

"*Me, nothing,*" Blackwood said. "*Him… probably everything, the way he talks.*"

Dubois sucked his teeth at the comment but smiled when Lucia shifted her gaze to him. "*I have taught some courses on the subject,*" he admitted bashfully.

"*Then you likely know that this mountain range, as with many of the lands of southern Germany, were disputed territories for much of the Roman's reign?*"

"*Oui, it is known.*"

"*…and that, despite their best efforts, the Romans could never quite maintain the foothold here that they so desired.*"

Dubois nodded. "*As I understand it, the German tribes had a rather… combative history.*"

She laughed. "*An understatement.*"

"*This is a Roman outpost then, this far out into the mountains?*"

"*Yes,*" she said. "*Though the men who built it were not from Rome itself. They were legionnaires — men pulled from all corners of the Empire and forced to fight on behalf of emperors and senates. A long time ago they were commanded to fight the tribes of the foothills. They were overwhelmed and beaten back, forced to take to the harshness of the mountains in order to make their escape. Low on resources* and without shelter or reinforcement, they were bound for death. Now that I think of it, you two might be able to relate." She paused with a smirk. "*That is when they discovered the cave that sits beneath us now. It was a sanctuary for them. It saved them from certain death. Here those men were able to hide and survive, cut off from the world at large and believed dead by their commanders. In time others came, many fleeing the wars that raged in the lowlands. Women, children, people in need. Melvilla was built and families were forged. The rest, well…*" She motioned toward the village below.

Dubois held up an inquisitive finger. "*Why did they not return to Rome once Bavaria was conquered?*"

"*Though I cannot speak to the reasoning of men who died eons ago, I imagine they preferred to build their lives here, where not even Rome could find them.*" Her tone shifted to melancholy as she stared out over the mountains. "*Would you blame them? Men torn from their own homes and forced to fight all across the known world for masters who cared for nothing but their own ego and greed.*"

Blackwood inferred the meaning behind her shift. "*That's what's happened to your men, isn't it?*"

She nodded, venom leaking into her voice. "*Our ancestors were blessed with anonymity. A fake name given at a trading post, a false identity used to procure apprenticeship in the cities. They kept our community secret and thriving. Unfortunately, this secret did not last through recent centuries. When the German soldiers first came years ago at the outbreak of the Great War, they took only those of fighting age. My brother was among them. Last he wrote, they had been sent south to fight the Italians. At that point we thought there was nothing else they could take from us. Then more soldiers came. They told us they needed working hands for the lands behind the front lines. Laborers to build fortifications and transport the wounded. That's when they took the young and the old.*"

"*I've never heard of this. That is terrible,*" Dubois said softly.

"*We are not city folk. Nor are we farmers. Though we keep some livestock, we hunt and forage most of our food. There is little tax to be drawn from wild game or mountain crops. Apparently, the Kaiser and his generals decided that we mountain folk had not given our fair contribution to the war effort. So, they decided that taking our fathers and brothers was not enough. That's when they came for our children and grandfathers.*"

"*I'm so sorry,*" Dubois offered.

"*It is I who am sorry. Perhaps if we had been stronger, put up more resistance, then maybe they would have taken less.*"

"*Non, non…*" Dubois tried. "*Your men and your boys will return. War is a monster, but it does not destroy all. There will be a time when this is all just an unpleasant memory.*"

A sad smile crossed her lips, but she said nothing in response. From far below came the clang of the tavern's bell.

Lucia cleared her throat. "*Apparently your masters want you back. I trust you can find your own way down?*"

Dubois looked to the door and groaned. Blackwood clapped him on the back. "Easier down than up, old boy."

Dubois led the way down into the darkness. Blackwood made to follow him, but Lucia grasped his arm as he passed. He met her eyes.

"*You'll need this.*" She pulled the lantern from its hook and pushed it into his hand. A cold gust of wind howled through the tower, blowing her hair into a wild halo. Blackwood felt his pulse quicken as she shook the wild strands away and leaned in close to his ear. "*Perhaps I will see you tonight at the festival, Herr Blackwood. I believe we have more to discuss, just the two of us.*"

"*Festival?*" He stammered over the word.

"*No one has told you what day it is?*" She scoffed. "*It's the twenty-fifth of December.*"

Blackwood, afraid to mangle his words once more, offered only a curt nod in response. Her hand fell away, and he left to follow Dubois.

Neither of the men spoke as they trotted down the winding staircase. Blackwood was grateful for the silence. It allowed him a moment of self-flagellation. He didn't like how off-kilter this woman made him, like a teenage boy struck dumb by a pretty girl. There was no time for all that — there was still a war going on, and despite the temporary comforts of the village, he was still an active player in that conflict.

Now is not the time, he almost said out loud. He reiterated it silently again and again, yet still he could not shake her from his mind.

When they reached the sprawling cavern, Dubois caught sight of the great relief on the wall for the first time in the lantern light. "This place is astounding," he muttered. "A relic culture, at least in some regards. What fascinating traditions they must have…"

"Get a move on," Blackwood grunted, shoving him forward.

The Frenchman gave a wistful moan but did not resist.

"They can't be that different from us," Blackwood offered in consolation as they trudged out into the plaza. "Apparently they celebrate Christmas."

16

THE GUARDS sat in the corner of the tavern's dining room. Hanz leaned forward against the table, picking lazily at his fingernails. The others ate loudly around him while his own half-finished portion of dinner sat lukewarm before him. Besides the intermittent shifts of sitting watch over the village plaza — a useless endeavor enacted only for show, since the prisoners had been dispersed well outside of their sight — the group of them had spent the day doing much the same of what they did now: nothing.

Evening had brought with it a horde of villagers who bustled about the tavern. They had shuffled here and there, arms loaded with covered trays and bundles of torches. The tables were rearranged and barrels of beer and cider rolled out. Sovilo had overseen it all, snapping curt orders like a frustrated factory foreman. Then, as fast as they had descended upon the tavern, the villagers were gone. Now the tavern lay silent and still, the only noise coming from the guards' own smacking lips and the gentle murmur of Wulfson scolding Klaus behind the closed door to his private quarters.

Johan scraped at a marmot bone with his teeth. He chewed the cartilage from the joint then tossed it down in disdain. "*They serve us scraps. Did you see what they brought to those swine upstairs? Venison, a whole damn slab of it. And here we are, chewing on rodents.*"

Victor slugged from a stein of beer he had pilfered from the bar and belched. "*I like marmot.*"

Johan scowled. "*That's not the point. We should be living like kings here. No men about, a whole slew of worthless hillwalker women running around like chickens with their heads cut off. With a party of respectable German warriors like us coming into town, we should be having our toes sucked at the same time as our cocks.*"

Hanz cringed and glanced at Dietmar, the only other man not participating in the foul conversation. He sat silently staring at the door to Wulfson's quarters. In his fingers he twirled a British boot knife — a prize he claimed to have earned in the trenches. The short blade glinted in the firelight as it spun in tight circles.

"*Ya, that's the way it should be,*" Johan whined to no one in particular. "*Show up, take a war wife or two for the winter, and have a pleasant vacation from that shithole Rothenspring. But no… no… The Major's got a hard on for these hill-walkers. I think he's trying to keep them all for himself, charm them with his little proper gentleman act. Too bad these uncultured mountain sorts don't go for that. No, women like this you've got to break in. Like a horse but with tits.*"

Victor grunted in agreement. He reached across the table and snatched the meat from Hanz's plate, his filthy fingers smearing across the boiled potatoes. Hanz accepted the slight without a word. He wasn't hungry, and what slim shred of dignity he had left wasn't worth the beating that would result from protest.

"*I like the one with the big cans. The miller girl,*" Victor drawled through a mouthful.

"*And you should be with her now, batting those melons around as you please,*" Johan snickered.

Hanz bit his tongue. Over the past twenty-four hours this topic had come to dominate the few discreet conversations the guards had shared. He no longer had to wonder if the rumors of Johan's crimes were true. Now the only question in his mind was how many rapes it had taken for them to pull him from the line and ship him off to Rothenspring.

"*Fuck the women,*" Dietmar muttered.

Johan nodded enthusiastically. "*Ya, that's what I'm saying!*"

"*No, you idiot.*" The knife came to a sudden halt, balanced across his finger as if he was testing its weight for the thousandth time. "*I mean forget them. We should be dealing with the swine upstairs. That's our job. That's what they brought us on for. Right now, they're up there thinking of nothing more than gutting us in our sleep. They're planning, plotting out how they'll do it. It would take a blind man not to see it.*"

"*I thought that went without saying,*" Johan grumbled. A short silence reigned until he hunched forward and smirked. "*Hey, boys, how long you think before old Klaus has enough? Pops that fucking Major right in the head?*"

"*I heard he's bulletproof,*" Victor grumbled.

Johan laughed. When the others didn't join, he pursed his lips. "*What are you talking about?*"

Victor nodded to Hanz, who realized that Johan had already been asleep on the night around the fire when he'd recounted the story he read in the newspapers. Hanz cleared his throat. "*He was in the papers some time ago. They called him the Hero of the White War.*"

"*Hero of the White War…*" Johan mocked. "*What did that prim asshole do to trick the papers into saying that?*"

"*They didn't really go into detail. Just that he was the lone survivor from his platoon,*" Hanz said, hiding his pleasure at the sudden downward shift in Johan's features. "*They said he killed a whole mess of Italians though.*"

Johan blew out a dismissive breath. "*We've all killed men.*"

"*Hundreds,*" Hanz went on. "*They say he killed hundreds. A score of Arditi at that.*"

Johan's bravado faded. "*How the hell did he do that?*"

Hanz shrugged. "*Didn't say. I suppose—*"

"*Be quiet,*" Dietmar hissed.

Johan shot a terrified look back to the Major's door. It remained shut. "*Don't worry, he can't hear us.*"

"*I said quiet!*" Dietmar snapped. Slowly he rose, eyes locked on the window to Hanz's back. Hanz followed his gaze. Outside a ring of torches had begun to form in the plaza. Dietmar squinted at the glass. "*Do you hear it?*"

Hanz did hear it. The noise came low and slow, an ethereal song that drifted through the walls like a gentle hum. "*What are they doing?*"

All four of them were standing now, migrating to the windows that lined the wall. Outside the song grew louder, and the ring of torches filled in one at a time at the center of the plaza.

"*I don't know,*" Dietmar rasped, jabbing the blade lightly against the windowsill as he stared out. "*But I don't like it.*"

17

THE VENISON roast was savory and still deep red at its core. Blackwood used a hunk of bread to sop up the blood from his plate then washed it down with a gulp of hard cider. The drink was overly sweet and, like nearly every bit of food they'd sampled since their arrival, carried a hint of honey. He savored every sip and every bite. He'd found that Rothenspring had torn away the memory of simple pleasures. Despite the gratification of the moment, he tried not to allow himself to grow accustomed to it. It was a luxury that he knew could be yanked away at any moment.

"Ah, I almost forgot." McCulloch reached into the pocket of the coat that hung off his chairback and withdrew a parcel wrapped in paper. He tossed it on the table with a thump. "Salt pork. That butcher, Frieda, she's a stout lass. Couldnae understand a damn word she said, but a kinder German I've yet to meet. Nae a bad day."

Across the table Enzo stared off as if in a daydream. He hummed a quiet tune and drummed his fingers on the table as he ate.

McCulloch eyed him. "Though not as good as this one's, it would seem…"

Dubois asked the boy something in Italian, and Enzo's eyes lit up. He spoke in quick bursts between mouthfuls, animating with his hands and grinning the whole time. When he finished, Dubois chuckled and slapped him on the shoulder.

"Well?" McCulloch demanded. "What the hell did he say?"

"Bah." Dubois rolled his eyes. "The fool thinks he's in love."

McCulloch snickered, and even Blackwood cracked a smile. Fletcher alone remained dour. He hunched by the hearth, greedily scooping the last crumbs off his plate and avoiding the others' eyes.

"You must lighten up, Englishman," Dubois prodded. "You make me nervous just looking at you."

Fletcher grunted dismissively.

"Aye, come now, *sassenach*, what's up your ass this time?" McCulloch mocked. "Ya see a black cat today — make ya piss yer pants?"

Fletcher gave an offensive gesture and McCulloch laughed.

"Enough, both of you," Blackwood weighed in. "Fletcher, did something happen today?"

Fletcher picked his teeth and assessed Blackwood's face for any sign of mockery. Finally convinced, he spoke quietly. "There was an old hag come visit me in the stables. Spoke perfect English, she did. Crotchety wench kept calling me a 'rube' or some such, acting like she knew me. Rube… She's the bloody rube."

McCulloch snorted, but Blackwood wasn't so quick to brush him off. "What else did she say?"

Fletcher shrugged. "Nothing of substance. Made sure to tell me them horses they've got can't make it out of here through the snow. I figure the old bat's full of it, likely just conniving to keep us here."

"Cannae blame her for that." McCulloch grinned. "A bunch of handsome lads we are. Except you, Englishman. I've seen handsomer faces on a beat dead donkey."

"Enough, enough," Dubois scolded. "You would think you two had been on the opposite sides of this war with all of this anger. There is no room in life for such animosity."

Blackwood stopped listening. Something else had caught his ear, a distinct melody that seemed to melt into the room from all around. He crossed to the window as Dubois went on. "It's Christmas. You both need to get along, if only for tonight. Give the rest of us some small moment of joy in this endlessly bleak endeavor."

In the square below, a horde of villagers had begun to assemble. They formed into a loose circle, each of them bearing a glowing torch. The murmur of their singing seeped through the frosted panes. Blackwood drew close enough to the glass that he could feel the cold radiating against his face.

"He can talk all the shite he likes," Fletcher spat. "Don't bother me none. If we make it out of here I'll be back in London while he'll be stuck crawling back under whatever shit-stained northern rock he came from."

McCulloch gathered a breath to retort, but he too must have heard the music as his eyes darted to Blackwood. "The hell is that noise?"

"The villagers." Blackwood pressed his hands against the glass, cutting away the reflections of the room to see more clearly. They came en masse now, emptying from the houses and streets as the circle filled in.

"Oh, hell…" Fletcher moaned. They were all at the windows now, watching as the glowing circle began to shift, spinning in a jerky revolution like an unoiled clock. The villagers marched slowly in lock step, the low, ethereal song setting their pace. The precision of their movements mimicked the tight discipline of soldiers. One step, two steps, pause. One step, two steps, pause.

What happened next did nothing to assuage the sinking paranoia that had begun to creep up Blackwood's spine. From the depths of the temple cave ahead came another light. This torch was more of a staff, its flames burning twice as bright as the others and illuminating the man holding it. It was Sovilo. He was dressed in a long robe, his stark white hair spilling out from beneath a crude wooden crown. In one hand he held the flaming staff, and with the other he led a scrawny bull by a rope. Together they calmly walked down the steps from the cave and crossed the plaza toward the flaming circle.

The bull was emaciated, its withers wrapped so tightly in its flesh that the bones looked like they might burst out with every movement. Its belly was sunken and its ribs were emboldened by shadowed recesses. As it drew closer, Blackwood made out the amber hue of its coat and a dark cloth tied tight over its eyes.

The circle parted before them. When Sovilo reached the center, the song died away and the villagers' slow rotation came to a halt. All of the figures shifted inward, tightening the ring until they were shoulder to shoulder.

The tavern door slapped open below and the guards emerged into the cold. Blackwood looked down on them as they fidgeted and spoke quietly amongst themselves — Hanz alone kept his rifle slung. The others clutched theirs before them, muttering back and forth and shooting darting glances around the darkness. Only Wulfson appeared unphased. He stood rigidly beside them. Though Blackwood could not see his face, he could imagine the Major's stony countenance.

Sovilo began to speak to the gathering. Blackwood could not make out the words, but he could hear the muffled drone of the old man's voice arcing high and low like a sermon. There was brief period of call-and-answer with the tight-packed crowd, then a chant began.

Dubois unlatched one of the windows.

Fletcher flinched at the sharp click of the latch. "Stop!" he hissed, staring at the Frenchman in horror. "Don't listen to them, it's a siren's song, I tell ya!"

Dubois ignored him, staring in awe at the scene unfolding before them. He cracked the window, and the chanting became clear.

"*Mortem ad vitam,*" the women called in unison. "*Mortem ad vitam. Mortem ad vitam.*"

"It's Latin," Dubois muttered. "'Death for life'…"

"We should bloody run." Fletcher, seized with terror, dropped back from the windows and eyed the door to the stairwell.

McCulloch blocked his path. "Hold now, sassenach. You go down them stairs, you'll get us all shot. You understand that? Dinnae get yer panties all bunched over some hens singing a bloody song."

"You heard what he just said, they're going to sacrifice us!" Fletcher spat, eyes darting around the room, no doubt searching for a weapon.

"*Non…*" Dubois muttered. "Not us…"

Another figure strode out of the darkness of the cave. Her robe was nearly sheer and white and far too lightweight for the cold of the night. It wasn't until she strode into the light of the circle that Blackwood made out her golden braids and realized who it was.

The Frenchman squinted against the glass. "*Mon Dieu.* Is that Lucia?"

Blackwood nodded. "Yeah."

"Is she their chief?" Dubois scoffed.

"Looks like it."

The villagers broke apart as she passed. In her hand Blackwood caught the shimmer of something short and metal.

"*Mortem ad vitam! Mortem ad vitam!*" The thrum of the chanting grew to a shout as Sovilo stepped to the side and held the flaming staff high over the bull. "*Mortem ad vitam! Mortem ad vitam! Mortem ad vit—*"

Lucia held her hand high, exhibiting the long-bladed dagger. All at once every voice cut off. In the sudden silence Blackwood realized just how loud the throb of his own heart was in his ears.

"*Mortem!*" Lucia shouted. Her voice carried through the frozen square like a horn and crackled with ferocity. "*Ad vitam!*"

The last syllable still hung in the air as the dagger whipped across the bull's throat. Blood spilled out over the icy cobblestones. The bull thrashed in a sudden panic, spinning toward Lucia and nearly goring her with its horns as it barreled by. She didn't so much as flinch. It stumbled before her, falling to the ground with a thud. Blood drenched its chest and pooled at its hooves as it regained its footing. It spun again, and again, searching desperately from behind the blindfold for some sign of its killer. A cold silence reigned as the hapless animal's legs began to quake. It shuffled back and forth, snorting jets of steam into the winter air and pawing at the ice. Its rear legs gave out first. It flopped down to a seat with a long, morose moan. None of the onlookers made a noise as the dark pool of blood grew. Finally the bull collapsed, writhing for only a moment as it heaved its final breath.

Lucia raised the bloodied knife high and called out to the crowd, "*In nomine Mithras! Mortem ad vitam!*"

"'In the name of Mithras,'" Dubois muttered. "'Death for life.'"

"What the hell kind of demon is a Mithras?" Fletcher demanded.

"Mithras is no demon. He is—" Dubois began. He never finished his sentence, as in that moment the entire circle of nearly one hundred women erupted in a cacophony of animalistic shrieks. The sheer volume of their screams pierced Blackwood's eardrums like needles. He fell back covering his ears. They screamed and screeched and ululated, the mountains echoing back their horrifying call as it filled every corner of the room. Some among them began to gyrate and convulse, others fell to the ground or spun in wild circles, caught in some savage dance.

As suddenly as it had started, the horrible noise cut off. Blackwood sucked in an uneven breath as he watched them break away from the circle. Many of them were panting and others even appeared to be laughing. They embraced each other as a cheer rose up from their ranks. Whatever they had done here, apparently they were satisfied.

"This is witchcraft," Fletcher proclaimed. He'd fled to a corner, his gangly frame half hidden behind a chair. "You can't deny it anymore."

"I have to say, it is… well, it is *something*," Dubois agreed. Blackwood gave him a worried look, which he returned in kind.

"Do you think we're in trouble?" Blackwood asked quickly, as much to anyone as to Dubois.

"No." Dubois sounded unsure.

The door below clapped open as the villagers began milling into the tavern.

"They're coming for us." Fletcher whined. "You mocked me! You *mocked* me, and now we'll all die here! All because you fools couldn't see what was right in front of you!" He stood and grabbed an end table, its contents spilling over the floor as he brandished it like a shield. "I won't let these devil worshippers take me, not alive, you hear!"

No one argued with him. Even Blackwood found himself unsure in that moment. Seconds dragged by to the murmur of voices and stomping feet below them. Blackwood half expected to hear the blast of rifles from the guards. But no such ruckus came.

"Yea, though I walk through the valley of the shadow of death, I will fear no evil," Fletcher prayed from his corner. Though lacking the Englishman's panic, Dubois's own hushed voice joined him in French.

From below, footsteps started up the stairs.

18

THREE SWIFT knocks came at the door. The prisoners looked to each other nervously. Blackwood didn't realize that his fists were balled until he saw them raised before him.

The knocks came again.

"*Come in,*" Dubois called in German. Fletcher balked at him, dipping deeper behind the cover of his chair.

The latch clicked and the door eased open. Sovilo's pale countenance greeted them with a toothy grin. He'd shed his robe and now stood before them in the same simple attire he normally wore. "*Come, it is time to celebrate!*" he exclaimed, waving them forward. When he saw the looks on their faces, his tone shifted to one of reassurance. "*Come, friends. I promise you that there is nothing to fear here.*"

As uneasy as Blackwood felt, he recognized that the old man was no threat. He stepped forward and let his hands fall to his sides. Dubois followed suit and then McCulloch and Enzo. Fletcher began to protest, but in the end followed along. Blackwood couldn't imagine the fidgety Brit wanting to remain up here all alone.

Sovilo flung the door the rest of the way open and motioned eagerly for them to follow as he descended the stairs. The tavern below swarmed with people. Blackwood spotted the scarred, sweat-glistened blotch of Klaus's head beyond the teaming sea of women. The guards sat on the far side of the room in a close huddle, each cradling a stein of beer and appearing dumbfounded.

The rest of the crowded tables rang with laughter, and the warm scent of honey mead filled the room. The woman from the woodshed named Maria spotted them on the stairs and her face lit up. "*Come! Join us, friends!*" She held a toddler in one arm and beckoned them over with the other. More villagers cheered along, repeating her call.

Blackwood led the line of men, following Sovilo to an empty table far from the guards. The innkeeper insisted they sit. They did and were immediately swallowed up by the jostling crowd.

A heavyset woman with kind eyes wove through the throng. She set down a tray and began to hand out simple wooden mugs brimming with deep amber beer. McCulloch didn't hesitate. He lifted the mug high and drained it. Frothy suds foamed over his moustache and dribbled down his beard. The woman beamed and immediately replaced his empty mug with a full one. McCulloch stared at her in awe, then he cracked a crooked smile and proclaimed, "I think we might've died up there, boys, because this feels a bit like heaven."

Though still on edge, they all grinned. All except Fletcher, who sat round-shouldered and defensive with his back to the wall.

The beer was thick and strong and held a hint of blueberries. It was good, Blackwood decided after the first sip. Then, as he quickly reached the bottom of the mug, he decided that it was in fact great.

As the drinks came and went, the tension that the ceremony had instilled began to fade into the warm joviality of drunkenness. Dubois drank heavily, as did Enzo. The young Italian was the only one among them who seemed fully at ease. That was the gift of his oblivious nature, Blackwood imagined. He followed the boy's glassy gaze through the crowd to the girl who worked the mill, the one with whom Enzo had been paired up all day. She was young herself. Perhaps older than Enzo, but not by much. Her ample breasts spilled from a low-cut dress and Blackwood suddenly understood the boy's obsession. She gave Enzo a shy smile before disappearing through the crowd. His face seemed frozen in a stupid grin.

"Ah, to be young and dumb and in love," Dubois commented over the ruckus of voices. He and Blackwood shared a chuckle. They drank more, and every time a mug would empty, another would appear from the crowd to take its place. Fletcher still left his first mug untouched. His beady eyes snapped in every direction, and he flinched every time one of the jostling bodies bumped into him.

Dubois poked a finger into Blackwood's ribs. "Speaking of falling in love…"

Blackwood looked toward the door at the Frenchman's prompting. Lucia had just entered. She shivered under a great bearskin coat that Blackwood recognized from that first night. She had been the one who had found them in the storm on the outskirts of the village, he realized. She pulled it off to reveal the thin dress from the ceremony. The beer had already begun unraveling his thoughts, and Blackwood could not help but stare.

"Go on, talk to her," Dubois prompted with a wink.

"No."

"Oh, *mon ami*, life is too short. You are young, you have no wife, and this girl's eyes sparkle when you are a rude ass. This means she likes you. If she is indeed a witch as Fletcher claims, then perhaps she has a special spell for you." Dubois slapped Blackwood on the back, spilling some of his beer on the table.

Blackwood continued to watch her out of the corner of his eye as she crossed through the crowded room and took a seat by the bar. She looked his way only once, and when they locked eyes, she flashed a smile. He looked away immediately, an embarrassed warmth radiating over his cheeks.

"I had not figured you for a coward…" Dubois teased relentlessly.

"Just shut up and drink," Blackwood grunted back.

Some time passed before the throng split apart near the bar, clearing a wide swath of open floor. From somewhere in the crowd came a call for silence. Others joined in until the ruckus died. Many of the older women sat in chairs while the younger ones knelt in the front so that those behind them could see.

A little girl emerged from the door of the kitchen beyond the bar. She wore a ragged red garment that hung past her knees. Straps of overlapping tin adorned her shoulders and chest — a rudimentary costume of armor. In one hand she held a blunt wooden spear, and in the other a heavy-looking rectangular shield that she had to drag across the floor.

"*Non damus misericordiam!*" she shouted, her voice high with a childish lilt.

"Latin," Dubois whispered. "'We give no quarter.'"

Blackwood flinched in his seat as the villagers bellowed back as one. "*Nec ille!*"

"'Neither does he,'" Dubois translated under his breath.

Two more little girls emerged from the door, each of them outfitted much the same. They grimaced and stomped their feet, putting on a show of their ferocity. Many in the crowd laughed and clapped. Blackwood watched Lucia across the room. She smiled at the children proudly.

"*Non damus misericordiam!*" the children shouted together this time.

A beat rose in the air as the villagers began to drum the tables and tap their heels. "*Nec ille!*"

The beat grew louder, and some began to clap. From somewhere in the crowd a woman ululated as others cheered.

"*Et ipse est!*" the little girl in the forefront called.

"'Where is he…'"

A deep drone filled the air. It reverberated through Blackwood's bones in a way that made his stomach drop and his heart throb in his chest. He spun, searching for the source. Sovilo stood to the back of the crowd, a tall, curved brass horn extending above his head. He blew hard into it. His pale skin flushed with effort and the unearthly tone blared from between the jaws that formed the trumpet's flare.

"*Hic est!*" the crowd cried.

Dubois was too enraptured to spout the translation, but Blackwood didn't need it. He understood from context well enough: *he is here.*

A bundle of fur exploded through the door. It barreled toward the little girls with a savage snarl. Instinctively Blackwood made to stand, but Dubois's firm hand was quick to stop him.

The bristling figure charged into the opening, dancing and whooping like a crazed chimp. Blackwood suddenly realized what it was — another child, only this one bound in a savage-looking rig of furs and strung bones. The caped head of a wolf hung over the child's face as they danced furiously before the little warriors.

"*Mors! Mors! Mors!*" the little girls chanted, leveling their spears. The creature fell upon them, batting at their spears and tossing the shields away. The girls dropped, one after the other, tossing themselves dramatically across the floor and flinging handfuls of red ribbon that had been hidden beneath their armor. The crowd erupted in deafening applause as the creature stood victorious. The child inside the suit howled along with them.

"*C'est fascinant*," Dubois muttered to himself.

"More deviltry…" Fletcher corrected with disdain.

McCulloch, wide eyed and grinning from the drink, shrugged. "It's a bloody good show, you ask me!"

Blackwood watched in silence. The little girls did indeed put on a good show, convulsing in death as the animalistic figure pulled away his hood. It was a little boy, no older than eleven, and the first male besides Sovilo that Blackwood had seen in Melvilla. The boy smiled wide as the girls leapt to their feet and scrambled to gather their props. Maria, toddler still balanced on her hip, rushed forward to hug the boy and whisper praise in his ear. Their striking resemblance made it apparent that she was his mother, alongside the way he wiped away her kisses with disgust before plunging back into the crowd.

The beer hit Blackwood's bladder as the throng unleashed itself once again into a bustling mass. He stood and made for the front door, careful to avoid the guards' eyeline. They didn't seem to spot him through the shuffling mass as he slipped outside.

The bitter cold of the night stung his face. It was snowing again, though not a storm as before. After a stumble that nearly put him on his ass, he realized that, after so long without a drink, the beer had a greater effect than he'd expected. He made for the row of outhouses that stood on the near side of the village outskirts. Though this newfound freedom of movement still weighed on him, he was beginning to feel more at ease with the solidarity. He opted not to enter any of the outhouses themselves. The idea of closing his senses off from his surroundings never failed to make him uneasy. Instead, he found a nearby tree and relieved himself in the snow at its roots. The cold felt good, and the night was quiet and his blood was warm with alcohol. All around him the shadows of the mountain peaks loomed on high, and he drew a distinct comfort from their serene overwatch.

"*You,*" a low voice hissed in German.

The hair on the back of Blackwood's neck stood tall and his stream cut off. He put himself away as he turned. Dietmar stood only a dozen feet away. His rifle was slung, but in his hand he held his beloved boot knife. He toyed with it absently as he watched Blackwood through narrowed eyes.

"*You…*" Dietmar repeated, and Blackwood realized this was the first time he'd ever heard the man speak. "*I don't like you.*"

Overhead a raven quorked, and Blackwood's pulse quickened. In an instant, his mindset shifted to violence. He considered the distance between them carefully, planning his steps.

Dietmar's thin lips curled. The blade in his hand glinted as he twirled it. "*What do you think you're doing out here?*"

"I don't speak German," Blackwood said flatly in English.

"*Too stupid to even speak right,*" Dietmar heckled, no doubt hearing Blackwood's words as gibberish. "*You are American, ya? You know, my father used to say things about Americans. He told me that, though you may have come from us, your blood was different. Corrupted from breeding with savages and siblings. That your existence is an insult to the pure European race. Is it true? Are you a savage sister fucker, American?*"

Fifteen feet. Eight good strides would close the distance. Dietmar was slight, but not scrawny. If Blackwood could fend off the blade, he might be able to daze the German with a hard pummeling and gain control of it. Then it would be silent work, and he would have his own rifle.

"*Is there a problem here?*" a woman's voice called from the darkness between the buildings.

Dietmar wheeled about. Blackwood dared a quick step forward but froze when the guard spun back and brandished the knife toward him. "*Don't you move, swine.*"

"*I've been looking for you.*" Lucia closed with them in quick strides. She paused when she saw the knife, then waved Blackwood toward her. "*Come. We must get back.*"

Dietmar eyed her suspiciously. She, on the other hand, ignored him completely. Blackwood didn't wait for another cue. He strode around Dietmar, giving the guard a wide berth as he joined Lucia.

"*Stop!*" Dietmar commanded.

"*He will not stop, guard,*" Lucia snapped with sudden authority. "*And you will do nothing about it. You would do best not to forget your place here. Do you understand me?*"

Dietmar glared at her without responding.

"*Do you understand me?*" Lucia demanded.

The guard spit on the ground and turned, stumbling to one of the outhouses and slamming the door behind him.

"*Thank you,*" Blackwood said as they made for the tavern.

"*You're welcome.*" She glanced back toward the outhouses. "*Watch out for that one.*"

"Yeah, you too," Blackwood muttered.

"*Come,*" she said as they reached the tavern door. "*I know a way that you can show your gratitude.*"

He immediately dismissed the illicit thought that came alongside her comment. She led him inside and together they made for the rear of the swarming room, pausing along the way for Lucia to quietly mutter something into Sovilo's ear. Blackwood caught McCulloch's booming laugh alongside Dubois's boisterous voice still cheering with mirth as she led him through the door behind the bar. It opened into a quaint kitchen with a narrow table at its center. The little girls stood around it, chattering loudly amongst themselves. They smiled at Lucia when she entered.

"*Go on! Find your mothers! Steal a drink!*" She swatted at them playfully and they dispersed back into the main room with a sputter of giggles. Once they were alone, she shut the door and nodded to one of the two chairs. "*Please, sit.*"

While he wasn't sure exactly what he'd been expecting, this wasn't it. He sat as she pulled a bottle of clear liquid from one of the shelves along with two short glasses, then took her seat across from him. "*You are less jovial than your friends.*"

It was true. Besides Fletcher, the other prisoners seemed happy enough to delight in the evening's revelry, as if they weren't one wrong move away from an agonizing death. The thought occurred to him that Dietmar might still be lying in wait by the outhouses. "*We need to warn them about that guard. He could still be out there, waiting for them.*"

"*I've already put Sovilo on it. They will be fine,*" she assured him. "*You owe me, twice over now.*"

"*Twice?*"

"*Yes. Twice. Once for just now, and once for saving you and your comrades from the mountain.*"

Blackwood nodded in acknowledgment, but he was still stuck on Dietmar. Though he was grateful for her intervention, a part of him wished she had never shown up. "*It might have been better if you'd cast us off.*"

"*I have had the same thought.*" She grinned ruefully. "*But enough of that tonight. Tonight is about celebration. About friends and happiness. So, about your debt… I will make you a deal. You play a game with me, and then we will be even. Ya?*"

"*What sort of game?*"

"*A game of introductions. It is one we like to play with the few travelers who pass through here, a way for us to get a measure of their character.*"

"*What is it called?*"

"*There is no name for it. But the rules are simple: I ask you a question and you answer. Then we drink to your honesty.*"

He pursed his lips. "*I'll admit that my German is not very good, but you said 'game.' I think you meant interrogation.*"

"*No, no…*" She chuckled. "*Your German is fine.*"

It suddenly made sense why the mugs at his table had been so seamlessly refreshed. The woman before him appeared to be stone cold sober while he already felt tipsy. This was indeed a game — a game of deceit. A well-choreographed effort to glean some information from the prisoners, though he could not imagine what the hell he might know that these people would find useful. As much as he didn't like the idea of it, her aura was magnetic, and he couldn't help his guard from lowering some small bit. "*If I play your game, do I get to ask questions as well?*"

"*Eh, why not? But I go first. Question: Why is an American fighting against Germany? As far as I know, your nation is still neutral in this war.*"

"*I enlisted with the Canadians.*"

"*I asked why, not with whom you signed on.*"

A dull warning went off in his mind. Why would she care? What was this leading to? Such a question was more becoming of a character like Wulfson, not some mysterious mountain queen. She was not involved in the war, at least not in any way that he could imagine. He decided to err on the side of vagueness. "*It made sense at the time.*"

"*Tsk tsk.*" She gave an exaggerated frown. "*That's not how we play the game.*"

"*It's how I'm playing.*"

"*You were a criminal then? On the run?*"

His eyes thinned. "*What makes you say that?*"

"*A hunch.*"

Blackwood sat back and shook his head. "*I don't like this game.*"

"*Well, you're not very good at it,*" she scolded, pouring a splash of the clear liquor into each of the two small glasses. "*Now tell me why you chose to travel halfway across the world just to go to war with my people.*"

"*I was ready for a fresh start.*"

"*A fresh start? Or a clean end?*" she asked. When he didn't respond, she took her glass and held it up. "*I guess that will have to do. I expect better of you in the next round though. Now, drink.*"

He took the other glass and tapped it to hers. Together they downed the schnapps. It burned like hellfire as it rolled down his throat, and he had to suppress a cough.

She looked bemused as she poured another. "*Your turn, I suppose.*"

"*What the hell was all that tonight?*"

"*The children's play? Just a piece of folklore the children like to act out; the legend of the Sarvàn. It makes them feel included in the festival.*" She held up her glass once more.

"*I meant with the bull—*"

"*No, no. You got your answer, now drink.*"

"*That's bullshit.*" He glowered.

"*Ask better questions then.*" She downed her shot. "*Now, question: where did you get the scar?*" She motioned to the X of pink scar tissue that sat prominently over his left eye. A token he had earned from friendly artillery on his final night raid.

He winced as the second shot went down, then refilled the glasses himself. "*Why do you care?*"

She gave a dramatic sigh. "*Will you follow the rules please?*"

"*Fine. Shrapnel,*" he said, then, before she could speak again, he downed his shot.

She feigned betrayal, but a smile slipped through as she drank her own. "*Well played, Herr Blackwood.*"

"*Why did you kill the bull?*"

"*The bull was a sacrifice. A yearly tradition to mark the birth of our Lord.*"

"*You killed a bull for Jesus?*"

"*No.*"

He thought back to the ceremony, to Dubois's translation of her words in the moment of sacrifice. "*For Mithras…*"

Her eyes narrowed. "*What makes you say that?*"

"*We have ears, you know.*"

"*Good ones, apparently.*"

"*What the hell is Mithras?*"

"*It's not your turn—*"

"*Lucia.*" His patience waned, and his voice took on an edge. "*Enough with this game. I don't know what it is you have going on out here, and honestly, I don't care. What I care about is how it's going to affect those bastards sitting in the corner out there. You've already got one of my people believing you're witches. If the guards take up that sentiment too then it won't end well for either of us. You understand that?*"

She was less offended than he thought she would be. In fact, she giggled. "*You think we're witches?*"

"*I don't know, and again, I don't care. All I know is that between whatever the hell that ceremony was and that god-awful howling last night, you've got us all on edge. If you knew what type of men you were dealing with you would not be sitting here playing at idle chit-chat. For the love of God, give me some answers so that I can at least keep the others from losing their damn minds.*"

Her grin faded. "*Very well,*" she said flatly. "*The noises you heard in the night came from my grandfather. He is quite old and quite ill. Unfortunately, I have found it necessary to keep him quarantined in my home. For the safety of our people, as well as himself.*"

"*Tuberculosis?*"

"*No. Nothing like that. An illness of the mind and of the soul. He's a good man, but such a thing requires seclusion.*" Her voice softened, and she reached across the table to clasp his hand. Her fingers were warm and stirred a pleasant feeling in his core. "*I can assure you one thing, Herr Blackwood, you face no threat* of danger from me, my people, or my grandfather. I give you my word, which is all I can offer. Now, may we get back to the game?"

It was a solid answer. Furthermore, her touch seemed to have calmed him. He forced himself to relax, letting the drunkenness seep past his defensive shield as he regarded the beautiful woman before him. "*Sure.*"

"*Good.*" Her smile returned and she drew away. "*It is my turn now, ya? Question: do you like it here in Melvilla?*"

"*It's definitely better than where we came from. So yeah, I'd say so.*" Blackwood waited for her to raise her glass. She did so without reluctance. They both grimaced at the shot. Afterward, he leaned forward as his next question slipped out. "*Lucia, why me?*"

She raised an eyebrow. "*Huh?*"

"*Why am I the one back here answering your questions, and not the others? I would think Dubois would be more suited to conversation.*"

She filled the glasses again, this time making an unpleasant face toward them. "*This is normally a much slower game... Why you? Well, I already spoke with the leader of the German soldiers. I wanted to speak to the leader of the foreign ones.*"

"I'm not their leader."

"*Tell that to them. We watch you just like you watch us. The Scotsman, he's too old and aggressive. The Frenchman is clever, but he is fragile. The British one, Fletcher, he has the demeanor of a frightened deer. And the Italian... I don't think he's even a man yet.*" She laughed. Even through the drunken pumping of blood in his ears, her laughter still sounded to him like bells. "*Maybe you don't see it, but all of them look to you with respect when you speak. Perhaps even reverence. I believe they will listen to you if you tell them to do something. So yes, I say you are their leader.*"

"*Agree to disagree,*" he muttered. She braced against the table and eyed the shot with trepidation. Despite his surliness he couldn't help but smile. Together they toasted and took their shot. Outside the door a woman began to sing, and in response someone drew a tune from a fiddle. Others began to clap along. The sound of dancing on the hardwood reverberated through the floor.

"*This is going to kill me!*" She gasped after slamming the empty glass down on the table. "*Last question, or else I might throw up: did you enjoy the war?*"

"*What the hell kind of a question is that?*" He rubbed his chest to alleviate the burning. It did not work.

"*I want to know what kind of men I let stay in my home.*"

"*In your home?*" he asked, perhaps a bit too ruefully.

Her eyes thinned. "*In my village.*"

He smirked. His arms were heavy and he felt the liquor emboldening him in his advances. He looked away, thinking back on the misery of the trenches. The muck and rats, the rotten stink of corpses and the terror in young men's eyes. He thought of the weeks of tense boredom and the incredible rush of charging against gunfire. He remembered it all so vividly he might be there right now. "*No*," he said, "*…and somehow yes.*"

For once, she seemed happy to accept the ambiguity of his answer. She nodded, and they drank. Afterward she leaned in closer until he could smell the sweet scent of lavender wafting off of her. "*The game is fun, ya?*"

"Sure," he breathed.

She hiccupped and winced. Her cheeks were flushed and her lips looked so soft that he nearly gave in to the temptation to lean forward and kiss her. "*We should play again soon,*" she said with a wink.

Faster than he would have liked, she drew away and stood. With only the slightest stagger she crossed the kitchen and opened the door. Outside he heard joyful cheers ring out and beer sloshing onto the floor.

Lucia held out a hand. "*Do you dance, Herr Blackwood?*"

"*No.*"

"*What a shame.*" She hiccupped again before disappearing through the door with a coy smile.

Blackwood pushed the half empty bottle of demon piss away and sucked in a deep breath in an attempt to sober himself. It was no use. He searched the small room for a door leading outside. There was none, only a wide window. He forced it open clumsily then hung his head outside and jabbed a finger down his throat. The liquor burned worse coming up than it had going down. It was a worthy pain, as he needed to keep some semblance of his wits about him. Once he had purged, he leaned back against the counter and closed his eyes, trying to focus on anything in the world besides the room around him, which had started to gently spin. In the darkness of his own eyelids, all he could see was her.

19

THE CELEBRATIONS continued well into the night as the snow picked up pace. Lucia had vanished shortly after their conversation, a development Blackwood didn't particularly mind. He was painfully aware that her hold over him had grown significantly during their short time alone. Only in her absence could he see clearly that there could be no positive outcome for such a romance — a harried affair carried out in secret under the cruel eyes of tormentors, destined to end in either his death or his disappearance over the mountains. Still, the fantasy lingered.

Eventually the raucous merrymaking began to fizzle. The villagers filtered away, and one at a time, the prisoners disappeared up the stairs. Blackwood watched them go as he sipped a beer. He waited until Dubois clambered drunkenly up the stairs before following.

Dubois stumbled into his room and shut the door. McCulloch sat before the fire. His snores were interrupted as he startled awake at Blackwood's entry.

"Aye, lad, did you bring more beer?" he slurred out through a glazed-over grin.

Blackwood meant to shake his head, but it had begun to throb. The Scotsman waved him down. "Hold on, hold on… I got something here, sit… sit…" He patted the chair beside him.

Blackwood was exhausted of talking, but the Scotsman was adamant. He sat, and McCulloch pulled a hidden bottle of schnapps from his coat. He took a swig before handing it over.

"That lass." McCulloch thumped his chest and belched between his words. "You screw her?"

"No." Blackwood might have refuted the crass wording with more vehemence if not for the goofy smile plastered over the old man's face.

"Ah, what a shame. Ol' Frenchie told me you two had a thing. Ya should get on with it, lad. No telling when you might have another chance to wet your pecker."

Blackwood took a drag from the schnapps, hoping that it might ease his headache. It was sweet and thick with the taste of mint.

"You don't talk much. I like that about you. The Frenchie, he talks a lot. The others, meh." McCulloch waved an errant hand. "But you, you're a fighter, not a talker. A *killer*. I can tell."

"Doesn't matter much now," Blackwood muttered.

"Aye," McCulloch grunted. He leaned in, the drunkenness dissolving a bit as his demeanor shifted to serious. "It might still."

"You're worried about the guards." Blackwood nodded. "Me too."

"I dinnae need to tell you that they've been itchin' to have at us since we first stepped foot in these mountains. Hell, before that. But it seems they've gotten a hair across their arses as of late. The tavernkeeper told us about the bastard by the latrines. You got lucky, lad, but I dinnae think their patience will last much longer."

Blackwood didn't disagree, but McCulloch was an aggressor. A capable warrior, no doubt, but he'd exhibited little restraint over the course of their journey. If any one of them was too eager to seek violence, it was the old man. Blackwood knew that striking blindly was worse than giving up, and he figured there was no need to stoke the Scotsman's fire. "I think the Major still has a grip on them. For now, at least."

"For now…" McCulloch muttered. He settled back in the chair. "Cannae imagine the Swiss will want to keep feeding us for long, if we ever make it there, that is. If this war keeps on the same way, I can see them sending us home. Then what? Is it back to the trenches wi' you?"

Blackwood hadn't given it a thought. "Most likely," he answered honestly. "What about you?"

"Aye. Aye, I suppose I'll end up back in that shithole, mud-caked and bleeding…" McCulloch's voice faded away. He looked sadly at the fire. "You know, I've got me a good woman back home. A farm, and a pair of braw boys too."

Blackwood didn't hide his surprise. "And you still wouldn't go home if given the chance?"

McCulloch shrugged. "It's no for me. I tried for many years. Came back from fighting against the Boers and settled down. You know, after spending so many of my years fighting, I figured it'd be a relief, being done wi' all that. I was tired of the bloody bugs and the crotch rot, of the crying women pickin' bones off the battlefield. I thought I'd relish it, normalcy I mean." He shook his head. "Nae. I dinnae make it long afore I was back to the bloody business." He belched again and turned to regard Blackwood with bloodshot eyes. "That's the dark secret they never tell you, lad. There's a thrill in the fight like no other. You know that well enough by now yourself, I'm sure. It's a sickness only the brave and the wicked contract. A hapless need for the violence of it. But if you chase that thrill long enough, you'll never be able to let it go. Take it from an old man: bow out while you've still got it in you to find some happiness among the living."

Blackwood didn't immediately respond. He took another sip and handed the bottle back. He knew there was wisdom in the Scotsman's words, but unbeknownst to the Scotsman, he had his own long history of violence. The truth was that as much as he despised the rotting filth of the trenches, it called to him like a siren in the night. It had become who he was — *la bête*. The whispered tales of reverence among the French and Canadian fighters had become him. He was meant for war, if nothing else.

"I need sleep." Blackwood patted McCulloch on the shoulder as he stood to leave. "I think it might do you some good as well."

McCulloch snorted and leaned back in the chair. "Just heed what I said before it's too late."

Blackwood didn't find sleep until the wee hours of the morning. His mind was a battle between the thousand rogue thoughts that throttled each other for dominance. He reminisced on before, on the years spent rustling cattle and robbing. On the summer spent hiding amongst the Indians and the countless winters he had suffered on the frozen mountains as a child with his grandfather, hauling traps and skinning furs. He'd never been one for soft things — not that he knew the way they felt to begin with.

As much as he fought against it, Lucia remained dominant in his thoughts. The woman with the green eyes and an easy smile had brought forth a strange new feeling in him. It wasn't the wicked lust that so often drove men. Not entirely, at least. No, there was something else. Something that made him uncomfortably open to the idea of leaving behind the harsh existence he had come to know.

Across the room Enzo mumbled something in his sleep. Blackwood watched him, perhaps a bit jealous of the boy's soft-cheeked innocence.

"Don't worry, kid," he muttered. "We'll get you out of here yet."

20

HANZ WOKE to a rough shake. He winced, his head pounding with agonizing fury. A blinding light shone through his eyelids, and he covered his face.

"*Get up,*" a harsh voice demanded. "*It's your turn for watch.*"

"*No…*" Hanz moaned and rolled away. Consciousness had come hand-in-hand with the punishment for his indulgences the night before. He felt as fragile as thin porcelain; ready to shatter at something so delicate as a whisper.

"*Get up!*" Johan's voice was more insistent, though only a hair louder. This time the demand was accompanied by a hard slap to the back of Hanz's head. It might as well have been the blow of a sledgehammer.

"*Not now. Go away…*" Hanz managed to wheeze out.

"*If you don't get up.*" Johan's breath stank of hops and it was clear that he was still drunk. "*I'm going to drag you out into the snow and fuck you like a pig.*"

Hanz gave in and slowly uncurled. When he opened his eyes, the white-hot beam of Johan's electric torch shined in his face once again. He slapped at it, but Johan was faster and caught him with a swift cuff behind the ear. Without a second's warning, the larger man grabbed Hanz by the arm and hauled him off the bed. He hit the floor with a thud. Both men froze, simultaneously looking over to where Klaus draped off the side of his mattress.

"*You think I'm bad? Force me to wake him, then see what happens,*" Johan warned quietly.

Hanz ignored him the best he could. He hauled himself onto the edge of the bed and tried to sit up straight. The aching in his head intensified so badly that he gave up, dropping into a deep slouch and fumbling with his uniform.

"*Get dressed already, wimp. I'm going to bed.*" Johan grunted as he took to his own rack. He farted loudly as he stripped off his bandoleer and coat.

Hanz wrestled to don his damp socks and push past the growing nausea. He stood to pull on his pants and nearly fell forward, instead overcorrecting and landing on his ass back on the bed. He waited for the vertigo to pass and managed to pull on his shirt and thick wool coat. Once his boots were laced he leaned back against the wall, granting himself a tiny moment of reprieve.

THE SARVÀN

"*Fuck you, Johan,*" he said so quietly even he couldn't hear it. Mercifully, Johan didn't either, as he had already rolled over in his rack and begun snoring loudly.

Hanz's eyes drifted around the cramped room then up to the ceiling. He imagined the prisoners above, situated comfortably in their private quarters. *Lucky bastards,* he thought for the first time ever. Never in his wildest dreams did he imagine himself being jealous of the poor sods that had milled about the tents of Rothenspring, dead-eyed and starved to the bone. His thoughts went to their journey over the mountains. At least it was not cold in here. It was warm. Enchantingly, wonderfully warm…

His eyelids fluttered. With a jolt he realized he had fallen back asleep. He had no idea how much time had passed, but those around him still lay where they had been. For that he was supremely grateful — to be caught sleeping on watch duty carried with it harsh consequences, especially from Klaus.

He stood and pulled on his belt and bandoleer, body and brain still aching. With his rifle slung over his shoulder, he eased quietly through the door. The tavern was dark and still. He must have slept for some time because the fire in the hearth had died to embers. From somewhere far away, a dog barked. He stumbled through the maze of overturned chairs and empty cups that littered the floor, finally reaching the fireplace. After stoking the flames back to life, he surveyed the room in the flickering light.

The swashbuckling affair of the previous evening was evident in the absolute mess that had been left over. Tables stood jammed against walls, pushed out of place to make room for dancing. Beer casks were scattered at random, and his boots stuck to the floor with spilt drink. The air itself was thick with the stench of beer. Hanz found himself once more fighting not to gag.

"*One more for the night before…*" he reminded himself. The old saying was one his father used to mutter on those rough mornings when he'd down a beer for breakfast. It seemed as good a hangover cure as any Hanz ever heard of. He rooted behind the bar for an empty mug then crossed to the nearest beer cask and unscrewed the tap. Only a few drops dribbled out. He groaned and checked the next, and the next, until he was sure that the partygoers had drunk the bar dry. In a final bout of desperation, he checked the steins that littered the tables. He found one that was still half full. The thought of drinking the flat beer made his stomach sour — it may as well have been donkey piss — but it was his only chance to cure the pain. With a deep breath he closed his eyes, raised the stein, and took a long drink.

The beer was horribly bitter. He choked on it halfway through, sending it cascading down his cheeks and over his jacket. He muscled on, gulping it down until the stein was drained. Just as he lowered it, he felt something soggy catch under his tongue. He spit it into his hand, glaring at it in the dull firelight.

It was the burnt stub of a cigarette.

The stein clattered to the ground as he stumbled, retching, to the door. The cold air nipped his ears and burned his face as he collapsed into the fresh snow that covered the street. He vomited, hunching on all fours as he heaved and heaved until his belly was empty. When he finally caught his breath, he stared down at the pool of melted snow and stinking bile before him and made the solemn wish that he might die right then and there. It would be a relief to this putrid existence, he thought. Anything would be better than this.

Snowflakes floated down around his face, and in the distance the dog continued to bark.

"*Be quiet, boy*," he muttered. He sucked in the cold air and wiped his mouth, his disgust transforming slowly into misery.

He sat back in the snow as the barks echoed through the plaza. He imagined the mutt somewhere beyond the outskirts of the town, yowling away at some squirrel or marmot. It was cold out — too cold for some poor dog to be left out in the elements, Hanz thought.

He'd had a dog of his own as a child. Bello. A wonderful little terrier that had followed him to school every day. He'd loved his mangey little friend right up to the day that she wandered off into the forest to die of old age. Now, as he listened to the desperate barking, he felt a sudden responsibility.

Struggling to his feet, he stared out over the village. The sky had begun to ripen into a dark blue hue with the coming of the sun. Up on the mountain slopes, the trees and boulders began to take shape. He knew from the volume and direction of the barking that the dog was to the north, likely just beyond the edge of the village. He glanced back at the tavern. The windows were dark and the night was otherwise silent. Everyone was asleep. The prisoners wouldn't escape. Hell, even if they did try something, Hanz didn't truly care in that moment. They could have Klaus. They could have Johan. They could have Victor and Dietmar. Hell, maybe it wouldn't be so wrong if they killed him too. It would be a sort of justice, he figured.

Shaking off the dizziness, he unshouldered his rifle and trudged off toward the baying dog.

THE SARVÀN

The dog was almost exactly where he'd imagined it. Just beyond where the buildings ended to the north lay a hundred-yard expanse of ice-crusted bushes and trampled snow. The far edge of the field met a sprawling forest that worked its way up the mountainside like a great bristling beard. The dog was at the tree line, little more than a blip in the slowly growing light.

Hanz tried to whistle, but his lips were dry and cracked. He called to it softly, then a bit louder as he realized that no one else was awake to hear. Unfortunately, the dog could not hear him either. He called again and again as he waded out into the field. The dog continued to ignore him, focused on something in the trees. Barking and barking.

He was only twenty yards out from the animal when he managed to make out its finer details. It was a small dog with a long coat of fur that curled out wildly in every direction. It bowed in a ready stance, glaring toward the trees and snarling between sharp yaps. It looked angry. No, not angry. It was downright furious.

It suddenly dawned on Hanz that it might not just be the two of them out there. The image of a snarling wolf manifested in his mind, and he tightened his grip on his rifle. Following the dog's line of sight, he spotted a dark shape at the base of a tree. He raised the rifle and squinted against the dark. At first the shape appeared still, then he began to make out movement.

It was writhing.

A cold breeze swept in from the north. The scent it carried with it transported him back to his short time spent behind the trenches. On one evening he had been charged with hauling away the carts of the dead recovered from No Man's Land. He remembered the putrid odor of soured bowels and the metallic tang of blood. It was the stink of death.

He flicked the safety of his rifle off. The dog didn't matter now — he barely noticed it at all. With one trembling hand he fumbled with the electric torch that hung from his belt. It sputtered to life, bathing the forest's edge in a cone of yellow.

As soon as the light touched it, the squirming black clump exploded into a cloud of ink black feathers and furious cackles. He lurched back in shock, tripping and sprawling in the snow with a shriek. The dark mass barreled toward him through the air at an impossible speed. He threw his arms over his face and kicked out wildly as his ears filled with the heavy thrum of wingbeats.

When it was over, he lay curled there, gasping in shock as the pre-dawn silence returned.

The dog's wet nose drew a flinch. It was at his side, hot tongue licking his hand. Slowly, he unraveled his body. The dog whined and stared off toward the village. Once again he followed its gaze to see the cloud of flitting black shapes circle the distant cliff top tower before disappearing inside.

He realized what it had been — that wretched cohort of ravens that always seemed to be about.

"*Fuckin' birds*," he got out. The dog whimpered again, and he rubbed a hand over its muzzle as he began to laugh. Despite it all, he laughed long and hard, pounding a fist into the snow and slapping the dog's rump. "*Hell, look at us, boy. Two cowards scared shitless of some dumb birds!*"

When he finally stood and brushed the snow away from his coat, his eyes caught on the shape still sitting at the base of the tree. His panic had passed now, and he lazily shone the light over the shadow, the embarrassed smile still plastered on his face.

The beam of light illuminated a torn corpse. Its legs straddled a thick root, the torso draped against the bloodstained trunk. It was naked, though in that instant Hanz could not have said whether it was man or woman as cracked, frozen blood coated its every inch. Its skin was torn and flayed. Thin strands of flesh and fat and muscle hung like so many glistening ribbons. Deep gouges shone dark against the bare white of broken bones. The head, what was left of it, dangled lopsided from the neck.

A single raven remained. It perched on the mutilated shoulder, wrestling with something beneath the slacked jaw. Hanz watched in silent horror as it yanked what appeared to be a worm from the dead throat. The raven struggled to tear it away. Finally, it snapped, the artery wriggling in its beak as it threw its head back and swallowed.

Hanz had thought his stomach was already empty. He had thought wrong. He gagged and the sour burn of acid overtook his palate. He didn't bother bending over, so caught in shock that the vomit spewed out over his chin and cascaded down his chest. The raven squawked and took flight. He didn't flinch. He didn't react at all. He just stared, his body rigid and mind unthinking. The eyeless corpse stared back at him, slowly freezing blood still oozing from its hair.

Short, blond hair that he recognized.

It was the British prisoner. The man they called Fletcher.

PART THREE

An excerpt from *The Lost Roots of the Monotheism* by J. Wyatt, associate professor of history, University of Western New England.

It is both an absurd and inconsolable tragedy that so much of the formative history of the west has been purposely destroyed in the wake of Roman conquest. Take, for example, the obscure Cult of Mithras — often referred to as the Mithraic Mysteries — a secretive cult once popular amongst Roman legionnaires before the state adoption of Christianity and subsequent religious purge.

Little is known about the Mithraic Mysteries or its origins. Their worship was a complex and clandestine affair of which very little was recorded. While it is impossible to know the exact period during which the Cult of Mithras was founded, the evidence that we do have points us to extreme antiquity, perhaps even prehistory. Unlike Mithraism's contemporaries, such as Zoroastrianism or Christianity, there is no evidence of individual prophets (i.e. Zoroaster or Jesus of Nazareth) whose exploits and writings can provide information that can help date the religion's founding. There is, however, one piece of evidence left behind by this ancient mystery cult that may provide some insight into its roots.

This is, of course, the *tauroctony* (more colloquially known as the bull-slaying scene). Nearly every known place of Mithraic worship displayed this same representation: the mighty god Mithras pinning down a bull while slicing its neck with a dagger. The sun and moon hang above, in specific alignment, and the scene is surrounded by the distinct figures of a snake, a canine, and a scorpion.

Many believe the depiction to simply be a presentation of the Mithraic creation myth wherein Mithras slays the sacred bull to conjure all life from its blood and seed. However, as first proposed by Donnelly and Rizzo in their essay *Visual Rhetoric of the Legions* (2003), the ancient people's relative obsession with the zodiac in combination with the commonplace use of these animals to represent constellations may lead to an alternative analysis wherein the scene itself may be interpreted as a time stamp rather than a simple depiction of mythological events. Through this lens we could potentially date the conception of Mithraism to the end of the age of Taurus (as the bull is slain), approximately 2150 BCE. If such a theory is to be believed, then it is crucial to note that this mystery cult would predate the founding of Persian Zoroastrianism — commonly believed to be the singular oldest monotheistic religion on earth — by nearly a millennia and Christianity by twice that number, thus solidifying Mithraism as the root monotheistic religion from which all others likely evolved.

If such bold claims hold merit, one must consider the relative effect that Mithraism would have had on the evolution of monotheism and the Abrahamic religions. This in turn begs the question: is the ancient figure of Mithras the root of the modern perception of God in the west? What answers might one find in the lost works of this long dead religion?

MONTANA, 1905

Edward Blackwood sat before a campfire hidden at the edge of the forest. It was hot, the hottest summer the boy of sixteen had seen yet. The chirp of crickets filled the night air as a rabbit sizzled over the flames. A dozen stolen cattle milled quietly about in the darkness of the of the prairie before him.

Beside him sat a man whom he'd recently come to see as a mentor. His name was Atticus. He was short and thick-bodied with coarse black hair that ran from his dome all the way to his knuckles. From what Edward knew, he was wanted from Billings to Missoula. After tonight, he might be able to tack another county onto that list.

"You think those dumb bastards have even noticed yet?" Atticus asked, referring to the ranchers they'd stolen the cattle from that morning.

Edward shrugged. "I doubt it. They've got two hundred head. Twelve won't bother them until they do a count."

Atticus took a slug of hooch and laid back in the grass. Edward pulled the rabbit from the flames. He tossed it down on a bed of fresh leaves before loading another onto the skewer.

"You're good at that, you know," Atticus said.

"Good at what?"

"That trapping shit. Your gramps taught you well."

Edward snorted. "He wouldn't agree with you."

Atticus propped himself up on an elbow, looking at the boy in the firelight. "He really go mad, or did you just say that so I'd take you in and you could get your name in a dime novel?"

"Oh, he's mad alright." Edward balanced the skewer over the flames. "Started with him just forgetting things, you know, getting angry for nothing. Wasn't long before he was raving about this and that, waking up in the middle of the night thinking he was back in the motherland. Swinging on me, thinking I was a redskin or a bandit."

"That's a shame. Maybe with you gone, he'll learn to miss you. You plan on headin' back there after we cash out? Take over his fur lease?"

"He don't want me back." Edward lifted his shirt to exhibit the peppered scars the birdshot had left on his side.

Atticus gave a low whistle. "Lucky he's not a better shot."

"He is. Don't think he was looking to kill me."

"Nah." Atticus waved him off. "That's luck if I've ever seen it. Same luck that's saved my ass more times'n I can count. All the mess I've been up to in my years, can't tell you how many men should have killed me by now—"

His voice dropped off as a shout echoed over the prairie. The snap of a bullet came on its tail.

"Get to the trees!" Atticus barked.

The cows scattered as more rifles opened up. Atticus let out a squeal of pain and toppled mid-stride as Edward fumbled with the six-gun on his hip. Edward saw him fall from the corner of his eye. He darted to his mentor and grabbed him under the arms, hauling him behind the cover of a thick maple as a volley of lead hissed by.

"Goddammit! They got me!" Atticus cried out. A red stain grew across his shirt.

Edward leaned out and fired the pistol blindly. The crack of a bullet sent him tumbling back behind the tree.

Atticus grabbed at him. "Stop! Stop!"

Edward ignored him. The pistol shook in his hand as he fired again. Atticus's callous mitts grasped his collar and yanked him in with a wheezing groan.

"Stop it! You've got to run, boy! There's too many of 'em!"

Edward couldn't form words. It was as if his tongue had grown too large for his mouth. His whole body trembled, he felt as if his skull was caving in on itself. Still, he shook his head no.

"Give me the gun and go!" Atticus demanded.

"N-no."

Atticus slapped him, leaving a smear of blood across his cheek. "Wake up, boy. You've no reason to die over some scrawny cattle. We shouldn't've stopped, it was my mistake. They'll be here soon and they'll have us both. Give me the gun and go. You're like a deer in them woods, they'll never know you were here." The old rustler groaned through his anguish. "I've given my life to whoring and gambling. It was a good damn ride, but they caught me in the lung. It's over for me now. Let me do something worthwhile in the end, eh?"

A bullet ripped across the side of the tree, showering them in splintered bark. The ranchers were closing in quickly. Hot tears rolled down Edward's cheeks. He didn't resist as Atticus slipped the pistol from his hand.

"Go on now." Atticus managed to flash a lopsided grin through a grimace of pain. "I'll hold 'em off. You can find a better way to die than this, eh? Now go!"

Edward disappeared into the night. He ran so swiftly through the trees that he barely heard it when the final shot cut through the night.

21

BLOOD COATED his teeth. It formed in clumps on his tongue and drooled down his cheeks. It pooled in the back of his throat, a thick, iron sludge that threatened to choke him. He tried to swallow, but the mire of curdy gore refused to go down. It gripped the inside of his throat, stabbing vicious legs into the walls of his windpipe like a spider clinging to a drain. He gagged, but the air wouldn't come. Far above a great shadow loomed. Though it hung beyond his focus, the blackness of its figure was so dark it burned his eyes.

Mortem ad vitam...
The words echoed through the black.
Mortem ad vitam...

Sweat-drenched sheets peeled from Blackwood's skin as he bolted upright. The bedroom came into sharp focus around him. The dull glow of dawn had begun to leak through the window. From across the room came the gentle rhythm of Enzo's slumbering breath. Alongside it came another noise. It echoed from outside, barely penetrating the glass panes.

Blackwood collapsed into his hands, fighting to calm his racing heart. The noise came again, louder this time. Despite the throbbing of his head, he made out the distinct timber of a man's voice.

Quietly, as not to wake Enzo, he eased out of their room and crossed to the windows overlooking the plaza. A lone figure stumbled through the sea of fresh snow. Blackwood recognized the uniform and the diminutive figure within — it was Hanz.

The guard staggered and fell. When he tried to stand, he slipped and collapsed onto all fours. His shoulders heaved in exhaustion, and his movements were jerky as if he'd just survived an artillery barrage by the skin of his teeth. His hoarse call echoed over the plaza once more. Blackwood could make it out now.

"*Alarm!*"

"Oh, no…" Blackwood's words were punctuated by a gunshot as Hanz raised his rifle skyward and fired. The sharp report echoed back from the mountains. The guard wrestled back the frozen bolt of his rifle and fired again.

The fracas of panicked waking came through the floor. Blackwood froze as a door banged open below and Klaus's muffled shouts filled the dining room. A slurry of tromping footsteps spread throughout the tavern. Blackwood looked back to his room. Enzo was sitting up, bleary-eyed and confused. Heavy feet stomped up the stairs.

Blackwood bolted, bare feet padding silently across the rough wood. He managed to shut the door to his room behind him just as the stairwell door burst open.

"*Up!*" Victor roared. "*Up, now!*"

The thought of barricading the door flashed through Blackwood's mind, but he had no time. A heavy kick broke the latch and sent it clattering across the floor. Victor stood there, eyes red with sleep and chest bare. His hairy gut hung over his belt, and his rifle pointed straight at Blackwood's chest.

Blackwood braced for the shot. It never came. Instead, the ogre jabbed a meaty thumb over his shoulder. "*Get out here! Now!*"

Blackwood complied, towing Enzo along with him. Victor moved to the next room and hauled Dubois out by the arm. He tossed the small Frenchman, still half asleep, to the floor. He kicked open Fletcher's door next. When he disappeared inside, Blackwood managed a fleeting glance out over the plaza. Another guard was yanking Hanz to his feet.

"*Where is he?*" Victor roared as he stumbled out of Fletcher's room. Just at that moment, McCulloch emerged from his room. He stood tall with his shoulders back, naked as the day he was born. Victor startled, and for a moment Blackwood worried that the Scotsman might attack. But McCulloch only grunted as he stepped forward to join the others, yanking his arm away when Victor tried to grab it.

Klaus came barreling up the stairs in his long johns. The sight of the stained garment stirred in Blackwood a deep rage. His mind went to Dickie, to the vile Unteroffizier wailing on him in the dark. Klaus descended on them with his rifle held high. "*What the fuck is going on? Where is the other one? The string bean!*"

"He's not here," Victor said. "*He must have escaped.*"

Klaus turned his rifle on Dubois. "*Tell me where your friend is, little Frenchman, or I will paint the wall with your brains!*"

Dubois's mouth flopped open, but nothing came out. The way his eyes turned to saucers betrayed that he was lost to shock. Klaus snapped his rifle upward, and the room filled with a thunderous boom. Blackwood ducked reflexively. When he looked back, Dubois was unmarred. A fresh hole marked the wall just above his head.

"*Tell me now, or the next one is through your head!*" Klaus racked the bolt and sighted in.

Dubois's words coagulated in his mouth. He stammered unintelligibly, exhibiting the same incoherent panic he'd devolved into on the mountain. Klaus closed one eye, focusing on the sights.

Blackwood knew that Klaus would do it. Out of other options, he cleared his throat. "*We don't know where Fletcher is,*" he said slowly in German.

Klaus's barrel snapped over to him, his brow knitting together. "*What did you say?*" he asked quietly.

"*I said,*" Blackwood went on in German, drawing a distinct satisfaction from the guard's stupid look of confusion. "*We do not know where he is. We have not seen him since yesterday evening. We believed he was in his room.*"

Klaus's face flushed red. He tightened the rifle to his shoulder with a grimace. "*You speak our fucking language? You miserable rat—*"

"*Lower your rifle!*" Wulfson barked from the stairwell. He filled the doorway, pistol held low at his side.

"*He is a spy!*" Klaus was nearly frothing at the mouth. "*He has been listening to us this whole time! He speaks our language!*"

"*I don't care if he can speak German, Unteroffizier.*" Wulfson's voice cooled. "*He is no spy. He is a prisoner, the same as he has always been. Lower your rifle. That is a command.*"

Klaus, still enraged, lowered the barrel reluctantly. Blackwood glared back at him, daring him to shoot. If he had only one last act on this earth, it would be taking the slimy bastard with him — even if it was Wulfson who got to pull the trigger.

"*The string bean is gone,*" Klaus growled.

"*Fletcher?*" Wulfson crossed to check the empty room for himself. "*The British one?*"

"*Ya…*" Klaus refused to break from Blackwood's stare.

I'm going to kill you, Blackwood thought, *I'm going to string you from a branch and watch you hang.*

"Where is he?" Wulfson asked in English, drawing Blackwood's gaze.

"We don't—" Blackwood began, but the clack of the tavern door below cut him off. A voice yelled and feet shuffled across the floor and up the stairwell. The door exploded open to reveal Hanz clinging to Johan, his legs rubber.

Johan dumped him onto the floor with disgust. Hanz gasped at the air as he rolled into a seat.

"*What has happened?*" Wulfson demanded.

Hanz's head shook slowly back and forth as he fought to catch his breath. He was pale and looked like he might add to the vomit that already stained his coat. Wulfson knelt before him. It looked for a second as if he might slap the private, but instead he reached out gently and took Hanz by the chin, tilting his head up to meet his eyes.

"*Tell me what has happened, Private,*" he said softly.

Hanz sucked in a quavering breath. His tongue caught in his mouth, but he managed to get out weak words. "*The British one…*"

"*Where is he?*" Klaus cut in forcefully from across the room. "*Have you found him?*"

"*He's…*" Hanz gasped out. "*He's dead.*"

22

IT WAS as if Hanz's head was submerged in a bucket of warm water. The world around him oscillated slowly outside his focus and the murmur of voices sounded distant in his ears. The villagers, all of them it would seem, were crowded onto the benches of the meeting hall. Hanz and the other guards sat in the back row as the women spoke quietly amongst themselves. Victor alone was absent, having been left in the tavern to watch over the prisoners. Klaus grumbled something, drawing a response from Johan. Hanz couldn't make out their words over the ringing in his ears.

His stomach was still sour, and his lungs still burned from his flight. He stared down at the stone floor and tried to ground himself. When he looked at his hands, he saw that they were trembling.

"*If I may have your attention…*" a faraway voice called out. Hanz couldn't comply. His thoughts remained fixed on the ragged corpse and the thrum of wingbeats. A slap upside his head brought him jolting back reality. Klaus glowered at him.

"*I have examined the body thoroughly,*" Wulfson went on, standing tall atop the stage before the gathered crowd. Beside him stood the headwoman, Lucia, and a step behind them were Sovilo and the old crone. Bags hung under the Major's eyes, and his hands were folded neatly at his front as he addressed the crowd with a solemn expression. "*After a cursory investigation, I believe this killing to be the work of a bear.*"

"*A bear?*" Hanz blurted out in shock. Another swift cuff from Klaus silenced him.

"*Yes, Private Hanz,*" Wulfson went on patiently. "*A bear. They are rare to see these days, but apparently one has been spotted in the nearby forest several times this autumn. It is likely that, due to the harshness of the winter alongside the absence of this village's men and the resulting lack of defenses, the beast has taken on a more exploratory nature than what was expected. Blood and prints found near the outhouses all but confirm this theory; the beast, driven out of its shelter by the elements,* caught the Englishman alone in the night as he went to relieve himself. It dragged him to the forest, where, after a terrible mauling, it abandoned him to scavengers."

Hanz couldn't believe what he was hearing. It was no bear. He'd never seen one himself, but he'd come across the carrion left by dogs and wolves back home. None of those unfortunate bits of prey had even displayed anything close to the degree of violence that had been inflicted upon the Brit. He'd been shredded, not dismembered. Beyond that, Hanz had *seen* the savage culprits ripping the body apart. He opened his mouth to speak again but flinched as Klaus's hand cocked back.

"*Enough, Unteroffizier. Let the man speak,*" Wulfson said.

Hanz paused, torn between the wrath of Klaus and the burning desire to protest against the absurd conclusion. "*Major, I apologize, but... he... the ravens...*"

Wulfson nodded. "*Yes. Ravens are carrion feeders. It is no surprise that they viewed his remains as a feast.*"

"*What are we going to do about this?*" a woman called out.

This time it was Lucia who stepped forward. "*As many of you are aware, bears are vicious creatures — this one especially, as it seems to be hungry enough to attack when it should be hibernating. They are an adversary that no person should ever imagine facing alone. That is why we have decided that it is in everyone's best interest that we instill a curfew over the village. Everyone is to be indoors come nightfall, no exceptions.*" She looked pointedly at the guards.

Klaus let out a dismissive grunt.

"*Furthermore,*" she continued, "*we need to be on the lookout for tracks or scat. If the creature is still about, then we must make it our first priority to deter it—*"

"Is it wild, or is it a pet?" Klaus asked evenly.

This time, Wulfson did not react so kindly to the interruption. He stepped forward, his ire evident on his face, but Lucia held out a hand.

"*Explain yourself, Herr Klaus,*" she said.

"We all saw that little show you put on last night."

"And?"

Klaus hunched forward, eyes dark and rifle balanced between his legs. "Your little monster play. Isn't that what that was in the tavern? You show us a mock beast killing children, and now a man is dead. Killed by a bear. Do you think us simple-minded? You keep ravens and mongrel mutts, what other rotten pets do you have hidden around here?"

Lucia's severity melted into a mocking chuckle. "*The Sarvàn? Is that what you are talking about?*"

"*I don't know what you people call it.*"

"*It's a children's tale.*"

"*Is it?*"

She laughed in full. "*How old are you, Herr Klaus? Do you fear every legend you hear? If so, you'd better steer clear of any rabbit tracks you come across. I hear there is a Wolpertinger about.*"

A cascade of snickers rippled through the crowd.

Klaus sank back in his seat, glowering.

"*Thank you, Herr Klaus. It is rare enough to find a moment of levity in such dark times. I'm glad you have found a way to be useful.*" Lucia returned her focus to the crowd. "*Moving on, we must be wary of traveling alone outside of the village proper. Until winter's end, we must only move in pairs…*"

The ringing overtook her voice once again as Hanz retreated back into his troubled thoughts. He saw Fletcher's corpse. It sat before him, flayed skin glinting with frost as the hollow sockets stared back at him. Staring into his soul. Judging him. Damning him for his part in all this.

23

THE PRISONERS spent the morning with their foreheads pressed to a table still tacky with cider from the night before. Victor ambled in an endless circle around them, chewing on salvaged meat and barking for silence at so much as a cough.

At noon Wulfson and the others returned to the tavern. He called the prisoners on line. After chastising Victor for their treatment, he set about explaining that Fletcher had been the victim of a bear attack. Despite Blackwood's suspicion that Fletcher had died at the hands of the guards, the theory seemed almost sound. Blackwood was no stranger to bears. He and his grandfather had hunted enough grizzlies for him to know what type of savage display they could transform a man into. Still, it seemed far too convenient that a man-eater would show up to take Fletcher from the same spot where Dietmar had been lurking the night before. Judging by the doubtful faces of the other prisoners, Blackwood suspected he was not alone in his misgivings.

Following his speech, the Major released them once more to their daily choring, much to the guards' chagrin.

None of them dared to speak as they departed the tavern. Even Dubois, still lost in a semblance of shock, remained silent as he accompanied Blackwood out to the woodshed. Gertrude and Maria awaited them there. When they set to the work of splitting logs, Maria intervened and instead sent Blackwood off with a wheelbarrow full of wood to what she referred to as *the Mithraeum*. When he expressed his confusion, she quickly clarified that she meant the cavern in the cliff. He didn't argue, sensing that he had been singled out for a reason.

Abandoning the wheelbarrow at the stairs, he took an armload of wood and passed through the door beyond the columns. A single brazier burned in the far corner of the cavernous space. A figure cast shadows over the polished floor as it moved back and forth before the flames. Blackwood drew in a breath to call out, but a pungent odor caught his nose. It was putrid and sour and carried a hint of iron. In the scant light from the open door, he spotted its source.

THE SARVÀN

Fletcher's corpse lay on a table beneath a thick blanket. Blood soaked through the wool in dark splotches and pooled on the floor below. A steady drip echoed back from the unseen walls.

"Sorry, old boy," he said quietly.

"*Hello? Who is there?*" the distant figure called out. Blackwood recognized the lilting voice.

"Blackwood," he called back, kicking the door shut behind him.

"*You brought wood. Good,*" Lucia said as he approached. She sat atop a short stool. The brazier beside her burned low. She nodded to it before turning back to her work. "*Place them in the fire, if you would.*"

He let the logs tumble into the flames. Sparks exploded outward, and the crashing of the wood echoed through the chamber. Suddenly the air was alive with a heavy droning.

Lucia snapped out a warning hand. "*Fool! Hold still and be silent!*"

The circle of light grew as the dry wood ignited. He saw what she had been fidgeting with. It was a conical wicker basket. Beyond it, dozens more stood in a neat row. A horde of insects buzzed around the firelight, hanging between the two of them in an angry mob. One landed on Blackwood's still outstretched arm, and he realized what they were: honeybees.

"*You could have warned me…*" he said, his voice barely a whisper.

She mouthed the word "silence" with a stern look

He obeyed.

In the lightest of voices, she began to sing. The song was woeful yet lovely, and her voice cracked when she struck the high notes. As the gentle tones washed through the air, the bees began to calm. They drifted back to their homes, disappearing into the baskets one by one until the air was once again still.

"*You have to be calm and quiet, or else they panic. Treat them like you would a baby and they will reward you.*" She held up a hand sticky with honey. A bee lay on her palm, entrapped in the golden liquid. It writhed on its side. With the finesse of a fine craftsman, she freed it. The bee, too exhausted from its struggle to fly away, wriggled onto her wrist. She watched it closely, muttering soft words in Latin.

Blackwood cleared his throat, but she did not look up, instead enraptured by the small creature. "*You wanted to see me?*"

"*Did I?*" she asked.

Blackwood, having already had one hell of a morning, was in no mood for her games. He made to leave.

"*So quick to run off.*" She simpered. "*How are you today, Herr Blackwood?*"

He stopped mid-stride. "*I'm fine.*"

"*You don't seem fine. Too much to drink perhaps?*"

He ignored her teasing tone and nodded across the cavern toward Fletcher's corpse. "*What will happen to him now?*"

"*We will burn him, as is our way.*"

The irony was palpable. He couldn't imagine Fletcher would think of this as anything less than an insult, being burned to ash by German heathens. Though perhaps it was kinder than burying him here. At least this offered an escape of sorts. "*They tell us it was a bear.*"

"*You sound skeptical.*"

"*You're not?*"

She understood his meaning well enough. "*I doubt it was your captors. It would take a truly demented soul to do those things to another man.*"

"*You clearly don't know them that well.*"

"*Yes. And for that I am grateful.*"

"*Bear attacks are common here then?*"

"*No. It's never happened here before. But the Major's conclusions make sense. We are weaker now than we have ever been. If there was ever a time for such a thing to happen, it would be now.*"

Blackwood had a difficult time gauging whether he believed her or not. While her inflection seemed honest, there was something else beneath her easy tone. A loose hint that there was more left unsaid. His eyes wandered the darkness, settling on the shadowed relief of the bull killing scene barely visible overhead. "*You'd best pray to that god of yours that your men return soon. It seems like you're getting overrun by predators these days.*"

"*Maybe that's why he brought you to us.*"

He scoffed. "*Your god had nothing to do with our coming here. Trust me.*"

A coy smile crossed her lips, but she didn't look up from the bee. "*Not a religious man then?*"

The mantra that had carried him through the trenches played through his mind: *There is no God. There is no judgement. The only thing to fear is death. And when death takes you, you won't even be around anymore to give a damn.* These words were the only religion he needed. "*Even you might second guess your god if you'd seen what I've seen,*" he muttered.

The bee had begun to fidget. She plucked it up and let it climb between her fingers. "*He is not* my *god. He is* the *god. There may be other spirits and powers* that are beyond our understanding, yes, but there is only one true god. And his name is Mithras."

"You sound more like a Christian than you know."

She shrugged. "*Perhaps they sound Mithraic.*"

He considered leaving, but realized that for once, no one was waiting for him. He knelt beside the brazier instead, resting his legs and enjoying the warmth of the flames.

"*Do you know why we keep bees?*"

He shrugged. "*The honey?*"

She shook her head. "*It truly is a wonderful gift. But no, that is not why. In ancient times they said that when a man's soul leaves his body, it rejoins the world as a bee. In this form, it may rest and mend from the wounds of a lifetime of human suffering. The hive offers it a simple, lucrative life that washes it free of sin, that it may start again fresh when the time comes. That is why we keep them so close, so that our loved ones may have a means to return to us after they die. That way we might meet again someday in the future.*"

"What if they die far away?"

"*The soul can travel much farther than a man. Do you have many bees where you are from?*"

"Sure."

"*Would you go back there? To be reborn amongst your people?*"

Blackwood didn't answer. At times in the past he'd found himself missing the great wilds of Montana. But it was the place he missed, not the sorry excuse of a life he'd left behind. That was something he never planned on returning to.

"Maybe you'll end up here," she said. "*Who knows? We do keep our bees quite happy.*"

"A missionary tried to convert me once. Why am I getting that same feeling from you now?"

"*You assume you're worthy…*" Her tone was only half teasing.

Blackwood smirked. "*Alright, go ahead. I'll hear the pitch.*"

She gave an exasperated sigh. "*As we sit here with the bees?*"

"It'd be better than hauling firewood," he deadpanned. She frowned, and he shrugged. "At least tell me what the deal is with all the ravens. I heard the guards muttering that they were eating Fletcher. I assume they're a part of all… this." He spun a lazy finger around the cavern.

"*Ravens are the messengers of Mithras. And yes, they do feed on carrion, like your unfortunate friend became.*"

"*Messengers, eh? They talk to you?*"

"*In a manner of speaking.*"

He quorked sarcastically.

She gave him a sidelong glance. "*Really, Edward?*"

Their eyes caught. He quorked again, apologetically this time.

"*Mithras was born from stone into chaos,*" she explained. "*He formed all of this — the mountains, the trees, the creatures of the forest. Even us he molded from the chaos that was before with only his two hands. He is in all things and speaks through all things. When he wishes to be heard, he makes himself apparent.*"

"*…through birds?*"

"*Through many things,*" she emphasized. Then her lips cracked into an inadvertent smile. "*And yes, often through birds.*"

They shared a quiet laugh. A tenseness melted from her shoulders that he hadn't realized was there. The bees hummed quietly in their hives. Blackwood looked down the line of baskets. They sat in long rows that disappeared into the darkness. He tried to imagine the countless souls she believed inhabited them. "*This god of yours, is he at least kind?*"

The bee in her palm began to buzz. She raised it tenderly to the basket. It paused, turned toward her, and flapped its wings as if in thanks. Then it was gone. "*I don't know if kindness is a concept for something so powerful as he. But he protects us, and for me that is kindness enough.*"

They sat in silence for some time. When she spoke next, her words were barely a whisper. "*Would you kill them if I asked you to?*"

"*The guards?*" he asked, taken aback by her abruptness.

"*Yes.*"

"*I would.*" Blackwood didn't feel the need to add that he'd gladly do it regardless.

"*And if I asked, would you let them live?*"

This time he hesitated. "*You know they won't think twice about hurting you, right?*"

"*They are only five against many.*"

"*Do you even have guns?*"

She didn't answer.

"*Lucia…*"

"*No. Ammunition is a luxury we are not afforded up here. We hunt the old way, with bow and spear.*"

"Well, they have rifles and plenty of ammunition. If they decide to kill the Major, to slaughter us, there's no reason to think they'd just leave behind so many witnesses to their treason."

"That won't happen."

"They know I speak German now."

Her eyes snapped up to his. "Why would you let them know?"

"I had no choice, they would have killed Dubois. I'm telling you this because it's just another crack in this fragile alliance. They're paranoid, and they're eager for blood. It won't be long before they break."

She swore as she stood, cautious not to bump the slumbering hive, and withdrew something from the belt of her skirt.

"Take this." She held out a thin item wrapped in cloth.

"What is it?"

"It's why I called you here."

He took it in his hands and unraveled it. The cloth dropped away to reveal a long-bladed dagger. The handle was cast bronze with an ornate pommel bearing a bull's likeness. The blade was razor sharp, and he nicked himself as he tested the edge.

She grasped his wrist. When he looked up, her eyes were clouded with worry.

"Don't lose it, and only ever use it to keep yourself alive. Please, do not initiate with the guards. It will do nothing but make your worries a reality."

"Why are you giving this to me?"

"I already told you." She nodded up to the relief. "Because I believe he sent you to me."

His chest tightened as he stared into her eyes.

"Lucia, you don't have to..."

She stepped close, her nose nearly brushing the tip of his. He could feel her breath on his lips and the warmth radiating off her body. He closed his eyes, giving in to the magnetic desire that tugged him toward her.

"Let them live..." she breathed.

A loud creak shattered the moment. Blackwood jolted back as if shocked by a bad wire. Daylight spilled across the cavern, and seven figures shuffled inside. He scrambled to rewrap the dagger and conceal it under his belt. Lucia stepped in front of him to obscure the motion with her body. All but one of the figures crowded around Fletcher's corpse. Together they hoisted the body up and carried him outside.

The one who remained, a woman bent crookedly with age, croaked out in English. "Blackwood, yes?"

He stepped away from the bees and called back, "Yeah."

"Your arms are needed at the woodshed."

"Sure." He cleared his throat and straightened his coat, making sure the dagger was well hidden.

Lucia's cheeks flushed with embarrassment. She spoke quietly. "*Go. We will burn your friend tonight. You may watch from the tavern. But do not come out into the dark.*" She reached up and brushed an errant hair from her brow. "*And please, do as I asked.*"

Blackwood caught her hand as it dropped away and gave it a soft squeeze. "*I hope you're right.*"

With that, he left. The low hum of the bees faded behind him as he strode back out into the cold.

24

LOUIS DUBOIS stood on a stool beside the pyre that had been constructed for Fletcher. He wrestled with the knot that bound a bundle of kindling. Eventually he resigned himself to using his teeth. The knot gave with a jerk, and the spindly branches clattered into the snow. He swore, stepping down and dusting them off before gathering them in his arms.

Blackwood was still at the woodshed. Upon his return from the so-called *Mithraeum* he had silently taken to hacking at the logs like the piston of a steam engine. At first Dubois didn't mind the lack of conversation. He'd found that the comfort and revelry of the past two days had left him entirely unprepared for the intensity of that morning. Even worse, he was ashamed of his ineptitude in the face of danger and desired nothing less than to draw the hardy American's attention. However, as the hours carried on, he found his mounting questions burning a hole through his skull.

When Dubois had finally tried to broach the subject of the morning's events, Blackwood had only muttered "later" with a stern finality. As if sensing the tension, Maria had asked the Frenchman to bring kindling to the funeral pyre at the center of the plaza. Dubois had accepted, but when he arrived and saw Fletcher's naked corpse already laid to rest atop the stacked beams, he immediately regretted it.

Now, as Dubois climbed once more atop the stool and began meticulously placing the kindling around the perimeter of Fletcher's body, he found himself alone in the plaza. A few villagers passed here and there through the surrounding streets, but even the guards had retreated inside at the late afternoon chill. There was only Fletcher to keep him company.

"I'm sorry, *mon ami*," Dubois muttered for the umpteenth time. He had so far avoided looking directly into the empty cavities that had been Fletcher's eyes. As a matter of fact, he'd done his best to avoid taking in the details of the disfigured corpse altogether. The Brit's already pale flesh had begun to grey under a thin layer of ice crystals — what little flesh was left, at least. Though the villagers did their best to clean his skin of the blood, his body looked as though he had been tied to a horse and dragged over a mile of cheese graters. Ragged straps of skin hung from torn fascia where the ravens had been at him. His chest was largely caved in and bore several raking wounds. His gaunt face was ripped open and his eyes had been plucked from his skull by sharp beaks.

Though Dubois was not a soldier, this was not the first dead body he had seen. None of the others had been like this though. The state of the corpse reminded him of an ancient practice he'd read about in old tomes — the act of flaying, where a man would have his skin peeled away like the hide of a deer. Only, rather than being sleeved like an animal, it seemed Fletcher had been peeled bit by bit.

Dubois gagged at the thought, then again as he looked over the body. For a moment his revulsion outweighed his remorse. He wished only to be done with the vile hunk of meat before him. His composure returned alongside his compassion. Whatever he might have thought of Fletcher in life, this was no way for a man to die.

"*Notre Père, qui es aux cieux,*" Dubois bowed his head and prayed. "*Que ton nom soit sanctifié, Que ton règne vienne—*"

"*Get back to work!*"

Dubois flinched. He glanced up to see Dietmar's thin silhouette in the tavern door. The guard stabbed a vicious finger towards Dubois. "*Are you deaf, swine? I said work!*"

"*Ya, ya!*" Dubois raised his arms in a submissive act of acknowledgement. Dietmar glared for only a moment, then was gone.

"You know, it was a choice," Dubois muttered to Fletcher's corpse as he finished laying the last of his kindling, then glanced around to make sure no one was watching. "Involving myself in this war, I mean. I didn't have to. I could have waited it out with the others of my… my privilege, I suppose. But I thought it was only right to do some little thing, lend at least a bit of knowledge to those who mattered. Now… now I think I may have been a fool. These days I worry only for my family. For my daughters. For what life must be like for them without a father. I knew that life myself, and I swore it would not be theirs." He felt the tears begin to well in his eyes. "I fear I have failed in the one great thing I was destined for."

He didn't know why he was speaking English to the corpse rather than his native French. Perhaps it was so Fletcher could have understood. Then again, he didn't know why he was speaking to a corpse at all. It felt good, he supposed. He smiled, forcing himself to look the dead man in the face.

"You're a good listener, *mon ami*. Thank you for that. As you English say, I wish you fair winds and—"

The words caught in his throat. Just below Fletcher's jaw hung the pale pipe of his exposed trachea. It was not the organ itself that caught Dubois's attention, but rather the crisp wound at its center. Ignoring the roiling bile that threatened to rise from his stomach, Dubois leaned forward and examined it. The cut was precise, almost surgical. Even through a crusting of ice he could see the cartilage on the other side bore a matching slice.

"What in God's name happened to you?" Dubois whispered. The question was moot, as deep down he immediately knew the truth. There had been no bear. This wound had been caused by a blade. A blade driven upward through Fletcher's throat. A blade that, at that angle, was meant to skewer the man's brain.

Dubois's eyes shot to the tavern. He fully expected to see the guards wading across the snow, murder glinting in their eyes. But he was alone.

Alone with a murdered man, he thought as a pit opened in his stomach.

25

AFTER DINNER Blackwood was the first up the stairs. He managed to slip away into his room as the others settled in. Barring the broken latch of the door with a chair, he made quick work of hiding the dagger Lucia had given him inside a slit in his mattress. When he returned to the main room, he found McCulloch and Dubois sitting before the hearth. He dragged a third chair over to join them.

"Where's the kid?" Blackwood asked as he took a seat.

"Apparently he's sick of yer company." McCulloch nodded toward the room that had previously been inhabited by Fletcher. Movement was audible beyond the closed door.

"Didn't think I snored *that* bad," Blackwood tried for levity.

Neither of the other men smiled. Dubois's head hung below his shoulders as he massaged his temples, meanwhile McCulloch's fingers strummed absently against the arm of his chair.

Blackwood realized that whatever he'd interrupted was serious. "What don't I know?"

Dubois looked up at him. His expression was dour and his eyes had lost their playful glint.

"Tell him," McCulloch muttered.

Dubois's voice was barely above a whisper. "It wasn't a bear that killed Fletcher."

"I suspect the same," Blackwood said.

Dubois shook his head. "*Non*, it is no mere suspicion, cowboy. I saw him today, his body. He was stabbed through the throat. The wound was too clean for a beast. It was made by a blade."

Blackwood's jaw clenched inadvertently. As much as he'd suspected that Fletcher had been murdered, the confirmation was still jarring. "What about the rest of his wounds? They say he was shredded."

"Who knows what horrid things were done to him. Perhaps it was the work of the animals that got to him afterward. The ravens, other scavengers, I do not know. All I know is that the killing blow was done by a man."

"You're certain?"

"*Oui.*"

Blackwood settled back in his chair and looked toward the cliff. Snow was falling outside, as it always seemed to be. A trail of smoke lilted up through the gentle flurry as Fletcher's pyre burned in the plaza.

McCulloch spoke up next. "It's high time we bring the fight to them."

"Nothing would please me more," Blackwood started, but his voice faltered as he remembered his promise to Lucia. "But we can't. Not yet."

"Why the hell not?"

"Because we'd die."

McCulloch snorted. "If I dinnae do things because I might die then I wouldnae be here, lad."

"You need a better reason?" Blackwood motioned toward the other buildings. "How about those people out there, huh? How about those kids? If I thought we could do this clean, I'd be right there with you. But we can't. If we lose, and they kill us — which *will* happen if we strike now — then the Major will be next. And then what? You really want to leave these people in the hands of those bastards?"

McCulloch was undeterred. "If they knew what was good for 'em, they'd fight too."

"They don't have rifles," Blackwood said then added quickly, "but Klaus doesn't know that. He thinks he's outgunned. I think that's the only thing keeping us alive right now. If we attack too soon, he'll find out the truth. Then it's over. For everyone."

"That pretty bird's been in your ear…" McCulloch's eyes narrowed. "You think she'll save you from all this? From them that's downstairs?"

"I think she can help us." Blackwood's voice was sure, though he was not.

"Then where is this help, eh?" McCulloch demanded.

"It's coming," Blackwood said. For a fleeting moment, he considered showing them the dagger as proof. He immediately thought better of it. The guards weren't above using torture to extract information from any of them. If they really were hunting the prisoners down one by one, then the fewer people who knew his secret, the better. "For now, we need to bide our time."

"We dinnae have any bloody time!" McCulloch snapped, perhaps too loudly. He sucked in a breath through his nose and went on in a hushed tone. "You're next, you know. Wasnae a bright idea to let them know you speak their language. What will you do when they catch you alone out there? Will you just lay down and let them take you? And for what? The sake of some bonnie German whore?"

Blackwood was on his feet before McCulloch finished the word. The Scotsman didn't flinch. He looked up at the American, a wry grin spreading across his craggy features.

"Aye. I see where your allegiances lie," the old Scotsman drawled. He turned his head, never taking his eyes from Blackwood. "What about you, Frenchman? What do you say to our lovestruck American's plan to tuck tail and wait?"

Dubois, who had until now been silently observing the fire, cleared his throat. "I think the two of you must remember who the true enemy is."

McCulloch grunted softly. His nasty grin faded, and he waved Blackwood off. "He's right. My blood's hot. I dinnae mean anything by it, lad."

Blackwood returned to his seat, his face still flush.

"I also think," Dubois went on, "that the cowboy is right. I'd rather win tomorrow than lose today."

"Fine," McCulloch conceded. The wind had left his sails, and he drooped further into the chair. "Did you at least get any information from the woman?"

"About what?" Blackwood asked bitterly.

"I don't know." McCulloch gave an exasperated shrug. "This place is a bloody circus. Was Fletcher right? Are they witches?"

"No," Blackwood said. He forced his anger away. Dubois had spoken truth — the only enemy was downstairs. "They worship a god called Mithras." He turned to Dubois. "Ever heard of it?"

"I have been thinking about that name since I heard it last night. Mithras. Mithras…" Dubois's voice faded away. When he spoke again, he sounded uncertain. "While my memory is not what it once was, I do recall reading that name. A Roman god, I believe. One that was eradicated when the Christians came into power — as happened to most heathen beliefs at the time."

"What do you mean by eradicated?" Blackwood asked.

Dubois gave him a sidelong glance. "I think you know what I mean."

"They were slaughtered."

"Presumably."

"I guess it makes sense why they've kept to themselves out here for so long, living in secret," Blackwood surmised. "Their ancestors were hunted down. They were hiding."

Dubois's eyebrows drew together, as if something troubling had just occurred to him. "Yes. That would mean that their existence truly has been a secret since the Roman empire. Nearly two thousand years. I doubt anyone in academia knows who they worship. Perhaps no one outside of this very village, even."

McCulloch grunted. "They dinnae bother to hide it from us."

"No." Dubois stared back into the flames, lost in thought. "No, they did not…"

Blackwood continued to watch the pyre burn well after the others had retired to bed. The moon was bright and cast the plaza in long shadows. As the fire dwindled to ash, he knew he'd regret not getting some sleep.

It was as he made for his room that something caught his ear. A light tapping. It came from Fletcher's old room, the one Enzo had claimed for his own. He pressed an ear to the door as the tapping continued. A cold draft seeped out from the seams. He eased it open.

The room was dark. A frigid breeze brushed his face as his eyes adjusted. The bed was empty, and beyond it the window was slightly ajar. Its latch tapped against the sill as the wind tried to blow it shut.

Blackwood darted to look out over the snow-covered alleyway. Twenty feet below, a rough impact shone in the snowbank. Leading away from it, toward the street, was a single set of footprints.

"Oh, you little son of a bitch…"

26

ENZO CREPT through the alley. The houses stood tall around him, and the snow came down hard. It had already accumulated to the point where each crunching footstep sounded like an avalanche to his wary ears. He thought more than once of abandoning his mission, of shimmying back up the tavern's drainpipe and returning to his warm bed. But the force that drove him was too great to ignore: love.

At least, that's what he believed it was. Truth be told, he'd never been in love before. He had imagined he was, once, back home in Italy. There was a girl in his village named Gabriella. She was kind and beautiful, but never once had she shown any interest in the shy young boy from down the street. She was the reason Enzo attempted to sign up for the army at only fifteen — to prove once and for all he was a man worthy of her affection. They had laughed at his crudely forged paperwork and told him to return in three years. But the Red Cross had been easier to fool.

Fantasies of Gabriella had dominated the countless hours spent shuttling medical supplies here and there behind the Front. One sad winter day he received the news that she had run off with an older man and was to be wed. At the time he'd considered the resulting heartbreak to be the worst pain a young man could possibly endure. A week later he was proven wrong when a miscommunicated order brought him into the clutches of the ruthless hun.

But it was different this time. He was certain of it.

Hilde was her name. He had worked with her for two days now at her absent father's mill. Initially, he'd been smitten solely by her looks. She was a short woman, robust in a way that appealed to him greatly. Her face was soft and round with deep hazel eyes that seemed to light up when she laughed. They hadn't exchanged many words, as he only spoke Italian and she German. Despite this seemingly insurmountable obstacle, they had managed a working method of communication through the most rudimentary of methods: charades. Through the language of movement, he had learned that she was only two years older than he was. He'd learned of her love for carrots and sweets and her affection for the orange tabby cat that followed them around the mill. He learned that she found even his silliest antics funny and that when she smiled, he could not look away. Unlike with Gabriella, his interest did not seem to be unrequited. Through stolen glances and kind gestures, they had developed a connection deeper than he imagined possible in such a short time. Deep down, he knew it was never destined to work. After all, being a prisoner of war had its limitations. Hell, he could be back out on the mountain and freezing to death tomorrow for all he knew. But that didn't matter. Now, after an afternoon of sneaking drinks in the mill between wonderful (though indecipherable) whispers, all he wanted was to see her once more before he closed his eyes.

Had he not been so lost in his fantasies, he might have thought better of venturing out into the night. He might have considered Fletcher's wretched death, or the Frenchman's brief warning about the guards as he slipped away into his room. But the schnapps had put Enzo's mind on a single track forward, and there was no getting off now.

The midnight streets were dead, and he managed to reach her house without being seen. It was a humble, single-story home adjacent to the mill where they'd eaten lunch together during their working hours. He had sat awkwardly in her kitchen while they ate, shamefully timid and wishing he could understand her words. He didn't feel timid now though. He knocked gently on the door.

There was no answer at first. He tried again, then a third time. All at once his hopes began to crumble. He considered skulking off in defeat and was a hair from turning away when a shadow passed in front of the window. The door cracked open.

"*Hallo?*" Her voice warmed the winter air.

"Hilde, *it is me, Enzo*," he whispered in Italian as he emerged from the shadows.

"*Enzo*," she gasped. "*Bist du hier alleine?*"

He turned his palms skyward and couldn't help from showing off a silly grin. She was clad in a thin nightgown that draped low, exposing her ample cleavage. Her initial look of shock melted into one of concern. With a quick glance around, she ushered him inside.

"*I'm so sorry to intrude, Hilde, but I needed to see you again. I've never felt this way before. It's not just your beauty that has me smitten. I—*"

"*Du weißt, ich kann dich nicht verstehen, Enzo. Du solltest nicht hier sein,*" she rattled off, stealing around the room and yanking curtains shut. When she reached the last one, she stared anxiously through its seams.

"*I...*" he started, but suddenly he felt foolish. Her reaction was not what he had anticipated. Now, as she stood at the windows, face drawn and eyes darting, he realized his stupidity. "*I've overstepped,*" he said quietly. "*I'm sorry. I will leave.*"

He backed toward the door. She abandoned her post, darting to block his way.

"*Wohin gehst du jetzt? Suchen Ihre wachen nicht nach Ihnen?*" she demanded.

He recognized a word he'd heard many times before at Rothenspring — *Wachen*. Guards.

Rather than continue his fruitless attempt to explain in words, he shook his head. He pointed to himself, then mimed the exaggerated antics of a burglar sneaking through the night.

Hilde sighed in relief, though her agitation remained. "*Sitzen,*" she ordered, pointing to a rocker before the fireplace. He understood and complied, sinking onto the seat as his smile returned.

"*I have something for you.*" He fumbled to unfold a piece of paper from his pocket. It was a page he'd torn out of a book he'd found in the tavern. One side was spattered in fine German print, but the other had been blank. Now, thanks to a pencil he'd nicked during the festivities, it bore a carefully drawn likeness of the beauty before him.

He held it out. She took it, and her face softened. "*Das bin ich?*"

He nodded, pointing to the paper then to her. If she could have understood him, he would have told her a great many things in that moment. But she couldn't, and he didn't. So, instead, he found his rear glued to the chair, a stupid smile painted on his lips to mask the slowly growing sense of panic he felt inside.

This was where his plan had ended. He hadn't thought of what would come next. In his fantasy, he imagined it might just sort of *happen*. Now, grinning like a buffoon, he was painfully aware of his own lack of experience. For a brief second, his mind flitted back to when he'd been summoned to the interrogation shed at Rothenspring. To when he'd first stood before Wulfson and told the Major his age. Dubois, standing dutifully to the side, had translated the Major's response: "*What are you doing here, son? You're just a boy, not a warrior. Have you ever even lain with a woman?*"

Too afraid to lie for the sake of pride, Enzo had admitted the truth. "*No.*"

Now, as he sat on the precipice of a harrowing failure, he began to mentally retreat. "*I must go,*" he insisted again, beginning to rise.

Hilde pushed him back down with a firm hand. "*Nein,*" she insisted, miming the action of drinking. "*Hast du durst?*"

He cleared his throat and nodded. "*Ya, hast… dooderst,*" he tried in his best attempt at German.

She smiled, though it didn't reach her eyes. Without another word she disappeared into the next room.

Alone now, Enzo removed his coat and took in the room around him. The house was humbly furnished. A few nicknacks and heirlooms dotted the walls and tables. One in particular stood out to him — it was a photograph in a gilded frame on the mantel. The boy in the photograph was handsome and young, maybe around his own age. It was her brother, he told himself. But the boy in the photograph looked nothing like her. If anything, he reminded Enzo of himself.

The resulting realization hit him hard. Dubois had explained to him that the village men were all at war. Was this another suitor? If so, was Hilde patiently awaiting his return?

Had Enzo misread her intentions that poorly? Risked his very life for the sake of a polite rejection?

His hands were clammy by the time Hilde returned bearing two steaming mugs. She handed him one. It burned his tongue when he sipped it, and he recoiled. She gave an affectionate *tsk* and they both laughed. After blowing away the steam, he tried again. The smooth taste of mint schnapps hid under the sweetness of the tea.

"I… I have to ask." He pointed to the photo. "*That photograph, who is that?*"

The smile fell from her face as she traced his finger to the mantel.

"*I'm sorry, I'm sorry. I just… Is that your brother?*" he asked hopefully.

A profound sadness filled her eyes. When she finally turned her gaze to him, she appeared immeasurably lonely.

"…*a lover,*" he surmised, trying to mask the pain as his heart sundered in two.

"*Tot,*" she said.

Enzo knew that word well enough. He'd heard it a thousand times from the guards. It meant *dead*. His selfish elation was immediately overshadowed by a great shame as a tear rolled down her cheek.

"*I'm so sorry. I do not mean to hurt you. I— I really need to leave,*" Enzo blurted out and started to rise again. For the third time she reached out to stop him, only this time her arm collided with his mug. The hot tea spilled out, burning his hand and causing him to drop it. The mug shattered on the ground, the deep amber tea splattering over them both.

"*Sind alle Italiener so ungeschickt?*" she hissed, eyeing the brown stains that marred her nightgown. Again, he tried to apologize, but she waved him off and eyed his stained shirt. "*Gib mir dein hemd, bevor der fleck fest wird.*"

"*I don't understand—*" he began, but she had already placed down her own mug and now pulled him to his feet. He felt like a toddler as she slapped his arms up into the air and yanked the soiled shirt over his head. She began to turn away, clearly intending to clean or at least dry the shirt. But he caught her eyes wandering over his chest. Without thinking, he gave in to his impulses and grabbed her by the waist. She looked at him in surprise and, as they locked eyes, he leaned in and kissed her deeply.

She didn't pull away. For a moment he imagined she might just be in shock. Then she kissed him back, and her hands clutched his bare skin. When she finally did retreat her expression was torn. At first, he thought she might cast him out of her house for his indecency. But she didn't. Instead, she stared into his eyes and frowned.

"*Das hast du nicht verdient…*" she whispered as a fierce look of determination came over her. The fabric that covered her shoulders slipped away, and the nightgown fell to the floor.

Enzo could feel his heart jackhammering against his ribs as his eyes took her in, and in a most inaudible breath he managed a single phrase. "*My God…*"

Enzo had no idea what hour it was when he finally pulled away from her. They had made love by the fire twice, and he knew he must have slept at some point. Now she dozed angelically on the fur rug beside him, curled in his arms in a way that somehow made every miserable step of this journey worth it.

He kissed her delicately on the neck before sliding away. The room around him swam a bit thanks to the now empty bottle of schnapps on the floor beside them. He didn't care. He had found something now, something that finally justified all the pain and horror and loneliness of the past several months. He decided right then and there that it would take more than the threat of a German bullet to keep him from this woman. Should he be forced to leave and make his way to Switzerland as the Frenchman had said they would, he would let nothing stand in the way of his return to claim his sweet Hilde.

He let her sleep as he dressed. She would be at the mill waiting for him in a few hours, of that he had no doubt. Now, as the sunrise drew ever closer, he only needed to sneak back to the confines of the tavern and wait.

"*Sleep well, my love,*" he whispered before slipping out into the night.

He found that the cold did not sting the same as it had before. The wonderful feeling of warmth that emanated from deep in his belly flowed outward through his limbs and all the way up to his head, and he couldn't help but hum.

Once more caught in the midst of his fantasies, he didn't notice that someone was staring down at him from a nearby window. Too late he saw them out of the corner of his eye. He froze, only half concealed behind a barrel, and stared back.

They loomed over the street in the second story window of a large house. A shadowed figure cut against the dull yellow glow of the room beyond. Though their details were shrouded in darkness, Enzo imagined he could feel their cold gaze upon him. All thoughts of Hilde fled his mind as he prayed that he had not been seen — that the primal feeling welling up in his gut was nothing more than his own mounting panic.

The earliest hints of dawn already showed over the houses to the east. Enzo steeled his racing heart and forced himself to think logically. Whoever this was, they were not one of the guards. It was almost certainly just one of the villagers, drawn awake for some unknown reason to stare boredly out into the snow.

He eased further out from behind the barrel, eyeing the alleyway that would take him back to the tavern. "*Go back to bed, stranger,*" he begged.

The onlooker did not obey.

With one final, shallow breath, he darted forward along the edge of the houses. When he reached the alley, he glanced back. The figure remained still. From this angle, the light of the room reflected back into their eyes.

Eyes that glowed yellow.

Enzo's blood ran cold. As if they could see the sudden shock on his face, the figure eased back, disappearing into the room.

The electric charge of adrenaline wiped his mind clean like a slate. He bolted. Abandoning stealth entirely, he sprinted for his life. He rounded a corner and could see the rear of the tavern ahead. It came as no comfort, as behind him came the unmistakable sound of heavy footfalls crashing through the snow in pursuit.

The drainpipe stood bolted to the building's corner. Even in his panic Enzo was not fool enough to circle to the front door and dive into the waiting arms of the guard on duty. He leapt high and grasped his fingers around the frozen metal, yanking himself up higher and higher as his pursuer closed in. As he neared the top, the window above flung open, and a man appeared in it. A strong hand seized his forearm and yanked him away from the drainpipe. He swung free, dangling over open air with only the grip of the outstretched hand holding him. A deep growl resonated from below and he swallowed a scream. With a great yank he was hauled upward and through the window.

Enzo collapsed to the floor. His breath came ragged and he felt dizzy. Blackwood stood over him, McCulloch and Dubois at his flanks. They glared at him with a mixture of concern and anger.

"It almost got me!" Enzo gasped as he rose and shoved his head back out into the night, searching desperately for his pursuer. At first, he saw nothing. Then, down near the bottom of the drainpipe, there was a movement.

A wiry mutt shuffled in a tight circle, sniffing the base of the pipe and wagging its tail.

Enzo fell back, suddenly overcome with the uncontrollable desire to laugh. The madness, the absolute *madness* his mind had conjured now seemed so absurdly stupid. He cast a toothy grin at the others. "*You wouldn't believe it. I thought I saw something so wild, a man with yellow eyes—*"

There was a sharp jolt against his cheek, and stars erupted in his vision. Suddenly he was on the bed, clutching his face. Blackwood stood over him, fist balled and cocked for another strike. Enzo whimpered and cowered behind his hands. Blackwood's fist slowly lowered.

"*I'm sorry,*" Enzo squeaked. "*I'm sorry, I'm sorry!*"

Blackwood grunted and stepped aside, making room for Dubois.

The Frenchman knelt beside him and spoke in Italian. His face was uncharacteristically hard. "*You have much explaining to do, you little fool.*"

27

THE EMBERS of the pyre had been smothered overnight, and the villagers spent the early hours of the morning clearing away the charred debris. Now, all that remained of Fletcher was nothing more than a soggy grey blemish in the freshly fallen snow.

Dubois refused to look at it as he passed through the plaza.

He and Blackwood had arrived at the woodshed that morning to find only Gertrude awaiting them. The plump older woman set Blackwood to his usual job of splitting logs, while Dubois had once again been tasked with delivering kindling — this time to the surrounding houses rather than to the corpse of a dead compatriot.

Gertrude called out to him as he meandered back from his latest delivery. "*The next one goes to the edge of the village, to a house with a cracked step and boarded window. The woman there is old and she will be very grateful.*" Gertrude's eyes took on a mischievous glint. "*If she offers you a pastry, be a dear and bring me back one as well, would you?*"

Dubois smiled kindly in return and hoisted a hefty bundle of sticks over his shoulder. Blackwood worked nearby, slamming the axe down in a steady rhythm. It was beyond Dubois how the American managed to work so tirelessly, especially after a night spent sleeplessly awaiting Enzo's return. While Dubois's eyelids were heavy and his thoughts drifted lazily away from his grasp, the American seamlessly chopped away, building a tower of broken logs around him as if he'd woken up fresh to a coffee and a smoke. It did little to dissuade the stereotype he'd come to see the American as — a rugged ranch hand with a strong jaw and a hard fist, and maybe not too many brains.

Dubois set off down the road that Gertrude had pointed out, trying his best to keep his exhausted mind on task. He was in no rush, and it took him some time to reach the invisible line that delineated the abandoned houses from those still inhabited. He searched among the houses for the one that matched Gertrude's description yet found none. With a groan, he realized that she must have meant the *actual* edge of the village, which stretched out another several hundred meters before him. He set the kindling down and paused to catch his breath.

From the shady alleyway to his ride came a distinct thud. At first he thought his ears were playing tricks on him. Then it came again, the heavy *whop* of a strike tailed by a muffled yelp. He glanced back. Clouds had amassed in the sky, casting the empty street in bleak winter shadows. He suddenly realized that he was alone.

The sound came again. His stomach clenched.

Mustering his courage, he crept toward the corner of the house. In the alley, a woman stood panting between two snow-covered barrels. It was Maria, Dubois realized, one of the women who had been overseeing him and Blackwood. She appeared furious, her cheeks beet red and streaked with tears. She spoke rapidly. He couldn't make out her words, but they dripped with malice. She wound back and delivered a sharp kick into the huddled mass before her. Another yelp came in return.

"*Rotten whore!*" Maria choked out, striking harder. "*What have you done?*"

Dubois stepped into the alley. "*Maria! What are you doing?*"

Maria recoiled in surprise. She scowled at him and wiped her nose on her sleeve before spitting on the figure curled at the base of the wall. "*You will not be forgiven. Ever.*" Maria feigned another kick, drawing a flinch from her cowering victim, then stalked off.

Dubois waited for her to disappear. Once she was gone, he darted forward. The girl looked up at him as he approached — it was Hilde. Enzo's girl. She huddled in the hard packed snow, a purple bruise growing around one eye and a spot of blood under her nose.

"*My dear, are you alright?*" he asked, reaching out to help her. She shrank away.

"*I'm fine,*" she managed between shuddering breaths. "*Just leave me be.*"

"*Please, you need someone to look at that eye—*"

"*I said leave me be!*" she snapped.

He stepped back, caught off guard by her vitriol. She curled against the stone foundation and folded her head into her arms. Dubois was dumbfounded. He never would have imagined Maria, a sweet woman as he knew her, to do such a thing. Whatever had led to this, it must have involved Hilde's night spent with Enzo.

"*My dear,*" he tried to sound soothing. "*It is not ever an easy thing, love I mean. Sometimes when you are young—*"

"You don't know what you're talking about," she mumbled through her arms. *"Please, just leave me be."*

She withdrew further into the folds of her sleeves. Instinctively, he made to place a comforting hand on her shoulder but thought better of it at the last moment and pulled away.

"I'm sorry, sweet girl," he muttered, retreating from the alley to retrieve the kindling.

For all the worldly wisdom gleaned from the hundreds if not thousands of books he'd devoured, he knew that the one enigma that would always baffle him would be women. The poor girl crying alone in the alley made his heart throb as he thought of his own daughters, Madeleine and Colette, two beautiful girls in their teens now. His memories of them filled his languorous mind like a drug — flaxen-haired twins dancing in the meadows outside his estate, giggling and hollering at the birds that flitted through the apple trees and making up silly stories of the grand places they have flown from.

Had his daughters been given cause to weep like Hilde in his absence? Had they been hurt? Has they discovered the horrible pain that this world could bring upon young women? How many times in his absence had they needed the soft words or loving embrace of a father but found none? The bitter pill of regret soured in his stomach, and his eyes grew misty with tears.

Caught in his lamentations, Dubois didn't notice the lone figure trailing him as he trudged further into the derelict outskirts of the village.

"A cracked step," he reminded himself as the houses grew sparse around him. *"A cracked step and a boarded window."*

Out here, the broken buildings brought on the memories of the lands surrounding the Front. Though he'd never partaken in the fighting — or even seen it firsthand outside of his capture — the grimy feel of the war was something that still brought him a great discomfort.

The buildings looked as if they'd been through a war themselves. The stain of soot marred the old stone walls. It was no wonder no one lived out here. A fire had torn through these homes, likely not too long ago based on the odd way the blackened timbers still balanced against each other. He wondered what had saved the rest of the village from the conflagration. A shift in the wind, perhaps, or a lucky bout of rain. If nothing else, the casual imaginings drew him out of his remorse and he managed a smile. *"You're alive, you fool. Be happy. Have hope, and you will see those sweet girls of yours again."*

He plodded forward until the buildings ahead ended, and still he did not see the cracked step.

"*Oh, Gertrude, you must learn to give better directions.*" He groaned.

When he turned back, he stopped cold.

In the center of the snow-covered street stood Johan. The guard's face was crinkled in a nasty sneer. He was just close enough that Dubois could make out the dull yellow hue of his teeth. He sized the Frenchman up. "*What do you think you are doing out here, Frenchman?*"

Dubois's tongue swelled in his mouth. "*Delivering kindling,*" he managed to get out, jiggling the faggot balanced over his shoulder.

"*And who, all the way out here, are you delivering it to?*"

"*An old woman. She… she has a cracked window and a boarded step, as I was told.*"

"*A boarded step?*"

"*No.*" Dubois was flustered. "*I meant a boarded window and a cracked step. I was sent by Gertrude, the woodcutter. You can ask her—*"

"*You are not one to give me permission to do anything, frog.*" Johan growled. Then his teasing disposition returned, and he nodded toward the burnt-out shell of a house nearby. "*Come. Let us have a little chat, ya?*"

Dubois didn't move.

"*Let's go!*" Johan jabbed a thumb toward the shadowy relic.

It was abundantly clear to Dubois that to do so was to die. This was it. His fate would be akin to Fletcher's — his life stolen on the fringe of town, the light in his eyes extinguished by some rabid mongrel of a man. "*My orders are to deliver kindling.*" He tried to sound confident in his delivery, but his voice shook. "*These orders come from Major Wulfson himself, and I will see them through.*"

Johan's lips pulled into a tight grimace. "*You know, of all the races, I've always detested you frogs the most.*"

Dubois had never been a brave man. Since childhood he had been called *soft* and *kind hearted*, an *old soul* with delicate hands and an affection for comfort over glory. He was a man of thought, not a man of deeds. He'd never fired a gun or so much as thrown a punch. He was a coward by the judgement of most, and, especially as of late, that was something he'd come to loathe about himself.

No more. If this was to be it, he would die a man, on his feet. Defiant and brave. Proud, even.

"*I am surprised you detest frogs so.*" Dubois steeled himself. "*As you yourself are a snake.*"

Johan snickered. His rifle hung loose in his hands. "*It seems to me that you are trying to escape. That's why you're out here, isn't it?*"

"*I told you why I am out here, guard. Need I repeat it?*"

This time Johan didn't snicker. He jabbed the rifle toward the derelict building, "*Get in there. Move your ass before I put another hole in it.*"

"*I will not,*" Dubois stated. Johan stepped forward but Dubois did not fall back. He stood tall. "*If you murder me, it will be here, in the open. That is what you have stalked me here for, is it not? Creeping in my wake like a hyena, waiting for the moment to lure me to the shadows and spill my blood? I will not give you the satisfaction. You are a wicked man, Johan. You and all of your lot. And let me tell you, wicked men never prosper. Do you know why it is you are driven by such evil impulses?*"

Johan stopped moving at this point, perhaps a bit stunned by Dubois's brash insolence.

"*It is not the work of God or Satan. No, it is a far sadder thing that guides your hand — envy. You are stupid and loveless. You are the bane of joy and the proliferator of shame. Your heart is a black hole, and in the end I think you will not descend into Dante's burning pit — I think you will be reborn here, only to live your miserable existence again and again until time itself gives in to nothingness. This is your hell, and it brings me joy to watch you writhe in it. And if I am wrong, so be it. You will still die someday, but I hope it is a long time from now. For you are a rotten peach squirming with worms, festering in the sun until some bird comes and plucks the meat from your barren pit. I only pray its beak is dull and its mercy lacking.*"

Johan let him finish, his grimace never melting. "*Are you done? You yap a lot for such a toothless little doggy. This backbone you've suddenly grown, perhaps I'll keep it as a souvenir.*"

When the guard started forward again, Dubois hurled the kindling down into the snow with a loud rattle. He leapt forward, beating a fist against his chest. "*Come on then! Do your filthy deed but know that I will not go without a fight!*"

Johan flinched at the Frenchman's volume. He glanced over his shoulder toward the village. "*Be quiet!*" he hissed.

Dubois saw the fear in his eyes and laughed. "*Are you afraid, son?*" he bellowed. "*You fear a man with no weapon? Does my voice alone frighten you?*"

The guard's rifle angled toward him. "*I said be quiet, swine!*"

Dubois puffed his chest out and shouted with all of his might. "*I am Louis Pierre Dubois! I am a father! I am a proud man of France! I will not be struck down in silence, you coward! Have at me then! Come on! Do your wicked deed and be done with it!"*

Spittle flew from the guards lips. *"Shut your fucking mouth!"*

In the distance beyond Johan, a figure stepped into the street, then another, and another. One began to run back toward the plaza, and a distant shout went up.

"I am the light to be shed upon your wickedness! Go ahead! Shoot me! Let them see you for what you are — a spineless murderer! See what they do to you then!" Dubois screamed even louder, his rage brimming. The words echoed back from the mountains as he jabbed a finger to the group of villagers forming on the street.

Johan, shaking with rage, dared a backwards glance. A tall figure emerged from the crowd, moving toward them in a dead sprint. Dubois could tell even at a distance that it was Wulfson. Johan swore and turned back to the sights of his rifle, keying in on Dubois's face. The safety clicked off.

Dubois knew it was over. He focused on the dark pit of the barrel and screamed again as he waited for the flash. *"Do it then, coward!"*

"Lower your rifle!" Wulfson's voice came hoarse over the wind.

Johan's panic was painted over his face. His rifle went slack for a moment, then he raised it once more with a grimace. *"I'll fucking kill you!"*

Dubois returned his hatred with a disgusted smirk. *"Go ahead,"* he spat. *"It will be the last thing you do."*

28

THE GUARDS stood in formation beyond the edge of the village. A bonfire raged before them, blindingly bright against the night. The air was frigid, and a harsh wind cut through their jackets and whipped the snow at their feet.

Wulfson paced a line in the snow. His regularly well-kept appearance had begun to erode. Dark bags hung under his eyes, and the shadow of a beard spread over his cheeks. His uniform, ever smooth and tidy, now bore creases and spattered stains.

Hanz shivered from his place at the end of the formation. Victor stood beside him, and beyond him stood Dietmar and Klaus. Johan stood away from them at rigid attention. He'd been stripped of his rifle which now hung from the Major's shoulder.

Wulfson came to a halt. His hands were clasped behind his back and his eyes passed from one to the next. "*What were your orders?*"

The guards stood silent. Hanz didn't know whether to respond or not, as such a question posed to a formation was traditionally rhetorical. This time, however, it was clear that Wulfson was waiting for a response.

Klaus finally spoke up. "*To ensure that none of the prisoners escape, by any means necessary—*"

"*No!*" Wulfson snapped, a rare moment of rage leaking through. He fumed at them. "*I have made it abundantly clear by this point that you are not to harm the prisoners. Yet here we are, with one dead and another chased down for slaughter by one of your men.*" He stabbed a finger at Johan. "*Was this man acting under your orders, Unteroffizier?*"

Klaus cleared his throat. He was oddly composed — void of the impotent fury he had come to regularly exhibit under such circumstances. "*Any orders I have given have only mirrored your own, Major.*"

"*You did not order him to kill the Frenchman?*"

"*No.*"

"*You did not order him to kill the Englishman?*"

Klaus appeared caught off guard. Hanz himself thought he had misheard. He glanced out the corner of his eye to Johan, who looked similarly perplexed.

"*Major,*" Klaus said. "*You told us the Englishman was killed by a bear.*"

"*He was killed by a knife. A knife driven through his throat. Then he was mutilated and tossed to the scavengers. Do you know why I did not tell you this?*" Wulfson looked disgustedly at Johan. "*Because I knew whoever did it would strike again if given the freedom to do so.*"

Johan balked. "*No… No, Major, I did not—*"

"*Silence,*" Wulfson barked.

Johan turned desperately to Klaus, who kept his steely gaze locked on the Major.

"*Did you order this man to kill the Englishman?*" Wulfson demanded once more.

"*No, Major.*"

Wulfson sucked his teeth and resumed his pacing. When he spoke next, it was to all of them. "*I suspect you are all at least somewhat aware of my past. Of where I have fought? The White War, they call it now. To us, it was simply hell. Do you know what happened to men who disobeyed orders in those unholy mountains?*"

Each man shook his head no. Hanz had heard enough of the harrowing stories of bloodshed in that frozen hellscape to fill a book. He had lain awake late at night poring over the newspaper articles and fantasizing about fighting the Italians on those daring slopes. He'd dreamed of enduring the harshness of alpine combat and proving his mettle against the infamous Arditi. Not now, though. After experiencing such proximity to a cold death in these ice-capped mountains, he could think of no place he'd less rather be.

"*Corporal punishment is a standard of our military. It is our only thin line of defense against devolving into a mass of scrambling savages. On the Front, men are whipped. Men are dragged behind carts until their legs give out. Men are even shot for their disobedience,*" Wulfson went on. "*But what do you do to a man whose skin is too frozen to feel the lash? How do you drag a man when you have no horse or cart? How do you justify shooting a man when there isn't a single bullet to spare?*"

Wulfson stepped back and pointed to the darkness beyond the bonfire. Hanz couldn't make out what he was motioning to at first. As his eyes adjusted, he saw the vague outline of a tall post standing in the shadows beyond.

Wulfson pulled his cigarette case from his pocket and plucked one of the few left. He turned his back to the formation. When he spoke, his voice was cold. "*Take his coat. Bind him to the post.*"

As one, the guards looked down the line to Klaus. Hanz felt a burst of adrenaline. Was this it? Was this the final straw?

Klaus didn't return their gaze. He turned his head and looked past them, toward the rows of houses that stood less than a hundred yards away. When he turned coolly to the guards, he nodded. "*You heard him. Do it. Now.*"

Johan staggered back, babbling in protest as they closed around him. He tried to run, but Victor grasped the nape of his coat and yanked him back. Together they wrestled him down and tore the garment free.

Johan cursed and howled. "*Stop, dammit! Stop! I didn't do it! I swear I never touched that bastard! Major, please! It wasn't me! Klaus! Klaus!*"

It struck Hanz that, in his desperation, Johan might turn on them, might betray the others' mutinous gripings. Victor must have shared a similar concern, as his hand clamped tight over Johan's mouth, muffling his cries into little more than weak yelps.

The post was eight feet of rough-barked cedar. Hanz held the ropes tight as Dietmar tied thick knots. In time, Johan abandoned his protests, submitting to whimpering against the inside of Victor's hand. When Victor finally let go, Johan was left gasping for air.

"*Will we leave him to die?*" Klaus asked evenly.

"*His judgement is up to God now. If the wind maintains its direction, the heat of the fire will keep him alive. If it shifts, he will freeze by dawn.*" Wulfson took a long drag from his cigarette and stood before the bound man. "*Tell me the truth now, Private: did you kill the Englishman?*"

Johan sank against his bonds in defeat. He shook his head no.

"*We shall see. If you make it to morning, you are absolved. Then you may rejoin us — with a renewed sense of discipline, one would hope.*" Wulfson flicked the half-burnt cigarette into the snow. He made to walk back toward the village but stopped and called back over his shoulder. "*The rest of you are dismissed. Should any man interfere with his punishment, he will find himself enduring a similar fate.*"

The guards remained in place even after Wulfson had disappeared back to the village.

Johan coughed as a plume of smoke blew into his face. "*Unteroffizier, please...*" he begged quietly. "*Don't let him do this. You need me — don't let him whittle us down any further.*"

"*Quiet,*" Klaus muttered. His gaze was once again locked on the houses, gliding over the dully lit windows. Hanz squinted to see better. Dozens of silhouettes hunched behind the sills, watching them. He suddenly understood — an insurrection would not have been five against one, but many against five. He wished desperately in that moment that he could switch sides, but he knew the villagers wouldn't have him.

Victor grunted dumbly. "*What do we do now?*"

Klaus fished the Major's half-burnt cigarette from the snow and re-lit it. His calm façade had taken on a sinister glint. "*The Major has shown his hand. Get your rest, boys. Tomorrow you will need it.*" Then, as an afterthought, "*Johan, try not to die.*"

29

IT WAS late, and the tavern was quiet other than the scratching of Sovilo's broom against the hardwood floor. Klaus sat with his back to the albino, silently strumming the table.

It was just the two of them in the dining room. The other guards had taken to their cramped quarters hours before. Now Victor's thunderous snores emanated from beneath the door. Wulfson had likewise disappeared into his room, and the prisoners remained silent and accounted for upstairs.

All Klaus had to do now was wait.

His plan was simple, as all good plans were. He'd been formulating it since their arrival. While he hadn't intended on executing it so soon, the Major now forced his hand. If he did nothing, then by morning he was likely to be down one more underling, as the odds of Johan's survival dropped by the minute. Klaus couldn't have that. He needed the numbers.

Once Sovilo had departed for the night, Klaus would kill Wulfson first. He figured that a bayonet through the heart would be an ideal manner since, for his plan to work, the ruckus of gunplay needed to be avoided at all costs. After the Major had bled out, Klaus would move upstairs. The prisoners each had their own rooms now, and he was confident that he could dispatch them in much the same manner as the Major — one by one, silently, without waking the others. He was considering bringing Dietmar in at this stage. The other two, an oaf and a mincing coward, would likely cause more harm than good. Dietmar alone seemed to be dependable and good enough with a knife. Klaus put a pin in the thought. An extra blade would be handy, but he longed for the satisfaction of looking each of the prisoners in the eyes as he delivered the killing blow himself.

Once the prisoners were all dead, he would send one of his men to free Johan. As dawn neared, he would dispatch his four underlings to the tallest of the nearby houses to slaughter its inhabitants and take up position in high windows. There they would patiently await his signal. Come first light, he would ring the tavern's bell and call for a gathering in Wulfson's name. This would doubtlessly lure the bulk of the villagers in — at least the ones who mattered. When the women flooded the dining area, he, hidden atop the stairwell, would utilize his secret weapon: the battered grenade tucked in his belt. He'd been itching to use it since he first confiscated it from an incoming German soldier at Rothenspring. Long nights had been spent picturing the carnage of tossing it amidst a teaming formation of prisoners. He liked to think of their piggish screams as they crawled from the crater, searching the mud for their limbs. Though he had always imagined the killing of women to be beneath him, he still felt giddy at the prospect of finally seeing the devastating results of his toy.

In the chaos of the aftermath, the guards would mop up whatever threats remained from the high ground. It didn't matter if some of the villagers managed to survive. They would make good servants until spring arrived. They were women, after all. Hardly a threat to men like them. He had no doubt of the lengths they would go to in order to secure their survival, and he planned to take full advantage. Of course, he wouldn't enlighten them as to the final step of his plan — a curt round of executions once the roads had thawed, followed by a series of fires that would wipe this place from the map. He would return to Rothenspring a hero. The Unteroffizier who saved his soldiers' lives by leading them through the horrendous prisoner mutiny that had ended Major Wulfson's life and decimated some insignificant village in the mountains.

It was a solid plan. Brutal and with enough wiggle room to account for small errors. He hadn't enlightened his men to it yet, nor would he. Not until the Major was dead and it was too late to turn back. His mind was made up, and it wasn't worth the spent breath.

A door behind him opened and footsteps tromped out. He glanced back to see Wulfson heading his way. Klaus felt the tingle of anticipation. He had hoped that their brief, one-sided conversations had come to an end. As Wulfson took the seat across from him, he knew his hopes had been in vain.

"*You don't approve of my methods.*" Wulfson's words came as a statement rather than a question.

Klaus swallowed his pride, promising himself it would be the last time he'd have to do so. "*It is not my role to question your orders, Major.*"

"*Yet you do. Often. Why not this time?*"

The question made Klaus uneasy. Did Wulfson suspect what was to come? He was not a stupid man, and the sudden change in Klaus's disposition had clearly been noticed. He shifted uncomfortably in his seat, unsure of how to deflect. "*If I've offended you in the past, Major, it was not my intention.*"

Sovilo's broom went silent. "*Gentlemen, it is time I retire for the evening. Is there anything I can get for you before I go?*"

"*Beer,*" Wulfson said, stabbing two fingers in the air.

Klaus listened to the albino fill two steins. He set them on the table, and Wulfson thanked him, then he was gone through the back door without another word.

"*For the Empire,*" Wulfson toasted.

"*For the Empire,*" Klaus echoed. He took a long drink. The beer had a bitter aftertaste that made him smack his lips.

"*Do you believe that Johan killed the Englishman?*"

Klaus shrugged. He highly doubted it, though the truth was that he hadn't given it much thought. A dead prisoner was a drop in the bucket for him. As far as he was concerned, it could have been a bear or a wolf or Johan or any of the others. It did not matter. "*I don't know,*" he said.

"*I'm not asking for facts. I'm asking what you think.*"

Klaus considered his options. Wulfson had never asked candidly for his opinion. "*You want to know what I think, Major? I think this place is wicked and backwards, and that we are all trapped here, for better or worse. I can account for my men. They follow my orders. Orders I receive from you. If they have disobeyed those orders, I believe I would know. On the night in question no man left my sight for long enough to slaughter the English swine.*"

"*What about while you slept?*"

"*I am a light sleeper.*"

The answer seemed to satisfy Wulfson. He took another drink. "*Unteroffizier, how many prisoners did you yourself kill at Rothenspring?*"

The hair raised on the back of Klaus's neck. While Wulfson's expression remained casual, Klaus swore that a minuscule shred of malice had seeped into his voice. "*I do not know.*"

"*If you had to guess.*"

Klaus let his next words slip out without thinking. "*Not enough.*"

A stillness settled over them. Victor's muffled snores droned alongside the snapping of logs in the fire. Wulfson was the first to break the silence. "*Do you understand the purpose of our mission?*"

Klaus suppressed a groan. He desired nothing less in the world than another lecture. "*Of course, Major.*"

"*And it is?*"

"*To shuttle these worthless swine to Switzerland.*"

"*That is the mission. But do you understand the purpose of it?*"

Klaus shrugged. "*I don't know.*"

"*Exactly. You don't know. You don't know because you don't need to know. This is a war of machines. Great, hulking machines that eat nations and spit out hundreds of thousands of corpses. You are a tiny cog in this machine, as am I. Our place is not to question why we must turn. It is only to turn. You must learn to put the whole above yourself.*" Wulfson finished his beer. He stood quickly, waving Klaus to follow him as he made for the door. "*Finish your beer. There is something I must show you.*"

A cold blast of air flowed into the room as Wulfson departed. Klaus watched him go. With a frustrated sigh, he downed the rest of the fizzing stein.

Wulfson hadn't waited for him. A thick screen of clouds masked the moon, and the Major was barely visible in the night. Klaus cursed and jogged to keep up. After only a few bouncing steps, his stomach began to sour. He ignored it, but in another few steps, a sharp pain sent him doubling over, clenching his gut. He gagged, then retched and vomited beer tinged with blood. He fell gasping to his knees. The next thing he knew, he was on his side and the world around him had begun to spin. The icy cobblestones stung his cheek as he struggled to stand. The effort was in vain. His legs were useless.

"*Help...*" he tried, but only a desperate croak escaped. The tavern door stood ajar a mere fifty feet away. For him it might as well have been a mile. He grasped feebly for the rifle slung over his shoulder. No sooner had his fingers found the strap than it was ripped away from above.

A shadow appeared over him. It shifted, blocking the light of the tavern.

"*You fucking bastard...*" Klaus drawled past a mouthful of saliva.

Wulfson crouched to look him in the eyes. Though Klaus could barely make out his details, he could sense the smug satisfaction radiating from the Major's face. Wulfson stripped away Klaus's bandoleer and belt and patted him down. His hands paused on the lump concealed in Klaus's waistband. With a look of bewilderment, the Major withdrew the grenade. "*What the hell were you going to do with this?*"

From beyond Wulfson, another shadow approached.

"*Take him to the cells,*" Wulfson said, tucking the grenade away in his own belt. "*We might need him later.*"

"*We should kill him now and be done with it,*" Sovilo came back coldly.

Wulfson jabbed a finger under Klaus's chin, checking his pulse. Klaus made to bite it, but he found that his jaw was no longer under his control.

Wulfson shook his head. "*No. If Mithras wanted him dead, he would be dead.*"

Klaus managed only a weak moan as Sovilo yanked him up by his arms. The world spun violently and he thought that he might vomit again. No heaving came, as his diaphragm was just as paralyzed as the rest of his body. Only drool spilled from his lips as the tavernkeeper wrapped him under the arms and dragged him across the plaza.

The world sputtered in and out as the blurred light of the tavern faded. Klaus teetered on the edge of consciousness. Everything around him melded into a sick dream. They were no longer on ice, but on smooth stone. He could feel it dragging beneath his fingertips as the grey light of the moon disappeared. Then there were sharp edges under him — steps, three of them, stabbing into his back as the old man dragged him mercilessly up them.

A door creaked open, ushering with it an unworldly sound. Someone was wailing. Horrible, sickening cries rebounded all around him as if he was trapped in a glass bottle. Flickering light shone fuzzy in his vision as Sovilo set him down.

"*What are you doing?*" a woman's voice demanded over dreadful screeching.

"*Bringing him to the cells.*"

"*Now?*" she objected.

"*Yes,*" Sovilo came back sternly. "*Come on, help me.*"

Another set of hands were on him. He was moving faster now. His thoughts were gone, rotted away with the raging pain in his gut. One of his tormentors shifted, causing his head to flop to the side. For only a moment he caught the scene before him as he passed.

Kneeling in the dancing glow of flames was a woman. She howled in agony as she cradled the lifeless body of a young boy. His skin was sallow and his body limp. A thin line of blood ran from the corner of his mouth and dripped into a pool on the stone floor.

Others surrounded her in a wide arc, looking down with demonic faces. Wooden faces.

Devils, Klaus thought as they disappeared from view. The word hung in his mind as the light faded away alongside his consciousness.

PART FOUR

A transcribed excerpt from motivational speaker Ken Watson's speech, "Finding Your Inner Killer: Unlock the Key to Weaponizing Your True Potential in the Boardroom"

"Here we arrive at Tucholsky's famous, or perhaps infamous, quote: 'Soldiers are murderers.' Now, I would be comfortable going so far as to say that these three words are the most succinct defining thesis for the modern pacifist movement. If taken at face value, their meaning is rather simple: the acts of violence committed in war — or really any other such 'condoned' arenas — are inseparable from criminal violence.

So is this true?

From a philosophical standpoint, the answer is as moot as the question itself — who knows? Who even gives a shit? Philosophy has few — if any —real world applications. And this is a question that needs *real* answers. I mean, how else are we supposed to define war crimes? Where is the line between right and wrong? Don't we need some sort of definitive terms by which we can judge whether violence is to be condoned?

While I don't have a rock-solid rubric for you, I can tell you one thing — Tucholsky was full of shit.

I get what some of you are thinking — I can see it in your faces. After all, killing *is* wrong. At least, that's something that most who adhere to the current zeitgeist can agree upon. The act of taking another human's life has been admonished in some way or another in nearly every widely practiced religion, every society, every government — every organization really. Yet despite this commonplace detestation of the act of killing, we as a species have time and time again allowed a special class within our society the proverbial 'license to kill.' I, of course, am talking about the warrior. The soldier, the law enforcer, the Praetorian Guard or the Green Beret. We didn't blink an eye when they gunned down Saddam's guys in '91. Hell, I watched it on the news at a bar and folks were cheering them on!

So the question becomes: why the hell do we allow this? Why do we permit some 'special' group of men to run around slaughtering folks just because someone high above us on the social food chain — someone who we've never even met in most cases — has designated them as an 'enemy'? Meanwhile the rest of us sit back and whinge at the very thought of stabbing someone who's wronged us. What is this miraculous social constraint that allows us to say, 'He's allowed to do it, but if I do, it's evil'?

Is it because some great authority, be it governmental or spiritual, grants these men the right to do so? Or is it because in those instances where we condone it, their acts of killing directly benefit us — so we silently applaud their own supposed damnation while reaping the rewards of their bloody labor?

I have to be honest with you all. I don't think it's any of that. I have a far simpler answer to this grand conundrum: we don't have a fucking choice.

I would argue that while most men are capable of violence, some small percentage of us are inherently drawn to it. Excel at it, even, as if it were a cardinal drive such as food or sex. This is not to say that those men are monsters. Just that they have a little extra spark in their DNA that drives them to violence. Some of you out there are balking, but you know what I'm talking about. Whether it's the valiant soldier returning from overseas or the creepy serial killer whose mugshot you see in the paper, some men just have that extra gene in their system that sets them apart from the average. And those men are out there, walking around amongst us — more of them than you might think.

I believe the reason war still exists in the first world is the same reason a hobo might feed a stray pit bull — give it a bone to gnaw at, lest you become the bone yourself.

Now, getting back to Tucholsky, you might ask what about that other group? Not the soldiers or cops — not those who we give permission to be violent to — but the killers we don't like? The spree shooters and serial killers and maybe that same hobo hopped up on PCP and wielding a hammer outside the local grocery store? What about them? Aren't you, like Tucholsky, implying that they're essentially the same as our beloved soldiers? How could you?

Well, there is a line between the two. And this line is a bit simpler than you may imagine because it's not some innate morality that we all share. The Nazis cheered on the SS. Genghis Kahn's subjects adored him. Assyrian peasants bathed in the barrels of blood that their soldiers brought back from their conquests. All of those men who committed all of those atrocities were not only right in their own eyes, but in the eyes of their gods, their wives, and their societies at large. They were cheered on the same way I myself cheered on the Marines rolling into Iraq. Which brings me to my point.

The only difference between a just killer and a murderer has nothing to do with god or country or some legal definition. It is based solely on how much *you*, as an individual, like them.

Nothing more.

Nothing less.

Now, if we take this same mentality and apply it to the boardroom, you will find that optics are the only significant factor in…"

WYOMING, 1910

Dead leaves scuttled in the breeze over a back country road. At the end of the lane, nestled between two stout maples and an old barn, a humble country house stood as a blip of light against the night. A body draped over the railing of the porch; its blood was still warm and dribbled down over the neat row of hostas below.

From inside the house came a muffled cry of desperation. Gruff laughter drowned it out.

Blackwood dismounted his horse and strung her reigns to a fence post. He checked his weapon before making for the door.

"Password," a low voice demanded from the darkness.

"Shut up, Larry," Blackwood grunted in return.

Larry shuffled back into the shadows. He was a great lout of a man. Nearly as tall as he was round, he'd worked a couple jobs with Blackwood back in the day. He was dumb and brutish but not mean. Something like this was out of character for him.

Blackwood pushed through the door. A heavy trail of blood streaked the freshly milled floor. He followed it to where a woman and a girl sat back-to-back, bound together by thick rope. Dirty rags hung from their mouths, and they wept in silent prayer.

In the corner a young man lay still against the wall. His chin drooped, and one hand clutched a wound in his belly. Blood pooled around him.

"Look who it is!" one of the two men standing by the fireplace chirped. He was tall and gangly, just like his brother beside him.

"What the fuck is all this?" Blackwood looked to the women. They stared back in horror.

"Needed fresh horses for the job. Saw these folks had a few extra round back. Figured we might help ourselves to some dinner while we was about." The second brother chortled. They were Harold and Josiah McCallister, new hires brought in on the recommendation from a dirty Pinkerton out of Billings. Blackwood would have words with the Pinkerton when this was over. Perhaps more than words.

"This isn't how we do things. I made that clear when you came on with me. We hit institutions, not people. This is cold-blooded murder."

"How'd you even find us?" Harold eyed him suspiciously. "We ain't even supposed to meet up 'til tomorrow."

Any air of respect the men had shown in the presence of the crew was gone. They stood before Blackwood with hunched shoulders and dogged faces, two sets of rot-gapped teeth glistening in the lamplight.

Blackwood's gaze drifted from one to the other. "Maybe I could smell your foul stench from the road."

The brothers' expressions soured. "That ain't polite. Thought you was polite, bossman. I think you best get to steppin'. We'll meet up with you in Glenrock tomorrow, like we said we was. That is, *if* we still feel like taking the job."

The girl whimpered, drawing a sneer from Josiah. "So long as we don't get caught up having too much fun here, that is."

"No. You're going to walk outside with me right now," Blackwood told them evenly. "And we're going to leave these people be."

"Who you think you are, bossman? You think just cause you sent for us that you can—"

Harold never got to finish his sentence, as the top half of his head splattered against the chimney behind him. His brother, whose hand had already been resting on the handle of his pistol, barely managed to pull it free from its holster before the second barrel of the sawn off concealed beneath Blackwood's coat erupted in a plume of flame and thunder. Josiah toppled, flecks of his heart and lungs staining the same bricks as his brother's brain.

Larry's heavy footsteps thudded over the porch. The door banged open. Blackwood's pistol was already leveled when the lout stepped inside. Larry came to a staggering halt, his gun still held at his waist as he took in the sight of the two dead brothers.

"Wha… what happened?" he got out.

"You chose to come here with them, yeah?"

"Yeah." Larry looked confused.

The pistol barked, and the enormous man fell dead.

The woman and her daughter cried out. Their eyes were wide and glistened with tears as they watched Blackwood check the wounded boy in the corner. He was dead.

Blackwood cut their bonds in silence. There were things to say, be it words of condolence or comfort or even an apology. But Blackwood didn't say any of them. Not because he wouldn't mean it. But because he knew his words were worthless.

30

HANZ WAS the first to wake. Sunlight spilled through the threadbare curtains and the peaceful sounds of slumber filled the room.

Something was off.

They had never been permitted to sleep in past sunrise. Klaus was a notoriously early riser, always eager to get them formed up before the break of dawn. Hanz looked to the Unteroffizier's bed. It was empty.

Did he do it? Hanz felt a sudden pang of nervous energy. Had the foul tempered goat finally had enough of the Major and put the whole issue to rest, once and for all?

The previous evening Klaus had stood the first night watch that Hanz had ever seen him stand. Hanz tried to stay awake in the darkness, debating on whether to intervene should the seemingly inevitable sounds of violence come. At some point he decided that he would — should the fight begin, he would not hesitate to charge headfirst into the fray. But not on the side of his companions. No. It was Wulfson who had earned his loyalty. He would rather die beside the Major and this horde of villagers than live alongside these wretched men. But the violence had never come, and his eyelids had grown heavy in the darkness.

Could Wulfson really be dead?

Hanz was melancholic at the thought. He had missed whatever happened in the dead of night — slept through it like a little boy too tired to wait up for Father Christmas. Klaus had doubtlessly killed the Major, and now he was likely sitting outside the door, feet kicked up on a table as he enjoyed a beer clasped in bloodstained hands.

Or perhaps they were both dead, two corpses knotted together in some horrible embrace.

Or Wulfson could have even struck first.

The more Hanz thought on it, the less Klaus's absence made any sense. Maybe instead of Klaus, it was Wulfson out there, feet up, sipping a coffee with his pistol at the ready.

Whatever it was they would find on the other side of that door, Hanz felt in his gut that it wouldn't be pretty. He sat up and checked his rifle.

Dietmar woke to the click of the rifle's bolt as it slid into place. He sat up quickly, eyes darting around the room before settling on the light leaking through the window.

"*Where is Klaus?*" he asked quietly, jabbing Victor awake.

"*I don't know. I just woke up,*" Hanz whispered.

Dietmar cursed and looked at Johan's rack. It was empty as well. "*And no Johan either. I suppose he's dead by now.*"

In his waking daze, Hanz had somehow forgotten about the man they had lashed to a post on the outskirts of the village the night before. He recalled the whisper of the frigid wind against the walls overnight, and he silently concurred with Dietmar. Johan was surely dead. Now, they were only four. And that was *if* Klaus was still alive.

From the back of his head, a voice spoke up: *Good. Good riddance to the lot of us.*

They dressed quickly. Each man checked his rifle as if preparing to step off for the trenches. They donned their bandoleers loaded with ammunition and belts that hung with their long, saw-backed bayonets. Even Dietmar, ever the stoic, seemed on edge. "*We need to be ready for anything. If Klaus has—*"

The muffled smack of the tavern's front door interrupted him. Footsteps thudded in the dining room, two pairs. One set steady and the other staggering and unsure.

"*Johan...*" Dietmar smirked. He slung his rifle and pushed through the door. "*Unteroffizier, we—*"

Dietmar's words cut off. Hanz nearly bumped into him as he followed. The dining area was exceptionally hot. He saw Johan collapse to his knees before the raging hearth. Ice and snow still caked the man's hair, and his coat was stained with what had already melted. He shivered so violently that he looked as if he was having a seizure. His rifle lay on the floor beside him, but his fingers, waxy and purple, looked too far gone to even grasp it.

Beyond him sat Wulfson. His face drooped, and his mouth sagged slightly agape. It was clear he had not slept. He didn't look up at them. His eyes remained fixed on the rifle laying on the table before him. Hanz recognized the deep brown stains of old blood that marred the wooden stock. It was Klaus's.

"*Sit.*" Wulfson's tone was curt. He fished through his coat until he found a silver flask.

One by one the guards cautiously complied, taking to the chairs on the opposite end of the table.

Wulfson coughed after a long pull from the flask. "*Klaus will not be joining us. The villagers have taken him into their custody. He now awaits judgement for his crimes.*"

An electric jolt passed through the three of them. Victor's jaw dropped while Dietmar's brow dove into a deep V. Hanz, on the other hand, had to mask the sheer relief he felt flowing from within.

"*The bastard may very well have killed us all,*" Wulfson went on, vision still locked on the rifle. "*He's committed a murder. Two of them now, actually. It's become clear that he was not eager to stay the winter here. Last night as we slept, he broke into the stables in an attempt to steal a horse. When the young boy minding the animals tried to intervene, Klaus throttled the life out of him. He was apprehended before he could escape. From what they've told me, he's admitted to killing the Englishman as well. As of this moment, I fear these people are on the verge of revoking their hospitality. If they do, we will have no choice but to brave the mountains. If this happens, have no doubt, we will all surely die.*"

A strained silence fell over the room. Hanz couldn't believe what he was hearing. He had expected the grizzled Unteroffizier to launch a violent coup, not sneak away like a coward in the night, leaving his men to face the village's wrath on their own. Then again, had Klaus ever displayed any true sign of grit? Despite his surly ruthlessness, he had never exhibited the virtues of a fighter, never gone toe-to-toe with a peer. His time at Rothenspring had been spent punching down rather than straight. Killing unarmed men did not warrant courage. Killing Wulfson would have.

Johan's quaking moan startled them all. All except Wulfson. It was clear that the frozen man lacked the faculties to understand that he was not alone in the room. He edged closer to the flames, his body still quaking in violent tremors. His face was burnt red from the wind and underneath the wet mop of his hair, his pupils were empty pits. Though his body had survived, Hanz wondered if his mind had not.

Wulfson cleared his throat, drawing their attention back to him. He held out a clenched fist. When he opened it, two thin strands of lace dangled between his fingers. They were the insignia of an Unteroffizier. From the frayed threads that hung from their borders, they had clearly been cut from Klaus's collar.

"*It is standard for enlisted men to be led by one of their own.*" Wulfson looked from one to the next. When he landed on Hanz, he tossed the ribbons across the table. "*Congratulations, Unteroffizier Hanz. I pray you fare better than your predecessor.*"

Hanz's face flushed. His fingers drifted across the rough wood of the table until they closed around the soft lace. He didn't understand. Was this real? Was this some strange game? Of the three of them, he was the whelp. The whipping boy. The last in the short line of succession when it came to authority. "*I…*" he stammered, then the shock subsided and he realized where he was. He stood quickly and snapped a rigid salute. "*Thank you, Major. I will not disappoint you.*"

Wulfson waved him at ease. "*I expect not.*"

Dietmar glowered from across the table. Once Hanz had settled back into his seat, he spoke up. "*Major. May I ask a question?*"

"*You may.*"

"*What will happened to Klaus?*"

"*I imagine that we will not be seeing him again.*"

Dietmar's nostrils flared. "*Then you would let these people have him? One of our men? A German soldier surrendered so easily for a crime none of us witnessed? A crime only evidenced by the claims of some savage whores?*"

Wulfson returned the contemptuous tone twofold. "*That man is no soldier, Private Dietmar. Soldiers don't murder little boys in the act of desertion. Such men are beneath the mongrels that feed on war carrion. They are animals worthy of nothing more than a bullet. I will not stand in the way of justice — that boy was the only male left in their village. Their last shred of hope, as many of them saw it. They will do with Klaus as they please and neither you nor I nor anyone here will stand in their way. Know that even if they were to give him back, I would drag him out to the forest myself and shoot him between the eyes like the rabid cur he is.*"

Dietmar withdrew into his seat without another word. The back door eased open, and Sovilo crossed the dining area. He delivered a steaming mug of coffee to Wulfson alongside quiet words. Dietmar offered a scathing glance across the table to Hanz, which the new NCO now felt empowered to return.

Sovilo departed, and Wulfson stood. "*Unteroffizier Hanz.*"

Hanz leapt once more to his feet. "*Yes, Major?*"

"*These people require a replenishment of lumber, as we have added yet another funeral pyre to their burden. As it has become apparent that I cannot trust your men to oversee such a working party, I will accompany the prisoners myself. It goes without saying, but I will say it anyway: you and your men are not to leave the tavern in my absence. Our very lives lay in the hands of those who now despise us. I will not allow any more nails to be driven into our communal coffin. Is this understood?*"

"*Yes, Major. Understood.*"

Sovilo spoke up quietly from behind the bar. "*Major Wulfson. I forgot to mention: Albert*—" He looked loathsomely at the guards. "—*the boy that your soldier murdered, he would deliver water for me around town every tenday. The ill and elderly have come to rely on this service. I would ask that you leave one worker here to assist me in this. One of our* upstairs *guests, I would hope.*"

"*Of course. I will give you the Scotsman. He is old but a good worker. Besides, I will need young muscles to cut trees.*" Wulfson turned to Hanz. "*Go, rouse the prisoners. There is work to be done.*"

31

"UP THE ridge here, just a bit farther," Wulfson called over his shoulder. He led a stout plow horse by the reigns. Behind it an empty lumber sled crushed a trail in the knee-high snow.

It was still early in the day, but Blackwood was dead beat. What little sleep he'd achieved the night before had been plagued by more sickening nightmares. Deep down, he worried that he might be going mad. The images that had haunted him in the dark remained with him into waking hours. A dreadful cawing, dark spaces and muddled faces and a horrible, morose cry. As before, above it all, that dreadful figure loomed — teeth glinting and skin writhing like a thousand black bees.

He shook the thoughts away, plodding onward toward a tall copse of pines amid a spattering of frozen stumps. Dubois and Enzo followed at his flanks.

Klaus's rifle hung from Wulfson's shoulder — a fact that had not escaped Blackwood's attention. Along with Klaus's absence at breakfast, Blackwood had heard Wulfson refer to Hanz by his new rank. This was just the latest in the bizarre string of events of the last twenty-four hours. The night before, Dubois had told them in hushed tones the story of his brush with Johan, and they had watched as the guards marched away into the darkness only to return missing one among their ranks. Now, having seen Johan half-frozen and crumpled next to the fire — alongside Klaus's mysterious absence — Blackwood knew that the prisoners had missed some significant event. While he hoped that whatever change had occurred was for the best, the ripe hatred that had been festering on the guards' faces that morning had left him more uneasy than ever.

The village had appeared miniature in the distance as they crested the hills leading to the forest. The dark stone of the cliff face had loomed over the quaint hamlet, masking the buildings in a cloud of shadows against the morning sun. Blackwood worried about McCulloch, about what the guards might do to him without Wulfson there to slap them back into place — or what antics the Scotsman might pull in the absence of his more level-headed companions. It may have been a foolish decision, but as they'd departed, Blackwood made a point to discreetly whisper the location of his hidden dagger into the Scotsman's ear. The way McCulloch's eyes had lit up made Blackwood immediately regret this decision. Still, Blackwood would rather see his ally armed than served up empty-handed to the enemy.

Hell, if everything went to shit, maybe the Scot *did* stand a chance. If Klaus *was* gone, and there really were only four guards now — perhaps only three considering the enfeebled state Johan was in — then McCulloch's odds were only getting better.

Wulfson untied the fasteners of a fat canvas bundle that was strapped atop the lumber sled. It thumped open, revealing long saws and felling axes. He re-slung his rifle crosswise, a bold move considering it would make it significantly harder to bring to arms, then took an axe in hand. "Come," he told them in English. "Each of you, take an axe."

The prisoners complied warily. Wulfson didn't shy away, remaining well within striking distance as he lit a cigarette and absently surveyed the trees. "Do any of you have experience in the felling of trees?"

Blackwood nodded. Beside him, Dubois translated for Enzo, who responded in Italian.

"The boy does not," Dubois said, then, ashamedly, "I must admit that I do not either."

"Blackwood, show them." Wulfson pointed out two sturdy pines on the edge of the copse. "Take those two first. We will collect a half dozen today. The harder we work, the faster we return."

They set to work, Wulfson moving to higher ground on the slope to work on his own while Dubois and Enzo shadowed Blackwood as he stripped the lower branches from his tree and set the initial cuts. He explained the basic principles of a wedge cut to Dubois, who mirrored his words in Italian. After hacking a V in the wood, Blackwood had Dubois take over. Dubois's weak axe strokes fell well short of expectation, leading to the decision that the small Frenchman would be better suited for trimming the branches of the nearby trees. Enzo stepped forward next. Unlike Dubois, he attacked the tree with the fire of youth. In no time he was panting like a dog.

Blackwood chuckled as he called out to Dubois. "Tell him to let the axe do the work."

Dubois did, but Enzo still seemed confused.

"Like this." Blackwood threw a sweeping chop, focusing the arc on the weight of the axe head. Fresh wood chips exploded from the gash in the tree.

Enzo nodded along eagerly. "*Si, si.*"

When Blackwood glanced up the slope, he swore he caught the hint of a smile cross Wulfson's face.

Soon they switched to the backside of the trunk, and the tree began to groan. A few solid chops later, it cracked and leaned, then finally toppled into the snow with a thunderous boom. The other two set to work stripping away the remainder of the branches while Blackwood meandered up the slope to Wulfson, who still labored away on his own.

"You want me to take over?" Blackwood asked as he approached.

Wulfson glanced up. His brow glistened with sweat, and his face was craggy and exhausted — he looked as if he hadn't slept in days. "*Ya,*" he said, shouldering his axe and stepping back. "I suppose I could use a break."

Blackwood hacked at the tree while Wulfson sat nearby atop a frozen stump. Wulfson's demeanor was uncommonly relaxed. Almost human. Maybe it was the weariness of the journey as a whole, or even the stress of keeping the peace amongst the varying factions he now found himself embroiled with, but the shell of the Major's cool façade had begun to crack. Blackwood was tempted to push his luck and ask candidly about what had happened to Klaus. He thought better of it as Wulfson rose and waved him off, taking his place at the tree once more.

Rather than sit, Blackwood moved on to the next tree down.

"You should rest as well," Wulfson told him.

"I'm alright," Blackwood said between strokes.

Wulfson considered him. "You look at home with this type of work. Is this what you did before the war? A lumberman?"

"No."

"What was it then?"

"A little of this, a little of that."

Wulfson didn't push further.

The group worked in this way for an hour. Two more trees fell and were stripped to long logs. When Enzo and Dubois fatigued, Wulfson rallied them all for a break. They sat upon one of the logs, and the Major handed out bread and salt pork.

"Thank you, Major," Dubois said as Wulfson took a seat beside them. He gave Blackwood a side-eyed glance which the American understood well enough — at this point, Wulfson's body language and proximity seemed to be purposefully eroding the station of his rank, as well as his role as captor. Even Enzo picked up on it, glancing down the log distrustfully.

Wulfson stared off toward the village. "You have something to say."

Dubois picked his words carefully. "Erm… my apologies, Major. It's just… I suppose it's a rarity for us to break bread with an enemy."

"You are not my enemy, Herr Dubois. I am your captor."

"I'm afraid the two are not mutually exclusive. Is not every captive an enemy of his captor?"

Wulfson chewed on the pork. "No. Not when that captor is working toward his captives' interests."

An awkward silence fell over them. Wulfson alone seemed unbothered. "There is something we must discuss. I wish to make peace with you. All of you."

The statement sounded sincere, but Blackwood found it oddly foolish considering their position.

"That is an admirable goal—" Dubois started.

Blackwood cut him off. "I don't think your men would agree with that."

"No. I don't think they would," Wulfson said. "But they are under my command, and they will do as I say."

"Are you sure about that?" Blackwood's tone ventured further than might have been wise.

Wulfson spit out a piece of hard gristle. "The guards I command are not good men. I know this is not news to you, but you should know that I see it too. It has become apparent that Klaus murdered your friend Fletcher. He killed a villager as well, a young boy."

Dubois, who had been translating the Major's words to Italian, cut to silence. He muttered something in French, and his face turned dark. "I have only seen one boy in this village." He looked to Blackwood. "Maria's son."

"Yes," Wulfson said. "Klaus killed him while attempting to steal a horse and escape. I have stripped him of his rank, and he will suffer the villagers' justice. As sorry as I am for his actions, I must accept due fault. A man like that should never have been given the power he possessed."

Blackwood ignored the thousand other burning questions he held, instead focusing on the one that mattered. "What is it you want from us?"

"Cohesion."

"In what way?"

"We cannot deal with any more infighting. We must become one unit, working together toward a combined goal. A goal that will benefit all of us equally: survival. The guards are driven by fear. A fear of you, a fear of me, a fear of the villagers. They are brutes, drawn from the worst reaches of the Empire, and I will deal with them in the manner that suits best. However, I do not wish to govern over you prisoners with threats of violence. You men have lived with that threat long enough. I chose this group because I saw something in each of you. Now we are here, on the edge of the map, and I must ask of you the impossible: I need not only your allegiance but your trust as well."

The Major's face was straight, unlike Dubois's, who looked uncertainly to Blackwood. "Major, if I might ask a question without giving offense…"

"Ask it."

Dubois hesitated. "Why should we trust you?"

"Because if you don't, and all of this falls apart, you will die," Wulfson said curtly. "Not by my hand, mind you. Either by the guards as they step over my body, or the elements themselves as you attempt to flee."

Wulfson's mention of his own death rang as a warning bell in Blackwood's head. The Major's control of the situation must be quickly fading — what other reason would he have for looking to the prisoners as allies? He looked east to the mountains above and toward Switzerland beyond. "We should just continue on. There's no reason to drag these people into all of this."

"No. The way is too dangerous."

"It's better than ending up like Fletcher."

Wulfson let out a disparaging sigh. "No. It is not. Trust me on this."

There was that word again: trust. Blackwood may not have hated this man like he did the other Germans, but he would never trust him.

Wulfson took a deep breath as if to speak but instead pulled his flask from his jacket and drank. When he lowered it, his face was somber. He stood and faced them, pointing to the Iron Cross that hung from his chest. "Do you know what this is?"

The prisoners all nodded.

"Two years ago, I faced an enemy in a place much like these mountains. They were your people, Enzo. They fought viciously and with great passion, greater than any enemy I've met since. Our regiment was beaten back across the slopes and peaks until they had us nearly surrounded. I was an Oberleutnant at the time with only two score of men under my command. We were mountaineers, men accustomed to such a climate. Or so we thought."

He tossed the flask to Dubois, who nearly fumbled it into the snow. The Frenchman eyed it before taking a tentative sip and passing it down the line.

"After months of fighting, the regiment was pushed back into a defensive position. It was our last stand. A hidden mountain pass was discovered to our west that would have allowed the Italians to surround us entirely. A thin gap between sheer peaks only the width of three horse carts. I was ordered to take my men and hold it by any means necessary. It had been weeks since our last resupply. For five days we suffered the elements on empty bellies as we awaited their attack. Half of my men fell, not to bullets but to the cold and hunger. When the Italians finally arrived, it was a bloody fight. We ran low on ammunition by end of the second day. I sent for more men and supplies, but by dawn, no reinforcements had arrived.

"That morning the Italians came at us with everything they had. It would have been over in minutes had they reached us. With no hope of survival, I did the one thing I could. I blew a charge set in the mountainside. There was no time to withdraw, no hope of retreat. The snow gave out beneath our feet and the avalanche carried us down, caught in its frozen grasp. The mountain consumed us all. My men. The Italians. Her wrath was indiscriminate. I do not know why I alone survived her fury.

"It was a pair of Italian scouts that ended up hearing my cries for help through the snow. When they dug me out, they saw my uniform and made to shoot me. I shot them first. Then I shot their friends, whatever ones I could find, until our reinforcements arrived and retook the slope. When they found me, I was nearly dead. That is why they gave me this medal. For killing my own men alongside the enemy. An enemy made up of young sons and tired fathers. They gave it to me because I survived when I shouldn't have — a cruel joke if you ask me.

"I tell you this now so that you will not doubt my next words: I know better than most the risks of the mountains. I have waded in the trenches and crawled through the tunnels, yet I have seen more horror at the hands of mother nature than at the edge of any weapon designed by man. This is a place designed by God to kill any man that does not respect it. You do not want to venture out into these mountains. You do not want to push on, or you will find yourself begging for the relief of a bullet." Wulfson looked to each of them, impressing his point. "Furthermore, I tell you this because I need you to know the extent to which I will go to accomplish my mission. I promised you your freedom from the clutches of my countrymen. This is a promise for which I would die to deliver. This is why you must trust me. Now come. We have work to do."

None of the prisoners spoke as they set back to work. Like Blackwood, and despite everything, they believed him.

32

DIETMAR PACED a wide circle around the dining room, head down and knife flipping between his fingers. Victor sat by Johan's side, prodding him every so often to ask some variant of the same dumb question: *"You gonna live?"*

Johan hadn't responded yet. He just trembled as he stared in the flames through glassy eyes.

Hanz, entirely lost in his own world, barely noticed any of them. He sat alone, staring at the twin ribbons in his hand. He was now a noncommissioned officer of the Imperial German Army — something that, up until a few hours prior, had seemed a more distant dream than returning home.

He rubbed the smooth ribbon between his fingers. It felt like everything he could have hoped for and more. With this promotion, he should be able to leverage his way out of his duties at Rothenspring — if there even was a Rothenspring upon their return. Rumor had it that Wulfson's convoy was just the start of decommissioning the disreputable camp. If this were true, as an Unteroffizier, Hanz would have his pick of his next assignment. He could rejoin the artillery or even push his luck and try to make it into the infantry. Hell, they might even let him in the cavalry. He'd always fancied the idea of leading a column of riders into battle. Of course, he'd have to learn to ride a horse. But there would be time for that later. And who knew? Maybe, if he truly proved his worth out here, Wulfson might even put him up for a medal.

He felt giddy at the idea and struggled to keep a smile from emerging. He forced his mouth into a hard line — his men wouldn't respond well to gloating.

Dietmar stopped his pacing and regarded the others. *"This is bullshit,"* he hissed. *"We cannot let them kill Klaus. Who the hell do they think they are?"*

Hanz fought his instinctual desire to shrink back and remain silent. He clenched the ribbons and willed courage into his voice. *"Private Dietmar. Enough with that talk. We have our orders."*

"Shut the fuck up, Hanz." Dietmar dismissed the new Unteroffizier as if he was still nobody. *"We need to find out where they're keeping him—"*

Hanz simmered with a sudden, indignant rage. He slammed a fist on the table and stood. "*Private! Are you deaf or stupid?*" He channeled every bit of gravitas he could. "*I am your—*"

Dietmar wheeled on him. "*You are a joke. A whiny little dog and a fuck up. If you wish to lick the Major's boots, then go out there and find him. Make sure you don't miss the shit on his heel.*"

Hanz shook the ribbons in his fist. "*These mean nothing to you now, do they? You are a soldier! You will do as you are ordered!*"

Dietmar snorted and feigned to turn away, then, in one swift motion, the rifle swung from his shoulder and leveled with Hanz's chest. Hanz felt time slow down as the air was sucked from the room. He looked to the others.

"*Victor...*" Hanz tried, his voice shaking — with anger or fear, he did not know.

Victor looked back and forth between the two men. He stood slowly and unslung his own rifle. Dietmar didn't bother to look back as Victor raised it and pointed the barrel squarely at Hanz.

"*What have you ever done to make you a soldier, boy?*" Dietmar demanded. "*While I pushed Belgium, what were you? A scrawny little schoolboy begging for sweets? When I gutted my first frog in France, where were you? Crying at your mother's feet or still suckling on her drooping tit?*"

Hanz's rifle leaned against the table beside him. His hand drifted toward it.

Dietmar laughed. "*I was a sharpshooter, you idiot. The best in my company. If I wanted to, I could thread a bullet through a man's head, earhole to earhole, at a hundred yards. Go ahead, reach for it. Imagine that you're fast enough.*"

Hanz froze.

"*Good.*" Dietmar's lips turned upward in a nasty smile. "*Now throw them into the fire.*"

"*What?*"

"*Those precious ribbons of yours. Throw them into the fire, or I'll sever your spine with lead and toss you in there yourself while you're still drawing breath.*"

"*No.*" Hanz shook his head. He realized that he was trembling as much as Johan now.

"*Very well.*" Dietmar flicked the safety off. The sharp click made Hanz wince. Dietmar's eyes narrowed. "*Last chance.*"

Hanz uncurled his fingers and stared longingly at the ribbons — at his future. At his hope. He couldn't do it. He *wouldn't* do it. These men had already taken so much from him, but they couldn't take this away. Not now.

Hanz had every intention of telling Dietmar to fuck off, but when he looked up and saw the morbid sincerity in the man's eyes, the fight drained from his body. He sucked in a deep breath, then crossed the room in long strides and tossed the ribbons into the flames. They curled and withered away to ash in a matter of seconds.

"You are a brat," Dietmar said smugly. "*A sniveling nobody. You are nothing, and you will die nothing. The best you can ask for is that you do not die today. Now, go sit down like a good little boy.*"

The rage returned twofold. Hanz felt his heart thrum in his ears, and an electric surge exploded through his body. Dietmar, still focused on his sadistic reveling, was caught off guard as Hanz lunged at him and swatted the rifle aside. The tackle brought the two men to the ground where they grappled over the weapon. When he could not tear it free, Hanz slammed his elbow down into Dietmar's face with a satisfying *crunch*. Victor's heavy footsteps came at his back, then a horrible pain erupted from the base of his skull.

⁓

When Hanz awoke, he was slouching in a chair. His head ached, and his hands were bound behind his back. A filthy dishrag stretched tight between his teeth as a gag, filling his mouth with the taste of mildew and rotten beer.

Dietmar wiped the blood from his nose and cursed. He and Victor stood over Johan by the hearth and spoke quietly. "*The first step is to free Klaus. Wulfson has gone too far; he's siding with the swine, just as he has all along. He'll let these savages have us next if we don't act now.*"

"*Where are they are keeping him?*" Victor asked.

"*He has to be somewhere around here. It's a small village, not many places to hide a man where he can't escape. A cellar or a jail cell, most likely. Somewhere underground, I would imagine.*"

Johan coughed weakly. "*He's in the cave.*"

Dietmar knelt before him. "*Why do you say that?*"

"*I heard them, in the night.*"

"*You were nowhere near that cave.*"

"*I heard them,*" Johan insisted. His voice rasped as though the wind had torn apart his vocal cords. "*Their movement. They were there. Lots of them, going in and out in the dark. We need to find him. Then we need to kill Wulfson, the mangey bastard.*"

Dietmar leaned closer, and Hanz could barely hear him. "*You are sure he is there?*"

"*Where else would he be…*" Johan muttered. "*In some old woman's attic?*"

A sly grin spread across Dietmar's face. "*Then what are we waiting for?*"

"*What about the Scot?*" Victor asked.

Dietmar considered. "*Victor, you go. Kill him quietly. Use your bayonet, or your hands, or whatever you like. Just no gunplay. There's no reason to bring this place to arms. Not yet.*"

"*And him?*" Victor jabbed a fat finger toward Hanz.

"*We should kill him now,*" Johan muttered.

"*No.*" Dietmar's nose bore a gash from Hanz's elbow, and his eyes had started to blacken. "*Klaus will want to deal with this traitor on his own.*"

They seized Hanz and hauled him roughly to his feet. He tried to resist, but Victor easily wrenched his shoulder painfully in its socket and dragged him across the floor. Johan's gaze broke from the fire for the first time, and he gave Hanz an empty smile as he passed. "*Not so fun when it's you, is it?*"

Hanz's head smacked off a bed post when they hurled him into the bunk room, leaving him dazed. Before he could reorient, the door slammed shut and a heavy scraping beyond it told him that they had barricaded it. He lay still, his mind reeling. In short order, he heard the footsteps in the next room depart. Struggling to his feet, he fumbled blindly with the latch with hands still bound behind his back. It was no use. Whatever blocked the door from the other side was too sturdy for him to push through.

"*No!*" he tried to scream through the gag. "*No! No! No!*"

He threw himself against the door with all of his strength. It didn't give an inch. He slammed it again and again to no avail until he finally collapsed in a heap against it. White hot tears streamed down his cheeks. He panted against the damp cloth, and the rope burned his wrists raw as he thrashed against it. The image of the others slaughtering Wulfson and the prisoners tormented him. He could almost hear the cries of shock and horror as the guards turned their rifles on the villagers, gunning them down ruthlessly behind evil smiles.

He'd been so close. So close to redeeming himself. So close to, for once, actually mattering. He should have fought harder, he thought bitterly. He should have been a man and made Dietmar shoot him. At least the shot would have alerted the villagers, given those poor women a chance.

He didn't know how many minutes he spent lamenting before he heard the grating sound of the barricade shifting once again. He rolled to a seat as the door opened, ready to spit curses past the filthy rag. But it was not any of the guards who stood before him. It was Sovilo.

The tavernkeeper stared down at him with concern. From his belt, he pulled a small pocketknife and clicked it open. Hanz recoiled when Sovilo leaned in, angling the blade toward his neck.

"*What has happened?*" Sovilo asked as he slipped the blade behind Hanz's ear and cut the gag away.

Hanz choked on the drool that had accumulated in his mouth. "*They've gone to free Klaus! They're going to kill Wulfson and the others.*" He bowed forward, offering up his bound wrists. "*Cut me loose, we have to stop them!*"

Sovilo stepped back. The concern on the tavernkeeper's face slowly melted away into an apathetic glare.

Hanz jabbed his chin over his shoulder toward the bonds. "*Cut me loose! What are you waiting for?*"

Sovilo folded the knife and retreated through the door.

"*Stop!*" Hanz insisted.

Sovilo ignored him, easing the door shut without meeting his eyes.

"*What are you doing? What are you doing!*" Hanz's voice rose to a scream as the barricade slid back into place. "*I have to stop them!*"

33

WATER SLOSHED over McCulloch's pants as he slipped on the ice. He swore, slowing his pace and adjusting his grip on the buckets. He'd already toted at least a dozen of them about town. Every time he'd drop one off, he'd return to find another full and waiting by the wellhead. Now he was headed back out once more, cutting through the alleys and trudging down streets, muttering angry sentiments as he went.

"Men used to follow you to their deaths under the tune of the pipes... Now they've got you wandering about in the cold, a delivery boy to old wenches. What's your life become, old man?" Despite his frustration, he couldn't help but snicker. He'd never imagined himself as anything but a soldier. Maybe in another life — the one he so often wished he'd chosen to pursue — a chore like this would seem normal. Not now, though. Now it seemed silly.

The mirth of the moment melted away as he rounded the next bend. In the shadows of an overhang stooped Victor. The lumbering brute stalked along, shoulders hunched and head low like a dog on the prowl. McCulloch knew immediately that something was off — the clumsy attempt at stealth was a dead giveaway to the guard's intentions. He was hunting.

McCulloch stilled. Blackwood's dagger was tucked securely inside his coat, still wrapped in thin cloth. It would take a moment to retrieve — a moment he might not get. Victor's eyes caught on him before he could slip back into the alley.

"Du bist da, Schotte. Komm her." Victor called just loud enough to be heard across the empty street.

McCulloch felt his pulse quickening. A metallic taste erupted over the back of his tongue, reminding him of the taste of every battle and skirmish he'd ever fought. It made him feel warm. It made him feel strong and fearless. He'd been waiting for this moment since the hun bastards had first scooped his unconscious body from the battlefield. Now it hardly surprised him that the guards had chosen to strike in the Major's absence. He'd expected it, mostly — though a part of him figured they didn't have the stones.

"*Komm her!*" Victor commanded again, his frustration mounting. His rifle hung from his shoulder, but his fist formed tight around the handle of the long bayonet sheathed on his belt.

"Aye," McCulloch barked back. His volume drew a wince from the German.

So you want to be quiet about it, eh? McCulloch thought ruefully. *Have it your way.*

It took less than twenty paces to close the gap between them. McCulloch went slowly, gauging the German's posture as he came within range. When only a few yards separated them, he pulled a trick that he hadn't used since the schoolyard. Looking over the guard's shoulder and feigning surprise, he asked, "Major Wulfson, that you?"

The childish mislead worked. Victor stiffened and glanced back, leaving McCulloch the opening he needed. Without warning he heaved the bucket at Victor's face.

Icy water dowsed the oaf, and the impact of the bucket sent him staggering back. McCulloch seized the moment to fish the dagger from inside his coat. It had already flopped out of its wrapping and into his palm before Victor recovered.

"*Du dummer hurensohn!*" Victor gasped as he shook the water from his face and yanked his bayonet free from his belt. It was a good two feet long, more of a sword than a knife.

McCulloch's wicked glee glowed on his face as he advanced. He hunched low, dagger held far in front while his free hand hovered defensively against the bottom of his beard. He was no stranger to a knife fight. More than once he'd employed his dirk in the hand-to-hand battles of the trenches, and his forearms bore the winding scars to prove it.

Victor, on the other hand, seemed unversed in the craft. He lumbered forward, the bayonet held high like a club.

The first cut was McCulloch's. He darted in, dipping beneath Victor's wild swing and slashing the inside of his opponent's bicep. Victor roared as the blade bit through his coat and drew a streak of blood. He recoiled, clumsily attempting to render McCulloch in two with his backswing. This time the Scotsman stepped in close, catching the German's elbow with his barrel chest and slashing high, cutting a deep gash across Victor's forehead. Victor stumbled back as blood cascaded into his eyes.

"Come now, lad," McCulloch goaded. "We're no finished yet."

Again, McCulloch attacked, landing a flurry of slices and jabs. Their blades flashed red in the morning sun, darting and weaving as the men engaged in their bloody dance. Despite Victor's reach, McCulloch had the upper hand in both skill and ferocity. He landed cut after cut, absorbing the bayonet's graceless blows with the hard bones of his forearms. His heart throbbed with exhilaration as his sleeves grew heavy with blood. The German fell back farther after each onslaught, desperately searching for the space to pull his rifle from his shoulder. McCulloch gave him just enough leeway to try, but with every attempt the Scot would launch another vicious assault, aiming for the German to get caught up in his own sling. Victor's panting turned to roars of frustration, his defense devolving to wild hacks as he stumbled backwards. McCulloch pressed on, stabbing, slicing, laughing.

"You should'a shot me, you rank bawbag!" McCulloch chided as he pushed forward, growing bolder as the grey of Victor's uniform blossomed red.

The guard's legs grew wobbly, and he collapsed to a knee. His breath came heavy, each exhale accompanied by a high-pitched whine. A mixture of hatred and fear filled his blood-soaked eyes as he stared up at McCulloch. The Scot smiled in return.

Perhaps Victor realized he was going to die. Perhaps something deep in his brain switched off and the animal inside took over. Whatever it was that happened beneath that thick skull, his lips lifted into a vicious snarl and he leapt forward, abandoning all semblance of defense. McCulloch was caught off guard. He managed to bury the dagger in Victor's gut before the blood-slickened handle slipped from his grasp. The German drove forward, pinning him against a wall. McCulloch caught the flash of the bayonet at his side just in time, managing to grasp the blade before it slid between his ribs. Rusty steel bit through the flesh of his fingers as he wrestled to keep it back. The rifle had slid from Victor's shoulder in the tussle. It hung by its sling from the crook of his arm. McCulloch grabbed for it, missing sight of the ugly head rearing back before him. He didn't feel the ferocious headbutt that cracked down on his nose. All he felt was the searing pain as the bayonet erupted through his chest wall and cut deep into his lung.

McCulloch gasped. In a swift motion he abandoned his grip on the blade and dropped his weight. His searching hands found the bulge of Victor's crotch, and he latched on with a bone crushing grip. Victor howled and drew back, toppling in the snow as McCulloch rode him down.

Blind with fury, the Scot mounted the downed guard and seized him by the throat. He bore down with every ounce of his strength. Victor's trachea crunched under his palms as the guard's hands, tacky with hot blood, clawed desperately at his face. McCulloch let out a hoarse scream and sank his teeth into the raking fingers. He gnashed against bone and tendon as Victor convulsed beneath him, not letting up until the fingers clenched in his teeth went limp.

McCulloch fell back. A sea of red spread through the snow beneath Victor's corpse. The Scotsman's mind was void of any coherent thoughts in the wake of his rage, and an all-encompassing pain took hold as his adrenaline ebbed away. Blood poured from his slashed sleeves and the bayonet still protruded from between his ribs. Deep red grew across his coat and every breath felt like fire.

"You did it this time, you daft fool." The words seared in his chest as he spoke them.

From somewhere down the road came the crunch of footsteps in the snow. He scrambled to untangle the rifle and bring it to bear. The barrel drooped when he saw who it was.

Sovilo approached cautiously, his face drawn. He stared at the dead German for some time before turning to McCulloch.

"What're you looking at?" McCulloch coughed out. Blood accompanied his voice, spattering out over his beard.

"*Das sieht schlecht aus.*" Sovilo nodded to the bayonet protruding from McCulloch's side.

"I dinnae speak kraut."

Sovilo said in perfect English, "Your wound, it looks bad."

"I've had worse," McCulloch lied. He knew he was going to die. He looked at the tavernkeeper with a raised brow. "You speak English then? This whole bloody time?"

"Yes. I speak many languages."

"Clever bastard," McCulloch snorted.

Sovilo crouched down, dropping to eye level with McCulloch. He pulled a thin vial from his pocket and held it out. "Take this medicine. Take it now."

McCulloch squinted at the flaking reddish-brown substance within the glass. His strength had already begun to ebb. He felt the cold of the wind now, and his whole body throbbed. He looked from the vial to Sovilo, then back to the vial. "Nae. If this is it, I'd rather feel the pain. Better to die awake."

"Take it," Sovilo implored.

McCulloch waved him off. His eyes drifted down to the dead guard next to him. "At least I got the one. The biggest one at that, eh?" He chuckled.

"Look at me, Scotsman."

McCulloch barely heard him. His mind was back home, in the rolling hills and deep moors of the Highlands. A hard slap brought him back. He scowled at the tavernkeeper, but the man's expression gave him pause. The morose grimace had been replaced by a cold glare.

Sovilo nodded down the street toward the plaza. "Do you not desire vengeance?"

"Vengeance, eh?" McCulloch took the vial and regarded it. The powder inside was only a teaspoon or so. He pulled the cork free and sniffed it. It stank of iron and sour meat. "Smells like shite."

"It will keep you here long enough to finish the job."

"What the hell is it?"

"It is the gift of power. It is the blood of the Sarvàn."

McCulloch laughed through the pain. "Your little beasty legend? Maybe Fletcher was right about you people."

"Perhaps he was." Sovilo leaned in and pushed McCulloch's hand toward his mouth. "Does it matter now?"

The lightheadedness threatened to overtake him. He poured the contents of the vial into his hand. It was dried blood alright, of that there was no doubt. "You're saying this witchcraft'll help me kill 'em, eh?"

"Yes."

"Sounds like Deviltry. Good thing for you I'm already damned." McCulloch chuckled as he pressed his palm to his mouth and threw his head back. The powder tasted as putrid as it smelled and left a tangy bitterness as it dissolved over his tongue. He licked his palm clean and braced for some sort of effect. None came, and he felt foolish for imagining something would. "You lot need better medicine. Now leave me to die, you fuckin' ghost." He leaned back on his haunches and sighed. "Though I suppose I'll be one myself soon enough."

His heart skipped a beat, and a wave of energy rippled through his core. It crashed over him as he jolted upright. In an instant, the murky brume of death washed away. The pain, which had been so insurmountable only a breath before, was gone and the air grew warm. His eyes, wide with shock, met Sovilo's.

The albino's approving smile pulsed before him. "All glory to Mithras."

"Where are they?" McCulloch growled.

Sovilo pointed past the houses to the cliff face looming overhead.

There was no pain as McCulloch pulled the bayonet from between his ribs. He didn't bother to stymie the blood that followed it, instead affixing the long blade to the end of the rifle. He rose to his feet and stumbled toward the cliff. In only a few steps, he found himself jogging. Then he was sprinting.

34

BLOOD POURED over Hanz's ear from where he'd used his head to shatter the window in his would-be cell. The numbness in his hands was dissipating now that they were free thanks to a broken shard of glass he'd used to cut the rope. Now, he ran through the plaza toward the cliff face. In the shadows beyond the pillars, the recessed door stood open.

He staggered to a halt at its threshold. Inside, the dull radiance of torchlight carved a path forward through the darkness. Hanz could hear the other guards' voices echoing from within. He clenched the sliver of broken glass — his only weapon — and advanced.

As he crossed into the darkness, he saw the death laid out before him. Two women lay in his path amidst a pool of their own blood. On a table nearby, wrapped in a thin cotton shroud, was the unmistakably small form of a child's body. Another dead woman was draped over it. He recognized her — it was Maria, the murdered boy's mother. Her arms still held him as if to shield him from the violence. Blood dribbled from the gaping knife wound in her back. Hanz felt his stomach turn.

"*It won't open!*" Dietmar's voice came from across the yawning expanse.

At the end of the torchlit aisle of pillars he saw them. Dietmar beat against the latch of a tall door with the butt of his rifle while Johan leaned weakly against the stone wall nearby.

"*We should go the other way,*" Johan's voice, though frail, carried through the acoustic chamber.

"*I said no. It leads upwards. If they are keeping him here, it will be this way.*"

"*You cowards!*" Hanz stepped forward into the light, his voice cracking. "*These were innocent women! What have you done?*"

Both men looked back in surprise.

Hanz stalked toward them, brandishing the shard of glass like a knife. "*You're not worthy of those uniforms! You're not worthy of life!*"

Dietmar balked and jabbed a thumb over his shoulder. "*Go kill that little shit already.*"

"*Gladly.*" Johan raised his rifle.

"*No! Do it quietly.*"

Johan looked annoyed. His frostbitten fingers fumbled over the stock of his rifle as he affixed his bayonet.

Hanz felt the flames of rage encompass his body. It was a deep rage, one that had smoldered in dormancy for as long as he could remember. It wasn't just the months of beatdowns and abuse at Rothenspring. It was years and years of being treated as trash. Of being made to feel small — the invisible, weak boy, always touted as useless or cowardly. A lifetime of shame and regret, of wishing he was better.

He *was* better now. It may have taken far too much horror to finally stoke those flames to life, but now they burned so bright that nothing else in the world mattered. He advanced, glass shard raised, feeling ready to die.

Johan started toward him stiffly. His legs were unsure beneath him, and though he tried to hide it, his face betrayed his trepidation. It was clear he still hadn't recovered from his night in the cold. Hanz came forward faster, driven by every moment of abuse he'd suffered at the hands of the rapacious bastard. The darkness hung around them as they closed on each other across the bridge of light, two enemies caught in a slow, steed-less joust.

"*I should have killed you a long time ago.*" Johan's voice shook. "*I'll tell you what: go back to the tavern and I'll promise to give you one final lick of Wulfson's boots before we string him up.*"

Hanz picked his pace up to a jog.

Johan froze, and his eyes grew wide. He jerked the rifle to his shoulder and a deafening gunshot filled the cavern.

Hanz flinched hard and stumbled. Only no bullet struck him. Ahead, Johan collapsed to his knees. His face screwed up in bewilderment then exploded out the back of his head as another shot split the air.

Dietmar turned and raised his rifle. His bullet snapped by Hanz, who, still stunned, spun to follow its trajectory. A figure cut against the brightness of the open door to the outside. It was the Scotsman.

McCulloch fired again. This time the bullet passed so close to Hanz's ear that he felt the wind hissing off it. He managed to drop and scramble into the darkness beyond the pillars as the other two men engaged in gunplay. As he jostled through the pitch black, his foot caught on an unlit brazier and he fell hard. Something crunched beneath him, and the air filled with unearthly buzzing.

"*Johan, over here!*" Dietmar screamed over the gunfire. Hanz spotted his silhouette at the mouth of a dimly lit doorway. He bolted toward it. Dietmar snapped his rifle up as Hanz dove inside. "*You!*" he hissed. "*Where's Johan?*"

"*Dead,*" Hanz panted out as another round ricocheted outside.

Dietmar gave a frustrated growl. He jabbed his chin up the spiraling stairs. "*Go!*"

Hanz went, scrambling hand over foot upward into the blackness as Dietmar reloaded behind him.

35

THE FIRST gunshot was distant and muffled. Initially, Blackwood imagined it might have been something else — the report of a blacksmith's hammer or even a cart clattering off its axle. He froze mid swing as the tree before him groaned in the wind. Nearby, Wulfson also stood rigid and alert.

There was another distinct pop, then they came in a flurry, echoing across the slopes from the direction of the village.

"Stay here," Wulfson barked as he struggled through the snow to the lumber sled. He hefted his axe, and in two swift strikes he severed the bonds to the plow horse's harness, then leapt atop the steed and wheeled her about.

Blackwood paid him no mind. He was already sprinting down the lane of compacted snow toward the village.

"I said stay here!" Wulfson repeated as he barreled after him.

Blackwood didn't care. He ran as hard as he could, knowing that with every distant gunshot people were dying. Heavy hooves beat the snow at his back. He turned just as Wulfson's boot caught him in the side and sent him sprawling in the snow.

The horse came to a skidding halt. Wulfson towered over Blackwood, rifle in hand and features hardened. As Blackwood floundered in the snow, something heavy landed on his chest. He grasped at it, his fingers closing around cold steel and stippled wood. When he made it to his feet, Wulfson was already galloping away. He looked down to find the Major's pistol in his hands.

"It's happening, isn't it?" Dubois panted as he caught up.

Blackwood checked to make sure a round was chambered and nodded.

"*Mon Dieu*... What do we do?"

"Come on!" Blackwood barked as he took off in a sprint toward the village.

36

MCCULLOCH TOOK the stairs two at a time. High above, the mad scramble of the Germans brought a smile to his bloodstained lips. His breath came in wheezing gasps, but the pain was gone. The only sensation that consumed him now was the electric buzz that permeated the air. Around him the blackened stairwell was alive with color, thrumming in and out with his own pounding heart. Bees crawled over his skin and wove through his beard. They stuck in his blood and wriggled under his clothes. He felt them like he felt his own flesh — buzzing.

Despite the mounting pressure of cold air filling his chest cavity and slowly collapsing his lungs, it was the most alive he'd ever felt.

The darkness above flashed with a gunshot. The bullet whizzed by, thwacking harmlessly into the stairs below. He cackled, firing blindly back. A German curse followed his shot, and he howled in glorious triumph. He was a predator, and they were his prey — a wolf stalking sheep in the inky black of night.

Another shot came hurtling down. Once more he returned fire. The rifle felt like a feather in his hands, its recoil nonexistent. In the darkness he did not need the sights. The weapon was a part of him. An appendage of its own, melded with his hands as if it had sprouted from the flesh itself. Far above, the Germans were desperate and terrified. He heard it in their voices as they jabbered back and forth in their scrambling ascent. Their panic washed down over him, and he bathed in it like spring rain.

In all his years at war he'd never experienced such savage elation. Not in the muck of the trenches. Not in the jungles of Bombay. Not even in the plains of South Africa, where he'd made his name hunting Boers under the beauty of the dying African sun.

He fired again. Once more a hoarse cry came in response. He laughed. He couldn't stop laughing. Bagpipes blazed in his ears, bursting forth with the grand marches of his beloved Black Watch. In the dark, he saw the rolling hills of the Highlands fading to the sky in perfect purple and green. He saw his wife, the beauty of her smile. He was there, inhaling the scent of damp earth and peat smoke, steeping in the droplets that hung in the air and savoring the soft caress of the moss beneath his toes.

He was home.

And it tasted deliciously like blood.

"*Ah cannae see the target!*" He bellowed the old war tune in unison with the rasping pipes that played in his head. "*Oh, ah cannae see the target!*"

Above they screamed and fired, but he didn't care. He reveled in their plight, ignoring the blood that spurted from his own lips with each gagging cough. "*Ah cannae see the target! It's ower faur awa'!*"

37

HANZ CRASHED through the door at the top of the staircase. Ravens cackled and exploded out of the tower top in a hurricane of black feathers and beating wings. His cramping legs threatened to give out as he stooped and heaved in the cold air. Dietmar came close behind, firing blindly down the shaft toward the madly howling Scotsman.

"*Die, you son of a bitch!*" Dietmar's shrieks rang high with terror. When his rifle clicked empty, he slammed the door shut and battered the bolt in place.

Hanz stumbled as Dietmar pushed past him. His burning legs betrayed him, and he toppled into a row of thin wooden birdcages. They scattered across the floor. He lay in a daze. He'd only ever been shot at once before. Even then, it had been a drunk old farmer with a weak scattergun. No one had ever actually tried to kill him — especially not a mad, bloodstained lunatic spouting out some guttural chant. For all his glorious fantasies of combat, this was about as far from his expectations as he could imagine. In his fantasies there had always been some narrative — some sort of meaning or hope that drove the violence forward. What was unfolding now was nothing more than chaos. Deadly, horrific, terrifying chaos that exploded all around him without an ounce of consent. He'd never hated anything more in his life.

Even Dietmar appeared overwhelmed. He paced back and forth, muttering under his breath as he reloaded his rifle. A stripe of blood ran up his coat where one of the Scotsman's bullets had grazed his side. His eyes caught on Hanz. "*Get up, you little shit! Get up and watch the door!*"

Hanz, barely in control of his own body, managed to crawl to the thick wooden door and press himself against it. Through the grated window in the door, he heard McCulloch's song from far below. To his profound relief, the Scotsman's voice had begun to faulter.

"*I— I think you got him...*" Hanz sputtered out. "*I don't think he'll be able to make the climb.*"

"*Good... good...*" Dietmar strode to tower's edge and scanned the landscape below. With a satisfied cackle, he raised his rifle and steadied it on the wooden parapet. "*There you are...*"

Hanz only faintly registered Dietmar's movements. He was trapped in the recesses of his own mind, desperately wishing to be home. Wishing he had listened to his father. Wishing he had never signed up for this godforsaken job.

The crack of Dietmar's rifle snapped him back to the moment. Dietmar chambered another round and adjusted before firing again.

"*What are you shooting at?*" Hanz got out weakly.

"*Shut the fuck up.*" Dietmar fired a third time.

"*Are you...*" Hanz started, taking to his feet and leaning over the short wooden wall. Far below, a lone rider cut against the white slope leading into the village. The horse pounded along a path of packed snow. Its rider ducked as Dietmar fired again. Hanz made out the slate grey of the uniform and realized it was Wulfson. "*Stop!*" he tried, but it was too late.

Dietmar's rifle cracked, and the galloping horse toppled. Its chest slammed into the ground, and it rolled, kicking up a spray of snow as Wulfson, feet caught in the stirrups, was rag-dolled underneath.

Hanz cried out and grabbed for the rifle. Dietmar was faster, yanking it away and delivering a hard butt-stroke. Hanz crashed to the floor, more wooden cages splintering under his weight.

"*I told you to watch the fucking door!*" Dietmar screamed. He fumbled to pluck bullets from his bandoleer, jabbing them one by one into the rifle's breech.

Hanz curled in a ball where he lay. He couldn't watch the door. He couldn't watch Dietmar as the man leveled the rifle once more. He couldn't be here at all — he needed to be anywhere else. Anywhere but here.

Dietmar squinted over the sights. "*Now,*" he growled through clenched teeth. "*Where are the rest of you swine...*"

38

BLACKWOOD SPRINTED down the horse's trail. The others were far behind, unable to keep up with his desperate pace. He'd lost sight of Wulfson around the bend of the wooded hill ahead. The gunshots rang louder now, coming clear and crisp in the open air rather than muffled as before. The sound echoed from on high, and he knew exactly where the shooter was located: at the top of the tower, precisely where he would have gone in their shoes.

All he thought of at that moment was Lucia. He imagined her cowering at the tip of a rifle, Johan staring down on her with a lurid smile and wicked eyes.

He made the bend of the hill, and the slope opened up before him. The village lay just ahead, a mere two hundred yards away across open ground. Halfway to it, the plow horse lay in a crumpled mess, the grey of Wulfson's uniform shadowed against its shaggy coat.

Blackwood skidded in his tracks and retreated to the cover of the hill. He didn't know if he'd been seen from the high vantage of the tower, but no bullets followed him.

Enzo reached him first. The young Italian looked petrified. Dubois came on his heels, sucking at the air like a winded racehorse. The gunshots continued in steady rhythm.

"What now?" Dubois gasped out.

Blackwood was drawing a blank. Their only chance was the pistol clenched in his grip — but the tower was laughably out of range. He searched his memory of the landscape around them, drawing from his short time spent atop the tower days before. The village was clear of trees or cover on all sides, there was no way to reach it without crossing through the open.

"Here." He shoved the pistol into Dubois's hands. "Listen to me. I need Wulfson's rifle. If I go down, you need to circle back around into the thickest part of the forest. Hide there until nightfall, then slip into the village and kill them all."

Dubois sputtered to come up with an argument, but Blackwood didn't give him the time to get one out. He was once again on his feet and running, the Major's rifle his only focus.

Snow kicked out from under his boots as he made it to the open. The firing paused as the shooter focused on his new target. A round snapped by. Blackwood zagged, cutting erratic angles back and forth down the hard packed trail. More bullets hissed and cracked in the cold air as the distant booms of the rifle followed each one. A round exploded the snow at his feet, and he stumbled, careening to the ground.

"*Va te faire fouttre!*" Dubois roared. Blackwood glanced behind him as he found his feet. Dubois was in the open, pistol raised high. The Frenchman let go a rapid burst of shots, then collapsed with a screech as a bullet impacted his stomach.

Blackwood grimaced but did not turn back. If he could not reach the rifle, they would all be dead regardless. Even if he could, their odds of victory were still close to zero.

A round thwacked into the dead flesh of the plow horse as he slid behind it. He thudded hard into Wulfson, who cried out in pain. Blackwood scrambled over him, chest to the earth and hands searching for the Major's rifle.

"Where is it?"

Another bullet hit the measly cover of the horse, painting them with hot blood. Wulfson was dazed. One leg was pinned beneath the beast's flank, and his arm was contorted at a sickening angle. Blackwood yanked him in closer, burying him as deeply as possible behind the bulk of the horse's body.

"Where the hell is the rifle?" Blackwood shouted.

"I… I don't know." Wulfson's eyes were vacant. "It… it must have flung away…"

Blackwood dared a glance over the horse. There was no rifle in sight. He looked to the snow on either side of the path. The disturbances that the bullets had kicked up in the white blanket masked any clear sign of where the rifle had fallen. "Goddammit!" He pounded his fist into the snow. "Goddammit!"

His mind raced. With no cover in any direction, there was no way forward without some sort of suppressive fire. They were pinned down.

Gathering his breath, he dove into the snow, hands clawing and searching for the solid wood of the stock.

39

THE TOWER rang with Dietmar's cackling mirth. He yanked the bolt of his rifle back again and again, raining insults down onto his quarry alongside deadly lead. Hanz curled in the mess of broken cages, eyes misted by tears. Through the grate in the door, the Scot's song had faded away to be taken over by sick, hacking coughs. It seemed the climb had sapped the last bit of life from the battered old man.

But Hanz wasn't there, not really. He was a thousand miles away, watching Dietmar's joyous massacre through the eyes of some paralyzed avatar that cowered uselessly in terror.

Dietmar reloaded. His bloodstained bayonet glinted in the sun as he turned his sights once more toward the village. He hooted after each shot, the pleasure of his deeds evident in his wicked sneer. A chorus of screams carried up the cliff's face in the wind. Hanz imagined the villagers then, sprinting through the streets in horror, cowering for cover as they bled. The same people who had taken them in from the cold. Who had fed and sheltered them. Who had made the mistake of saving their miserable lives.

"*Fuck you, bitch!*" Dietmar squawked. "*And you! And… you!*"

The screams brought with them the fresh memory of Maria's body — her limp form draped over her son's cold corpse, protecting his memory even in those final, horrible moments.

"*Don't you run, little lady!*"

What Hanz did next wasn't driven by bravery. It wasn't some vengeful, justice-fueled action of redemption. It was sourced entirely in the thought of his own mother — the woman who had held him on cold nights as a boy and wiped away his tears as he lamented over the cruelty of the world. He saw nothing but her in Maria's last act as it played out in his mind. Now, as his eyes locked onto the bayonet still wet with her blood, his hand closed around one of the jagged wooden spindles beneath him.

Dietmar yanked the trigger, and the rifle clicked empty. He cursed, searching his bandoleer for more loose rounds. He turned to Hanz. "*Give me your ammunit*—" He never finished his demand. Instead, his mouth fell open and his eyes bulged wide as they drifted down to the thin stake protruding from his chest. He moved to strike, but Hanz shoved him, ripping the rifle away as he did. Dietmar fell hard on his back. His hands gripped the spindle as he gasped in agony.

Hanz loomed over him. The rifle shook in his hands, and his mind went to Fletcher, to the horrors of finding his torn corpse. He remembered when Wulfson had told them how the Brit died. Slowly, he slid the bayonet up the seams of Dietmar's coat until its steel tip pressed against his throat. Dietmar's scream turned into a wet gargle as Hanz pushed the blade forward, penetrating the hard flesh of his windpipe and easing into his brain. His dull grey eyes rolled back as his body gave one final, violent twitch. Hanz stared down into them as the life faded away. Despite the curdling sickness in his gut, a profound feeling of righteousness welled in his chest.

Barring the whisper of the breeze, the tower was silent. It was over.

Hanz felt weak. He stumbled back, colliding with the parapet. Holding back vomit, he tried to steady his mind.

It was over.

It was finally over. And they were all dead. Dietmar, Johan, Victor no doubt. Even Wulfson, he figured, remembering the violence of the collapsing horse. It was just him now. Him and the prisoners, however many were left — if there even were any. They would want his blood next, not to mention the villagers. He would have to explain. He would have to beg for their mercy. Maybe they would kill him. Maybe he deserved it. But it wouldn't happen right now. In this brief moment in time, he was safe.

The bolt exploded away from the door with a shower of wooden shards. Hanz stiffened as the Scotsman stumbled into the light. He was a terrifying sight to behold. He'd shed his coat, shirt, and cap somewhere along the way. He stood hunched, drenched from face to boots in glistening crimson. He met Hanz's gaze with wild eyes. Beneath a beard thick with the molasses of clotting blood, he wore a mad smile.

"*It's over now. No more.*" Hanz slowly raised a hand in peace, nodding to the body before him. "*It's over.*"

The Scotsman's barbaric laugh sprayed blood at his feet. Hanz realized too late that he was well beyond reasoning. All he could do was feebly raise his own rifle as the Scot charged. He winced as his bayonet, still dripping with Dietmar, buried itself in the Scot's chest. Then the Scot's own blade drove through his belly. They stood still for a moment, locked together by the protruding weapons. Then the Scot fell, pulling his rifle with him.

Hanz had never experienced such pain as when the jagged sawback of the blade ripped free of his guts. He screamed and collapsed to the floor, squirming backwards against the wall. The rifle fell from his hands, and he grasped at the slimy cord of his intestines as they spilled out.

Tears came freely as he looked down at the gaping wound. It was too painful to apply pressure as he'd been taught, but he tried anyway. The act brought with it a scream, and his hands fell away.

"*Help*," he tried weakly at first. But his voice built with panic as the cascade of blood began to spill out over his lap. "*Help me! Help!*"

A raven quorked overhead. Then another. They were returning, slowly lining the rafters. Watching him.

"*Help...*" he begged, turning to the Scotsman. But McCulloch was dead. Horribly dead, his eyes glassed over like hazy marbles. All that lay before Hanz now was an empty vessel of meat and inert blood. The sight of this brought with it a horrifying epiphany — he was staring at his own immediate fate. He might have minutes, but not hours. It was too late to stop the bleeding, and the wound was too egregious to treat.

"*Please, somebody help me!*" he screamed. Nothing came back to his ears besides the echo of his own words and the flutter of wings overhead. There was no one else to help him. He was alone, hundreds of feet above the nearest villager, who would probably rather throttle him on sight than help him stuff his innards back into his belly.

He began to panic. The blood that spilled over his quaking hands kept pace with his heart as it raced faster and faster. When he tried to stand, his legs gave out. He stumbled, falling into a shelf of nests which snapped under his weight. Then he was on the cold stones of the floor again, his blood mixing with the yellow slime of broken eggs. His arms were heavy, and his thoughts became fewer and less coherent. He tried his best to seek comfort inward — to picture his father, the old man's soft smile. But his father's face was vague and details few. His mind went to that last hug before the train. That last fleeting moment.

Why the hell had he gone? What was he thinking? This is what he wanted, wasn't it? Combat? War? Blood? He'd foolishly yearned for such things for as long as he could remember. Now, bleeding out in this frozen tower that stank of death and bird shit, he wished desperately that he could take it all back.

This is it. This is really it. He felt numb as the cold truth of the matter solidified. He tried to manifest some final pleasant thought. Anything but the truth. But his mind drew blank.

The shadows of the tower's ceiling grew darker. Wavering spiderwebs danced in the cold breeze and ravens shuffled above, their heads cocked curiously and black eyes darting.

Hanz began to weep. His shoulders shook with sobs, and the tower filled with his quiet cries. A burst of anger brought his own hand slapping across his face. *"You're a man, dammit!"* he croaked out.

If he was going to die here, it would be as a man.

With great effort and greater pain, he managed to climb to his knees. He pulled in a deep breath. The sloughing mess of his own innards stank like a paunched deer. He accepted the putrid stench with a grimace. If the long dark was coming, he would see light first. Climbing up the jagged stones of the wall and the rough wood of the parapet, he struggled to his feet.

The light off the snow was blindingly bright. He balanced his weight against the parapet and looked out over the majesty of the mountains. They were serene, stretching out before him with a beauty that stole what little breath he had in him. Neverending rows of white peaks were blemished only by the darkness of forests and crags and deep dipping fingers, all of it teeming with life. He could suddenly imagine the marmots and the foxes and the deer dancing on the slopes. He smiled through his tears. His father would have given anything to see this place. To stand beside his son in this tower and witness the grandeur of an untouched world. And Hanz would have given anything in that moment for the old man to be there with him as well. To hold him by the shoulder and just watch, silently, as the wind caressed the snow and the trees shuddered away their downy jackets. Just one last joyful instant. One little moment, and he could die happy.

He didn't feel the bullet slam into his chest. He didn't feel the impact of his body on the hard stone floor. He didn't even feel the ravens' sharp beaks as they began picking at his flesh before his heart had stopped beating.

Because for him, he was still staring out over those mountains, arm in arm with his father.

Smiling.

40

BLACKWOOD BRACED the rifle against the dead horse's rump, steadying himself for another shot. The smoke that lilted from the barrel obscured his view of the tower. He shifted, scanning the distant parapet for any further signs of movement. None came besides the black cloud of ravens circling above.

Seconds dragged by in cold silence, then minutes. Blackwood kept the rifle tight to his shoulder and his breathing shallow. Time was a fickle thing in combat — a lesson he'd learned many times over. Hours could feel like minutes, and minutes like hours.

"Is it over?" Wulfson got out between gritted teeth. He huddled against the horse's back, coherent now but still trapped beneath the beast's weight.

"I don't know," Blackwood replied. Something moved in between the houses ahead. He jerked the rifle to focus on it then back to the tower as he recognized a rider emerging from the village. It was Lucia. Her golden hair flowed out behind her as she galloped toward them.

"*Get to cover, dammit!*" he shouted in German as she approached.

She yanked on the reigns, and the horse skidded to a stop beside them. The ebony Oldenburger stomped and spun in a tight circle. "*It is done. The guards are dead.*"

"*You're sure?*"

"*Very.*"

Blackwood shoved through the tavern door. Wulfson stumbled in beside him, his good arm draped over Blackwood's shoulder and the other dangling uselessly at his side. Blackwood set him in a chair and took in the scene before him.

The dining area, once so warm and welcoming, had transformed into a bustling field hospital. The room filled with the pained groans of the wounded villagers. Women rushed about, tending wounds and shuttling supplies. Dubois writhed in pain atop one of the tables. Sovilo stood over him, a bloodstained apron tied over his chest and a leather surgeon's kit unraveled beside him.

Blackwood crossed to the Frenchman's side and grasped his hand. A dime-sized pit of mangled flesh marked where the bullet had entered just below his bottom rib. Sovilo retrieved a slender pair of forceps and squinted at the wound. A bead of sweat ran down his temple. "*You must be still for this, my friend.*"

"*Oui, oui,*" Dubois panted weakly.

Sovilo eased the tip of the forceps through the hole. Dubois flinched as they made contact. When they pushed deeper, he cried out and shirked away. Sovilo pulled back and wiped his brow. "*Anneliese, fetch me the laudanum.*"

A nearby woman abandoned her own patient and darted to the back room. Dubois's eyes were crimped shut and his cheeks puffed in and out like a blowfish as he sucked at the air.

"*You'll be fine. You'll be fine,*" Sovilo repeated quietly. He looked up at Blackwood. "*Tell him. Tell him he will be fine.*"

Blackwood did as he was bid, whispering the words to his friend with far more confidence than he felt.

Anneliese returned, a small bottle in hand. Sovilo, who was focused on the wound, nodded to Blackwood. Blackwood took the concoction and poured a dribble into Dubois's waiting lips.

"*More,*" Sovilo said.

Blackwood hesitated. He was no stranger to opiates nor to the dangers of overdose.

"*More!*" Sovilo insisted.

Blackwood emptied half the bottle into Dubois's mouth.

"*Now hold him down.*"

"*We have to wait for it to—*"

"*There is no time. It will work as we go. Give him something to bite down on.*"

Blackwood yanked his belt free and shoved it in between Dubois's teeth. He pressed the Frenchman's shoulders to the table in a vice grip. Once more the forceps dug into Dubois's side, and again he shrieked and convulsed as the tool burrowed deeper.

"*Almost, almost… Hold him still!*"

Blackwood bore down with all his weight.

"*Come on now… Wait. Wait, there it is — I have it!*" Sovilo grunted triumphantly. Blackwood heard the soft clatter of the bullet dropping onto the table. He eased off as Dubois went still but for his heaving chest.

"*This is good.*" Sovilo stepped back and patted his brow dry. "*The bullet did not penetrate too far, and it does not smell as if it struck his bowels. With any luck, the kidney was not damaged. It should heal well so long as we manage to avoid infection.*"

Blackwood assessed his friend. "You're lucky that shot was from so far away. If it had any more power, you probably would have been a goner."

"Eh," Dubois got out. "I would have been luckier if the *bâtard* missed."

Blackwood patted him gently on the chest. "Welcome to the war, my friend."

Dubois managed a weak chortle before the opiate cocktail overtook him.

Blackwood stepped back as Sovilo set to work applying a bandage. He scanned the half dozen wounded villagers strewn around the room. "*Where are the guards' bodies?*"

"*Why?*"

"*I need to know that they're dead.*"

"*I assure you they are,*" Sovilo said.

"*I'll see it for myself.*"

"*The big one is in the street to the east.*"

"*And the others?*"

Sovilo, concentrated on his work, jabbed his chin toward the tower.

Victor was easy enough to find. He lay spread eagle in the center of the street, a bed of red snow beneath him. Blackwood followed the trail of McCulloch's blood over the icy cobblestones to the Mithraeum. For the first time, the cavern was well lit. A score of braziers burned bright, illuminating three fresh corpses shrouded in bloodstained sheets. They'd been arranged neatly beside the table bearing the dead boy. Blackwood passed them without pause. There was no time to lament. Regardless of what the others had said, he needed to be sure that this was over.

The slate grey mound of a German uniform lay in the aisle near the rear of the cavern. Johan's cheekbone had cratered into his skull and his brains were scattered in a mess over the floor. Despite the certainty of his demise, Blackwood still landed a solid kick into his ribs. Just to be sure.

Bees buzzed lazily around Blackwood as he lit a torch and continued along the blood trail to the base of the tower stairwell. As he ascended, he passed a young woman on her way down. She looked ill from what she had seen and avoided his eyes as he squeezed against the wall to let her pass.

At the top of the tower, he found himself amongst the putrid remains of a veritable battlefield. Blood pooled between the stones and dribbled in a thin stream over the edge of the stairs. McCulloch lay dead, shoulder to shoulder with Dietmar. Hanz had crumpled atop them both, completing the morbid pyramid of death. Blackwood was not gentle in casting the guards aside. He pressed two fingers against McCulloch's neck in search of a pulse. The flesh was already cool to the touch, and the gore that matted the hair of the old Scot's chest had begun to coagulate.

Though the ravens had already been at the others, somehow McCulloch remained untouched. His features were still frozen with the palpable glow of mirth. Even in death, it seemed he reveled in his victory. Blackwood returned the look with a sad smile. "I'm sorry I wasn't here." He glanced to the dead Germans. "Not that you needed me anyway."

He eased McCulloch's eyes shut. Hooking his arms under the Scotsman's shoulders, he dragged him to the edge of the stairs. He stopped when he noticed that the lid of one of the crates beside the door was askew. A coil of rope was visible inside.

He set McCulloch down and turned back to the dead guards. Their lifeless bodies were a satisfying sight. Still, it didn't feel like justice. His thoughts went to the horrid atrocities he'd witnessed at Rothenspring — skeletons of men dropping to the dust from starvation, forced to crawl and grovel until they begged for death, all for the amusement of these demented bastards. He thought of Dickie, to the last time he'd seen his only friend in that rotten place. To the way Dickie's body swayed from a branch as he'd passed by on his final march out of that desolate hellhole.

He took his time tying the nooses. They were precise, knotted just the way the guards had done it many times over. Once he'd stripped their gear and uniforms, he tied the ropes to the rafters above and hauled the two dead men to the edge of the tower and tossed them over. Despite the fact that they were already dead, the wicked *pop* of their spines brought a vengeful satisfaction.

He left them hanging there off the side of the tower, bloodied and naked for all to see. With the weapons and gear hanging from his shoulders, Blackwood took his dead friend in his arms and began the painstaking journey down the winding stairs.

41

IT HAD been pitch black for days. Maybe weeks. Klaus had no idea. Time was nonexistent in a place where the sun could not touch. All he had to base his guess on was the curdling hunger in his belly and the parched rasp of his throat.

He curled in the corner of the cramped stone cell. The sound of dripping water echoed through the stale air. At first the sound had drawn a deep yearning. He didn't care if it was clean or even if it was dribbling sewage runoff, so bad was his thirst. Now, after a thousand iterations, the gentle noise did nothing but threaten to drive him mad.

But he wasn't mad yet. That much he knew. He'd made the decision that he wouldn't allow his sanity to slip away from him in the horrible darkness he'd awoken to. He had vengeance to dole out.

His memories of that night had grown clearer as Wulfson's poison filtered from his system. He could now recall the weeping woman cradling her child. He could see that bastard albino dragging his limp form and hear the familiar way the Major had spoken to him. Wulfson was a traitor. He'd betrayed them all. If Klaus was to suffer this horrible fate, all he wished was for Wulfson to suffer worse.

He'd already blindly explored the subterranean cell more times than he could count. The only surface his wandering hands had felt besides the jagged touch of stone was a sturdy wrought iron grate. He knew he was underground. The air was thick and wet like a cave, the only movement being the rare draft of frosty air that passed through the grate.

If there was a draft, there had to be a way out.

With chilled fingers, he searched the wall beside him once more. One of the stones, a rather small one, was loose. He worked at it, pushing and yanking until the old mortar began to flake away. Finally, it came free in his hands. He used it as a hammer, chiseling away until another baseball-sized chunk of stone fell free. It was slow work, and he was already weary before the third stone broke away. He didn't slow, striking harder and harder until he felt the warmth of blood on his fingers.

He had no idea what lay on the other side of the stone wall. It could be another sealed cell. It could be the sheer wall of the mountain's belly. It didn't matter. The hatred that boiled inside drove him onward. The others were already dead — he could feel it in his bones. Soon they would come for him as well. He needed to escape. Escape from this damned cell. Escape from this damned village. Escape from these damned mountains.

If he could somehow make it back to Rothenspring, then he would return here, and with him he would bring the full weight of the Imperial Army to crush these swine into dust.

PART FIVE

The following is the transcription of a self-guided audio tour cassette from the British Museum's featured exhibit on Ancient Mysteries, 1994

Over here on your right we have evidence of one of the most fascinating ancient mysteries you'll see today. These intricately engraved stone reliefs hail from all the way back in the second century AD, where they were carved by a mysterious cult devoted to a deity named Mithras.

Mithras's followers were called the Mithraic, and their religion was one of utmost secrecy. The Mithraic existed all throughout Rome's many territories and was especially popular amongst soldiers and conscripts. Unlike the more well-known Roman pantheon, Mithraism was actually monotheistic, as in its followers believed in only one God. Some academics speculate that since what little we know of Mithraism has so much in common with Christianity (and because the religion was particularly active at the same time among a shared populace), Mithraism likely had a significant influence on Christianity. However, one of the aspects that really sets Mithraism apart was its class system. This brings us back to the stone reliefs you see before you now.

Most scholars agree that the symbols exhibited in these reliefs are representative of the grade system that existed within Mithraism. By that we mean it was likely that a worshipper of Mithras would find themselves working their way up a military-style rank — or grade — as they advanced in their knowledge and devotion — similar to modern secret organizations such as the Freemasons.

If you look to the first relief, you'll see that the carving is of a raven, also called *corax*. This animal was believed to have acted as a symbolic intermediary, or messenger, between the heavens and the earth.

Second in the row, you'll see a carving of an ornate veil. This is believed to represent *Nymphus*, the bridegroom or male virgin. Across the ancient world, many cultures often viewed virgins and chastity as a symbol of purity. It is believed that the Mithraic held similar views.

Third comes the helmet and spear. These are meant to represent *Miles*, the warrior. Mithras himself is speculated to have been a warrior, so it's no surprise the cult gained such popularity amongst the military ranks.

Fourth in the row is the mighty lion, *Leo*. Even today, the lion is traditionally seen as a noble creature. It is believed that the lion symbolism in Mithraism is akin to our very own British coat of arms, this grade representing royalty and power of man on earth.

Fifth in the row we have *Perses*, or the Persian, represented by the Phrygian cap. This is one of the more enigmatic grades of Mithraism. Even the best scholars often argue over its meaning. It is important to remember that despite being known as a Roman religion, Mithraism seems to have originated in the Middle East. Thus, it stands to reason that this grade represents the cult's cultural origins or even the ancestral root of its practitioners.

Sixth comes the radiant crown. This grade is often associated with *Heliodromus*, or the sun-runner. In legend, this figure carried the sun itself through the sky. When Mithras defeated the sun, he subjugated both it and its runner. This being the penultimate grade level of Mithraism, it is hypothesized that a person reaching this grade was considered a keeper of sacred truths, or one who would shed the light of knowledge onto others.

Lastly we arrive at the final relief. This carving is of a shepherd's staff, and is believed to represent *Pater*, or the father. This was the final level of Mithraic worship, and is a grade believed to have only been achieved by the most devout of worshippers. A person in this grade would likely have been one of great religious and social significance.

Now, it's important to remember that the Mithraic left behind no written documentation before mysteriously vanishing around 400 AD, so much of what we know today comes from anthropological speculation as well as what little archaeological evidence we have managed to find. In layman's terms, that means that the experts have to make some educated guesses in order to fill in the blanks.

To learn more about the Mithraic mysteries, please ask a docent about our considerable selection of literature located in the gift shop.

MONTANA, 1914

Sun-scorched dandelions wilted in the dust by the roadside. The road itself shimmered through a haze of midsummer heat, and the horse riding down it left behind a dribbled trail of sweat.

Edward Blackwood plodded through the valley. Flies buzzed in a cloud over his head. They danced along the exposed flesh of neck and arms and crawled under his salt-stained shirt. He didn't care. His shoulders sagged as if he were a candle that had been melted to its base.

It had been over a decade since he had been out this way. A decade spent accruing little more than scars and regrets and a heap of useless dollars.

At first, a life of crime had seemed a necessity. As the years dragged on, he'd made the habit of promising himself that each job was the last. But violence begot violence as right had blended into wrong in his slow spiral down the drain of damnation. Now he couldn't even remember his life before. He knew what he was now though, and he didn't like it.

Maybe the geezer would know what to do.

That thought alone had carried him back up the Rockies to his boyhood home. The old man had done things in his own youth, things he was not proud of. Things that had haunted him in his sleep. If there was any hope to be had, the old man would be the one to know it. If not, there was always the solace of a rope.

The cabin was in disrepair. The shingles were cracked and a window had broken. When Blackwood knocked, there was no answer, but the door was unlocked. The air stank and was filled with the buzz of insects as he pushed it open.

His grandfather sat in his favorite chair. His shoulders were splayed out on the table before him along with what remained of his head. His favorite twelve gauge, a double barrel Ithaca, lay on the floor by his side, his naked toe still hooked in the trigger.

Oddly enough, Blackwood felt nothing. His life had already devolved into a putrid circle of death. He'd killed a bounty hunter in Carson City only a week before. The man was arrogant and drunk and had shot first. Still, when Blackwood found a photograph of a young woman and five children tucked in the man's breast pocket, something in him had finally broken.

"*I get it,*" he muttered in German, the only language his grandfather had let him use in the house. The old man had been dead at least a week given the maggots that squirmed in his neck. On the table lay a pile of mail and newspapers. Only one envelope had been opened. Blackwood searched the floor until he found the blood-splattered letter that had come from it.

It was from the bank and postmarked nearly a month ago. The sentences were short and crisp and coldly professional. The bank was sending notice that they had decided to prematurely terminate the hundred-year lease his grandfather held on the land. They went on to offer a paltry hundred dollars for his troubles. This was the same land that the old man had built the cabin on with his own two hands. Land he'd spent four long decades hunting, trapping, and cultivating. Land that had been his life.

Blackwood looked to the header. He knew the bank. He'd been inside its vault before. Though the letter didn't accuse it outright, he had no doubt that his past transgressions had been a factor in their decision.

That meant someone had talked. Spilled his name in a manner that connected him to the job. In the past, he might have sought vengeance. Now he just considered the shotgun. Two barrels, one still loaded.

Beneath the envelope a dramatic image centered the front page of one of the newspapers. Though the details were fuzzy through the mottled black and white print, it was clear that the brawny young soldier depicted was meant to be stained with blood. He held a victorious smile, and behind him flew two flags, one British and one American. Above was printed in all capital letters:

AMERICAN BROTHERS, SHOW YOUR LOYALTY! FREE THE MOTHERLANDS OF EUROPE FROM THE GRASP OF THE WICKED HUN! ENLIST NOW IN THE CANADIAN ARMY!

When Blackwood left, he did not take the road he had come in on. He went north instead, leaving the burning cabin to fade into a distant column of smoke behind him.

42

DARK SHAPES clawed at the inside of his skull, and a searing pain engulfed his chest. As always, the shadow lurked above, watching him, glaring down with yellow eyes and black wings spread wide.

Blackwood woke with a start. His head felt like it had been run over by a truck.

He wasn't hungover. The night before had been a solemn affair. While drinks had been poured to the dead, none among them had drunk to excess. He'd forgone much of the somber festivities, instead committing a considerable effort to hauling both Victor and Johan's corpses to the tower top and hanging them beside their compatriots. Afterward he'd gone to bed more or less sober, rifle by his side and pistol still tucked in his belt. In the next room over, Enzo had slept in a chair watching over a still drug-addled Dubois. The Frenchman's labored moaning had been audible through the wall into the wee hours of the morning. Now it was silent.

Blackwood took to the parlor and sat in silent contemplation until daybreak. When the sun finally came, he spotted a group of villagers amassing in the plaza. They carried woodcutting tools and were heading west toward the pines he and the other prisoners had felled the morning before. Knowing he couldn't sit and lament all day, he decided to help finish the job they hadn't had the opportunity to complete. He had to jog to catch up with them.

It was a tedious process. With the plough horse dead they were forced to use the swaybacked old mule, who struggled under the weight of the sled and required frequent breaks. Upon their return, he found that some of the women had taken to pillaging wood from the collapsed houses along the village's outskirts. With this wood, three fresh pyres were built: one for the slain villagers, one for the boy, and one for McCulloch. Though it seemed odd for them to be cremated separately, Blackwood was too tired and frazzled to question their customs.

He spent the remainder of the day drowning himself in toil and sweat, heaving old planks free from the crumpled houses and hauling them along the windy streets. The ever-growing pyres cast long shadows in the fading light of the sun. To the north, a dark hedge of clouds hung like a halo over the mountain peaks. He'd heard the murmurs go up amongst the villagers of the storm to come. It would be fierce and unforgiving. A true blizzard, they said with fear in their eyes.

At that point he wouldn't be surprised if it was accompanied by a volcanic eruption or an artillery barrage. Hell, if the moon itself were to hurtle down on them from the sky, it would seem par for the course.

Blackwood set McCulloch to rest atop the lashed together beams himself. He took comfort in the subtle look of contentment that had frozen over the dead man's face. It was an odd thing to take solace in, a violent death. But it was exactly what the grizzled old warrior had wanted — to go out a bloodied hero basking in a victory earned against the odds.

The winter days were short, and it took until dusk to complete the work. Blackwood wasn't sure if he was disappointed or relieved that he had not crossed paths with Lucia since the day before. Between the lingering headache and the overall aura of mourning, he was in no more of a rush to speak to her than he was to speak with Wulfson, or anyone else for that matter. The urgency of the situation regarding the guards had died with them. He needed a chance to breathe and think before dealing with whatever was to come next.

The villagers formed a wide circle around the pyres as darkness came. They were six less now, and six shoulder-width gaps in their formation were left open. Many wept openly while others just stared on with slacked faces and sorrowful eyes. Blackwood stood off to the side. He felt it wasn't right to take a place amongst them. Enzo stood beside him. The young Italian looked as if he'd aged a dozen years overnight. His shoulders, once square and strong, slumped forward in a tired hunch. Blackwood had seen the transformation too many times to count — Enzo finally had the look of a soldier after he's sampled the cruelty of combat. Now, the rifle strung over his shoulder seemed nearly at home. If it weren't for his fleeting glances to where Hilde slouched under a cowl, Blackwood might have forgotten that he was still just a boy.

When they had all settled into position, Lucia emerged from the meeting hall alongside Sovilo and the old crone. Lucia stood rigidly between the pyres and recited words in Latin. When she finished, the bundled thatch at the base of the platforms was lit, and a fire crackled to life.

THE SARVÀN

The scent of woodsmoke filled the air as the flames grew to encompass the sleeping dead. Soon the stench of burning hair and crisping skin joined it. The circle of villagers began to chant in their low tones. The ambiance was mesmerizing. Blackwood didn't know if it was a trick of the dusk or the pulse of their song, but slowly, the aching smog that had strangled his mind all day long began to clear. As their volume built, many broke away, weeping and gasping and collapsing to their knees. Soon only a few remained standing and chanting. Lucia was among them. Her skin reflected the orange light of the flames as she stood solemnly, lips moving slowly to form the same words over and over again.

She embodied a feral power in that moment. One that enraptured Blackwood and captured him in a way little else in his life had before. The bristling fur of her bearskin coat and the stark white fangs that hung over her face seemed a part of her very being — a beautiful emissary of something wild and terrifyingly powerful. Blackwood wondered if he'd fallen in love.

Evening quickly sank into night. The pyres cracked and collapsed inward in showers of sparks. The wind picked up, drawing the raging flames ever higher as snow began to drift from the heavens. In time, the chanting faded and with the dark came a cold stillness. Blackwood stood in place as the circle dispersed and huddled figures wove away down the icy streets.

The wind-whipped smoke washed over Blackwood. It stunk of scorched meat. He didn't shy away from it, rather sucking in a deep breath and letting it flood his being. It was a familiar stench. One that grounded him to the reality of his past and the bleak outlook of his future. Craning his neck, he looked to the tower that hung over the cliff high above. The four guards hung naked from its side, now little more than shadowed silhouettes in the moonlight. They deserved no pity. No funeral. No tears. They were carrion for crows, and they would freeze and rot and freeze again until the maggots and birds tore away the sinew that held their bones together.

Good.

When his gaze drifted back down, he caught sight of Lucia disappearing into the shadows of the pillars at the cliff's base. He followed after her.

The Mithraeum was dark once more. He followed the glow of her torch until he came up on her amongst a handful of smashed wicker beehives that were scattered over the floor. She'd shed her primal coat and now picked up the broken fragments piece by piece. He approached quietly, and when she looked up he saw the reflection of tears in her eyes. He knelt beside her and began to help.

"*I'm sorry about your friends,*" Blackwood ventured softly in German.

"*They were cousins and aunts, women I've known my whole life. They were not friends. They were my family.*"

He wished he knew a soothing response, a way to assure her that the pain would pass, that they were at peace and that she would be okay. But such words were beyond him.

She withdrew a thin wrap of cloth from her belt and held it out. He recognized the shape of the dagger.

"*I gave this to you,*" she said. "*Please, do not lose it again.*"

He pressed her hand shut around it. "*I can't take it.*"

"*Yes, you can,*" she insisted.

"*I can't. It should stay here with you.*"

Her eyes darted up to meet his. "*Where do you think you are going?*"

"*Switzerland with the others.*"

"*You can't. The mountain—*"

It was his turn to look away. "*This isn't a question, Lucia. I have to leave. Once Dubois has healed—*"

She lunged forward. Her swiftness caught him off guard, and before he could react, her lips pressed against his. She was warm and sweet and he couldn't resist kissing her back as they pulled into a tight embrace. For a moment, everything else melted away and it was just the two of them lost in the endless void of darkness.

She finally pulled away. Still, she held his face close. "*I need you to stay here, with me.*"

Blackwood had never heard a more enticing proposal. For a moment, everything that had happened — not only in the village, but throughout his whole wretched life — felt like nothing more than a faded nightmare.

He shook his head. "*I can't.*"

"*We can have a good life. No one will find you here. No one will know that you are not one of us.*"

"*You don't know that—*"

"*I promise you.*" Her words had the strength of being etched in stone.

"*Your men will return when this war ends. They'll know what I am, where I'm from. I won't hide what I've done. They will either kill me or drive me away.*"

"*No they won't.*"

"*Of course they will.*"

"*No,*" Lucia said solemnly. "*They won't.*"

"What do you mean?"

"They're dead."

Blackwood scoffed. *"Lucia… They can't all be—"*

"We kept it secret for the sake of your guards. They needed to fear the idea of retribution. They thought that there would be vengeance doled out should they do something to us. But now that doesn't matter. So I'll tell you the truth: our men are not coming home."

"There must be some who—"

"Those they took first, the able-bodied, they were killed in Italy. All of them. The others…" Her voice drifted off. A single tear rolled down her cheek, but her face hardened. *"The army lied to us. They were just boys and old men. The soldiers who came here told us that they were just to be workers. Then they threw them to the wolves of the Front. They didn't make it a week before they were killed — butchered like dogs while they slept."*

Blackwood tensed. A flood of bloody memories rushed back to him — the old man twitching under the torrent of blood, the jolting rhythm of the machinegun, the horrified screams of agony. *"Where did they die?"*

"What does it matter?"

"I want to know."

"In Lorraine."

Blackwood felt his heart lurch out of rhythm.

"What is it?" She looked concerned.

He realized he had stopped breathing. *"Nothing. Nothing, I…"*

It was not possible.

It was beyond impossible.

"Where are you going?" she called after him.

He hadn't been aware of his own retreat. He nearly stumbled as he erupted from the cavern back into the cold. The snow was coming heavily already. He crossed the windswept plaza in a rush as his thoughts knotted together into a cluster of horrific memories and desperate denial.

43

DUBOIS SLIPPED gently between the worlds of dream and reality. The laudanum had done its job well. The fear and uncertainty that had come to dominate the last year of captivity had been washed away by a soothing flush of euphoria. It tingled over his skin and kept him dozing comfortably as the candle on his bedside melted down.

Those few coherent thoughts that managed to slip through the opiate's mist were of his home in France. He could feel the smooth oak of his dinner table and the polished silver forks. It was as if he was there, seated in his dining room overlooking the river, a heaping serving of seared ham before him and his fingers wrapped delicately around his wife's palm. His daughters, still young in his mind, giggled and caroused and begged for dessert under the warm blanket of his gaze. He laughed along with them.

It was the sound of his own laughter that woke him to the night. He didn't know how long he'd been asleep. Now the snow was swirling outside the windows, and the air carried the subtle scent of charred meat. His mouth began to water.

"You alright?" Blackwood's voice startled him. He sat up reflexively. The pain in his side sent him collapsing back.

With some exertion, Dubois shifted to prop himself up on the pillow. "I was having the most wonderful dream."

"You should probably go back to it then."

Blackwood sat in a chair in a darkened corner of the room. A rifle laid across his lap. Dubois ran a hand down to the bandages on his side. They were cinched tighter than he would have liked, but the red spotting of blood was minimal. "Dear Lord, what have I done? Getting myself shot — *eugh*. A stupid thing to do, even for a fool like me."

"What you did was brave," Blackwood said. "Stupid, but brave."

"Stupid indeed. Brave though... *heh*. Perhaps I wouldn't have been such a terrible soldier then, *oui?*"

"I wouldn't recommend testing that theory."

Dubois smirked. "Don't worry, *mon ami*. I know I am as far from a soldier as a man can get, and I am not ashamed of this. If we make it out of this mess, I swear I will never set foot near a battleground again for as long as I live."

Blackwood only grunted in response.

"What about you? Will you return to the war?" Dubois asked.

Again, Blackwood only grunted.

"You were in it for some time, yes? I heard you tell our friend McCulloch that you were at Ypres. I heard about that place, about what happened there. You are a true veteran. I… I was only on the Front for less than a day. Just the wrong day, I suppose… *Oui*, it was a bad stroke of luck that put me in the Germans' hands. Now that I think of it, I'm not sure if it's a story I've ever had the chance to tell." Dubois waited for Blackwood to respond with interest. This time he didn't even get a grunt. In the dim light of the candle, Dubois could not make out his friend's face. "Are you asleep, cowboy?"

"No."

"You are quiet tonight," Dubois offered.

"You really shouldn't be talking this much."

"My lungs are just fine. I'm sure that expelling a bit of hot air will not kill me."

"It's not *your* health I'm worried about."

It took a moment for Dubois to process the jab. When it clicked, his barking laugh quickly devolved into a pained whimper. "You cannot choose now to grow a sense of humor. Not when it pains me to laugh!"

"Just try to relax and be quiet."

"To relax the body one must relax the mind, and there are too many worries trapped in my head to do so. What I require is distraction."

"Fine."

"Then I will tell you a story," Dubois went on. "As I said, you will be the first to hear it. Isn't that the best way to hear a story? A first recounting before it's had time to grow legs of its own and transform into an embellished fairytale, before the teller has had the opportunity to bend the facts to his will…" Dubois realized he was rambling and struggled to get back on track. "Anyhow… I was not supposed to be anywhere near the war. As a professor at a fine university, I was above conscription — at least in the eyes of the government. There was a boy I taught, long ago, a very promising young pupil from a good family. He took a commission shortly after leaving school and rose through the ranks of the army. I think he did it to seek out glory, but by the time the war had begun he was too high among the brass to serve in a way that might earn such a thing. Instead he was assigned to lead a cryptology unit. His duty was to crack the German codes as they came in, and he was good at it. Still, the Germans are tricky, and there was one dastardly code he and his men could not break for the life of them. With the Germans ever on the advance, he called on me for help. Like a fool, I agreed to make the journey.

"For me, it seemed a truly courageous act — I kissed my wife and daughters goodbye as if I was taking up a rifle myself. They begged me not to go, but I felt I had to. It was a small contribution, and it might save the lives of some poor young boys. I rode out only hours after receiving the dispatch. It was a three-day journey by horse, and by the second evening I came across a rather lively tavern. My nerves were frayed, and in an attempt to soothe them I overindulged to the point where when I woke up the next morning, I was barely able to walk. I believe my horse to have been a German spy because in my stupefied state, she took me straight through the forest and landed me directly in the hands of an enemy patrol. I was still so drunk that I asked them for directions."

This drew a chuckle from Blackwood.

Dubois laughed along with him. "The worst part is that I probably could have played myself off as a drunken civilian fool, but in my patriotic hubris I had pinned a fleur-de-lis to my lapel! They took me at gunpoint, and that was the last time I saw my beloved homeland."

"So you're just some civilian? How the hell you end up at Rothenspring?"

The grin faded from Dubois's face. "That was due to yet another chance meeting between poor luck and stupidity." He wriggled the bandages down to reveal the edge of the tattoo on his chest.

Blackwood leaned forward into the light. "Is that what I think it is?"

Dubois couldn't see it himself, but he knew damn well what it looked like. Three golden lions blazed against a red shield. "Yes. The British royal coat of arms. They saw this and imagined that I was more important than I was. The commander at the first camp I was interned at wanted a ransom from the royal family. When they laughed at his request, he became furious, branded me a spy and had me banished to die at Rothenspring."

"You're lucky McCulloch never found out that you're actually a Brit."

"*Non, non.* I am no Englishman, *mon ami.*"

"That tattoo says otherwise. I wouldn't have figured you for a monarchist either."

"I am neither of those things. This is not a mark of politics or of patriotism. It is the sigil of my father's family."

Blackwood scoffed. "What?"

"I am a bastard." Dubois felt a bit of pride in the proclamation. It had taken him much of his youth to come to terms with the title. Yet as a man, he'd learned to embrace it. "My father's proclivity for promiscuity was well known. Many summers of his youth were spent sowing his oats in the French countryside. Lucky for me, he made the mistake of taking up with a wealthy politician's daughter for a night. When my mother fell pregnant, he, along with the Crown, refused to acknowledge my existence. But unlike those half siblings I surely have scattered over Europe, my mother's father was just important enough to make a stink. Such a scandalous thorn in the side of a beast such as the monarchy does not go unacknowledged. After that, we were always well taken care of, though it was in exchange for our silence."

"Who was your father?"

Dubois smirked. "I'm sure you can guess. I decided very young that I would not speak his name until I met him myself. I'm sorry, *mon ami,* but he is dead now, and I am a man of my word."

"You won't say his name, yet you've got his crest inked on your ribs."

Dubois sighed. "A youthful act of spite. They could deny my existence, but I suppose I believed that the truth needed to live on in some way. And I am luckier for it. It was this tattoo that drew Major Wulfson's eye to me. When I was first summoned to the interrogation shed, I imagined that I was to be tortured. Instead I found him sitting there. He said he'd read my dossier and wished to hear my story. In the end I believe it was my heritage rather than my linguistic abilities that impressed him the most. He said such lineage would doubtlessly be accompanied by a sense of honor. Such is life, I suppose. You get a little, then it takes, then you get a little more."

Blackwood settled back in his chair. "You're full of surprises."

"*Oui,* well, I'd rather be full of something else. Would it be too much for me to ask for a drink?"

"There's water in the pitcher there."

"Oh no, not water." Dubois winked.

"Then no."

Dubois sighed. His fingers searched the bedside table until they closed around the small bottle of laudanum. There was only a dribble left. "I guess this will have to do," he muttered before finishing it.

Time passed as the wind battered the window. Frost formed like spiderwebs on its corners and snow caked the outside of the glass. "Another storm?" Dubois asked.

"Yup."

"Perhaps tomorrow I will build a snowman," Dubois joked. "Do children build snowmen where you are from, cowboy?"

"I don't know."

"How would you not know?"

"I don't know any children."

"Were you not one yourself once?"

Blackwood didn't answer, and Dubois didn't push. "My daughters always dreamed of building snowmen when they were small. Alas, there was never enough snow where we are from. Maybe they would like it here, eh? After the war, I mean. It is a place I would not mind visiting again." The laudanum had begun to hit, and Dubois felt his mind once more unraveling. "I think this place would be nice to visit. I mean, academically it's a gold mine. The masonry alone — *ooh la la*. They are a very unique people, these villagers. I think they are hiding something truly fascinating under the guise of simpletons. Their culture, I mean. What secrets are they keeping?" He chuckled and the room felt fuzzy. "I think… I don't know what I think. What was I talking about?" He looked to Blackwood. Even in the darkness, Dubois could sense his brooding. "You're quiet again."

"Huh?"

"What is keeping you so busy in your own mind?"

"Nothing."

"Come now. You are moodier than usual. One joke is all I get for the night? *Non*. Tell me what is troubling you."

"It's nothing."

"It's that woman, isn't it?"

Blackwood didn't answer.

"She is a beauty and seems kind. It is a hard thing, having to leave someone like that behind. Perhaps she will draw you back some day." A funny thought occurred to him. "Maybe the two of us will make the trip, *oui*? Two old friends reunited to find the love one of them left behind in the war. It sounds like a fairytale, doesn't it? You know, I may even be able to get the university to pay for it. A research trip — the ancient practices of the Mithraic revealed! Hah! Can you imagine?"

"I don't think these people would like that very much."

"You're probably right. Still, it would be good for you to see her again."

"She wants me to stay."

"Eh?" The idea hadn't occurred to Dubois. With all that had happened, he hadn't had time to imagine any outcome besides Switzerland. He considered it. "Perhaps you should."

"I have you and Enzo to look after."

"Come spring, I'm sure Enzo and I will be able to make our own way — given that Major Wulfson does not pose a problem in that regard."

"I'll deal with Wulfson."

"So, you'll stay then?"

Blackwood stood and slapped Dubois gently on the leg. "Enough talking for you. Try to get some rest."

Dubois waved him off. "Fine, leave me hanging. And don't you worry about me, cowboy. I'm a soldier now, remember?"

"Enzo is out here. Call out if you need something."

Dubois lay back. The drugs embraced him, and he found solace in the darkness behind his eyelids. He liked the rough and tumbled American. He was a good man despite what he might think of himself.

Sleep came easily now, only this time his dreams were not of home. This time, he dreamed he was a honeybee floating in a warm breeze.

44

OUTSIDE, THE storm was worsening. Wind ripped at shingles and howled through alleys. Despite the brutal weather, the upstairs parlor held a cozy warmth. Enzo slept peacefully in a chair beside the fire, his rifle leaning next to him. Blackwood felt for the boy — he'd been on steady watch over Dubois since the shooting the previous day. At this point, it was no doubt exhaustion, not comfort, that had lulled him into such a deep slumber.

Blackwood stoked the fire absently. He felt fragile in the quiet of the night. The sight of young Enzo brought him back to the horrible memories he'd been rehashing since leaving Lucia's side. To the boy he'd slaughtered with a knife on his last night in the war, and all those who came after. He knew his worries were foolish — thousands of men died every day in this war. No matter how much his gut screamed at him, he had to believe that the odds were that he had never stepped within miles of the men from this village.

In the corner of the room was a neat stack of the guards' remaining rifles and gear. The spattered stains of blood on the tan canvas bandoleers conjured the image of the corpses whipping in the wind high above. He felt no remorse for those wicked bastards. They had earned every bit of their fate, the same as he would someday doubtlessly earn his own. He took a rifle and bandoleer and headed downstairs.

Wulfson sat at a table before the larger of the two hearths. His splinted arm hung from a sling, and, as usual, his nose was buried in a book.

"*Herr Blackwood*," Sovilo called from the bar. "*A beer?*"

Blackwood accepted the offered stein and took a seat across from Wulfson. The Major took his time finishing his page before placing the book down and regarding Blackwood with tired eyes.

"Are you feeling better?" Blackwood asked.

"Yes. Thank you." Wulfson considered him. "The tables have turned quite abruptly, haven't they?"

"How do you mean?"

Wulfson nodded to the rifle. "It would seem that I am now the prisoner, and you the captor."

Blackwood drank. "You know, in my old unit... it was never our way to keep prisoners."

"I have heard that about the Canadians. *Sturmtruppen*, as we call them. Bloodthirsty and never the type to shy from breaking the rules of war."

"You're not wrong."

"So, your way was to cull men rather than take them prisoner. Dare I ask if this will be my fate as well?"

Blackwood scoured the Major's face. If he had any fear, he did not show it. "You gave us your word that you would deliver us to Switzerland."

"I did."

"I would ask that you keep that promise. With an addendum."

Wulfson's expression did not shift. "What sort of addendum?"

"For now, we will stay the course. We will over-winter here and help these people as we can. Come spring, you'll escort Dubois and Enzo through the mountains to Switzerland as planned. However, you will not deliver them to the Swiss camps. Neither of them were combatants, and neither deserves to be held in captivity for the duration of this war. They have served their time. After you cross the border — when they are safe from your countrymen — you will release them to their own accord. From there, they will be free to find their own ways home."

"You don't plan to join us?"

"I... I don't know," Blackwood admitted. It was the truth, one that he wrestled with even in that moment. "If I weren't to join you — if I were to stay — would you give your word to never speak of me or this place ever again?"

Wulfson didn't appear to be put off by the request. He strummed the table. "I would agree to this, as well as give you my word that it will be done as you have asked — given that you spare me the indecency of spending the rest of the winter locked in a cold cell."

"Like I said." Blackwood placed the rifle on the table and slid it toward Wulfson. "I'm not the sort to take prisoners."

Wulfson's lips cracked into a wry smile — something Blackwood realized he'd never seen. "You're a man of honor, Herr Blackwood. Do you still have my pistol?"

Blackwood's eyes thinned. "I think the rifle is gesture enough."

"I only mean—" Wulfson reached below the table and withdrew the holster from his belt along with a spare magazine "—you will need these. It is yours, though I hope you do not need it."

Wulfson offered his hand. Blackwood leaned in and shook it firmly.

The wind howled louder as the front door swung open. Lucia entered, glancing to the others before settling on Blackwood. "*Herr Blackwood, would you join me? I would like to finish our conversation from before.*"

Blackwood tried not to let his discomfort show. As much as he had convinced himself that his concerns over the village men were invalid, the feeling of revisiting the topic still made him uneasy. "*Ya. Just a moment, please.*"

She waited patiently as he returned his attention to Wulfson. "There's one more loose end."

"And that is?"

"Klaus. Where is he?"

"No one has told you?" Wulfson asked.

"Told me what?"

"He's dead."

"How?"

"I shot him this morning. His crimes deserved nothing less. I believe it to have been a just end."

Blackwood scowled. "You should have left him for me."

"It was a fitting death," Wulfson said. "Trust me. Nothing you could have done to him would have given you the satisfaction you desire."

"I want to see the body."

"To hang it from the tower like you did the others?"

Blackwood could see Dickie's dangling corpse as clear as if it was before him now. "Yes."

"I… Very well. I will not deny you your…" Wulfson struggled to find the words. "Yes. You deal with what you must. Sovilo and I will retrieve the corpse in the meantime."

Blackwood considered insisting on retrieving it himself. But it would only be in a weak attempt at avoidance. No, he needed to find the truth, whether it set him free or damned him. "Very well."

He stood, donned his coat, and followed Lucia out onto the icy streets.

45

WULFSON WATCHED through the ice-crusted window as his sister and Blackwood faded away into the driving snow.

Sovilo strode up behind him.

"*She's done well,*" Wulfson muttered. "*I was worried about the avalanche — it was a dangerous mission, but she got it done.*"

"*She always gets the job done, Anselm. She's grown into quite a woman. Your father would be proud.*"

"*I am proud enough for the both of us. Though it is still hard for me not to see her as a little girl.*"

"*I feel the same, dear nephew, but I am confident that she will lead them well once you and I are gone.*"

Wulfson nodded along, stifling the thought of his own looming demise.

"*Why did you lie about Klaus?*"

"*Necessity.*" Wulfson awkwardly pinned the rifle under his splinted arm and checked that a round was chambered. "*Our American friend wanted to kill Klaus himself. Would you have let him go down there? Into the depths of the Mithraeum? Would you have allowed Klaus the opportunity to reveal what he has witnessed? No. Blackwood is not ready for that. Not yet. Let Lucia do her work. I will take care of Klaus myself.*"

"*I will help you.*"

"*No. You stay here and watch after the Frenchman. He cannot succumb to his wounds. We will need him soon.*"

Sovilo retreated to the bar in silence. He paused halfway there.

"*What is it?*" Wulfson asked.

"*I have a bad feeling about this. We should have killed Klaus long ago.*"

Wulfson didn't respond immediately. This had been a point of contention since their arrival. The old priest had notoriously good instincts, but in this matter Wulfson had ignored them. Now was not the time to be drawn back into an argument. "*As I told you before, he was apt insurance to make sure that the*

Scotsman died properly in combat, as the ritual calls for. Imagine, uncle, if McCulloch had survived? Who else would we have to stand against him?"

"I still think it was a mistake."

"If it was—" Wulfson slung the rifle over his shoulder and headed for the door "—then it is one I will remedy."

The great cavern of the upper Mithraeum was empty. Wulfson strode alone through the dark, the torch in his hand barely illuminating the pillars as he passed them. The bees were quiet tonight, and the only sound that filled the dank air was the sharp *tap* of his own footsteps.

The sealed door at the far end of the cavern bore a handful of splintered dents and cracks where the guards had attempted to beat through the lock. Wulfson slid the old key into place. It stuck at first, but with a hard twist, the lock disengaged with a loud *clack*.

A steep tunnel lead downward, and the light of his torch evaporated into the gloom. While the polished floors and columns of the upper Mithraeum had been tooled by the hands of men, only the chipped stairs here stood apart from the naturally formed shaft of jagged granite and limestone. He took a deep breath before stepping off.

Down and down he went. The passage wound back and forth haphazardly as though it had been burned into the mountain's bowels by the arcing path of a lightning bolt. The air grew staler with each winding step. Finally the stairs gave way to flat ground and the walls opened up into a maze-like network of chambers and passageways. The floor here was uneven and littered with debris. Crumbling walls separated chambers, and the rusted remains of long dissolved hinges hung from empty doorways. A long-abandoned kitchen stood beside an armory still laden with rotted blades and pitted spearheads. There were bunkrooms and a bath, even a narrow meeting hall. Wulfson knew this place well. Countless hours had been spent exploring these hallowed halls as a boy while he imagined his forefathers surviving down here through that first horrid winter a millennia and a half before.

Only one door still stood intact. It shone a glossy black from the countless applications of oil over the centuries. It was the central point of the subterranean complex, all other rooms expanding outward from it. This was the heart of the mountain, and it called to him now.

He placed a hand on the latch. The electricity in the air made his neck tingle, and a funny taste teased at his tongue — bitter iron and sweet honeysuckle.

A gentle thrumming vibrated over his flesh, drawing goosebumps, as if some thunderous frequency was resonating around him in the silence.

"*I shouldn't...*" he muttered to himself. Despite his own words, he lifted the latch. The door eased open. Inside, the tall ceiling swooped down in a dome of shimmering obsidian. It glistened in the torchlight, a kaleidoscope of oranges and yellows trapped in the black volcanic glass. In the chamber's center stood a statue — a great man-like figure chiseled from some inky stone that had no name. Its feet were planted securely together, and it wielded a rod and a dagger in its hands. A thin viper coiled from its feet up its legs and around its body until passing between the two arcing wings that sprouted from its back. Wulfson's eyes locked onto the leonine face — thick lips curled back in an enraged snarl, and the narrow cat eyes reflected the torch's flames...

Wulfson took in a shuddering breath. He didn't know how much time had passed, but he realized that his mouth had grown dry. The eyes followed him as he stepped forward, his heart pounding against his ribs. "*I always thought it would be me,*" he whispered. "*I thought it would be an honor, a privilege even. One that I could earn. That sort of power... I yearned for it. But not anymore. No. Now, I understand the truth. You are a curse. You have always been a curse.*"

In the darkness beyond the statue something moved. Wulfson stepped back, grasping for the rifle on his shoulder as a hunched figure materialized into view.

"*Grandfather...*" Wulfson gasped, averting his eyes as a child might when caught in some shameful act.

The old man's only response came in the form of a rasping cough. He was slight, barely more than a shadow cut before the glimmering obsidian. Still, Wulfson cowered.

"*We're so close,*" Wulfson whispered.

The black silhouette of the old man's head tilted like that of a curious dog. His slitted eyes were yellow in the torchlight.

Wulfson hesitated. "*Forgive my surprise, father of fathers. I...*" He found himself lost for words. "*I promise that it will be over soon. We have a new vessel. One marked by Mithras himself. He will do well by them. He will keep it contained, as you have these many years.*"

Without a noise, the old man slunk back into the shadows.

Wulfson backed slowly out of the room, easing the door shut behind him. His whole life he'd never seen the old man leave his den in the village. The fact that he had ventured here, now, to the place of his ascension, meant that the time was indeed drawing near.

Banishing the chill from his bones, Wulfson forged ahead. He had come here for a purpose.

The dungeon stood on the far side of the complex. There were a series of bricked-off cells along one wall, each sporting a stout iron gate. He did not bother to disguise the noise of his arrival as he strode by the first. Its gate was open, as was the second. Only the third was sealed and bound in chain. Wulfson bracketed the torch and awkwardly unslung the rifle with one arm before stepping in front of the cell.

Nothing moved in the dark.

Wulfson felt a nervous twinge. He eased closer, searching the shadows for his quarry, but he could not see Klaus. By all rights, he was alone.

"*No...*"

Something slammed into him from behind. He was launched to the ground, and the rifle clattered away across the stone floor. Meaty hands were on him before he could fight back, grasping at his face as a heavy knee dug between his shoulder blades.

"*No!*" Wulfson managed as the grip tightened over his jaw and the back of his skull. It was too late.

With a horrendous crunch, his head torqued out of place.

A voice slithered from the darkness above. "*Hello, Herr Wulfson.*"

Despite the violence of the attack, there was no pain. He couldn't move, and there was a sudden, horrible numbness. His breath came short, and the world phased in and out with the beat of his heart as he was flipped onto his back. A rough hand grasped his face and angled it upward. Klaus stood over him, his bald head gleaming with sweat in the torchlight.

"*You're still alive?*" Klaus gave a look of shock which was quickly replaced by a crooked grin. "*Splendid. Are you still in there, Herr Wulfson? Can you hear me?*"

He jabbed a sharp toe into Wulfson's ribs. There was no sensation at all.

"*Can't speak, can you?*" Klaus taunted. "*No? Can you even fill your lungs? It's always different, you know, a broken neck. I've seen plenty of men in your condition. Sometimes the branch breaks when you hang them. Doesn't finish them, not entirely. They tend to just lie there in the muck, alive, but not really. Is that what you are now? Alive, but not really? Just an uppity soul trapped in a useless bag of meat?*"

What was left of Wulfson's mind began to withdraw. The cave was growing dark now, as if the flame of his own candle was slowly flickering away in a gentle breeze.

"*No, no, no! Don't go yet! You always loved to talk so much... Well, it is time for you to listen, you fuck.*" Klaus squatted close and searched the Major's body.

THE SARVÀN

He found the cigarette case and lit one, making sure to flick the ash over Wulfson's face. When he finally reached the Major's inner pockets, he let out a barking laugh. "*I'm so glad you kept this.*" He pulled the grenade free and looked it over. "*You know, I had nothing but time to think down here. Time to remember. Time to contemplate. That's when something occurred to me: how did you see this godforsaken village? That day in the storm, we couldn't see ten meters in front of us. Yet you somehow saw this place from a league away...*" He tucked the grenade into his belt and pressed the rifle's barrel into Wulfson's ribs as his voice darkened. "*You knew it was here, didn't you? You brought us here to this place on purpose. Ya... When I realized that, another question formed: why? Why would you bring us here? I think I know the answer now, but I want to be sure. This is your home, isn't it?*"

Wulfson felt a deep dread take hold. By Klaus's evil snicker, he knew it must have been evident in his eyes.

"*Of course. Of course it fucking is.*" Klaus plucked the torch from the floor and stepped back. "*For a long time I have imagined all the ways I would kill you. At first, I figured a bullet would have done well enough, or perhaps a rope. Then when you cast me down here, I reveled in the thought of flaying you alive. But now it would seem that fate has given me an even more delicious opportunity.*" He turned and strode away, the torchlight fading with his voice as he called back over his shoulder. "*I hope you live long enough to imagine all the horrible things I will do to those you love, dear Major. Though even your imagination may not do the truth justice. If you survive long enough, you might just be able to hear it.*"

No. Wulfson tried to scream the word, but his lips barely quivered.

46

THE HOUSE that Lucia called her own was the largest in the village. It was two stories of mortared stone reinforced by thick timber braces. She pressed a finger to her lips as she led Blackwood through the door and nodded toward the other end of the parlor. A little girl was curled atop the sofa there, just beside the fire. Her leg was bound in a thick bandage, and even in sleep, her face bore a pained grimace. Blackwood recognized her — she was one of the children from the Christmas play.

"*My cousin*," Lucia whispered. "*Those bastards shot her and her mother from the tower. She was lucky. Her mother was not.*"

Lucia took his coat and hung it alongside the great bearskin coat by the door as he clicked off his electric torch — one of the few worthwhile items he'd pilfered from the guards — and secured it back on his belt. He took in the details of her home as she shed her snow-caked boots. The place was tidy and spartan, well taken care of despite its antiquated ambiance. Tattered tapestries of animals and what appeared to be religious scenes hung from the walls, and books filled every shelf and table.

The girl on the sofa whimpered in her sleep. The delicate sound hurt his soul. War was one thing; men died killing men. It was fair in its own way, and not something he shied away from. But this wasn't war. Looking at this poor child trapped between the pain of her wound and the agony of loss, he felt his hatred for the guards rekindled. She didn't deserve this. None of them did.

Not for the first time, he wished he could go back to that day in the ravine. Knowing what he did now, he would never have stopped McCulloch from charging. He would have let the old man bring death to them all rather than allow their misery to accompany them here.

Lucia tenderly laid a blanket over the girl before motioning for Blackwood to follow her up the stairs. He obliged, moving quietly in an effort to not wake the child.

The second story landing stretched out into a long hallway. The air was heavy with the scent of upturned earth and old straw, and a faint buzzing reverberated all around. A honeybee crawled lazily from a gap in the clapboards, and it was clear that the source of the buzzing came from their nests within the walls. The first three doors in the hallway stood open. At the end, the fourth was shut. Three large keyholes adorned the outside.

Lucia noticed his focus on the closed door. "*That is my grandfather's room.*"

"The one who's sick?"

"*Yes. Perhaps someday you will meet him. But not yet.*"

She took his hand and pulled him into her bedroom. More overstuffed bookshelves lined the walls and a lantern burned bright from a desk.

She sat on the bed and patted the spot beside her. He hesitated. Though she wasn't smiling, the energy about her was pleasant. Her eyes were narrow as they drifted over him, and he could sense her hunger.

"*Take your clothes off.*" Her words came more as a tease than a command.

"Why?"

She smirked. "*Are you that obtuse?*"

He fought against the impulse to comply. There were things that needed to be said. A glaring issue that needed to be ironed out before. He needed to know.

"*Fine.*" She darted to her feet and crossed to stand before him in one fluid motion. Her fingers worked deftly down the buttons of his shirt. When he tried to say something, she abandoned her work to pull his face down and silence him with her lips.

He gave in, grasping her by the backside and lifting her to straddle him as she yanked away his shirt. Without grace he threw her down on the bed and pressed his body against hers. She moaned in his ear, the noise sending a shiver of pleasure down his spine.

"No…" He managed to tear his lips from her neck. "*No, not yet.*"

"*Get back here.*" She grasped at him as he pulled away and stumbled back. They both panted as she stared at him, ravenous.

"I need to know something."

"*No, you don't.*" She crawled toward him across the bed, her breasts exposed from where he'd torn the buttons from her blouse.

He stopped her with an outstretched hand. "*I do. I…*" He caught his breath. "I need to know… I need to know what happened to the men here…"

She looked cross. "*What do you mean? I told you that—*"

"Specifically. In the war."

"*Edward, this not the time—*"

"You have to humor me."

She sat back, crossing her legs as the mood shifted. *"Do you know anything about women, Herr Blackwood? This is not how a man typically acts when he is—"*

"You said they died in Lorraine, ya?"

Her eye twitched. *"Ya..."*

"Tell me what happened to them."

She took a moment to collect herself, pulling her blouse together and combing a hand through her hair. *"Fine, Edward. Fine. I suppose..."* She gave a frustrated grunt. *"Fine."*

"Thank you."

From the bedstand she plucked a framed photograph and looked down on it as she spoke. *"When the army came the second time, my father was among those they took. He was our leader, as my family has been for as long as this place has existed. He was a good man — fair, just, clever, and kind. But he was not a warrior. Not like my brother. When my father left, he asked me to stand in his stead until he returned.*

"I never spoke to him again after that. The only word I received as to what happened came in an official notice from the army. They said that our men and boys had been formed into a platoon and placed in a trench along the Front. At some point in the night, the enemy struck, slaughtering those on watch and gunning down the rest in their bunker with one of their own weapons. An act of cowardice and espionage, they called it, and they assured us vengeance would be paid."

The blood drained from Blackwood's face.

"I don't want to speak of this anymore," she said abruptly. When she made to return the photo, Blackwood stopped her. He took the gilded frame in hand, forcing himself to look upon it. A face looked back at him in warm sepia tone. The man stood proudly before the camera. Over his shoulders hung the bearskin coat Blackwood had seen so many times now. His features were sharp and clean cut, and a single silver streak ran through his hair. Blackwood recognized him from a thousand nightmares — only here he was not gasping in horror as the blood of his people cascaded out beneath him.

"Hilde's carrot stew..." he breathed.

"What?"

"Hilde. Her carrot stew..."

"What about it?"

"She had a man — a boy who loved her."

Lucia's eyes narrowed, this time in suspicion. *"Yes. Gustav."*

The photograph fell from Blackwood's trembling fingers. It landed softly on the mattress as Blackwood retreated. *"I have to leave."*

"*No!*" Lucia was on her feet again, just as deftly as before. She made to reach for him, but he pulled away.

"*Lucia, stop…*"

"*No.*" She sounded desperate.

"*Stop!*" he shouted.

She jolted at his volume, falling back and staring in bewilderment. "*What is it?*"

He couldn't look at her. Her face was too kind, too full of compassion and reverence. He knew that if he told her the truth, he would never see her look at him like that again.

Good, the nasty voice in the back of his mind said. *You don't deserve it.*

"*Edward, tell me what is wrong.*"

"It was me."

"*What was you?*"

"Gustav." He sucked in a deep breath. "*I put a knife in his belly. He died in pain.*"

"*What?*" The word escaped weakly from her lips. She shook her head in disbelief. "*What are you saying?*"

"They were talking about Hilde when I did it. I killed the man with him as well, and two more down the line. It was an old…" He stopped, forcing himself to say the word. "*That man in the photograph, your father… he caught me. They were in a bunker behind the machinegun nest. I turned the gun on them.*" He held up his left hand, showing the glossy scars that the hot barrel had left. "*I shot them in their bunks, on the floor, as they scrambled to escape. I didn't stop until the gun ran dry.*"

"You're lying," she said quietly, staring through him with red eyes. "*You're lying because you don't want to stay.*"

"I wish more than anything that you were right. I don't know what kind of cruel twist of fate brought me here, Lucia — brought me to you. But you needed to know. You needed to know."

"You're a monster…" Her words came as a whisper, but they crashed over him like a scream.

"*I…*" he began. But there was nothing left to say.

As if an echo of his past sins, a gunshot shattered the night.

At first he thought it was his imagination. That the anguish of the moment had awakened some deep sickness in his mind. That the shellshock had finally come to claim him. Then another shot rang out. Lucia heard it too, her eyes shifting to the window.

Over the rooftops an orange glow pulsated through the falling snow. Another gunshot boomed, followed by a scream.

Any thoughts of his confession to Lucia were gone by the time Blackwood reached the stairs. He was still shirtless, and more gunplay came as he reached the front door. The cold wind blasted him as he threw it open. He grabbed the closest garment to him, the bearskin coat, and threw it over his shoulders as he charged out into the street. The fresh snow had already grown past his ankles as he sprinted toward the commotion. A sixth gunshot came, then a seventh, each growing closer as he crossed through the plaza. His ears caught the thunder of hooves as he rounded a corner and a shadow tore past. Before he could level his pistol, the rider fired, sending him diving to ground.

Hateful laughter pealed above the stomping hooves. It was a sound that Blackwood would have recognized anywhere.

"I'll be back! And I'll be bringing hell with me!" Klaus's voice echoed through the plaza as he barreled into the darkness. Blackwood fired after him until the pistol clicked empty. He reloaded, slamming the spare magazine home, and waited, panting, praying for the bastard to turn back. But the only sounds audible over the growing storm were the panicked calls of the villagers. Klaus was gone, disappeared into the haze of the tempest.

The barn was already pouring flames by the time Blackwood reached it. A torrent of smoke billowed from the open doors, and the old timbers groaned. A scattering of villagers fought desperately to quell the raging inferno, but it was too far gone, and their efforts were in vain.

He grabbed one of the passing women roughly by the arm. *"Where are the horses?"*

She jabbed a finger toward the barn before yanking herself free.

"Goddammit!" he shouted, edging closer to the flames. Inside, the horrible screech of livestock burning alive cut through the roar of the fire. With a heaving breath, he plunged into the smoke.

The air was non-existent. Smoke seared his eyes and tears blinded him. Dry hay crackled in the loft above, and the beams of the stalls stood as pillars of flame. He stumbled forward blindly, batting the hot doors for their latches. One by one he managed to wrestle them open until his lungs ached for relief. Somewhere along the way he must have found the horses' stall, as a panicked whinny accompanied an impact that knocked the last of his breath away and sent him sprawling. He gasped at the smoke as his empty lungs spasmed. It scorched his throat like chlorine gas.

The fire surrounded him now. Its deafening intensity destroyed any semblance of direction he had. He was trapped, choking and wheezing as spittle spilled from his lips and tears poured down his cheeks.

A hand seized hold of his arm. It hauled at him, dragging him through the showering embers as he scrambled on his knees to keep up. When he was free of the smoke and heat, he hunched on all fours in the snow, gasping in the frozen air and wiping the soot from his eyes.

"*What were you thinking?*" Sovilo stood over him, eyes bloodshot and wrought with concern.

"*The horses,*" Blackwood managed to cough out. "*Where are they?*"

Sovilo glanced over his shoulder. Blackwood followed his gaze to where a group of women struggled to calm the frightened beasts. The mule was bucking and wild, but the old nag stood calmly, pawing at the snow and tossing her head. Blackwood found his feet and pushed past Sovilo.

"*Stop!*" Sovilo tried to grab him. "*You cannot go!*"

Blackwood shrugged him off. Only Klaus's words rang in his ears — *I'll be back! And I'll be bringing hell with me!*

The son of a bitch wasn't just escaping. He was headed back to Rothenspring. There he would tell a story, and they would believe him. When he returned, it would be with an army. Nobody would survive.

He was out for vengeance, and he had to be stopped. No matter what.

The nag snorted as Blackwood hauled himself atop her. She was slick with sweat. He was bareback, and he thanked the heavens that she did not try to buck him off. "Come on," he urged, grabbing hold of her mane and digging in his heels. She complied, spinning in a tight circle and galloping up the street in Klaus's wake.

Enzo was standing outside the tavern when he passed. The boy had no idea what was going on, as was apparent from his confounded state. "*Che diavolo sta succedendo?*"

Blackwood yanked on the nag's mane, and she skidded to a halt. "Give me the rifle!" he commanded.

For once, Enzo understood. He passed the weapon up into Blackwood's waiting hand.

"*No, non puoi andartene!*" Enzo tried desperately, then in broken English, "No go!"

"It's not a fuckin' choice, kid," Blackwood growled.

He kicked the nag into a canter, riding off into the night without a backward glance.

PART SIX

An excerpt from *The Lost Roots of the Monotheism* by J. Wyatt, associate professor of history, University of Western New England.

However, unlike many monotheistic religions, it would appear that Mithras was not believed to be the sole creator of the universe. According to modern analysis of the hundreds of hidden Mithraeums discovered across the former Roman Empire, we now have some generalized insight into the Mithraic creation myth, or rather its lack of a creation myth, which may shed further light onto the cult's roots.

According to the Mithraic doctrine, Mithras burst forth from a rock into a world (or universe) already inhabited by the beasts displayed in the *tauroctony* (i.e. the sacred bull, snake, canine, and scorpion). The sun and the moon were already in existence and, presumably, the earth as well. Even if one were to maintain the assumption that the beasts are in fact astrological representations of the heavens, the fact that the physical universe already existed means that Mithras was not seen as the creator of all matter, but rather just the molder of life as it has come to be.

This idea begets the question: if Mithras was not the creator of the universe, who was? What other spiritual forces exist within this mythos? If Mithras only created a portion, then who else had a hand in weaving the whole?

While no answer is abundantly clear, one clue we have comes in the form of the *leontocephaline* (lion-headed) figurines that appear in a number of Mithraeums. These figures remain shrouded in mystery and appear to play no part in the rituals as we understand them. The figure itself is often depicted as a naked, winged, lion-headed man with a snake wrapped around his body. No clear markers survive to aid in our identification of who or what the statues or reliefs are meant to depict, however a single broken nameplate found near a statue in a Mithraeum discovered in Britain suggests the name associated with this entity is *Arimanius* — a latinized counterpart of the Persian god *Ahriman*, an evil spirit in Zoroastrianism. The presence of such a figure in Mithraism is doubly interesting when considering the theory that Mithraism may predate even the earliest of its monotheistic counterparts by a millennium, including Zoroastrianism. If true, these mysterious lion-headed figures may in fact be representative of the earliest known human depiction of the villain in the duality of good and evil, which later developed into *Ahriman*, the dark one. Or, as modern Christians have come to know it, *Satan*.

FRANCE, 1916

Three miles behind the Front, the streets of a quant French town bustled in the night. An entire company of soldiers had descended upon the town to take their leave. Drunken men stumbled between taverns and brothels, shouting and singing as they drowned their misery in the fleeting dream of normalcy. Blackwood sat alone outside an alehouse, sipping a whiskey and watching them filter by.

A gentle hand laid on his shoulder. "*Bonjour beau gosse. Vous êtes ici pour vous amuser?*"

He glanced up to the woman who had slipped beside him. She wore a blouse so thin he could see through it. The smile plastered over her face was as fake as the warmth in her tone. Beneath it, she had the same burnt-out look as the soldiers she made her money pleasuring.

"*Non,*" he muttered. Her smile, unflinching, turned to the next man before the syllable had finished leaving his lips.

His drink finished, Blackwood took to wandering the dark streets. He wasn't looking for anything in particular — the wages in his pocket would no doubt remain unspent, as they had every leave from the front lines he'd been forced to take. Upon his return to the Front, he would likely continue his tradition of bestowing the wad of bills onto some lucky young man who had a family back home.

Down an alley and across from an abandoned apothecary, a sign caught his eye. Carved into it in blazed red letters read "C*hiromancie,*" and below it, scratched in English as if an afterthought, "Palm Readings."

The windows were dark, shrouded by fabric, and it was his curiosity alone that drove him inside. The room was warm and smelled of sweet perfume and earthy incense. Ornate drapery billowed from the walls and ceiling, and in the room's center stood a short round table with a glistening glass ball.

There was a shuffle of movement beyond a beaded door to the back, then, "*Allo?*"

"Hello," he answered.

A woman slipped through the beads. She was slight with olive skin that appeared to glow against the red of the walls — a Romani, best he could tell from the style of her dress and her large, hazel eyes. She looked him up and down. "*Vous êtes ici pour chiromancie?*"

"You speak English?"

She smiled, the thin-lipped grin of a predator that knew it had cornered its prey. "I do. Come, sit."

He obeyed, sitting across from her and placing a franc on the table. She took his hand in hers. Her fingers were thin and fragile, and she traced gentle lines across his palm.

"Yours is not an easy fortune to read," she began. "Tell me, what is it you seek in this life?"

"You tell me."

"I read fortunes, not desires, soldier. Tell me what you seek, and perhaps I can tell you if you will find it."

"I don't seek anything."

She clicked her tongue. "*Tsk.* Come now, every man seeks something. Why else would you come into my shop?"

He shrugged. "Impulse."

She chuckled. "Impulse, hm? Yes… You are a man of impulse, but also of matching restraint."

"You read that in my hand?"

"No." Her finger tickled his palm. "I say that because you have found your way here rather than one of the whorehouses down the street."

The edge of his lip inadvertently raised into a rare half smile.

"Your palm is… interesting," she went on. "I have never seen one quite like it. It reads of great power and sadness. Violence unending…"

"You could say that about any one of the poor saps that come walking in here."

"I could, but I don't."

"What else does it say?"

"A great many things. Things I don't think I should say aloud…"

He pulled away and stood with a disinterested grunt. "This isn't worth the franc."

"Stop." She gave the curt command as she rose. She crossed to stand before him in languid movements. When she drew close, her hand brushed down his chest and straight to the fold of bills hidden in his pocket. She pulled them free. "You have no desire to keep these, do you?"

"You think I'll just let you take them?"

"No." Using the bills, she brushed the strap of her dress low over her shoulder.

He didn't resist when she took his hand once more and led him through the hanging beads. The back room was cramped and ornate. Trinkets and skulls of small animals covered most surfaces other than the bed and a wide wash basin. He didn't react as she pressed against him and began to kiss his neck and strip away his shirt. Her lips migrated up to his as her fingers unclasped his belt. When he did not return her passion, she paused with a quiet snicker.

He flinched as she bit into his lip. A hard smack landed against his cheek without warning. He caught her wrist as she followed up with a second strike and wrestled to hold her at bay. She was strong and lithe, and his resistance was weak. Soon her teeth had sunk into his lip once again. The pain awakened a fire deep inside, and in a single violent motion he ripped her dress down the back. Her cry of protest transformed into a gasp as he shoved himself inside of her. Pinning her against the wall, he went at her like a buck in rut. She managed to seize a handful of his hair and wrenched him away. Her feet slapped the floor as she hauled him to the bed and dragged him down atop her, her nails clawing bloody tracks across his back.

Afterward she laid on the bed while he gathered his scattered garments.

"You should know that is not a service I offer to many."

He grunted.

"...and you don't have to worry," she continued, lighting a cigarette. "I am barren."

"Good."

Her face soured only a bit. "Perhaps for you. Still, that was pleasant. You should come back on your next leave."

"I doubt I'll be back."

Her eyebrow raised. "Not worth the money?"

"Not what I meant."

"What then? You think you will die?"

He didn't answer, tightening his belt and pulling on his shirt.

Her eyes narrowed. "You're one of *them*, aren't you?"

"One of who?"

"A raider. One of the quiet ones who slips through the night to murder the Germans as they sleep."

"I don't kill sleeping men." He pulled on his boots.

"Mm... You'll die out there, you know."

"You see that in my palm?"

"No," she admitted. "But your type always does."

"What type is that?"

"A hound."

It was his turn to raise an eyebrow. "A hound?"

"'Cry havoc and let slip the hounds of war'."

"It's dog."

"What?"

"'Let slip the dogs of war'."

"He is well-read." She grinned.

"A well-read hound and a mystic whore. A bedtime story for your children." He remembered her words from only a moment before. "Or not."

The teasing glint faded from her eyes. "Go home, dog of war. Be done with this place. You have been here too long, you have dead eyes."

He pushed through the beads. Behind him, she stood in a hurry.

"Do you want to know what I really saw in your palm?" she called out as he reached the front door.

"No," he muttered, stepping out into the cool of the night.

47

ENZO'S HEEL bounced against the floorboards. He was on the edge of his chair, his fingers drumming on his thigh and unfocused eyes lost in the fire. It had been hours since Blackwood left. Now, as midnight approached, he knew that the American's odds of survival in the ever-worsening storm were rapidly plummeting.

Though his eyes itched with sleep, he refused to give in to the urge. Dubois was asleep in his room, wounded and doped up on drugs. After all that had happened, Enzo was scared and confused, but the one thing he knew he needed to do was keep his guard up. Anything could happen, as proven by Klaus's escape. Now was not the time to relax.

The tavern below was silent. The whole place still stank of smoke. Or maybe it was just his clothes and hair, or even his soot-stained skin. He'd spent much of the first half of the night rushing to and fro in the cold, battling the flames of the barn by hurling heaps of snow. Now all that remained of the barn was a burnt-out carcass of smoldering beams and charred meat. They'd been lucky that the fire had not spread to either the houses or the second barn. Still, they'd lost a good portion of their livestock, and two more villagers to Klaus's rifle.

"*Oh, Mother Mary, please see us through this,*" Enzo whispered to himself.

The door below opened and soft feet padded up the stairs. He waited, a new rifle resting at his side, until Hilde emerged from the stairwell. She glanced to the gun before meeting his eyes. Like everyone else in the village at this point, she appeared to be broken and running on fumes. Her brow sagged low, and the shadows exacerbated the yellowing bruise under her eye.

He hadn't had the chance to ask her about her injury. She'd avoided him like the plague since the night they'd spent together. In his inexperienced mind, he'd first taken this as a slight to his performance. But when he'd seen the bruise, he realized that her avoidance likely stemmed from something well beyond his control. Either way, he hated the fact that someone had hurt her.

"*Enzo,*" she said. "*Ich muss dir etwas zeigen.*"

He had no idea what her words meant, but they were like a song to his tired ears. He crossed to her and ever so gently brushed his hand against her cheek. It was rough with the salt of dried tears.

"*Are you alright, beautiful?*" he asked softly in Italian.

She fell into him, and he held her as she began to sob. His own vision began to blur with tears.

"*It will be okay,*" he whispered into her hair.

She withdrew and pulled him toward the stairs.

"*I can't leave.*" He motioned toward the room where Dubois groaned in his sleep.

"*Vertrau mir.*" She tugged his hand.

While he didn't understand her words, her tone was one of reassurance.

Why not? he thought. Klaus was gone, there was no one out there left to hurt them, and Dubois was peacefully sleeping and healing. He repeated the thought over and over in his mind until he was convinced. If there was one place in the world that he desired to be in that moment, it was in her little house, wrapped in the warmth of her arms. The very idea of it soothed his soul.

Enzo didn't argue further. He slung the rifle and followed her down the stairs and out into the cold.

48

BLACKWOOD DROVE the nag forward through the storm. The hours had dragged on since he'd ridden out of the village, and the weather had only worsened. He pulled the bear skull cowl low and slivered his eyes against the raging wind as it whipped stinging ice against his cheeks. The jagged molars of the beast's skull dug into his scalp and its yellowed fangs hung before his face. The night was dark, and his only light came from the dying beam of the electric torch. It barely illuminated the tracks immediately before him in a grainy yellow hue.

Klaus had at least had the sense to ride in conjunction with the lowest levels of the snow drifts along the mountain slope. Even so, every few yards the nag would stumble and sink in deep. Hot steam jetted from her nostrils as she waded slowly onward.

"Come on, girl," Blackwood urged. They hadn't made it far, but she was already exhausted. The horse Klaus had stolen, the ebony Oldenburger, was young and spry. Blackwood's only hope of keeping pace lay in the fact that he was traveling in the trough Klaus had already cut in the building snow. Still, he needed to go faster. The nag whinnied and thrashed her head in protest as he goaded her on. "You can do it, girl. Come on now."

Time dragged on as the elements beat down on them. Ahead, a spectral shadow materialized — a dark split in the wall of grey. Blackwood recognized the ravine they'd taken shelter in a week before. Somehow it felt like it had been so much longer ago — as if he'd stumbled across some ancient relic left over from a past life. Only now, instead of the promise of safety, it exuded the aura of danger. If Klaus suspected he had a pursuer, this would be the ideal place to launch an ambush. Despite the fact that the bastard would have the upper hand, Blackwood realized that this would be the best-case scenario — better to be done with it here and now than to risk losing his trail to the storm.

To Blackwood's chagrin, Klaus was not waiting in the ravine. According to his tracks, he hadn't even paused to take shelter from the wind. The nag plodded through the thin gap in the stones, and they emerged on the other side to find that the trail led down the slope toward the vast alpine forest below.

He pulled to a halt and stared out into the darkness. The snow was coming thicker by the minute and the fierceness of the wind grew with it. What was left of Klaus's trail was little more than scant divots in the pale sheet of snow. There was no doubt that at this rate they would disappear faster than Blackwood could follow them. Without a trail, riding down the German would be impossible.

He cursed. Quietly at first, then louder until the screams burned ragged in his throat. The howl of the wind ate his words as it whipped over the canyon's mouth. Under him, the nag pawed restlessly at the snow. She was in bad shape. To take her any farther would likely be a death sentence — for her as well as for him. It was becoming increasingly apparent that finding his quarry would take an act of god.

He's probably already dead, the voice in the back of his mind whispered.

The voice was right. Klaus couldn't be faring any better than he was. Their initial trek had taken several days on foot. A horse might be able to make it in half that time, but not in a storm like this. The odds were that the snow would swallow Klaus whole somewhere along the way.

But if Klaus did make it... If he did somehow manage to get through the forest and over the mountains, then they were all damned. Even if the prisoners were to escape to Switzerland, the villagers stood no hope of survival if the German army were to come seeking their vengeance. And for what sin would they be punished? For saving some sorry bastards who should never have been saved?

There were two paths ahead. Forward to his own demise. Or backward to a warm bed and a few friends and the agony of knowing that they might be swarmed and slaughtered at any given moment. It wasn't really a choice at all. If there was any redemption to be had, it lay ahead, not behind.

Over the wind came the sharp cackle of a raven. A shadow swooped through the sky overhead. He watched it glide into the storm to the east, toward the forest. Steeling himself, he kicked the horse forward.

49

PAIN WASN'T the only thing that kept Dubois from finding sleep. The last of the laudanum had worn off, and the wound on his side throbbed worse than ever. Still, his thoughts remained on Blackwood. Earlier that night he had managed to hobble to the windows at the sounds of gunfire and screams and had watched as the American rode off into the storm. Recalling vividly the brutal desperation of their initial journey, he couldn't help but envision Blackwood back out there now in the thick of another storm. The imaginings drew a shiver. He bent his head and prayed for the cowboy's safe return.

A gentle knock drew his attention to the door.

"Enzo?" he called.

The door cracked open, and the light of his bedside candle revealed Lucia.

She entered, shutting the door behind her before taking a chair beside his bed. "*How are you feeling?*"

"*I am alive, so I suppose I cannot complain too much.*" He tried to hide a wince as he struggled to sit upright against the pillows.

"*I brought you more medicine.*" She held out a small bottle.

He pushed her hand away gently. "*No, my dear. Too many things are going wrong. I must keep some bit of sense about me. The pain will keep me sharp.*"

"*That's brave, but not necessary. Please, take it.*"

He shook his head resolutely. "*No. Thank you.*"

Her shoulders sagged, and she did not meet his gaze.

"*You're worried about him, aren't you?*" he asked softly.

"*Ya.*"

"*As am I. But he will return. Men like him, they always survive. It will take far more than a bit of snow and a wicked troll like Klaus to…*" He stopped short, not wanting to utter the words "kill him" aloud.

"*Is he a good man?*"

The question caught Dubois off guard. "*Pshhh…*" He blew out through pursed lips, stalling as he tried to formulate his response. "*He is a fine fellow. As fine as I have met. Sure, a bit gritty, but war will do that to a man.*"

"But is he good?"

"Did he do something wrong?"

She opened her mouth to speak but reconsidered and remained silent.

He could tell from the look on her face that the storm in her head mirrored the one unfolding outside. *"You know, our friend McCulloch — God rest his soul — he wished only for bloodshed and vengeance against the guards. Time and time again, it was Blackwood who quelled the Scot's urges. This whole time he's proven himself to be more concerned with what might happen to you and your people than what might happen to us. Beyond that, I can say very honestly that he's saved me more than once, often to his own detriment. Given me strength when I would otherwise have faltered. So in short, I would say yes. Yes, he is a good man. At least as much as an American can be,"* he finished with a wink.

She gave a sad smile that didn't reach her eyes.

"You care for him?" he asked

"I believe so."

"You wish him to stay here, even after the war, ya?"

"He told you that?"

"Yes. Did he not give you an answer?"

"No."

"He will stay. Trust me. But you must understand that things like this take time. He is like… like a feral dog." Dubois chuckled. *"I mean no offence to the man. Only that like a cur you'd come across on the street, you cannot just expect him to enter your home and behave as a proper pet. You are asking him to change the foundation of his being in order to fit your mold. That takes patience. Sure, he may chew up some furniture or chase your cat, but you must give him time to acclimate, or you risk him rejecting you and running off back into the wilds."*

"You have a funny way with words, Monsieur Dubois."

"And big ears." He wiggled his ears, a talent that had never failed to draw a giggle from his daughters.

It was slight, but for the first time tonight, Lucia's smile looked genuine.

"It is late," he went on. *"Or perhaps early. You should get some sleep."*

"Too much to do," she muttered quietly. *"I came here for a reason. To tell you a story. I wanted to… I wanted you to understand."*

"Understand what?"

"Who we are, and why we must do what we do."

"I imagine your reasons are not much different from anyone else's."

Lucia ignored his comment. Her focus shifted vacantly to the window. *"Do you remember what you asked me in the tower, about why our ancestors stayed here?"*

"*I do.*"

"*I told you I didn't know. That was not the truth. They stayed here for the same reasons we have — a duty. A duty that we remain loyal to even now.*"

"*A duty?*" Dubois leaned forward. The academic curiosity that had once driven him bled through the callus of survivalism that he'd built up over his time in captivity.

"*It was not the barbarians our people were fleeing from. It was their own brethren. We are the remnants of a very ancient faith. The church of Mithras, the monolith of heaven. Lightbringer and Lord of truth. You are a Christian — I have heard you pray. I don't expect you to believe what I am about to tell you, but you must understand that to us it is absolute truth.*"

"*Very well, go on.*" Though he was unsure of why she was telling him this now, he felt a flutter of excitement. Firsthand insight into one of the great lost religions — he could not have asked for anything more.

Lucia didn't speak right away, but when she finally did, her voice was resolute. "*When Mithras first created man, he did so with purpose. A purpose only the most devout are privy to. To ensure we fulfilled our roles in his grand design, Mithras raised up seven disciples. The father, a man most righteous and the keeper of the great secret of life. The light bearer, master of earthly knowledge. The son, whose duty was to carry on the blood of the first creation. The king, the ruler of human domain. The warrior, defender of the just. The bridegroom, the purity of youth incarnate. Lastly, came the messenger, the voice between nations and men.*

"*With our world secure, Mithras moved on through this cosmic realm. He left us here to fulfill our duties to him, his presence reduced only to the whisper of his name. It was not long before man grew neglectful and forgot their true creator. Nations rose and fell in the names of false idols, and within thousands of years, the old ways went dormant.*

"*It was in the time of the Romans that the word of Mithras once again emerged. A leak had sprung in the vat of knowledge, and our secrets spilled out to those unfit to keep them. In short time they spread beyond control. The word of Mithras coursed through the legions like lifeblood. The emperor of Rome, a weak man obsessed with power, saw his soldiers flock to these ancient ways and realized the threat of our truth. He knew that in the growing fervor, men he considered his lessers could have him trampled with as little as a whisper. As a result he grew devious and turned to the Christians for help. They gave him their book in exchange for his fealty, and together they launched a campaign of blood and conversion.*"

"*You speak of Emperor Constantine?*" Dubois cut in.

"*Yes.*"

Dubois sucked his teeth. "*To my knowledge, he was not one to massacre people for their faith.*"

"*I'm sure you've read that in your books, ya? I ask, who wrote those books?*"

Dubois yielded with a shrug.

"*There are dark places in the world. Places where man was never meant to tread. Places where Mithras hid things that were never meant to be discovered. When those with weak will gave up names in exchange for coin and comfort, the true believers were found. Conversion was forced at the edge of a sword, and the devout fell in droves, whether to spears in their chests or daggers in their backs. Few of the old blood, the true believers, managed to escape the persecution in Rome — less than two score. They were pursued relentlessly. With nowhere else to go, nowhere to hide, and no means of escape, they sought out one of those dark places Mithras had hidden beneath the earth. A place that held a power so horrible that it might just save them.*"

Dubois's thoughts went to the inexplicable cavern in the mountainside. "*You mean this place?*"

"Yes."

"You speak of your home as if it was cursed."

Her eye twitched. "*A cohort of soldiers managed to follow them here. The Mithraic retreated deep into the cave, searching for something ancient and terrible. Five hundred Roman soldiers followed in their wake, frothing at the mouth to slaughter those who were once their brothers.*" She paused.

"*And?*" Dubois demanded eagerly.

"*…And they were all killed.*"

"*No, impossible. How would you be here now to tell me the story if all of your ancestors were killed like this?*"

"*I wasn't speaking of my ancestors.*"

"*The cohort of Roman soldiers then? Heh, killed by less than forty men? Quite an unbelievable feat. The stuff of legends, I dare say.*"

"*It wasn't the men that killed them. Not entirely.*"

He cocked his head, sure he had misheard.

"*It was the Sarvàn.*"

The word sounded familiar. It took Dubois a moment to place it. "*The beast from the children's play…*"

"*Yes. Only it is not a beast. Not… not truly. What they unleashed from deep in that mountain has no form of its own. It is a fragment of something that lived in the darkness long before even Mithras himself came to be, a force of nature with no consciousness, no thoughts, just hunger. They used sacred words and bastardized rituals of old to unleash this wickedness. A wickedness that Mithras himself had entombed in this mountain.*" At this, she paused again and took a shuddering breath. "*They felt they had no other choice. They were fools. The spirit melded with their leader, empowering him beyond his mortal state. He rose with fury; unstoppable, terrifying, and monstrous. He tore through the Romans with bare hands, ripping them limb from limb and scattering their entrails down the mountainside.*

"*When it was over, what was taken from beneath the mountain could not be returned. They didn't understand what they had trapped in that man's body. A spirit like that could never be let free. To do so would be our undoing. It would be to bring a plague upon the world unlike anything we've ever known. Their only saving grace was the strength of their leader. He managed to contain it. To control it. To force it to bend to his will. Because of this, our forefathers came to view this abomination as a gift. An act of salvation. A great warrior empowered by Mithras to protect his most devout. But now we know the truth: what they did was cursed and a burden left for their descendants to forever bear.*"

Dubois struggled to put together the pieces of her tale as she finished speaking. "*So this is the duty you spoke of. Some sort of loyalty to this Sarvàn figure?*"

"*Yes.*"

"*Almost Christ-like, isn't he?*" Dubois mused. He shot a quick glance upward before doubling back on his blasphemy. "*I of course only mean that a man sacrificing himself for his people is… You know what I mean. What happened to him?*"

"*It took many, many years, but like all things, he grew old and weak. The darkness inside ate at his soul and malformed his body. He lost solace in the company of his people, and in time took to the wilds, preferring the company of beasts over that of men. As the centuries passed, he disappeared from memory and morphed into legend.*"

"*So he is no more?*"

She didn't answer, her focus instead returning to the bottle in her hands. "*You should take more medicine.*"

Dubois settled back against the pillows. "*The wild man, a fascinating story. You know, I have heard many similar tales in my life. The English, they have their Woodwose, and we French have our 'homme sauvage.' I am most assuredly no expert, but there are some interesting things that—*" Dubois cut himself off, realizing that she was paying no attention to his rambling. "*Do you and your people believe it is still alive? I mean, in your tradition, is it believed that the creature — or man or whatever he is — that it is still out there in the forest?*"

Her next words were barely a whisper. "*He's not in the forest anymore.*"

"*What was that?*"

She drew in a trembling breath, and when she finally looked up at him, tears stained her porcelain cheeks. "*You're a kind man. A good man. I wanted you to know that we didn't have a choice. That all of this had to happen as it did.*"

The deep sorrow in her voice made the hair on the back of his neck stand on end, and the warm sense of safety he'd been basking in suddenly dissolved. He looked squarely at her, his face dropping and his words coming slow. "*Your story… It's not finished yet, is it? Tell me what happens next.*"

Dubois had to strain to hear her next words. "*The Sarvàn grew so weak that the spirit threatened to escape him.*"

A lump had begun to build in Dubois's throat. He choked it down, willing his mounting nerves not to constrain his voice. "*If this leader of yours who contained this spirit within him was the Sarvàn, then what was the spirit itself called?*"

She didn't answer.

"*Lucia, what was it called?*"

"*Arimanius.*"

A chill ran down his spine. "*I know that name. Why do I know that name?*"

"*Because you are a learned man. He is the one the Jews took their story from, and you Christians after.*"

"*What story?*"

"*You know what story.*"

"*Say it.*"

"*They called him the opposer. The adversary. Belial. The beast.*"

"*You cannot mean…*"

He tears came quicker now. "*He cannot be released from his mortal bonds. We needed a new host. Someone strong enough to contain him. We… we needed others as well. Men… for the seven rites to complete the transfer.*"

"*What?*" Dubois sat fully erect now, his heart thumping against his ribs. "*What are you talking about? What have you done, Lucia? Answer me!*"

She sat still, lips pursed and eyes glued to the floor. In the sudden silence, the soft scuffle of feet came from the sitting room. Shadows moved in the light that spilled beneath the door.

"*For so long we thought that Mithras had abandoned us for the sins of our forefathers, left us to contain this evil on our own as a form of punishment. We suffered sickness and blight. When the army came and took our men, we imagined it was over — that we would fade away along with the Sarvàn, and that when he died all would be lost — for everyone, not just us. But Mithras has not abandoned us.*"

He guided my brother's hand to deliver us our saviors. The messenger. The virgin. The warrior. And you, the lion."* Her eyes dropped to where his tattoo peeked out from beneath the bandage. *"The blood of kings runs in your veins. Mithras chose you, and for that you should be profoundly proud,"* Lucia whispered.

"I don't understand." Dubois clenched the mattress and he glared at her. "What are you telling me? Lucia! Look at me!"

She wouldn't.

Deep under the layers of Dubois's psyche, beneath the warm joviality of his character and the decades of hard-earned knowledge and wisdom, the part of him that was still animal seized hold. He lunged forward, grasping for her. She was faster, darting away toward the door as the chair toppled behind her. He hit the ground hard. When he tried to stand, the pain at his side sent him keeling over. *"Stop! What are you doing?"*

She was by the door now, holding back sobs as she looked down on him. "I'm so sorry."

"Lucia!"

She opened the door.

Sovilo stood outside. A gnarled wooden crown sat atop his white dome, and a stretch of thick rope hung from his hands. Beyond him, the light of the fireplace was blotted out by a mass of shifting bodies.

Dubois recoiled against the bed. *"Stay back! Enzo! Enzo, where the hell are you?"*

The crowd filtered into the room, bearing down on him en masse. He swung wildly as a dozen hands seized him. Again and again his fists connected with soft flesh, but they were too many. A harsh blow landed against his wound, and he toppled, blinded by pain. Then they were upon him, yanking his arms behind his back and dragging him out into the light of the sitting room. He fought them the whole time until another blow to his wound sent him reeling. They forced him into a chair and bound his hands behind him.

"Stop, goddamn you! Lucia, stop this! Please! I have daught—"

Sovilo looped the rope over his head and pulled it tight between his teeth. The rope yanked back over the chairback, contorting his head upwards. The rough beams of the ceiling above filled his vision as he bit down desperately against the dusty fibers.

Lucia's voice rose in Latin above the ruckus of shifting bodies. *"Light maker! Fire-driver! Master of sun and moon! Mithras, hear us!"*

Dubois tried to scream. The rope cut off his pitch, and all that escaped was the muffled howl of a wounded dog.

Sovilo's breath came hot against his ear. "*Hush now, brother, be at peace. You do all of us an honor. Take solace, for we are chosen. Soon enough, I too shall join you in the hive.*"

"*We return to you the blood of kings! Hear us and hear our plea!*" Lucia cried. "*Death for life!*"

The room exploded in a fracas as the villagers bellowed the mantra over and over.

It struck Dubois then, as his sweat ran cold, the true horror of knowing that he was about to die. Of knowing that he was utterly helpless, and that whatever was to come next would be entirely beyond his ability to combat. With his head wrenched back and throat exposed, the memory of the bull came rushing back — of its staggered steps as its blood spurted out across the snow. His tears began to flow as he threw the last of his strength against his bonds.

The villagers' chant grew until it drowned out his own gasping whimpers. He braced for the cold bite of steel against his flesh. It never came. Instead, a large clay carafe appeared overhead clenched in the twisted hands of an old woman. Slowly she tipped it until a thick, yellow liquid began to drizzle from its spout. It oozed down onto his chin and glided over the rope, saturating his lips and seeping slowly through his teeth until it found his tongue. It hit his palate with a horrible sweetness that he immediately knew.

It was honey.

"*No!*" he coughed against it. The gentle cascade did not slow. He flailed with all his might as Sovilo yanked the rope tighter. The honey began to pool in the back of his throat. Dubois grappled desperately for some semblance of control, but his mind was nearly gone, obliterated by the panic. He needed to swallow. He needed to gulp it down in order to keep from drowning. He choked as he tried, his throat burning as he hacked up the thick sludge.

"*Death for life!*" The horrible words rang from every direction.

The honey was coming faster now, filling his mouth, overflowing from the corners of his lips and cascading down his cheeks. He squeezed his eyes shut, closing off his throat the best he could. It was nearly impossible to do from the contorted angle, but by the mercy of God he managed to pull a heaving breath in through his nose.

The chanting died away as a sudden gasp filled the room. In an instant, there was silence. The rope loosened the slightest bit as Sovilo's focus shifted to something toward the stairwell. Dubois managed to jerk his head just enough to spit some of the wicked honey from his mouth.

He saw it then. The throng of villagers had parted before him, exposing a bent figure standing in the shadows of the doorway to the staircase. It was a man by all rights. But somehow Dubois knew it was not a man at all. He was haggard and old, draped in a thin blanket and clutching a knotted cane. Even in the darkness the irises that centered his bloodshot eyes were an impossibly black void. As the women gave berth, the light of the fire washed over him. His eyes reflected back in a flash of pale yellow. A patchy beard stained the craggy skin of his face, and a grey wisp topped his mottled head. Thin lips bulged out over concealed canines, and the thin quill of a black feather erupted from beneath the yellowed flesh of his cheek.

Dubois stared on in utter disbelief as the will to fight fled his body. His thoughts erupted in a silent scream, for he recognized what he was seeing.

It was the devil himself.

"Mithras. I give unto you the lion, blessed and anointed in honey." Lucia spoke softly. She alone stood facing him now, her face soaked in tears and lips quivering. She met his eyes and her voice cracked. *"Let it cleanse his skin. Let it cleanse his hands, his tongue. Let it fill him from the inside and purify his soul so he may bask in your light, a true servant once more. Oh, Lord of wisdom. Lord of life. Lord of truth. Accept him as your child."*

The rope yanked tight. Once more the jar filled Dubois's vision. Shadows danced across the ceiling beyond it as the dribbling honey shifted upward past his moustache, finally cascading over his nostrils. His sinuses burned, and one final scream evaporated into a thick gargle as the image of his family flashed in his mind.

Then his thoughts withdrew, replaced with the thrashing, dead-minded panic of a mackerel ripped from the sea.

50

BLACKWOOD RODE through the alpine forest. The night had drawn on for an eternity and the storm had only just begun to ebb. The moon broke through the clouds above, casting the barren trees as black phantoms in its silvery glow. They creaked in protest as the wind thrashed clumps of snow from high pine boughs. It spattered down, beating an uneven rhythm of muted thumps and pockmarking the otherwise smooth sheet of the forest floor.

His cowl had grown heavy with snow and ice. He shook it off and slapped the remainder from his shoulders and legs. The electric torch had died some time ago. He'd discarded it on the side of the path. Now he operated solely off the scant grey of the moon. His hands were shaking, and the chill had begun to penetrate his bones. The chatter of his teeth filled his ears and exhaustion clouded his mind. He wasn't the only one in bad shape. The nag was hurting as well. Her steps had grown staggered and her breath devolved to labored wheezing. He leaned forward against her neck. It was hot and coated in a thin sheen of sweat. There was no question now — she would not have the strength to carry him home.

Ahead, the raven cackled. It had been following him since the ravine. He'd figured that it saw him as little more than a meal — a lump of warm meat plodding slowly toward its own demise. It was perched on a low branch ahead. In the snow beneath it rested a dark shape.

He readied the rifle, approaching cautiously until he could make out what it was. The Oldenburger lay on its side, a thin layer of snow coating its coarse hair. He pulled the nag to a halt and dismounted. The wind stilled, and he heard no sign of Klaus. He advanced, rifle raised and darting between the trees. When he reached the dead horse, he found that it was already cold to the touch. Tracks led away into the dark. Those of a man on foot.

"I've got you now, you son of a bitch," Blackwood muttered. It was too late for him to turn back, but maybe his horse could make it on its own. He turned back to the nag. "Go on, girl, go home. If you still can."

The raven quorked as it took off, circling the body thrice before flying low through the trees to the east. He set off down Klaus's trail in its wake.

51

ENZO CURLED into the warmth of Hilde's sheets. They were soft against his naked flesh and still held the sweet honey scent of her hair. The turmoil he felt inside had largely dissipated. It was as if the hours spent tangled in the arms of his lover had managed to release some rigid spring coiled tight inside his chest. Now, perhaps for the first time ever, he felt that everything would be okay. He had her. Just her touch could cure any ailment he could imagine. Not only would she get him through the night, but she would also get him through all the nights to come. Of this he was certain.

She'd left moments before, climbing from the bed and padding out of the room without a word. He'd barely noticed, caught too deep in his own ruminations to worry — not that she could understand him even if he had spoken up. He would learn German eventually. They had time. All the time in the world.

His thoughts drifted to back home. What would his family think of him now? What would his mother say when she met his German love? He thought of his home, a small village nestled on the coast of the Mediterranean. He'd grown up with a view of the ocean from their kitchen window. He thought fondly back on those times — the heat of the sun on his face, the gentle noise of the waves lapping the beach. Hilde would like it there. And if she did not, then they would return here, or go anywhere she liked. It didn't matter, so long as they were together.

Footsteps came from the hall. They were too heavy to be hers.

"*Hello?*" Enzo sat up alert.

Sovilo stepped through the doorway. He cradled Enzo's rifle, which the boy had left leaning by the front door.

"*What has happened?*" Enzo blurted in Italian, knowing even as the words slipped out that they were useless. He made to stand, but the tavernkeeper motioned him to stay seated.

"*Stay there.*"

Enzo froze. Sovilo's words were in fluent Italian.

The tavernkeeper appeared morose. He went on gently, "*Enzo, my young friend, you and I must have a difficult conversation.*"

"*You speak Italian?*" Enzo didn't hide his shock.

"*I speak many languages. Yours is among them.*"

"*Why did you not tell me?*"

"*Because you did not need to know.*"

The answer did nothing to quell the boy's building sense of dread. "*Where's Hilde?*"

"*She's gone. Not far, but you will not see her again.*"

Enzo stood, the sheets falling away to reveal balled fists. "*Like hell—*"

Sovilo's hand slipped up the rifle's stock. "*You need to listen now, Enzo, not speak. Do you understand?*"

"*No, I don't. I want Hilde.*"

"*I'm sorry, but that cannot happen.*"

"*What have you done with her?*"

"*Nothing. She is perfectly safe. Her absence is of her own free will. She knows this is the only way. Now, I need you to get dressed.*"

Though Enzo did not believe a word out of this man's mouth, he was reluctant to continue the conversation naked, especially since the situation seemed bound to go sideways. He dressed, never taking his eyes from Sovilo.

"*The mule is tied outside — I believe you know him well by now, he is a fair steed. The saddlebags are laden with food, equipment, and even some money. I brought you my best coat as well, which you will find by the door. The mule knows the way east, to Switzerland. In case it gets lost, you will find a map in an envelope in the left bag. Burn it when you arrive there.*"

"*I'm not going anywhere.*"

"*You are. If you do not, I'm afraid I will be forced to kill you. If you somehow evade me, then the others will see it through. This is not a choice, my young friend. You serve no more purpose here.*" The coldness in the tavernkeeper's voice gave away his sincerity. "*I don't expect you to understand, and I know I cannot ask you to trust me, but you will have to. I am doing you a great kindness. The others, many of them do not approve of setting you loose.*"

"*You would cast us into the cold to die? How is Dubois supposed to survive out there? He is wounded!*"

"*He is dead.*"

The news hit Enzo like a barreling train. He glanced to the window. If he were to launch himself through the glass, he might beat the bullet that was sure to follow.

"*Don't*," Sovilo warned. "*Think of Hilde. She loves you, you know. When she took your purity, she did so to save you from your true purpose. A boy was made to die in your stead. She took a great risk in saving you. Now you must do the same for her. If you were to cause more havoc here it would only end in your death and her banishment. Do you imagine she would be able to find her own way in these desolate mountains? Leave now, peacefully, for her sake. That she may find redemption in the eyes of her people.*"

"*She wouldn't ask me to go…*"

"*No, she wouldn't. Not in person. That is why I am here. Go now, do not come back. Do not speak a word of this place to anyone you meet, and as I said, when you reach Switzerland, burn the map.*"

Sovilo stepped back into the foyer, the rifle now held ready at his waist. Enzo walked past him to the door. He donned his boots and a thick winter coat that Sovilo pointed out. When he was ushered outside, Sovilo followed him. Down the street the flickering light of a freshly lit pyre filled the plaza.

"*Untie the mule.*"

Enzo did so, circling the animal to place it between himself and the rifle. Sovilo walked a wide arc to offset his cover.

"*Get on.*"

Enzo struggled to climb atop. He'd never been much of a rider.

"*You will start east, along the northerly edge of the mountain ahead. Do not stop until you are far from this place, and do not ever return. Not for her, not for the others, not for anything.*"

Enzo eased the mule forward, caught in a thousand calculations. He searched desperately for a way to outsmart the situation. He couldn't leave her. Maybe they would let him take her — if they were willing to banish her, then why not let them go together?

He turned back to say this, but the rifle was now tucked in Sovilo's shoulder and pointed directly at his head. The albino tavernkeeper glowed nearly translucent in the moonlight. "*Go now, in silence. I will not tell you again.*"

He rode forward, toward the plaza. The horizon stood a dull blue beyond the mountains. The sun had not yet erupted. Still, a yellow glow emanated from the open space ahead. His heart caught in his throat.

The villagers were gathered in a great circle once more. In the center of them stood a pyre, just like the one they had burnt the bull on. Just like Fletcher's, the boy's, McCulloch's…

One by one, villagers turned to him. It wasn't their faces he saw, but rather the crude masks that adorned them. Ravens and lions and horrible caricatures of men carved crudely into cracked wood. They watched him in silence as he passed.

He squinted to see past the growing brightness. The skin of Dubois's naked corpse reflected the yellow glimmer of the flames, as if coated in a thin sheen of oil. Only the scent of burning sugar illuminated what it actually was. Honey.

"*Go!*" He dug his heels in. The mule grunted but ignored him. He kicked it harder, leaning forward and willing the beast on as it began to trot toward the distant mountains. The villagers watched him depart in silence.

All thoughts of Hilde had fled his mind, replaced by the rhythmic chant of the Lord's prayer through fear-stricken sobs.

52

DAWN WAS on the horizon. The pale tint of rose and butter yellow filtered through the scraggly pines above. The wind had died out, and now the forest was still. Low boughs tugged at the bearskin coat as Blackwood tramped onward. He'd lost feeling in his feet and face and hands, and now even his limbs had begun to grow numb with cold. Still, he kept on. Klaus's tracks had grown erratic and staggering before him, and he knew the German was losing steam.

The scent of woodsmoke carried over the breeze. He paused and peeled his eyes until he could make out a thin column of smoke rising through the canopy ahead. Rifle readied in his shaking hands, he stalked forward.

Klaus was huddled close to a fire made up of little more than a few broken branches and flame-wilted pinecones. It popped and sizzled as the German pressed his hands close. His fingers, purple and enflamed, steamed like fat little sausages. Even from a distance Blackwood could see that they glistened with the waxy tint of frostbite.

Blackwood circled into view, taking up position across the fire. Klaus did not bother to look up. His rifle lay abandoned by his side. It was obvious that his hands were too far gone to even operate the weapon.

Blackwood lowered his rifle to his hip. *"You look cold."*

"Go to hell," Klaus hissed. His voice vibrated to match the violent shivers that raked his body.

"I've already been there. Now it's your turn."

Klaus snorted. *"You think you're clever? Look at you. Look where you are. You caught up to me, good for you. It doesn't matter. You've nowhere to go. Neither one of us will see tomorrow, you pathetic swine."*

"It matters to me."

Klaus leaned closer to the fire, letting the flames lick his dead fingers. *"It's over. We're both going to die. Just fuck off and leave me be."*

Blackwood watched the miserable wretch trembling before him. Instead of pity or righteousness, all he felt was disgust. He knew too well the agony this little man had so gleefully imparted. All the murder, all the torture, all the cruelty… It just didn't seem right that he go peacefully in the cold. A numb death was unbecoming of such a rancid pile of shit.

"*I said get away from me!*" Klaus barked. "*Go on! Find your own hole to die in!*"

"*I'm afraid you don't get to give the orders anymore, Unteroffizier.*" Blackwood lowered his rifle. The monster before him was so small now. Those fleshy hands that had stolen the lives of countless unarmed men were now just useless hunks of frozen meat, never to torment again. Ice fell away from the scruff of beard that covered Blackwood's face as he grimaced and began unhooking the metal clasps that held the sling to his rifle.

Klaus looked up at the motion. "*What do you think you are doing?*"

"*Do you remember a prisoner named Dickie?*"

The German's brow crinkled. "*Who?*"

"*Dickie.*" Blackwood got the first buckle free and moved on to the second. "*He was a friend of mine. He was from Oklahoma. His mother was a baker. He told me she used to make apple pie for him every Sunday as a boy. That was all he dreamed about at Rothenspring — it kept him sane through all the torture, all the back-breaking labor, just that tiny hope that he might someday taste one of those pies again.*" The second clasp came loose and Blackwood stabbed the rifle into the snow. He worked the sling's buckle, lengthening the leather strap to bringing the loop to size. "*You hung him outside the gate days before we left. He was a good kid. Barely twenty, just starting his life. You know what the crazy thing is? He'd never even killed a man. When I first met him, he thought that was a mark of shame, being in a war and all. Of course, after seeing the things* you *did, I think he was proud of that in the end — to die with clean hands and a clean soul. He was a good man.*"

"*You think I give a damn about some American swine that I put to the rope? If I could go back, I would have strung you up with him.*"

"*You should give a damn.*" Blackwood finished adjusting the sling. He let the loop dangle from his hand. "*Because what comes next is for Dickie.*"

Klaus's eyes drifted to the makeshift noose. It took a moment for his frozen mind to process, then they went wide. In a mad rush he scrambled to get ahold of his rifle. His dead fingers fumbled to close on the long wooden stock. Before they could, Blackwood had circled behind him in long strides. He kicked the rifle away.

"*Get back!*" Klaus shrieked. He managed to make it to his feet only for Blackwood to shove him back down. His hands swung wildly behind him as Blackwood slipped the noose over his neck and wrenched the buckle tight. Clumps of snow flew up into the air as he thrashed. It was no use. Blackwood was stronger. He hauled the German backward to the trees, to a stout, low hanging branch.

With a heave Blackwood hauled Klaus to his feet. He looped the sling over the branch. It was barely higher than his own head and bowed under the German's weight. He pulled harder until the German thrashed, suspended by his throat. As Blackwood tied the knot, Klaus reached frantically over his shoulders, clawing at Blackwood's face in one final, desperate attack. A meaty thumb jabbed into Blackwood's mouth and he bit down, snapping through the joint like a carrot. Klaus didn't flinch, and the wounded flesh was so frozen it didn't even bleed. With the knot secured, Blackwood stepped back.

The branch bowed further until the tips of Klaus's boots found purchase in the snow. He gasped — weak, furious words escaping his cracked lips. "*You can't even hang a man properly, can you? You fucking swine!*"

Blackwood leaned close enough to Klaus's ear that he could feel the heat from his own breath reflected back onto his cheek. "*…and this is for me.*"

The gunshot echoed through the frozen mountain air like a thunderclap. The pistol pressed against the base of Klaus's spine jerked in his hand, and the guard's legs went limp. Klaus's weight dropped hard, wrenching his throat against the unforgiving embrace of the noose. Leather bit into the flesh of his neck and cut off his agonized scream. Useless fingers tore at his throat as he swayed slowly back and forth.

Blackwood stepped back as hot blood spurted from the still smoking hole in the German's coat. Harsh crimson dribbled over the pure white snow. He circled slowly to stand before the dying man.

Klaus's face glowed beet red. Fat veins threatened to explode from his frost-covered dome, and the foam of spittle dribbled from the corners of his mouth. His lips clenched and unclenched, desperately attempting to form some final word that would never come. Blackwood looked deep into his tormentor's eyes. They were bloodshot and ripe with horror and tears.

Blackwood had spent countless hours imagining this moment — imagining what scathing words he might utter as the last thing this mongrel would ever hear. Now they all seemed so… unimportant. He watched for only a moment, then tucked the pistol into his belt and trudged back to the fire. Behind him,

Klaus's death rattle mixed with the soft thudding of snow as it fell in clumps from the trees.

Blackwood didn't need to see it. He'd watched enough men pass through the gates of death. Soon enough, he knew he'd be there himself.

He was nearly to the fire when another noise came — a crisp pop that he would have recognized anywhere. The hair on his neck stood on end, and he spun. Klaus's coat hung open, the buttons ripped away. The wooden handle of a grenade emerged from his belt. A thin line of smoke poured from its end. The pull-cap fell from between Klaus's frozen hands, and his dying gasps contorted into short, wheezing bursts.

He was laughing.

Blackwood froze for only a second. Then his legs buckled and he fell to the side, shielding his face. The grenade exploded with a blinding flash, a wave of concussive energy washing over him as he sank into the snow. Shrapnel hissed overhead like a horde of furious wasps fleeing the deafening boom.

For a moment the air filled with the wet *schlop* of meat and organs as they slapped down around him. The great boom echoed back in a symphony from all over. When it was over, Blackwood gasped at the air. His hands worked down the bearskin coat and the frozen wool of his pants. Blood dappled his fingers, but as far as he could tell, none of it was his.

With a groan, he climbed to his feet. His bones ached, and his head throbbed. Before him, only Klaus's head and shoulders still hung from the tree bough. A ragged mess of entrails had replaced his belly and legs. Half of his face had peeled away and now dangled from the broken remains of his jaw.

"Missed me," Blackwood muttered. His own words sounded distant over the horrendous ringing in his ears. As he turned back, he heard another noise — a deep, distant rumble from up the mountain. He looked past the dripping remains hanging before him to the frosted peak far above the alpine forest. A gentle mist had formed near its tallest point. It sank slowly down the slope, building speed as the thunder grew louder.

His first instinct was to run. He dismissed it. There was no point. There was nowhere to escape to, no hope of fleeing the maelstrom of churning ice and stone and crushing snow. It barreled down the mountain, a mindless cavalry charge building and roiling as if driven by the hand of God himself.

"It's all nothing," he assured himself through gritted teeth. "There is no God. There is no judgement. The only thing to fear is death. And when death takes you, you won't even be around to give a damn." For the first time, he realized that his voice held far less conviction than it once had.

Above, the raven screeched as it departed. He watched it go as the trees ahead snapped and buckled under the avalanche's rage. Then his breath was gone, and he was flipping and turning and crashing as the world turned white.

PART SEVEN

An excerpt from *Ritual Science* by S. Kensington, PhD candidate, University of Wales.

Thus the debate transforms from the theory of anthropologically defined *magic* into one of cause and effect. Through the lens of scientific theory, we must consider the genuine possibility that ritual magic may in fact create real and substantial effects on the physical world.

Take for example Dr. Saul Poller, a renowned anthropologist who spent nearly a decade embedded in the Koin Pora tribe of New Guinea to study their traditions and history. Poller came to the (at the time absurd) conclusion that their ritual practices did indeed seem to have some veritable causation in regard to real life events. In one instance, he observed the elaborate sacrifice of a goat which he claims led directly to an increase in fertility amongst those tribe members who had so far proven infertile. In another instance, a wronged weaver engaged in a ritualistic prayer followed by the killing of seven roosters, resulting in the offending party's sudden and unexpected death. While these instances of success could easily be attributed to sheer coincidence, Poller claimed that similar rituals actually resulted in a success rate of 2:5. When compared to his own calculated odds of positive results occurring out of sheer chance at only 1 in 10,000, it is easy to understand how his conclusions were drawn.

Such findings, though often considered anecdotal in academic circles, lead to the complex question as to whether traditional modern views on ritual being merely "hocus pocus" are actually, in themselves, unscientific. What is science if not simply the formation and testing of a hypothesis? When ancient man discovered the concept of medicinal herbs, did he not do so through a complex process of experimentation? Is it not possible that this same concept has been applied to ancient ritual practice? If every action has an equal and opposite reaction, could it still be considered science even if we don't understand the full nuance of the action and the reaction?

It is worth noting that nobody can say *why* gravity works. We only know that it does, at least in the capacity in which we understand it to. In this way, could ritual magic not simply be a drawn-out experiment in cause and effect? Anthropologists so often get caught up in the *why* of religious ritual that they become eager to dismiss the purported outcome. Is it not possible, nay, probable, that the continued practice of something for hundreds if not thousands of years likely comes as the result of a decent success rate?

BAVARIA, 1916

Lucia Wulfson crouched atop the icy peak. She bundled tighter in her coat, wishing she could risk a fire. But she couldn't. No one could know she was there.

Far, far below, the convoy of broken prisoners milled along the winding road between the mountains. From up here they appeared as little more than a cluster of ants trudging in tight columns. She could barely make out her brother riding in the front, his horse merely a black dot against the road. They had made better time than he had estimated — she had only just made the peak that morning. Had she been delayed, it all would have been for nothing.

It might still be, she lamented. The plan was desperate, even for them. The village had suffered over the past few years. Their people were hungry, on their last legs. Even more frightening, Fausta was sure the Sarvàn was reaching the end of his life. *Imminent,* she had put it. His demise was *imminent*, and their own would surely follow. It would take an intervention from Mithras himself for them to pull off this last desperate effort.

The convoy approached the marker — a long dead tree that stood tall beside the road. She watched her brother closely, awaiting his signal. A dozen halting breaths came and went before he spun and rode his horse in a tight circle, feigning to observe those behind him.

She slammed down on the plunger. Its mechanism zipped as a current shot out along the long wires that lead away in the snow. From the next peak over came a tremendous *boom*. She grabbed the rope anchored into the stone at her side, praying it wouldn't give way as the snow below collapsed in a sheet. Whispering a prayer, she crimped her eyes against the deafening roar.

Slowly, the noise faded to a growl. When it was over, she opened her eyes.

The guards far below were shooting — she saw their violence long before the distant pops and screams echoed up. Her brother rode through the ranks, waving them down until the commotion died away. Several lay unmoving. She hoped desperately that his chosen weren't among the dead.

She didn't bother to stick around. Gathering her things in the cold, she carefully picked her steps down the backside of the mountain, back toward the forest where the Oldenburger waited. A storm was coming, a bad one, Sovilo had said.

"*Good luck, Anselm,*" she whispered as she climbed. "*May Mithras watch over you.*"

53

THE MITHRAEUM was dank. Sovilo stoked a second brazier to life, pumping a heavy set of bellows to drive the flames into a rage. Fausta, the glass-eyed old crone, hunched nearby snapping kindling between gnarled fingers.

Wulfson was laid out on a low table. His head lolled to the side, held in place between two pillows at the same wretched cant as when they had found him. Lucia sat beside him on the cold stone. Her hand rested gently on his arm. She knew he couldn't feel her touch, but it was more for her own comfort than his. His pulse was weak beneath her fingers, and his breath shallow.

"*He stopped taking liquids last night,*" Fausta said. "*The time has come.*"

Lucia took in his frail state. His skin had grown sallow, and the only visible sign of life came in the the occasional flutter of his eyelids. Still, she liked to think that he could hear them.

"*Even if things were different, he could never heal from this, could he?*" she asked.

"*No.*" Sovilo joined her by Wulfson's side. "*The heat and the herbs might prolong his life, but his vertebra is severed. For that, there is no cure. It is not something to dwell on, Lucia. He knew his fate, and that has not changed. He will still die with pride and dignity as he wished.*"

Lucia winced at the finality of her uncle's words.

Fausta shuffled over and laid a clammy hand atop Lucia's. "*He was always such a strong boy. Only he could persevere so long with such a wound. He holds on for us, my dear.*"

Lucia clenched her teeth and fought back the memories that had tormented her as of late. Memories of childhood, of happiness, of the older brother who'd taught her both mischief and loyalty. "*We can't just let him die first?*" Lucia let the foolish words slip out.

"*No,*" Sovilo said. "*The scriptures are clear. His is the rite of Perses, of the old blood. He's known his fate for quite some time. His current condition, though tragic for us now, is a blessing for him. He won't feel a thing. We must thank Mithras for his mercy.*"

She did so, silently.

"*We must go now.*" Fausta gripped her shoulder. "*They are waiting.*"

All sixty-seven remaining adult members of the village had packed into the meetinghouse. They filled the rows of benches and stood along the walls. The hall, once meant only to hold those within the community who had been deemed head of household, now somehow fit their entire population. Lucia's stomach churned at the realization.

She sat in her place at the center of the head table and faced out over the rabble. Fausta sat beside her in the same seat she had filled since long before Lucia was born. The air was stagnant and carried the mixed scent of woodsmoke and body odor as the gathered women murmured amongst themselves. A palpable unease filled the room, further exemplified by wringing hands and furtive glances.

Lucia hated what was to come next. As a child, she'd always looked forward to ascending to a leadership role within the village. She might have thought twice about such aspirations had she known what was in store for them. With a deep breath, she reminded herself of everything her brother had suffered in order to get them this far, and of what he would soon endure. This steeled her heart.

She stood, banging her fist twice on the table. "*Let us begin.*"

The room went silent, all eyes turned to her.

"*We've reached a critical point. With the sacrifice of the Frenchman, the fourth rite has been completed. As you all know, what comes next will be no less horrid. My brother lies dying in the Mithraeum. Tonight, we will send him to Mithras. Let us pray now for him.*"

Heads began to bow, but a woman's voice called out in the silence. "*How could you let the Italian go?*"

Lucia scanned her audience, her eyes finally finding the speaker. It was Esther, an older woman whose snobbish attitude had grated at Lucia's nerves since childhood. "*What would you have done, Esther? Killed him in cold blood?*"

"*It would have been the right choice. He will return to his people and tell them of this place,*" Esther proclaimed. A strained murmur of agreement resonated through the hall.

Lucia lowered her voice. "*You're eager for blood now, are you? You speak as if you have the backbone to have pulled the trigger yourself. Or are you complaining to me because I wished to keep my hands clean of senseless murder?*"

Esther shrank back a bit, then gave a snide look. "*You didn't have a problem killing the others.*"

Lucia winced. "*Acts done in the service of our lord are free of sin. Are you second guessing our path? Or do you need another lesson on the scriptures? Sister Fausta, perhaps Esther here should sit in on your lessons with the young ones.*"

Fausta let out a long groan as she shifted to look out over the crowd. "*Esther, be quiet now.*"

Esther went silent, but another spoke up. This time it was Frieda, the butcher, and sister to the slain Maria. "*What about Hilde? Will she be punished?*"

Lucia scanned the crowd. Hilde stood alone in the back, her head low and shoulders slumped. "*Punished for what, exactly?*"

"*For soiling the virgin! It is because of her that my nephew was forced to stand in his stead. It is not right. It is not just! That child was the last male heir to the village, now that your brother is gone.*"

"*My brother is not gone. Not yet. And whatever Hilde did, her actions were guided by Mithras, do not forget that—*"

"*Then it was Mithras who held her legs open for that heathen boy?*"

More mutters of agreement came, and Lucia felt her control of the room slipping. "*Frieda, do not blaspheme. I understand your pain. We have all lost loved ones to this cause—*"

"*I lost my nephew to nothing more than the lust of a whore!*"

"*You forget yourself, woman,*" Lucia barked with sudden power. "*Do you not remember the tribulations of youth? If I recall correctly, your own budding judgement was questionable at best. Wasn't it you who took to the flatlands at her same age, only to return with a bastard in your belly? Or are you so righteous that you have somehow managed to erase the past?*"

Frieda was a large woman, stouter than any other in the village. She also had a temper to match her size. She stood, cutting an imposing figure over the others. "*You sit in that chair because of the blood in your veins, not by the virtue of your actions. Who are you to speak for our god? Look at us! Look at what has happened! They took your father from us, our true leader, and left us with a girl young enough to be my daughter! You and your brother have launched us into chaos. How many of our people have died under your clumsy hand? How are we to know that you even have the slightest idea as to what you are doing?*"

Lucia's knuckles ground into the table. "*Chaos?*" she spat. "*Chaos, you say? First went the raven, Corax, messenger to men, set upon by his own winged disciples. I made the cuts as that man screamed and drove the final strike home myself.*

Second went Nymphus, the bridegroom, pure and without pain, with poison poured with these two hands." She raised her hands before her for all to see as her voice grew to a crackling shout. "*Third went the warrior, Miles, slain in the heat of battle, a conflict orchestrated by these two lips! Fourth came the lion, Leo, the blood of royalty, purified by honey and the words of our god! Do you not call that order?*" She felt herself growing unhinged, her furious gaze breaking from the butcher to pan the worried faces before her. "*Have you forgotten who we are? Why we are here? Have you lost faith in our cause? Or need I get* him*? Must he stand before you himself, let you see the weakness of his legs and the clouds that hang over his eyes? Too many of you have forgotten what it is that our ancestors imprisoned within him, the burden they left us with. You think this is chaos? Imagine what will become of you if the spirit breaks free!*"

She stabbed an accusatory finger at Frieda. "*Your discomfort does not matter, Frieda. Not any more than mine. Mithras has guided us through the dark. It's his hands that control our world and usher us along the path. He is the light, and all that he asks in return is our faith. Have you so easily lost it?*"

The self-righteous outrage that had radiated from Frieda moments before fizzled. She dropped back into her seat without another word.

"*Tonight at midnight, the fifth rite will be enacted,*" Lucia went on harshly, daring another to interrupt. "*I will give my brother to our god with a smile on my face and hope in my heart. If there are any here who no longer have the stomach for this, then go. And never return. If you stay, then you must be prepared for—*"

The door burst open. A young girl collapsed through it, gasping at the air as she tried to speak.

Lucia's heart caught mid-pump. The children knew better than to interrupt, lest it be a matter of life and death. "*What is it, girl?*"

Several women surrounded the girl, hauling her to her feet. She panted hard, fighting to get the words out. "*Riders… on the far slope… They… They're soldiers…*"

Lucia's stomach dropped.

Fausta was on her feet with a deftness unbecoming of her age. Her shrill voice filled the meeting hall. "*Go now, all of you! Make yourselves busy!*"

54

SIX RIDERS bore down the slope. Lucia stood alone in the windswept plaza watching as they approached. Even from a distance she could make out that their uniforms were haggard and their horses exhausted. Wherever they had come from, she had no doubt that it had been a long, arduous journey.

As the riders closed in, one of them took to the head of the formation. He was middle-aged with a bristly umber beard. He wore the rank of an Oberleutnant on his shoulder and bore a weather-beaten mountaineer's kit.

Despite the warmth of the bearskin coat wrapped around her, Lucia felt a chill run up her spine. This was a very dangerous development.

"*Where is your leader?*" the German officer demanded as he pulled to a halt before her.

"*I am the leader here.*"

"*You?*" His thick eyebrows drew together as he scanned the plaza. A score of women moved about, seemingly busy in their daily chores. "*Where are your men?*"

"*At war.*"

He snorted and dismounted, nodding to his men to do the same. "*Very well then. Our journey has been long and hard; we require food and a warm place to eat it.*"

Lucia bid him to follow her as she led them toward the tavern. "*I must ask — what is it that has brought you all the way out here?*"

"*We can speak once we've filled our bellies.*" His eyes caught on the cave opening of the Mithraeum and the pillars at its depths. "*What the hell is that?*"

"*A cold, foodless place,*" she answered curtly.

He only snickered in response. She followed his gaze upward to the tower. By the grace of Mithras, one of the women had made it up there in time to reel the corpses in and stash them behind the palisade.

The soldiers hitched their horses to the posts outside and followed her into the warmth of the tavern. They took seats near to the fire and bantered amongst each other. Lucia took to the kitchen, fetching a plateful of bread and cheese along with a pitcher of beer. Taking advantage of the brief moment of solitude, she forced herself to focus. What were they doing here? Was there a chance that Klaus had made it through the storm? It was impossible. Besides, even if he had, they would not have been this quick to return. This was something else. A new factor, one that they had not accounted for at all.

She spotted the rifle hidden behind the door as she left the kitchen. It was not a fight she could win, but if it came down to it, she would try.

"*As I asked before.*" She regarded the Oberleutnant once she'd set the food down. "*Why have you come to my village in the middle of winter?*"

The Oberleutnant tore into the bread ravenously. He didn't bother to answer her until he'd washed it down with a gulp of beer. "*This is a nice place you have here. What do you call it?*"

"*Melvilla.*" As much as she hated being disregarded, she knew to expect little else from outsiders. Especially armed ones.

"*Huh… Melvilla. Never heard of it. Do you have many visitors this time of year?*"

"*No. Never.*"

His focus drifted from the food, sizing her up. He stopped at the waist of her coat. "*Something happen here recently?*"

She followed his gaze down to the dark stain of old blood that marred the fur. "*An unfortunate repercussion of hunting our own food, I'm afraid.*"

"*Mmm…*" he grunted. "*We're looking for someone. A whole group, actually. We believe they came this way.*"

"*No one has passed through these parts since summer.*"

"*I didn't say when they came through.*"

"*Well, when was it then?*"

He finished a hunk of cheese before answering. "*These men, they were led by a German officer, Major Anselm Wulfson. A traitor who falsified orders with the aim of wreaking havoc amidst the ranks. We think he's on the run up here attempting to escape the Kaiser's retribution. Have you seen anyone like that?*"

"*As I said, no one has been through here.*"

"*Mmm…*" he grunted again, turning back to his food.

As they drank, she realized how simple it would be to slip something into their next pitcher. Behind her easy smile, she frantically tried to recall where Sovilo hid the nightshade.

"More beer?"

The Oberleutnant laughed and slapped one of his comrades on the shoulder. *"You were right. A village without men, and the first thing she tries to do is get us drunk! We must have died and gone to heaven in that storm!"*

The men laughed heartily along, and the Oberleutnant waved her off. *"No, Fraulein. No more beer, not yet. We are on a mission."*

Lucia fought the urge to go for the rifle. *"If you are not planning on staying, might I suggest you push on? We are expecting a hard freeze tonight. If the pass ices up, it will be nearly impossible to traverse in the morning."*

The German thinned his eyes. *"Are trying to get rid of us?"*

"Yes," she answered bluntly. *"As you can see, we are a poor people who have sacrificed much in the name of the Kaiser already. In just what you are eating now you have depleted our resources. Resources that were already scant enough before your arrival."*

He stood and spun in a slow circle, taking in the tavern. *"Your bar looks well stocked enough. If you are low on food, then it seems to me like you may not have your priorities in order."* He walked to the bar and began nosing around behind it.

Lucia resisted calling him off. The blatant disrespect was jarring, but the stakes were too high for anything rash. Even so, her anxiety was building to a crescendo. She thought of the bloody equipment and uniforms still piled upstairs, to her brother's belongings still folded neatly just a room away, to the corpses hidden in the tower high above. Each image put a new knot in her belly that refused to let go. She suddenly felt helpless. All she could do was pray that they did not look too hard.

The officer took a bottle of schnapps in hand and read the label. *"A good brand. You clearly have trade out here. Have you ever left this village?"*

"Of course."

"So you know the mountains well?"

"Well enough."

"Are there many other villages up here?"

"None. We enjoy our privacy."

"The route these men took, it wove northwest from the main road. It would have brought them close to here, ya?"

"There are many mountain paths that lead to Switzerland. Not all of them cut through here."

He paused, eyes still locked on the bottle. *"I never said anything about Switzerland."*

Lucia cursed herself silently. "*You said they were headed west. What do you think is west of here, soldier?*"

"*It is Oberleutnant to you, Fraulein.*"

"*Is it?*" She let the politeness fade from her voice. "*Or is it invader? Or perhaps marauder? When armed men show up at my doorstep and demand food and drink under the implication of force, I think those names are more applicable. Is that what our army does now? Rudely harass the widows and wives of their own fighting men? I've told you what you wanted to know, now I must ask you politely to leave.*"

His eyes cut thin, and the men at the table stiffened. Slowly he looked up to her. His glare only lasted a breath before his features exploded into a pandering smile. "*My sincerest apologies, Fraulein. If we've been rude, it was not our intention. Just… a long journey is all. You say the pass will freeze by morning, ya? Then we shall be off. Men! Mount up!*"

The soldiers groaned as they stood, filling their pockets with the remnants of the tray and finishing their beers in a hurry. The Oberleutnant made to follow them out but doubled back at the door. Lucia was already halfway to the kitchen, nothing but the rifle on her mind, when he caught her by the arm. She spun to see his smile just inches from her face. He held up the schnapps. "*Do you mind? Something to keep us warm on the mountain. I wouldn't want to take it without permission.*"

She pulled her arm free of his grasp. "*Yes. Of course.*"

⁓

From the upper story of the tavern, Lucia gripped the rifle tight as she watched the soldiers ride off. She felt sick. It was the same sick feeling she'd gotten when her brother had ridden into the village that fall, a crate of explosives lashed to the back of his horse and a desperate, last-ditch plan on his lips.

All she had to do was set off the avalanche to block the prisoner convoy. At least, that's what he had said at the time. Everything since had been a slow devolution into madness. *Chaos*, as Frieda had so furiously put it. She wasn't wrong, Lucia knew. But they had gone too far to change course now.

The stairs behind her creaked. She turned to find Fausta shambling through the door.

"*What did they want?*" the old woman asked.

"*They were looking for Anselm and the others.*"

"*Do they suspect anything?*"
"*No…*" Lucia said. "*At least I don't think so.*"
"*We're lucky then. Has our guest awoken?*"
"*No.*"
"*Let us hope he does. I fear we may need him soon.*"

55

REALITY WAS a distorted hellscape. Blurred scenes of havoc played against a backdrop of pure black. A searing void ripped his torso apart as blades slashed and gored him from all sides. A putrid sweetness clogged his throat, and jagged beaks tore at his flesh. He raged against it all, thrust in and out of the horrendous torment like a blade pumped through a forge.

When he could take no more, the darkness washed away to reveal a dome of dancing lights.

It was a cave. One he'd never seen before yet somehow knew. Men surrounded him. They were filthy, clad in mud-stained tunics underneath scaled cuirasses marred with dents and broken plates. Behind broken eyes they watched him, swords and spears and great wooden shields hanging from bloody hands.

But they were only on the periphery. Before him, a horrible figure stood cut in stone. It rose from the shimmering floor, legs wrapped in the embrace of a wicked serpent and arms stretched triumphantly to its sides. Its face… its horrible face, the snarling maw of a beast, looked down on him with blood red eyes that bore no mercy. He felt his nakedness in the cold air.

"*Mortem ad vitam.*" The chant filled the shallow chamber, bouncing from the thousand sharp edges of the walls as it came again and again, reverberating through his chest as it escaped his own lips in a bellow.

"*Mortem ad vitam. Mortem ad vitam.*"

The muted drone of a horn echoed down the stone corridors. The men around him stiffened. The clamor of heavy boots and rustling armor filtered through the door, followed shortly by the shrill screams of death and battle.

A deep, hateful voice shouted above the ruckus. Though he didn't understand the words, he somehow knew their meaning — *Give them no quarter!*

His hands moved without his consent. But they weren't his hands, he realized as he saw them raised before him. They were darker, muddy and coated in blood. The veins that bulged over their surface pulsated along with his beating heart. In them, he held a dagger. One that he'd seen before.

Lucia's dagger.

With hands that weren't his own, he lifted the blade to the head of the statue. The steel tip scraped against the monstrous folded flesh of the thing's face. Dust fell onto his face as he carved an even-sided cross above the eyes.

The sounds of battle grew louder. Far louder, until it seemed that the combat was happening all around him. Blood began to bubble and leak from the cut stone. It dribbled down over the creature's maw and dripped into his waiting mouth.

An explosion of pain sent him to the floor. He gasped and retched, clawing at the cool stone underneath him. A dozen hands seized him and hauled him back to his feet as the pain gave way. Burnt-out faces looked on solemnly, waiting, hoping. The dagger lifted once more, this time to his own arm. His blood spilled out into their waiting lips. They suckled ravenously at the wound, each man dropping back to make room for the next as their eyes grew wild above snarling, red painted teeth.

The fear that had held them evaporated.

Now the horn was close. Others, men for whom he held an unspeakable revulsion, erupted through the gap in the stones. They formed a wall of shields, their spears jabbing and stabbing and their own grunting chant drowning all other noise.

He looked on them and smiled as a great hunger rose in his belly.

The images faded to blackness, replaced by a bleary view of himself, his true self, from afar. He was in Lucia's bed, tossing and turning and groaning in pain. Bandages patched his body. Only he was still someone else. The body he felt himself inside of ached with age. His joints creaked as he shifted, and the heavy weight of exhaustion threatened to overtake him. Beyond it all, he felt a great sadness… yet also relief.

"*You must wake,*" a woman's voice filtered softly through the pale.

Blackwood opened his eyelids. They were heavy, and the air burned his pupils.

Lucia was over him. A warm mug pressed to his lips. "*Drink,*" she whispered, tilting his head gently forward. "*Drink, so you can rest.*"

He did as he was bid, taking a mouthful of the sweet concoction. Then he took another. Before he reached a third, he felt himself fading away once more. This time in peace.

56

THE MOON watched through a clear sky as the villagers laid Anselm Wulfson atop the pyre. The only sign of life he showed was the gentle rise and fall of his chest, though even that had grown sporadic. Behind closed lids, his eyes flicked back and forth, caught in one last unknown dream.

Lucia stood alone by his side. She clutched his hand and spoke softly enough that the others could not hear. "*One of my earliest memories is of you and that stupid horse. Bombulum, you used to call her. I don't even remember what her real name was, just that you thought it was so funny how she would break wind every time she'd hit a trot.*" She remembered it so well. He had been nearly a man already and she just a child. She'd wanted to learn to ride so badly. Their mother had just died, and their father was off on a hunt. Her brother had taken it upon himself to teach her. Thinking back, she knew it was likely just a way to distract her from the pain of her mother's passing. She was so happy up there on Bombulum. It had felt like she was flying when the old horse began to trot, and when she fell, it had hurt so badly.

She slid the sleeve of her coat up, revealing the scar that still wound its way up her forearm. She could remember the white bone jabbing out of her skin like it was yesterday. Her eyes wandered to the splint still covering her brother's arm. "*I was so scared. Not because I was hurt, but because I thought I'd disappointed you. You were always the hardest on me. I thought you hated me up until that day. But you weren't mad. You ran to me and held me tight, whispered that it would be okay. You told me not to cry, and you were so proud when I didn't. You said I was the strongest girl in the world, the bravest too. And when I rode that horse a week later with the splint still on my arm, you were even prouder. You've made me who I am, more than any other. All I hope now is that I can still make you proud.*"

The rest of the villagers had begun to gather. They formed a circle around the pyre and muttered quietly amongst themselves. Morose faces met her as she lifted her head high, holding back the tears. She would not cry now, just as she would not then. That wasn't their way. They were the children of the wolf, of the blood of old Melvilla. Weakness was not their way — they were the backbone of this place. The keepers of the Sarvàn. And it was not in her to be weak.

"*Goodbye, dear brother.*" His forehead was cold when she kissed it. "*You've done everything you could for us. More than any other. I swear to you it will not be in vain.*"

Her voice shook as she began the prayer. The dry thatch stuffed at the base of the pyre caught quickly. Flames spewed around its edges like a writhing crown of fire rising around an ancient king. Her voice caught in her throat as it licked at his living flesh. Black smoke swirled in the wind and choked her. She pushed through, bellowing the ancient words from her belly, ignoring the horrible thoughts that manifested behind the curtain of her faith.

Her words began to blend together as her thoughts spiraled and her brother disappeared behind the raging wall of fire. *Be stronger*, she demanded of herself. But her focus was broken, and each inhale brought with it the stench of her hope dying.

This was madness. This was not how it was supposed to be. The rite of Perses, how could it be her brother? How could that be Mithras's divine justice? To roast him alive like a pig while he choked on his own boiling spit? Was that a righteous reward to his blind devotion?

She lost control of her thoughts, the image of Dubois manifesting instead — of the horror on his face as the honey bubbled and oozed from his mouth. Of Fletcher's gagged screams as the ravens picked his flesh to ribbons, of the inharmonious droop of his eyes as her dagger mercifully slid into his brain. Of little Albert and his brave tears as he sipped the poison from her hands. Of the anguished wails of his mother as he collapsed into her arms…

"*Mortem ad vitam*," she finished, her words barely audible over the crackling flames.

"*Mortem ad vitam! Mortem ad vitam!*" the chant resounded around her.

The words were still echoing back from the mountains when she broke away from the gathering. When she passed Fausta, the old woman attempted to stop her with a feeble hand. Lucia brushed past, picking up speed as she made down the street for her home.

She shut the door without looking back and collapsed against it. Her breath came heaving. Could it be true? Could they have lost the path? Could all of this have been some horrid mistake?

And why was it only occurring to her now? Hadn't she denounced Frieda just that morning for the very same sentiment?

"*Get ahold of yourself*," she gasped out. Shutting her eyes, she focused on the words her brother had spoken months before when their plan was laid.

"*Mithras will guide us. We are only tools in his hands. If it is his will, then this will work. If not, then we need not worry, for he has abandoned us, and all is for naught.*"

He'd been so confident at the time. He'd always been so confident. But what if he was wrong?

"*No*," she muttered, straightening up against the door and clenching her jaw. That was nonsense. He knew the truth. So did she. This would work. It had to.

Her breath slowed, and the dizziness subsided. The ritual had to be completed. She knew what had to come next. She knew what she had to do. Gathering herself, she went up the stairs.

The hallway was dark. Even so, she knew something was off. She'd spent her life in that house, knew every creak and every draft. Now she felt, rather than saw, that something had changed. When she lit a candle, she realized what it was. The door at the end of the hall, *his* door, was ajar.

She paused. In the stillness she could hear his wheezing breath beyond it. He had always had the freedom to come and go as he liked, when he liked, as it had been since long, long before she was born. Still, she'd never seen the door open.

Maybe he had been watching over Blackwood. She grimaced at the thought. He had saved the American, after all. For decades they'd believed him too weak to return to the wilds, but he had appeared the morning before, Blackwood's broken form borne in his arms. Blackwood, who now thrashed in fever dreams through both night and day, owed him his life. And now his soul, she thought with a shiver.

Her fear of him was not new, and the fact that he was her own direct ancestor did little to stymie it. For 1500 years he had watched her family come and go, one at a time. What was she to him? Another meaningless name inscribed on the endless scroll of time?

Only once, as a little girl, she had seen him outside of his room. It was summer and she'd been picking mushrooms for her mother to make a stew. He had been huddled in the shade of a tree, his pale, bony legs pressed to his haunches in a low squat as he gnawed at the fur of a mountain hare. She remembered the deep red of the blood that leaked out over his lips. The cat-eyed stare that returned her horrified gaze. There was nothing behind those eyes. Just empty hunger.

They said he used to be a man. A real man. They said that for many, many, many years, he was a hero. A leader. A righteous follower of their god who guided them through the turmoil of history.

That he'd been able to control it.

Whatever he might have been, all she knew now was that he had become something else entirely.

A horrible thought floated in the back of her mind. What if Mithras *had* abandoned them?

Would that not make this thing their true god now?

57

THE DARK beams of a ceiling materialized alongside the gentle buzz of bees. Blackwood's temples throbbed dully as he coughed. His breath wheezed in his throat, and his tongue felt like rough leather left out in the sun.

Gentle hands guided his head upward until the lip of a mug pressed to his mouth.

"No…" he rasped, pushing the mug away. "No more sleep…"

"*It's not medicine. Just water.*" Lucia whispered tenderly.

He stopped resisting, instead pulling the porcelain to his lips and drinking greedily.

"*Slow down,*" she urged.

He ignored her until she pulled it away.

It took time for his surroundings to come into focus. They were in her room. It was dark outside the window — sometime in the late of night. She sat on the bed before him, a relieved smile on her lips. Behind the smile, her eyes looked sad.

"*What—*" He tried to speak but was cut off by his own coughing. She caressed his shoulders, guiding him to sit up and propping pillows behind his back.

"*Try not to talk. Not yet.*"

As he rubbed the sleep from his eyes, he felt the rough gauze of a bandage on his head. He took more water, and when his throat finally stopped burning he managed to speak. "*What happened?*"

"*I was waiting to ask you the same thing.*" She leaned in and felt his forehead. She was in nothing but a low-cut nightgown, and he was too moony to avert his gaze.

"*I…*" He tried to remember. There were only flashes. The cold, the exhausted horse, Klaus hanging from the branch. Then the great wall of white. "*There was an avalanche.*"

"*An avalanche, really?*" she chided. "*No wonder you're so banged up. What really happened?*"

He ignored her sarcasm. "*How did I get here?*"

"*You rode back the morning after you left. You don't remember?*"

"*No…*"

"*You and the horse were both nearly frozen to death.*"

"*I don't…*" he stuttered. It didn't make any sense. Even through the haze, he recalled leaving the old nag behind. "*I left her out there. She couldn't have found me after.*"

"*She must have. She managed to get you back here just in time. Sadly, she died last week—*"

"*Last week?*" Blackwood made to bolt upright, but a pain sent him back down. "*How long have I been asleep?*"

"*Ten days.*"

"*Oh, Jesus…*"

"*It's alright. You're fine. I'm just happy to have you back.*"

He scanned the room, remembering too well the last time he'd been there and the look of utter betrayal that had been painted across her face when he told her of the night raid. "*I thought you would hate me.*"

"*No. No, I couldn't even if I wanted to.*" She brushed the hair from his face with a warm smile.

It was a profoundly alien experience, being somehow so easily forgiven for something so atrocious. His life had been one of hard edges and vengeance, and the idea that this woman could ever look past what he had done made him uneasy. He didn't deserve it. He suddenly desired to change the subject. "*How's Dubois holding up?*"

Her face sank. "*He's… Well, he's gone, Edward.*"

"*Gone? Gone where? They left already?*"

"*No.*" She took his hand in hers. "*There was an infection. We didn't catch it in time. He went peacefully in his sleep. There was no pain.*"

The news landed like a ton of bricks. "*My god… He had daughters, you know? That's all he wanted. To be with them again.*" A sudden anger swelled inside of him. "*Goddammit!*"

She winced at his volume. "*There's more. Enzo's gone as well. Alive, last we saw. The night you rode off, he must been scared that you wouldn't return. Or maybe that Klaus would succeed in bringing the army back here. He took the mule and headed west—*"

"*He left? He abandoned Dubois? That fucking coward.*"

"*He's just a boy—*"

"*Who else then? Where's Wulfson?*"

Lucia's voice hitched. "*Klaus killed him in his escape. I'm afraid you are the only one left.*"

Blackwood fell back against the pillows and crimped his eyes shut. They were gone, all of them. Yet here he was, tired and broken. And now alone.

No, not alone, he realized as Lucia squeezed his hand. When he opened his eyes, she still sat before him, a beacon of warmth in the cold stretch of mountains that had swallowed so many. He lay there in silence. After some time, she retrieved a damp towel and dabbed his forehead.

"*Will you stay now?*"

"*Why do you want me to stay here so badly?*"

"*Because I... Can't you tell by now?*"

All he could think of was the boy falling from his knife in the wet muck of the trench. Whoever that boy was, his mother was out there in one of the houses beyond the window. His sisters, his aunts, they were there too. They would never forgive him, of that he was sure. "*I'm a bad man, Lucia. You know what I did to your people. I don't know how it happened that I ended up here, but I do know that I cannot—*"

"*I've told you why you're here.*" She forced him to look at her. "*Mithras brought you to us. We are not fickle or stupid, and divine intervention is nothing to scoff at. You must trust me.*"

As outlandish as the idea was, he had no better explanation.

She must have taken his silence as acceptance, because she leaned in and gripped his arm tightly. "*You can hear it now, can't you? His voice, guiding you?*"

The memories were bitter cold, and he struggled to push past the pain of the avalanche, but he recalled well enough the black speck of the raven in the greying storm. Still, he remained silent.

Her eyes diverted to the floor to hide her disappointment. "*Did you at least find Klaus?*"

"*Yes.*"

"*And you killed him?*"

"*Yes.*"

"*And was it worth nearly killing yourself? Just to kill that rat?*"

"*I had to be sure.*"

"*The mountain would have taken him.*"

He shook his head. "*I couldn't risk him getting away, not knowing what he would bring back here.*"

Her voice was low, and her eyes wouldn't meet his. "*You did it for us?*"

"*No. I did it for you.*"

She stood. He thought she would leave, but instead she went to the lantern that sat atop the bureau and wound the wick down. The flame died, blackness overtaking the room.

Something soft and light hit the floor. Before he could imagine what it was, the blankets lifted, and he felt the warmth of her skin as she straddled him. Her mouth caressed his neck, and he had to withhold a pained grimace as she lowered her weight onto his hips. She didn't notice, gently gliding back and forth as her breath grew hot against his ear. "*Don't ever leave me again.*"

Her words morphed into a moan as he slipped inside her. His pain evaporated in a cascade of bliss. She ground against him, their bodies intertwined as he grasped her tight with calloused hands.

"*Say it,*" she gasped.

"*What?*"

"*Say you won't leave…*"

He barely comprehended her words. It didn't matter, he meant it when he pulled her down tight to him and whispered in her ear, "*I won't.*"

58

A HUNK of mud fell from the treads of Hauptmann Felix Neff's boot, adding to the pile that already stained the corner of his desk. He didn't care, reclining further in his seat and eyeing the plate before him that was strewn with hard tack and a pair of burnt eggs. Pained sounds of forced labor bled through the thin wooden walls. What had once been a haunting din had grown dreary to his ears as of late. Still, mixed with the lackluster rations, it managed to dull his appetite.

Much had changed at Rothenspring over the past month. After assuming Major Wulfson dead in the mountains, Neff had returned with the convoy only to find an irate Generalleutnant berating the camp commander — who also happened to be Neff's uncle. The Generalleutnant's furious shouts revealed that not only had Major Wulfson not been acting under orders in his organization and dispatchment of the convoy, but that the orders he had presented were in fact a forgery. As far as their records showed, Major Wulfson had simply taken leave from the Front, and, contrary to his claims, the Kaiser had no intention of dismantling Rothenspring.

The fallout from the debacle had been grand. Wulfson had been branded a traitor, and Neff's uncle had been demoted and sent to the Front himself. Neff had managed to sneak by without similar treatment purely due to his lowly rank. When no other officers in better standing stepped forward to take command of Rothenspring, the duty had been left to him, along with a hesitant promotion. At the time it seemed like a rare stroke of luck. A month later, he'd come to realize it was anything but.

The camp's rations had been slashed. Even the guards were now often forced to feed on the same gruel as the prisoners. He himself enjoyed very few comforts — he hadn't even had a cigarette in a week. A constant menu of hard tack, eggs, sauerkraut, and maybe an occasional bony sausage had left his belly cramped and him miserable. Now the word from higher up was that even more cuts were coming.

There was only one person to blame for all of this: the traitor Anselm Wulfson. If he was still alive somewhere in those mountains, Neff was going to find him and skin him himself.

A knock came at the door. Neff grunted just loud enough to be heard.

Private Kucht poked his head in. "*Hauptmann, the mountaineers have returned. Their Oberleutnant is here.*"

Neff stood quickly, swiping the crumbled mud from his desk and straightening his uniform. "*Send him in.*"

The few mountaineers he'd managed to wrangle were a rugged bunch. They'd been lent to him from an Austrian cousin commanding a unit down south in Italy. Their Oberleutnant strode inside. He was tall and broad with a fleecy beard and a rough demeanor. He moved with the swagger of a man who put combat experience above rank and therefore showed little respect to men like Neff. Despite Neff's rank as a superior officer, the mountaineer took a seat without bothering to salute.

Neff bit his tongue at the slight, sitting stiffly himself. "*Well, what did you find?*"

"*Not much.*" The mountaineer's eyes caught on the plate. "*Are you going to eat that?*"

"*Yes.*"

The mountaineer grunted. "*Well, there is a village up there in the direction they went. Only one we came across. If they're not frozen on some mountainside then I'd say that's where they'd be.*"

"*You didn't check?*"

"*We stopped in. It was a whole village, and there were only six of us. Our commander sent us here as a favor. To scout, not to stumble about poking hornet's nests.*"

Neff ground his teeth. If it were up to him, he'd have this arrogant bastard flogged for insubordination. But at the rate things were going, his own guards might not even listen to him. "*How big was it?*"

"*Hard to say. Could've held… I don't know, maybe a few hundred people. Though a lot of the buildings looked like shit. They're poor mountain folk, nothing out of the ordinary.*" He paused, considering. "*They did say that all the men were off at war.*"

"*So you spoke with them?*"

"*Yes.*"

"*And?*" Neff grew flustered. "*It's like pulling teeth with you!*"

The Oberleutnant gave a dramatic scowl and leaned back. Once again, his eyes migrated to the plate. Neff swore and slid the plate across the desk.

"*Oh, why thank you.*" The mountaineer's scowl flipped to a sardonic smile. "*Yes, I spoke to their leader. She was some woman. She claimed your friend hadn't come through there. Although...*"

"*Although what?*"

"*She seemed quite nervous. Some of the things she said, it was almost like she knew something she shouldn't have. She brought up Switzerland unprompted. Maybe it was nothing, but at the time I felt it was a bit odd.*"

"*So she knew where they were going.*" Neff felt his heart beat faster. This was it. He could feel it in his gut. His ticket out of this damned place. If he could deliver the traitor, there would be no more hard tack and eggs, no more wretched wails in the night, no more bloody Rothenspring.

The mountaineer spoke between bites. "*Maybe. Maybe not. It was hard to tell. She was quite a looker.*"

"*Oh, they're there. They have to be.*"

The mountaineer gave a disinterested shrug.

Neff's excitement was building. Even if Wulfson wasn't there, all he needed was a body. Some torn remains he could return with and claim were Wulfson's. He couldn't stand another day in this shithole. No, this was it. "*Kucht!*" he shouted through the open door. "*Get in here!*"

The scrawny private scrambled into the room.

"*Rally the spare guards, then send word to the regiment — we need a platoon, and horses, more mountaineers if they can spare! And Jägers! Get me Jägers!*"

Kucht hesitated. "*Hauptmann... I... I don't know that they will give us that many men over such a weak lead...*"

Neff puffed out his chest. "*Weak lead, eh?*" He looked to the mountaineer. "*No, our lead is not weak — you saw him there, didn't you? Those villagers were harboring him, ya?*"

The mountaineer paused in his chewing and raised a bushy eyebrow.

Neff leaned forward on his fists. "*You know this man is among the most wanted in the empire, ya? A national hero turned traitor. They know his name all the way up to Berlin and back. I imagine that anyone who were to aid in the delivery of his head to the Kaiser — or even his desecrated, unidentifiable corpse—*" Neff accentuated the words "*—would be due for just rewards. Promotions, I mean. Medals. Other grand rewards as such. And besides, you said it yourself: there's nowhere else he could be.*"

The mountaineer swallowed the last of the egg. "*Ya.*" He nodded slowly, then glanced back to the private. "*Ya, we saw him there alright.*"

59

BLACKWOOD COULDN'T sleep. It'd been three days since he'd awoken to Lucia. Now she curled peacefully in the blankets by his side. The gentle sound of her breathing came as the only noise above the constant ringing in his ears.

He'd never liked the deep quiet of winter nights. It left a man alone too long inside his own head. It gave him leeway to open doors that were best left shut.

Lucia groaned in her sleep and rolled over. Her eyes cracked open as her hand fell on his arm, then, sleepily, she muttered, *"You're awake. What's wrong?"*

"Nothing."

"Tell me," she prodded.

"Would you ever consider leaving this place? Together, I mean."

She let out a long exhale. For a moment, it looked as if she might consider it. *"I can't. I have responsibilities here."*

"I'm sure they'd be fine without you."

Her eyes narrowed.

"That's not what I meant," he corrected quickly.

"I know. But I couldn't, even if I wanted to. My family has led our people for… for longer than even I know. I can't leave. My duties are too important."

"But what duty is it really? This village is dying. The world is big, we could get lost in it."

"No. My duty is to Mithras. To keeping the old ways alive and preserving the sacred truth. I can't do that anywhere else but here."

There it was again. Her god, her profound devotion to him. Blackwood didn't understand it, and he feared he never would. *"What truth?"*

She gave a languid smirk. *"You'll have to stick around to find out, won't you?"*

He didn't push. His brain was burnt out from overthinking. Never before had he been laid up for so long. All hours of the day he spent stuck in this bed, slowly mending from the toes up. The first time he'd tried to walk shortly after waking, he'd collapsed to the ground under his own weight. Even now his hips throbbed and he could feel the yellow remnants of the bruise that circled the broken ribs of his chest. "*You really think the others here will accept me? Knowing what I did?*"

Her eyes opened in full. She sat up, the blankets falling away from her, and reached out to his face. Her delicate fingers ran over the raised scar above his left eye. "*You know, in ancient times they said that Mithras would mark his most deserving disciples with an even cross on their foreheads. I knew the moment I saw you that you were meant to come to this place. So did they. My people already see you for who you are: his chosen. What you did before does not matter now, only what you will do next. They won't just accept you, they will love you, as I do.*"

Her words caught him off guard. It was a ridiculous assertion, and not even one that made sense. "*That scar is an X, not a cross.*"

"*Close enough.*" She smiled. "*Even a god can make mistakes. Mithras is often subtle in his will. Will you make me a promise, Edward?*"

"*That I'll stay? I already did that.*"

"*No. Something else.*"

"*What then?*"

"*There will come a time when I will ask something of you. Something you will be reluctant to do. I need you to trust me. I need you to promise me that you will do it.*"

"*What will you ask me to do?*"

She shook her head with a chuckle. "*That's not how this works. I need you to trust me. Will you trust me?*"

As odd of a request as it was, he didn't have the willpower to deny her. Deep down, he knew she'd become the only thing he had left. There was little in the world he wouldn't risk to avoid losing her. "*I will.*"

She settled her head against his chest. In only a few breaths she was asleep once more. He lay awake, a sudden and horrible thought weaving its way into his head. His scar — it was one of the first things she'd asked him about. Could it be that her interest wasn't based on passion or love, but rather some perceived mark of her faith?

He banished the thoughts from his mind.

Even if it was true, he didn't want to know.

60

IT WAS midday. The sun was warm, a sign that spring was edging ever closer. With less than two weeks left in January, the winter days had been passing quickly since Lucia had lost her brother. She sat at a table in the tavern peeling onions for that night's soup.

Fausta stood at the window nearby. Lucia knew she was watching Blackwood as he chipped away icicles from the houses across the plaza with a long pole. He'd been on his feet for a few days now and was healing well. Despite her chastising, he'd refused not to work. Yesterday he was hauling snow, today he was clearing icicles, and by tomorrow he'd probably be trying to split wood and rebreak his damned ribs.

"*He's healing well,*" Fausta croaked.

"*He is. Not as well as he would put on though.*"

The old woman gave a low chortle. "*That's how they are, men. If it was up to him he'd probably break himself again just so you'd have to pick up the pieces.*" She turned from the window. "*Does he trust you?*"

The knife in Lucia's hand slipped, opening a cut along the side of her thumb. She cursed and pressed it to her mouth.

"*Does he?*"

"*Should he not?*" she asked.

"*This isn't the time for games, Lucia.*"

"*Yes. He trusts me.*"

"*And when you ask him, will he do it?*"

A frustrated growl leaked out as blood dripped down onto Lucia's dress. "*How do you expect me to know that?*"

Fausta left her post at the window. Her feeble gait brought her to the much younger woman's side. With the condescending nature of a mother, she pulled Lucia's hand from her mouth and examined the cut. Satisfied with her assessment, she fished a loose stretch of cloth from one of her many pockets and tied a tight bandage. "*You will live,*" she uttered hoarsely. She didn't let go of

Lucia's hand, instead clasping it between her own. "*It must be soon. I have heard whispers in the wind. Something bad is coming. We must finish this.*"

"*We have time now,*" Lucia insisted. "*We must let him heal.*"

"*Why do you try to put this off, child? You know it must be done.*"

Lucia averted her gaze from the cracked face before her and pulled in a deep breath. Her words were quiet, as if she herself didn't want to hear them. "*What if it doesn't work? What if we lose him?*"

"*Enough of that talk. With all you have seen, where is your faith?*"

Lucia didn't answer. The old woman's words brought with them a certain shame that made her feel like a child again.

"*You love him, don't you?*"

"*Yes,*" she whispered.

Fausta squeezed her hand. "*That is a good thing, child. But you must remember, he belongs to us all.*"

61

FEBRUARY CAME with a false spring. For a week the temperature peaked just above freezing and the midday sun beat down warm on the melting snow. Blackwood had healed well enough. His ribs still ached by the end of each day, and the chill of night left his joints creaking, but he could walk and work and even run if he had to.

The villagers had taken to him just as Lucia said they would. Despite the aura of mourning that still permeated the air, everywhere he went he was met with smiles and kind words. While he was grateful for this, he would have preferred simple anonymity over the growing adulation they seemed to be placing on him. He was still unsure if Lucia had told them about his role in the slaughter of their husbands and sons, but if she had, they seemed eerily unfazed.

It was evening, and he sat in the cozy confines of Lucia's den. A fire smoldered in the hearth, and the sun was low in the sky outside. Minna, the little girl who had been staying with them, sat across the coffee table from him. She glared at him over a pair of playing cards.

"*Check,*" she said.

"*Bad idea,*" Blackwood muttered. He looked to his own cards: an ace and a seven. With the three cards already face up on the table, he had two pair. He plucked a handful of painted pebbles from the pile beside him and tossed them into the pot. "*You don't stand a chance.*"

Minna scowled. She looked back and forth from her cards to those on the table. Finally, she matched his bet. He flipped the next card. It was another seven. Minna's eyes lit up, and he immediately knew she had the last in the set. She broke out in a goofy grin and shoved her entire pile of stones to the center of the table. "*All in!*"

Blackwood groaned, faking disappointment. Despite the fact that his odds of winning were astronomical, he tossed his cards face down. "*Ya, ya, fine. I fold. You win again.*"

The little girl cackled as she swept her winnings into a pile. Their evening poker games had become a ritual at this point, and though he didn't make it easy on her, he had purposely never won. She was a smart child, only ten but already better at reading than he was. Even after her leg had healed, Lucia never pushed the child to return to her own home. It was clear that she had no desire to. The small house on the edge of town now sat derelict, like so many others, and served only to remind her of her dead parents.

Though she didn't show it, Blackwood could tell Minna was hurting. Sometimes he'd hear her crying from upstairs. He wished there was something he could do, something he could say that might offer her some bit of relief from the torment of loss, but teaching her card games and letting her win seemed to give her some semblance of joy, however trivial. That was the best he could do.

He was shuffling the cards when Lucia came through the door.

"*You win again?*" she asked the girl.

"*Of course,*" Minna chortled. "*Tell him we need to play for real money now.*"

"*You'd make him broke.*" Lucia smiled at them both.

"*You just going to stand there and run your mouth, or are you going to join us?*" Blackwood feigned gruffness.

"*I'm afraid not. Sovilo has asked to see you.*"

"*At the tavern?*"

"*In the ravenry.*"

Blackwood groaned. The countless stairs loomed in his mind, and his hips were already sore. He tossed the cards down, eyeing Minna and pointing to the measly pile of stones he had left. "*Don't get sticky fingers. I've counted them.*"

The little girl rolled her eyes.

Despite the disappearing sun, the air was still tepid compared to the frozen days of January. He pulled on his coat as he crossed the plaza. High above, the dark blips of the ravens circled the tower. In the plaza, a score of villagers were constructing a new pyre. He didn't bother stopping to ask who or what it was for — Sovilo would hold any answers he needed.

The Mithraeum was empty when he passed through it. Though the crimson stains of violence were gone, the yawning expanse still brought with it the memories of the carnage that had occurred there. He refused to reminisce, instead focusing his dread on the long climb ahead.

It took him a full half hour to climb the stairs. His breaks were frequent and long, and by the time he emerged at the top of the tower he was panting and covered in a thin sheen of sweat.

Sovilo stood waiting for him. He was clad in only a thin white robe which Blackwood recognized from their odd Christmas ceremony. The flailing bull and the shrill screams felt like a lifetime ago. After weeks spent living amongst these people, the fear he'd felt that night now seemed silly.

Blackwood leaned on the parapet beside the tavernkeeper, catching his breath. "*You must be cold in that.*"

Sovilo smiled. "*I carry my own warmth inside today.*"

Though Blackwood didn't know what he meant, he decided to move on. "*What's the pyre for? Did we lose someone else?*"

"*No. Tonight is a special night. There will be another sacrifice to Mithras.*"

"*I thought you were all out of bulls.*"

"*No, not a bull this time.*" Sovilo chuckled.

"*Then what?*"

"*You will see.*"

The sun had sunk just beyond the mountains ahead. The clouds blazed orange and cast the village below in their smoky hue. The two of them stood in silence, enjoying the beauty of it.

"*You know, Lucia is my niece,*" Sovilo said after some time.

"*Is that right?*" Blackwood fumbled to come up with a better response. Considering their relationship, he initially took the statement as one of protectiveness, but Sovilo's voice was soft and his expression friendly.

"*Yes. Our bloodline has been here since this village's founding. For nearly fifteen hundred years our ancestors have watched over this place. Protected it and kept its secrets.*"

"*That's a hell of a long time.*"

"*It is. A very long time. And something you should know if you plan on becoming one of us. Is it true, what I've heard? That you will stay?*"

"*Lucia asked me to. I told her I would.*"

"*Good.*" Sovilo slapped him gently on the shoulder. "*They will need a strong protector. I believe you will excel in that role.*"

"*I don't know. Seems you've been doing a decent job at that already.*"

"*Ha!*" Sovilo balked. "*Me, no. I have bones like a bird. That is not my role, friend.*" He paused, searching Blackwood's face. "*Has she told you yet?*"

"*Told me what?*"

Sovilo's gaze shifted out over the village below. "*I suppose not. You see, there are things you must understand about this place in order to be a part of it. I was born here, raised into it, so I suppose it was never hard for me to understand. You are not so lucky. You will have to keep an open mind to it as it goes on. Were you raised with religion?"*

Blackwood's mother had been Catholic, and though he vaguely recalled attending Sunday school before she died, any semblance of a religious upbringing had died with her. *"Not really."*

"But you know the story of the Bible?"

"To a degree," Blackwood said, then admitted, *"To a small degree, let's say."*

Sovilo nodded along. *"You know, I have read the Bible. I have also read the Jewish texts and the Quran. They all see it the same way, more or less. Their god is one of omnipotence. He created all matter and formed the world from nothing. I've always found that premise to be a bit silly myself."*

"Mithras didn't make all of this?"

"No, no. Mithras did not create all matter. How could such a being as him be born from nothing at all? Like a baby or a seed, such power must grow and form from something that already is. Mithras was thrust into the quagmire of life much as you or I. His role was to bring order to the universe, not to create the stars themselves. He molded what you see before you from what already was. Before him, chaos alone reigned. There were no creatures or forests or mountains or even seas. Only spirits convulsing and consuming and writhing together in an eternal struggle of death and rebirth. One among those spirits, perhaps the most powerful of all, strove for nothing more than havoc and violence. We gave a name to that spirit eons ago. We called it Arimanius. It thrived in its endless pursuit of destruction for an eternity until Mithras finally managed to defeat it and bring order to things. That was when our world was born. Even then, in Arimanius's defeat, Mithras found that he could not destroy it. How can one destroy the very spirit of destruction? Would that not give it life once more?"

The light was fading now, and Blackwood felt a chill setting in. He had figured that the villagers would try to convert him to their ways eventually, but this was an odd lesson to start with. *"So that's your devil then? This Arimanius."*

"No, no." Sovilo chuckled. *"Not in the way the Christians see it. Their Satan is a being of venality and trickery — a fallen angel intent on corrupting the human soul. Arimanius is not an immoral spirit. It has no interest in the souls of men. It is a force of pure chaos and destruction, the maw by which matter is obliterated for no reason and without sensibility. It is not selfish or conniving. Just hungry and single-minded."*

It started to feel as if the old man's musings were leading somewhere specific. Blackwood wondered if his own actions were being targeted. *"What does all of this have to do with me staying?"*

Sovilo's voice dropped. *"Lucia told me that you were the one to kill our menfolk."*

Blackwood's blood ran cold. He took a half step back, but Sovilo placed a reassuring hand on his arm. *"Stop, please. It is fine. I'm telling you this because you must understand it to move forward. When you committed that act, it was the spirit of Arimanius moving through you. We all have some bit of him inside of us. That is why we as men exist — why Mithras created us. When he defeated Arimanius, he shattered him into pieces and hid them deep in the earth. Fragments of a whole, never to be reunited. Still, the worst parts of this spirit were too powerful to hide. Mithras knew that they would escape, that they would find each other, that they would unite once again and consume all that he had created. Thus, he decided that they needed to be safeguarded in his absence. That is when Mithras made man in his own image. Only a being who bore some bit of his own strength could hope to contain even some small fragment of that horrid spirit. You see, that is what we are: lockboxes. Lockboxes meant to contain those tiny fragments of destruction. He spread what remained of Arimanius thin through us all, knowing that it would power our worst aspects — our hatred, our rage, our blind propensity for ruination. He gave us in turn his own strength, his honor, his courage, so that we might contain this evil in his absence.*

"These things he did not trust to any of his other creations. A wolf does not torture a hare for pleasure. The birds in the sky do not wage war." He kicked at the ropes coiled on the tower floor. Their nooses still bore the rotting grime left by the guards' corpses which now lay somewhere in the forest. *"How many friends did you watch die slowly at the hands of those men? Did they not take some barbaric pleasure in it?"*

It was more true than Sovilo knew.

"I am telling you this," Sovilo went on. *"Because Arimanius is strong within you. Yet, as I've seen with my own eyes, you have proven your ability to control it. You can guide it and unleash it when just. Actions in war do not reflect actions in peace. Whatever you did in those trenches, Mithras saw it. He blessed you with his own hand."* Sovilo nodded to Blackwood's scar. *"And he guided you here for a purpose. The same way he guides us all. You must accept this. You must also accept what Lucia will ask of you soon."*

Blackwood shoved aside the score of burning questions to focus on the last and most crucial in his mind. *"What is she going to ask me to do?"*

"*To embrace that part of you. To let it grow and to control it. She will ask you to become the Sarvàn.*"

Blackwood scoffed. "*What are you on about?*"

"*I'm afraid that is all I can say. You will get your answers, but it is her place to give them.*"

Blackwood stared at Sovilo for some time. The old man seemed finished with his odd speech, simply looking off toward the darkening sky as he began to hum. Though his message was cryptic, his delivery was one of extreme confidence — he actually *believed* all of this. At first, Blackwood imagined that maybe he was just a bit mad. Then the idea snowballed as he thought of the village itself, of how austere this place was. Of what a lifetime spent in such seclusion would do to a person's mind.

"*You're a strange man, Sovilo.*" Blackwood shook his head. "*Have you ever left this place?*"

Sovilo laughed. "*Once. I went to the flatlands with my father to trade pelts for steel. I remember people stopping in the street to point and laugh at the pale little boy with white hair. They mocked me for my complexion. I imagine that if I had been born amongst them they might have come to hate me for it. Here, it is not like that. Here, I am special. A child born as I was holds the light of the sun beneath his skin. I am blessed by Helios, the sun runner. Like you, I am chosen.*"

His devotion suddenly made sense, Blackwood realized.

"*You must go now. Find Lucia, she will tell you what comes next.*"

"*Hopefully a chilled beer and some warm food,*" Blackwood joked, trying to hide his discomfort.

"*Yes. Hopefully.*" Sovilo shot him a sad smile. "*Always trust in Mithras. He is the light.*"

Blackwood didn't delay any further. The air of the tower had grown too peculiar for his liking. He left Sovilo behind as the old man muttered a prayer in Latin. In the darkness of the stairwell he found it hard not to dwell on Sovilo's words. With each step he only grew more perplexed, until he finally pushed the thoughts away. He was tired and hungry, and his bones ached worse than ever. He wanted a hot meal and the warmth of Lucia's bed. But most of all he found that he wanted the truth.

He passed through the Mithraeum and out the stone doorway that led to the plaza. He had only just made it down the trio of steps when a shout rang out above. A blur of white hurtled from the sky and smacked the ground with a bone crunching *thwack*. Blood spattered over his boots.

Sovilo lay in a crumpled pile before him, brains spilling out and ribs smashed nearly flat from the impact. A growing pool of deep crimson stretched out around him, and the once pristine robes shone red.

Caught in shock, Blackwood stared upwards. The ravens circled the tower far above in silence.

62

LUCIA SANK into the sofa. Minna was gone, sent away with the other women to prepare the pyre. The parlor was warm, and a small teacup steamed on the coffee table before her. She uncorked a bottle of her father's schnapps. Despite the fact that he never drank, he'd kept it in a cabinet in his room for as long as she could remember. She'd always imagined that he'd saved it for the day that his son took his place as head of the village. If only he'd known how things would turn out, then maybe he would have indulged sooner.

She poured a splash into her tea. When she picked up the porcelain cup, it rattled against the plate. Her hands were shaking.

The door opened. Blackwood strode in, his footsteps heavy. Small drops of blood stippled his pant legs. His face was drawn underneath the beard that had come to fill his cheeks, and his voice came low. "*Why did he do it?*"

"What do you mean?"

"*Sovilo. He just threw himself off the tower. None of your people even blinked an eye. Hell, they were already building him a pyre. You knew that though, didn't you?*"

She sipped the tea. It was too hot, and she wished she'd just drank the schnapps from the bottle. "Yes."

"*Why did he do it?*"

"Because he had to."

"That's not an answer."

"*It is.*" She drank again, this time taking a gulp that burned all the way down.

"I can't play these games anymore, Lucia," he warned her. "*Tell me what's going on. Tell me what it is you want from me. Tell me why everyone keeps dying around us.*"

"I didn't want you to find out like this. They, the others I mean, they felt it was time. But I don't know that that's true."

"*If you don't tell me, you know I will leave.*"

The truth in his words hurt her. "*I know.*" He opened his mouth but she cut him off before he could speak. "*You made me a promise, do you remember?*"

Doubt clouded his face. "*Yes.*"

"*I need you to fulfill it now. I need you to… to do something that will frighten you. I need to become something… unholy.*"

Blackwood scoffed.

"*Come.*" She finished the tea in one gulp, wincing as it burned its way down. Then she rose and nodded for him to follow. He did so hesitantly. Together they ascended the stairs and passed down the hallway to the final door. The bees buzzed in the walls as she pulled the lantern from its hook and finagled a key into the oversized lock. When it clicked open, she stopped. "*Whatever happens, you must stay calm. Do you understand?*"

"*I do.*"

She pulled the door open. The air stank as it had always stunk. The room was large, taking up nearly half of the second floor. Old straw lay in heaps against the walls and dirt was scattered over the floor. In the corner lay a pile of bones, mostly small things like rodents and hare, but a few gnawed-at deer skulls lay among the mess. She repressed the urge to turn around, to leave and lock the door behind her before Blackwood could see what she didn't want to show him. But they'd come too far. It was time.

There was a small alcove. That's where the old one spent most of his time. Even before they rounded the corner she could hear his rasping breath. He recoiled as the light of the lantern peeled around the corner. Only the glistening dome of his head shone over a threadbare blanket. A tangle of wispy grey hair hung from the filth-mottled flesh.

"*Jesus Christ…*" Blackwood muttered beside her.

She shined the light closer and spoke softly. "*It is time, grandfather.*"

The old man only shivered in response.

"*Can he understand you?*" Blackwood took a step forward.

Slowly, the blanket lowered and the old man's face lifted into view. Blackwood's momentum suddenly reversed as he stumbled back in horror. The dirt that had stained the old man's skin for centuries flaked and peeled from pale flesh. His pupils, vertical black strips centering dark orbs, darted to follow the American's clumsy retreat. A jagged mess of yellow teeth hung behind cracked, protruding canines and red lips still stained with the blood of his last feeding. He crouched there, unnaturally long and bony fingers clutching the blanket tight.

Despite its monstrous appearance, Lucia felt a deep sadness. He was so frail and broken, yet he still held on.

"*I didn't want you to see him like this,*" Lucia breathed. "*I didn't want you to be afraid of him.*"

"*What the hell is it?*" Blackwood had fallen back against the wall and one hand clutched the handle of the ornate dagger on his belt.

"*He is the Sarvàn.*"

Blackwood stared in horror, lost for words.

"*Long ago he was a priest. He led the men who founded this place. It was he who Mithras guided to these caves. It was he who discovered the power hidden here beneath the mountain, and he who took that power, and used it to save his people. Without him and his legacy, Mithras would have been forgotten. But we are here now, in Mithras's name, to secure* his *legacy, and to keep a great evil from the world.*"

"*You're mad.*" Blackwood's head swung back and forth, as if trying to shake away the image before him. "*This is a demon.*"

"*He is not, despite everything. You owe him your life, at that. He is the one who brought you back from the cold. My whole life, he has never left the village. My father would say the same, and his before him. He has grown too old and too weak for the wilderness. Yet he climbed through the ice and the snow to rescue you. You would be dead if it were not for this man.*"

"*Stop calling it a man.*"

"*He is a man. A servant of Mithras. But there is a demon inside of him. A piece of a spirit so wicked that it would tear through our world without cause or distraction, laying waste in its path and leaving nothing but death in its wake. You promised me you would do as I ask. Just this once, I need you to fulfill that promise. You were chosen by Mithras to take his burden. To alleviate this poor soul and take his place.*" She nodded to the dagger in his hand. "*You must do it tonight, after we burn Sovilo.*"

Blackwood's eyes went wide. He looked from her to the Sarvàn, then back to her. "*No.*"

"*Please—*"

"*No! Of course not! Are you— Have lost your goddamn mind?*"

She knew he was spiraling. For all of his quiet self-assuredness, she'd never imagined him devolving into hysterics. "*You need to do this. For the sake of us all.*"

"*It's a goddamn monster, Lucia!*"

"*He's not a monster,*" she came back sharply, her patience waning. "*He was a great man, a godly man who has held the burden for far too long—*"

"*Is this why you've been fucking me? You— you what? You're saying you want me to turn into this... this thing?*"

"*No! It won't be like that! You can control it! For the longest time my people were too cowardly to do what was needed, to find a new host. Their faith had faltered and with it he grew weak. Now we are strong! We will not falter again! If this spirit escapes him in death, it will be a plague upon the earth, you understand that? Yes?*" She reached slowly for Blackwood's hand, her voice softening. "*If you do this, if you take it into yourself, you will be a saint. A godly man free of sin and with the adulation of all who follow you. With this power, you can protect us and we will love you in return. Is that not what you want?*"

He yanked his hand away. "*You used me,*" he spouted with vitriol.

A flash of anger ignited inside of her. "*And you killed my father. You killed my cousins. Those women out there, you killed their husbands and sons and lovers. Each of them were men with the courage to have accepted this burden with grace. Despite this, Mithras chose you, not them, and now you must fix what you broke. That is why you are here. Can't you see it? That is why he brought you to us!*"

Blackwood gave her a bitter look. "*You're a fanatic. And I'm just some fool who fell into your lap.*"

She tried to grab him as he shoved past and stomped down the stairs. She scrambled after him. "*You gave me your word!*"

"*Then we're both liars.*" He slammed the dagger down on the table by the front door as he left.

63

BLACKWOOD BARGED into the tavern. The dining room was dark. The fire had smoldered, and the air carried an unfamiliar chill. The villagers had just finished lumping Sovilo's broken remains atop the pyre as he'd stalked by them in the plaza. He'd refused to look at them. They were no longer innocent victims of circumstance. No, they were willing participants in whatever madness was unfolding here. The kind the madness that ragged pastors had screeched about on the street corners of Billings over their crudely painted signs. Only this wasn't some invisible existential threat. These people had a goddamn demon in the flesh.

He bolted the door and managed to mute the screaming voices in his head long enough to secure the building in what little ways he could. Circling its inner perimeter, he slammed open the doors to the side rooms and ripped curtains shut. It was a meager attempt at security. If someone wanted to get in, they could and they would. Knowing this, he kept his rifle slung tight to his shoulder.

Sovilo was dead. As far as he was concerned, this building belonged to him now — at least for tonight.

He finished on the first floor and moved to the second. Each of the rooms had been tidied. The beds were made and the furniture arranged as it had been the night of their arrival. He stopped in the room that had been Dubois's. It was cold and lifeless. In that moment he realized how much he missed the odd Frenchman. In his life he had made few friends whom he didn't simply consider to be amicable results of his circumstances. Dubois was not that. He was a kind man, one Blackwood cared about. Now the Frenchman's daughters were doomed to fatherlessness. They would never know the bravery he showed in the face of his enemies. They would never learn of his fortitude or the strength he mustered in that dreary little village in the mountains. They would never know that he died wishing only to see them again. For them he would just be another memory, cursed to fade away in the haze of time.

As he crossed the sitting room his heel stuck to the floor. He peeled it away and knelt to feel the tacky residue. He held a finger to his nose. It was sweet and floral, the smell of honey.

Muffled voices bled through the windows. He leaned against the edge of the frame, concealing himself as he looked out over the plaza. The pyre had been lit. Smoke poured from Sovilo's shattered and bloodied carcass. Lucia had taken her place at the head of the circle that surrounded it. He couldn't make out her expression, but he heard the murmur of her words in Latin. The others echoed her every so often as the prayer built. The sight made him sick to his stomach.

When they finished, the women dispersed. He hustled downstairs and watched the door. The rifle hung heavy on his shoulder. He was unsure if he would even be able to bring himself to level it should one of them — especially Lucia — come in. But no one came to the door.

Finally satisfied that he would be left alone, he crossed to the bar and hunted through the rows of stacked bottles. In the back of the third shelf he found what he was looking for. The old paper label was faded and flaked away, but when he held it to the light he managed to make out a trio of words written in English — Single Malt Highland.

Scotch. Thank god.

A glass wasn't necessary. The old cork crumbled in his grasp when he pulled it out, and he drank straight from the bottle. It took three solid slugs for the flush of warmth to reach his hands. He took a fourth, and then a fifth and set about building a fire in one of the hearths. When it was raging, he pulled a chair before it and sat, gazing into the flames. Everything had been a blur since Sovilo had splattered over the stones before him. He knew he needed to slow down, to reestablish order to his psyche before he went any further and did something rash. Without a plan, he was no better off than the dead.

No matter how hard he tried to focus, those slitted cat-like eyes burned in his mind.

Blackwood was no stranger to evil. He'd seen things that would iron the folds out of most men's brains. But this… this was otherworldly. Ungodly even. The more he thought on it, the more he realized that it was not just the creature's image that had shaken him so. It was something deeper. Something so innate and recessed inside of him that he had not immediately comprehended it.

He had recognized something in that horrible face. Something so familiar that it had, in a way, felt like staring into the distorted reflection of a funhouse mirror. As if some part of him existed inside of it, or it in him. As if they had been in each other's skin.

These thoughts disgusted and terrified him. He muscled down another hefty gulp of scotch and coughed hard. The liquor was doing its work, dissolving his inhibitions by the minute. It drowned his fear, eating at it like acid until all that was left was an empty clarity. He sat back and closed his eyes, concentrating.

Lucia had betrayed him. There was no other way to see it. She had never loved him, likely never cared for him above her wicked desire to please her wicked god. She'd played him like a fiddle, targeting him and drawing him in since that very first moment they met while shoveling the plaza. His anger grew as he recalled her flirtatious game on Christmas night, the way she'd so inexplicably forgiven his past. He was nothing more than a means to an end to her.

This realization hurt him more than he ever thought possible. Despite knowing the truth, he also knew his own feelings toward her were real, and they remained. This alone made him hate himself as much as he now did her.

A knock at the door brought him crashing back to the moment. He stood too quickly, swooning with drunkenness. The knock came again as he seized the rifle from the table beside him.

"*Who is it?*" he called through the door.

"*Silja,*" a delicate voice answered.

He paused, trying to recall anyone he'd met by that name. "*Who?*"

"*It's Silja.*"

It was the quake in her voice that drove him to unlock the door and ease it open. Still, he kept the rifle ready in hand.

A young woman stood out in the cold.

"*What do you want?*"

"*I saw you come here, and…*" her voice petered off. She was thin and young, no more than in her early twenties. She was not dressed for the cold and shivered under a thin shawl.

He looked beyond her for others, but she was alone. He opened the door further, allowing her to pass into the warmth.

She stopped just inside the door as he closed it and slid the bolt back into place. "*I'll ask you once more,*" he said sternly. "*What do you want?*"

She was shaking, and her eyes were avoidant. "*I saw you come here earlier. I know you must be concerned. Perhaps even afraid—*"

"*Afraid?*" he scoffed. She flinched, and he realized that he was drunker than he'd thought. He brushed by her, back to the fire and the waiting bottle. "*I'm not afraid. I'm fucking terrified. Do you know what Lucia has locked up in her house?*"

"*I do. We all do.*"

Blackwood took another drink. Whiskey sloshed out as he slammed the bottle down on the table. "*You all need to leave. Nothing good can come from this place — from that thing.*"

"*I have considered it in the past. But I couldn't do it. This is my home, I don't want to leave.*"

"*Then you're a fool.*"

"*Please,*" she said softly. "*I didn't come here to argue.*"

Blackwood stared into the flames. "*Then why are you here?*"

Instead of an answer, he heard the soft flutter of fabric over the snapping flames. When he turned, her dress was already lowered to her waist, revealing her breasts. He stammered to tell her to stop, but before he could find the words, the dress had slipped away completely. She stood before him naked and unashamed.

"*What are you doing?*" he managed.

She shifted nervously. When she spoke, her voice swelled with sorrow. "*I was with child once. She died inside of me. That was four years ago, before they took my husband away. Though I never met her, I loved that baby girl with all my heart. Mithras, in all of his ultimate wisdom, he spared my child from the pain and hunger of these last few years. He knew that we wouldn't be able to give her the life she deserved. That's not true anymore. You've come to heal our wounds, to make us whole again. Please, Sarvàn… I beg you to give me another.*"

Blackwood's jaw slacked. "*What are you— Stop this. Put your clothes back on.*"

Her lip quivered as her eyes slowly rose to meet his. Without another word she began to advance on him.

"*No.*" He held out a hand to stop her. She seized it and pressed it to her breast.

"*Please,*" she pleaded as he yanked it away.

"*Stop!*" he commanded with a sharp step back. The fireplace stood behind him, and he found himself pinned.

"*Do it*," she whispered as she pressed herself against him. Her hand slipped under his belt before he could stop her. The rifle clattered to the floor as he seized her by the arms and pushed her back, but he hesitated as her soft grip closed around his manhood.

She looked up at him with desperate doe eyes, pleading and seductive, and for a moment he almost broke and gave in.

"*No!*" He jerked away. He stumbled on a set of cast iron fire pokers and nearly fell as they clattered to the ground. She came after him once more, but this time he managed to hold her off. "*Get out, now.*"

"*We can do it however you want, Sarvàn. You call me her name—*"

"*Get out!*"

She stopped. The firelight glinted off her naked skin as tears filled her eyes.

He braced himself against the table, ready to ward off another advance. "*Leave, now. And don't come back here.*"

Without a word she returned sullenly to the pile of clothes by the door. She wept while she dressed, and before she left, she paused. "*I'm sorry to have bothered you,*" she said, her voice barely a whisper. Then she was gone.

Alone once more, he collapsed to his chair and drank heavily. Head in hands, he cursed this place. The room swam around him. "What have you become?" he asked out loud. "You came here to end it all, not damn yourself further."

It was true. That day, long ago in his grandfather's cabin, he'd made a choice. He'd followed the long path of war rather than the short path of the shotgun's second barrel. Still, the result was always intended to be the same. Yet here he somehow was, the subject of an insane religious clan's affection, being asked to become some abdominal beast in exchange for what? A new hope? A life somehow more wicked than the one he came from?

But was it more wicked?

If there was something he had no desire to confront, it was the unacknowledged temptation he felt to go along with it all. Despite the blaring alarms that filled his head, a part of him wanted to do it. To do it all. To take this on. To become this thing. To have taken that enticing young woman and given her exactly what she had come for. Deep down, a fire burned in him that begged to be released.

That part of him was what he hated most of all.

No.

He would not do it.

He could not do it.

He could not give in.

The memory of Fletcher's erratic voice came to him. "They used old Sawney for his brawn and seed, ate up his soul and his sons, and spit him right out in the end. Bloody witches. They'll get what they want in the end."

There was no question in Blackwood's mind anymore — Fletcher had been right all along.

64

"*HE IS leaving,*" Fausta said over the wind.

She stood beside Lucia atop the tower. Together they watched Blackwood's shadowed figure cross the plaza in the moonlight. He was headed west, away from the village.

"*We can't force him to do it,*" Lucia muttered. "*You know that's not how it works. He must accept it willingly.*"

"*If he doesn't, then all is lost.*"

Lucia bit her tongue. "*What more can I do?*"

"*You can pray. Pray to Mithras that he finds his way back.*"

"*And if he doesn't?*"

Fausta remained silent, letting the truth Lucia already knew hang in the air.

65

NEFF LED the way through the shadowy confines of the ravine. In his wake came a mounted cohort of thirty men. Half their ranks were a mix of Rothenspring guards and mountaineers while the rest comprised of the dreaded Jäger — huntsman and foresters who were already well accustomed to a life of hard living amongst the elements long before the first shots of this war. Where the others had suffered the trail, the Jäger seemed at home on it.

The Oberleutnant of the mountaineers rode up to join Neff. He was the same disrespectful lout who had originally discovered the village, and he and his men were the only ones who knew the way. "*We should make camp here, in the shelter of the ravine,*" he proclaimed.

Neff pulled his horse to a stop and looked down to his watch. The full moon above illuminated the face as the short hand ticked past midnight. "*How much farther is it?*"

"*As we're riding?*" The mountaineer considered. "*Four hours, maybe five. It depends if the weather stays calm. I say we regroup here and arm up before we make our entrance.*"

"No. We push on. There's no reason to let them see us coming in the light of day. I don't want to have to give chase."

The leader of the Jägers rode up to them. Though he was older than them both, he was a meager enlisted Oberjäger. He stared ahead into the dark. "*The Oberleutnant is right. We should send scouts ahead to discover the layout, that we may come up with a proper strategy. Tomorrow night we could be among them as they sleep, striking in silence before they even know we are there.*"

"*How many times must I remind you who is in command here?*" Neff puffed out his chest. This one, much like the mountaineer, spoke with a lack of respect that irked him. "*You Jägers, always so eager to sneak about in the dark. These are women we are speaking of. Do you imagine it will be some sort of battle that you cannot handle?*"

The Oberjäger gave a look to the mountaineer, who smirked back. Neff knew the meaning of their silent exchange, and it scathed him to the core. No, he wasn't a hardened veteran of combat. No, he'd never fired his gun in anger. But that didn't define a man's character. He was a goddamn Hauptmann now, and he would be much more than that once he delivered Wulfson's corpse to his superiors.

"*Then what exactly is your plan?*" the mountaineer asked, not bothering to hide his exasperation.

"*I want to glean the truth from them. I want to see this woman's face when she lies to me. I want to watch the life fade from that bastard Wulfson's eyes after I pull the trigger myself.*"

"*You just want to play with them first, don't you?*" the mountaineer muttered, followed under his breath by, "*Sick Rothenspring fuck.*"

Neff bristled. "*What I want is for you to follow orders! You forget your rank, Oberleutnant.*"

The mountaineer made a show of looking around, counting aloud as he waggled a finger toward the trailing column of troops. "*Six, seven, and… eight.*" His finger landed on Neff. "*I count eight of you out here with us. Eight little guards among twenty-two big, strong men. Perhaps you forget your position, Herr Neff. Don't forget how easily men disappear in these mountains.*"

Neff stuttered for a response, but the Oberjäger held out a hand. "*Enough. He means nothing by it, Hauptmann. Tell us the plan now so we may get on with it.*"

Neff steadied himself atop his horse. He was fuming, but the mountaineer's words had held truth. Among the rows of soldiers at their back, only the seven other men he'd brought with him from Rothenspring looked out of place. While the true soldiers were trim and organized, the guards looked like a ragtag assortment one might pull out of a deadbeat alehouse at the end of the night. He cleared his throat. "*We will surround them before first light. When they wake, I will find their leader, and I will find the truth.*"

"*And if this Major of yours is not amongst them?*" the Oberjäger asked.

Neff eyed the three flamethrowers lashed to horses amongst the ranks. "*As I told you before — burnt corpses are hard to tell apart.*"

66

A ROOSTER'S crow hung in the air as Lucia awoke to a shake. Minna stood over her. "*Lucia! Wake up! There is a man here!*"

"*Edward?*" Lucia mumbled, still caught in the daze of sleep.

Minna shook her head frantically. Her cheeks were red and her breath came hard as if she'd been running. "*A soldier.*"

Lucia bolted upright. Dawn graced the streets as she slammed the window open and shoved her head outside. The morning was unseasonably warm, and the air was pregnant with a thick fog that rose from the snow. Through it, she saw the lone figure straddled atop a horse in the center of the plaza. His uniform was grey, the same as her brother's had been. Beyond him, barely visible through the fog, she made another figure moving about the edge of the village. Then another. When she looked down the opposite street, she saw them there too.

They were surrounded.

"*Minna, I need you to hide,*" she said as rushed to dress. The little girl complied, scuttling away to whatever nook or cranny the children had deemed the best hiding spot. As Lucia left her room, she paused at the door across the hall. It was unlocked as it always was. She fished the keys from her pocket and clicked each of the three sturdy locks into place. It was in cases like this when the Sarvàn had saved their people in the past. But he was too old now. Too weak. It was better that he remained concealed, lest they manage to kill him and release what roiled inside.

By the door, she donned her bearskin coat. It had belonged to her father and his before him — the last bear in these mountains to be seen. Her grandfather — her actual grandfather, not the creature who had sired her ancestors — had slain it alone with a bow and a spear on a cold spring morning. He had died wrapped in the folds of this coat. It seemed only appropriate that, should this be her doom, she do so as well.

When she made to grab the ancient dagger that Blackwood had left on the table, she realized it was gone. "*Minna...*" she hissed. She didn't blame the girl. Perhaps it was better off with her anyway.

The soldier in the plaza gave an empty smile as she approached. His steed flinched unsteadily beneath him, revealing a gross inexperience in horsemanship — odd, considering the land he must have traversed to get here. Similarly, his eyes betrayed a lack of hardiness. He was no warrior, Lucia could tell, yet he wore the rank of Hauptmann all the same.

"*Where is your leader?*" he demanded once she came to stand before him.

"*I am the leader here.*" She stood tall and glared.

"*You?*" He raised an eyebrow. "*Never found a husband to hold your leash? I find that hard to believe.*"

"*That's her,*" a second rider called as he rode into the plaza. Lucia recognized this one — the mountaineer from weeks before.

"*You again,*" she said as he kept the horse in a trot, circling the both of them.

"*You don't look too happy to see me,*" he said nonchalantly.

"*Why have you come back?*"

The mountaineer shrugged. "*Perhaps I was drawn back by the schnapps. Perhaps by your beauty. Perhaps both.*"

Lucia scowled. "*You're in luck, on one account at least. I have a whole case of schnapps for you if you leave now.*"

"*Enough,*" the Hauptmann commanded. "*Oberleutnant, have you found anything?*"

"*Mmm...*" The mountaineer didn't take his eyes from Lucia as he spoke. "*Tracks. Leading out of town. Two sets of them on foot.*"

Two sets, Lucia thought. Someone had gone after Blackwood. Who?

"*Then you know what to do,*" the Hauptmann said. "*Perhaps the Major has already flown the coop. Find out if it's him, and don't return without a body.*"

The mountaineer pulled his horse to a halt. His gaze went from Lucia to the Hauptmann, then back to Lucia. "*Don't harm this one. I like her. She's got… spirit.*"

"*I'll do as I damn well please. Now, go.*"

The mountaineer gave her a wink before riding off. As he disappeared into the fog he let out a shrill whistle. "*Come on, men! There's a hunt afoot!*"

The Hauptmann took a moment to gather himself and dispel the frustration that was clear on his face. "*I am Hauptmann Neff. We are here to arrest one Major Anselm Wulfson.*" His eyes thinned. "*Does this name mean anything to you?*"

"*Only in that your underling there has said it to me before,*" Lucia said. "*I will tell you the same thing I told him. No one has come through here since before the snow fell.*"

"I implore you to think critically here." Neff leaned in and his words came with a false gravitas. "*This Major Wulfson, he is a traitor to the German cause. I know the man well enough. If you have harbored him, I will find out. Make this easy on yourself. Tell me the truth.*"

"*I have,*" she said sternly.

He grunted and leaned back, fiddling to unstrap the clasp of the holster on his belt. "*This man I am hunting, he forged orders and tricked many men into actions that have cost us good German lives. Beyond that, his actions cost me and my uncle dearly. So when I tell you that I will do anything to uncover the truth of his whereabouts, I mean it.*"

"*You've yet to tell me what this has to do with my village.*"

Neff surveyed the surrounding houses. More riders had emerged from the fog. They filtered through the streets, staring back at the frightened faces peering out from behind drawn curtains. "*I know he was here. There is nowhere else for him to have gone. I think he is still here, in hiding. Bring him out, or you will suffer the Kaiser's wrath.*"

Lucia scoffed. "*We are German—*"

"*You are nothing but hillwalker scum.*"

Lucia spoke over him. "*We are German! How dare you threaten us. Our men fought and died for the Kaiser. You will not harm us, and understand that if you do, you will be strung up by the very superiors you are trying so desperately to please now.*"

Neff sucked his teeth. "*Not if he's here. Empty the houses. Get everyone out in the open where I can see them.*"

"*No.*"

In a clumsy motion, Neff yanked his pistol free and fired a shot in the air. Lucia didn't flinch. The other riders paused to look to their leader.

"*Empty the houses! If they resist, kill them!*"

Lucia winced as doors crashed open and her people cried out as they were dragged from their homes. More men materialized from the fog. They were more than a score and armed heavily as if headed into the maw of battle. They rode to and fro, shouting orders and firing into the air. As one passed she caught sight of the black steel pack on his back and long spout in his hands. A flamethrower. Her heart sank.

Neff smiled at her. "*Do you want to change your answer now? Or would you prefer the hard way?*"

She shook her head, staring into those nasty eyes. They were ripe with an evil pleasure. They were eyes she wished to close forever. "*I can't give you what I don't have.*"

"*I'm not here for what you're willing to give, hillwalker. I'm here for what I can take.*"

67

BLACKWOOD TRUDGED beneath the green umbrella of the conifers. The snow was wet and heavy and stuck to his boots with every step. His pace was slow and his mind elsewhere, caught in the quagmire of self-doubt.

Had he made the right decision in leaving? The alternative was horrible, yes, but what was he traveling towards now? Would it be back to the Front for him, to inflict more pain and suffering on desperate men just trying to survive? Or would he go home to a place where no warm welcome waited? To another range of mountains just like this one — empty and cold? He'd come to this continent for a simple purpose. A purpose that he thought he had given up on. That he would have, had this whole endeavor not become a card game with the devil himself.

In truth, what drove him away from Melvilla now more than anything else was the burning need to put that slippery seductress's betrayal far behind him. He'd never been duped before. Not by a woman, at least not in that way. His hard countenance had saved him from the pain of heartbreak his whole life. Yet his past avoidance of it only made it hurt more now.

He knew he could forgive her, in time. He knew he was weak like that. But he couldn't go back. Every time he considered it, he saw that horrible thing huddled in the straw — the wretchedness and misery in its eyes as it had looked up at him from the shadows. He shuddered at the memory.

A noise came at his back. At first, it sounded like melting snow thudding down from the trees. He paused, peering through the forest and listening until he made out the distinct timber of voices and beating hooves. He didn't move, instead preparing himself for Lucia to emerge through the brush. Then it hit him: there were no more horses in the village.

He slipped behind a large rock just as the German soldiers came into view. The first was young and thin with a clean-shaven face and narrowed eyes that were glued to the trail of footprints Blackwood had left behind. Behind him came another, and another, until six were in view. They were less than a hundred yards away through the forest and closing quickly. Each appeared well-armed and vigilant.

With nowhere to run and no way to conceal his tracks, Blackwood steadied his rifle on the rock. He picked his targets as they flitted between the trees.

His opening shot hit the first man, the scrawny one, in the center of his chest. He fell without so much as a scream. One of his feet caught in the stirrup and his horse fled in a blind panic, dragging his corpse along with it. The gunshot sent the others scattering for cover. Blackwood's rifle followed them, and he struck the next before they knew the direction of their ambusher. This one cried out and clutched desperately at the blood that jettisoned from his throat before dropping limp to the snow.

Blackwood missed his third shot, and before he could place a fourth, the riders spotted him and returned fire. Bullets exploded against the stone and whizzed overhead. Splinters flew from trees and mud and snow kicked up in spurts. Blackwood held steady, lining up the bead of his front sight with a protruding head. Past the flash of his barrel, it erupted with a fine pink mist. He ducked behind the cover of the stone to reload.

Hooves pounded the earth as he shoved round after round into the rifle's breach. He managed to get the bolt closed and roll to the ready as a single brazen rider closed within yards of him. The rider, a gruff looking man with a short blond beard and the rank of Oberleutnant emblazoned on his uniform, fired at the same time as Blackwood. The horse fell dead, and the Oberleutnant was launched forward into the snow. Blackwood didn't see him land, as he himself was spun around in a violent circle by the bullet that tore through his shoulder. His rifle flipped from his grip.

A surge of adrenaline drowned the pain as he yanked his pistol free and scrambled for better cover. A shadow darted into view between the trees accompanied by a yellow flash, and a horrible pain ripped through his chest. He fell face-first to the ground gasping for air.

"*I got him!*" one of the soldiers called out to the others.

Blackwood struggled to roll over. He managed to raise the pistol in the direction of his attacker and fired it blindly. The soldier yelped and dove for cover. More bullets snapped overhead, and he roared as the Luger bucked in his hand. It clicked empty. In a final act of desperation, he pulled himself to his hands and knees and crawled toward where the rifle had fallen. A bullet tore through his thigh, and he crumpled.

"*Did you get him?*" a desperate voice called.

"*Ya, ya I think so!*" another answered.

"*Is he dead?*"

"*I don't know!*"

"*Oberleutnant! Are you alive?*"

The man beyond the rocks, the one whose horse Blackwood had shot from beneath him, groaned. "*Ya. Ya, I'm fucking alive. Is he dead?*"

"*I don't know!*" one of the panting voices repeated.

Blackwood lay still, enveloped on all sides by the wet snow. He felt a terrible warmth spreading beneath him.

"*He's down!*" the Oberleutnant's voice came louder as he stepped over the bullet-riddled stone. He scanned Blackwood over the sights of his rifle.

"*Is it the Major?*" one of the others called.

"*How the fuck should I know?*" The Oberleutnant bent low and slapped Blackwood gently on the cheek. "*You alive? Come on now, you're alive. Are you this Wulfson we've been looking for?*"

Though it was weak, Blackwood managed a laugh.

"*Oh, this is funny, ya? You kill three of my men, and you think it's funny?*" Beneath his scruff, the Oberleutnant's face was stained red with anger. He jabbed a finger inside Blackwood's shoulder.

Blackwood didn't cry out. He let the pain wash over him. His eyes felt heavy, and he thought of his grandfather's stories, of the boatman that would come to take him away. He'd always known it would end this way. He was just surprised at its suddenness.

Better now than later, he supposed.

"*Calvin, gather the horses. Bruno, come here. Help me load him up. We need to get him back to the village. Neff says he knows the bastard's face. If this is him, we can be finally done with this whole charade.*"

The name brought Blackwood back to consciousnesses. Neff. He knew that name from Rothenspring: the stringy little officer who'd helped run the place. He imagined Neff and his pack of sadistic guards descending on the village and what they would do to those unarmed women. What they would do to Lucia.

When Blackwood opened his eyes, the Oberleutnant faced away, addressing the underlings still concealed in the forest. "*Did you hear me?*"

"*Yes, Oberleutnant.*" Only one voice answered.

The Oberleutnant paused. "*Bruno, do you fucking hear me?*"

No answer came.

"*Where is Bruno?*"

"*He was just here,*" the soldier answered in confusion.

One of the guard's bayonets hung from Blackwood's belt. His grip was weak as it closed around the smooth handle and slipped it silently from its sheath.

"*Bruno!*" the Oberleutnant shouted, scanning the trees.

"*Bruno, where are you?*" The other soldier's voice had grown fearful. "*Oberleutnant, the second set of tracks, maybe there is anoth—*" His voice cut away in a wet gargle.

The Oberleutnant's rifle snapped to his shoulder, and he stepped back, nearly within Blackwood's reach. "*Calvin!*" he shouted. "*Calvin, what happened?*"

The forest was silent besides the slow drip of melt.

"*Calvin!*" the Oberleutnant retreated further, nearly stepping on Blackwood's leg.

Blackwood lunged. The Oberleutnant shrieked as the bayonet plunged into the back of his knee. When he toppled, Blackwood rolled atop him, grappling for his throat. Blackwood was too weak, and the Oberleutnant easily cast him aside, reversing their position and mounting him. Rough hands closed around Blackwood's throat, and the gruff face that glared down screwed up and flushed with effort. Blackwood clawed weakly at the hands. It was no use. He was outdone.

The edge of Blackwood's vision had already begun to darken when five pale, bony fingers clasped the crown of the Oberleutnant's skull like the talons of a raptor. Their yellowed nails burrowed through red flesh. Blood dribbled down over the German's astonished face and, with a single mighty lurch, his head ripped back with such violence that it shattered every vertebra in his neck.

68

IT HAD been nearly two hours since Neff and his men had descended on the village. They had searched it in a grid, smashing doors and attic hatches and burrowing beneath floorboards. He sat in the tavern now, a pint of beer in hand as he waited for his men to finish their ransacking.

"*I found something!*" one of his men called from a side room. He strode into the dining room, a German-issued pack held out as if displaying a trophy fish he had just caught.

"*Is there more?*"

"*Ya. Stuffed under the bed in there, more packs, some uniforms but no rank. You want me to get it all?*"

"*No, no. That is all the proof we need.*" Neff settled back in his seat and sighed. A wave of relief coursed through him. He had come to have his reservations over the Jägers' and mountaineers' loyalty. Should he have lied about Wulfson to his command, one of them might have ruined the whole thing. But this, this was proof enough that the contingent of men he'd watched tramp away from the convoy had found their way here. "*Is there any sign of Wulfson himself?*"

"*No, not yet. He could be hiding, but this gear looks to have not been used in some time.*"

"*Maybe they had the good sense to kill him.*" Neff stared out through the window to the nearly seventy women kneeling on the melting cobblestones. Only one stood among them — the one called Lucia. The one who had lied so blatantly to his face. He seized the pack and strode out the door.

"*You! Woman! How would you explain this?*" He brandished the pack as he approached her.

She looked unimpressed. "*As I told you, our men served in the army. They were cut down in Italy and France. What you will find in the tavern belonged to the few who returned.*"

"*And where are they now?*"

"Dead. They brought a sickness with them. It took many from us this winter. That is why those things have remained untouched. I would not be holding it so casually if I were you."

Neff recoiled instinctively, tossing the pack aside and swiping his hand across the waist of his coat. He knew she was lying. He was pretty sure, at least. "*Tell me the truth! Where is the Major?*"

The woman's face curled into a grimace. "*You know, it was a man just like you who came and took our men from us. A daft flatlander with less sense than a braindead mule—*"

"Watch your mouth."

"*The only thing I'll be watching is your bones as they decay in the depths of the outhouse where they belong—*"

"*Hauptmann! There is something here you should see,*" one of the Jägers called from up the street.

Neff didn't shift his glare from the uppity headwoman. Her cavalier attitude in the face of death put a bad taste in his mouth. He had rather expected — no, *desired*— the satisfaction of forcing whatever shell of lies these people had maintained to crack open. It seemed she would deny him that.

"*You, come with me.*" He flicked his pistol toward her. "*One false move, and I'll have to dig my answers out of your brain.*"

Two of the Jägers awaited them outside a large house. Its parlor was still warm, and when they were led upstairs, Neff caught the odd sound of buzzing from the walls. The soldiers stopped at the end of the hallway and nodded toward an open door. Neff prodded Lucia to enter first. When he followed, he found the Oberjäger awaiting them. For such a callous man, he looked as if every ounce of courage had been stripped from his soul.

"*What is this?*" Neff kicked at the piled straw and bones. "*It stinks like a barn. Do you people all live like this?*"

Lucia didn't answer.

"*Fucking hillwalkers. I don't know what I expected. Not this, that's for certain.*"

"*Why were there so many locks on the door?*" the Oberjäger asked quietly.

Neff glanced back to the shattered locks that had been kicked in, then to Lucia. "*Well?*"

"*To keep people like you out.*"

"*What were you keeping in here?*" The Oberjäger's voice remained hushed, and his eyes darted along the claw marks that marred the walls.

"*Oberjäger, what is wrong with you? Speak up like a man,*" Neff demanded.

The Oberjäger's leather face had grown sallow. He grabbed Neff forcefully by the arm and yanked him out into the hall.

Neff pulled away with a squeal. "*What the hell do you think you are doing, man! Keep your fucking hands off me, or I will have you—*"

"*Shut up!*" the Oberjäger snapped. "*Shut up and listen to me. We need to leave this place. It is not a godly place. There is no good that will come from staying here.*"

Neff stared into the battle-hardened man's eyes. They were full of panic. "*Get a grip, soldier. What is wrong with you?*"

The Oberjäger spoke through gritted teeth. "*I have been throughout the world and seen more horrible things than you can possibly imagine, boy. You need to trust me now — this place is not what you think. These people, they are not like us. Places like this... they do not exist for you and me. These women are witches, or demons, or both. You don't feel it in the air? In your bones?*"

Neff scoffed. "*Have you lost your mind? And you call me 'boy' once more, I'll have you court marshaled. Is that understood?*"

The Oberjäger looked away and shook his head slowly.

"*If you're so afraid, then perhaps you'd be better off guarding the old women.*" Neff meant for the words to be scathing, but the man before him didn't seem to notice.

"*He's right, you know.*" Lucia smirked from the doorway.

"*Is he?*" Neff spit on the floor at her feet and looked back to the soldiers waiting down the hall. "*Take her to the tavern. Then burn this place first.*"

69

BLACKWOOD FELT his life ebbing away. The canopy of trees bobbed in his vision as thin arms cradled him. It was carrying him, to where he did not know. All he knew was that his death was close at hand.

The trees gave way to blurred images of home and of the village. He could see things that were and things that were not. He saw his grandfather's cabin and the old man's weathered smile and crooked teeth. He saw the first girl he'd ever been with, Emilie, the daughter of a pastor from Billings. She was kind and sweet but had been too good for him in his own eyes. He saw Dickie and others, men he'd fought beside in the trenches, men he'd saved and others he'd watched die. He saw Dubois and McCulloch, Enzo's boyish face, and even Fletcher. But more than any of them, he saw Lucia. He saw her playful glances and warm smile. He saw their daughter and their son. Both had her green eyes, and he felt his own filling with tears as he mourned what never was or would be.

The creature, this thing they called their Sarvàn, set him down against an old tree stump. It was rotten and soft, and when his head fell back against it, he saw the ravens circling above. They sang to him now, their voices no longer a harsh cackle to his ears but a rippling ballad of sorrow and regret.

Cold fingers gently clasped his face and guided his eyes forward. He looked upon the Sarvàn. Whereas before he'd felt disdain, now, in the light of day, he saw beyond the monstrous features to something else. There was a weariness in the ancient folds of its skin. A glint of humanity nestled deep behind those cat-like eyes.

"*Why did you do it?*" Blackwood's lips formed the words, but the breath to fuel them came shallow.

The Sarvàn didn't answer. Blackwood didn't know if it even could. Yet its hand gently caressed his cheek, and the edge of its mouth lifted in the most subtle way, revealing a sad smile. Blackwood understood. Not just the creature's meaning, but all of it. He had his answer, and it was good enough. He nodded.

Blackwood could barely feel it as the Sarvàn pressed the cold metal of the ornate dagger into his hand. He didn't resist as it raised the blade to its own heart and pressed the steel tip to a fleshy gap between its ribs. It held it there, waiting, and Blackwood knew that what would come next was up to him.

"Fuck it," Blackwood muttered in his native tongue. "Why not?"

He pressed the dagger forward with what little strength he had left. The blade bit easily through its papery skin. Black blood oozed over the steel but the creature did not recoil. Instead, thin, ragged wings — like those of a fledgling bird — arched out from beyond its shoulders as it drew a single, long breath. Its hands shook as it gathered the dribbling blood in its palms. Then it raised them to Blackwood's face.

"*Oblatum est...*" The words rasped from its lips, and the ravens echoed them above.

"Yeah..." Blackwood breathed. "Yeah..."

The hands tilted forward, and the blood seeped into his mouth. It tasted of iron and fire, and Blackwood choked as he drank.

70

NEFF SAT across from Lucia. They were alone in the tavern. On the table between them stood a bottle of schnapps and two glasses. Outside, the distant roar of flamethrowers mixed with the desperate wails of the villagers as they watched their homes go up in flames.

Neff took his time pouring a glass, letting the sounds play out for her benefit. He took a sip. It tasted of honey and mint. *"Know that it was you who forced my hand here, headwoman."* He filled her glass, but she didn't take it. *"It is not personal. You have put me in a tight spot, and your choices now matter more than ever. Produce me a body or the man himself, and I will forgive you this slight. If you do not, I will be forced to dispense justice as I deem fit."*

"You mean you will leave no witnesses to your crimes against your own countrymen."

He shrugged. *"Semantics."*

"As I said before, your Major is not here."

Neff groaned. It would seem he had no other choice than to put the interrogation methods he'd learned at Rothenspring to the test. He finished his glass and rose from his seat. Before he could place it down, the door opened. Hugh, one off the heavyset guards that sported the metal pack of a flamethrower, shambled through. Smoke poured in behind him. *"The Jäger are leaving!"*

Neff was caught off guard. *"What? No, tell them to stay! Tell them I command it!"*

"They don't care," Hugh panted out. *"They are already mounting up."*

Neff hurled the glass across the room where it exploded against the bar. "Dammit! Superstitious cowards! You, gather the others and go watch the women in the plaza. If they move, shoot them." He called to the two guards who stood outside the door. "You two, get in here. You will stay here with me."

The two men entered and took positions by the door, but the one bearing the flamethrower looked nervously over his shoulder. *"The villagers have already begun to disperse. Without the Jäger there are only a handful of us. We can't gather* them back up through all this smoke and chaos. Should we not just shoot them and be done with it?"

Neff returned Lucia's stony glare as he considered the question. "*We will, if this one does not start talking!*"

"*I told you all I know. Do with it what you will,*" she said evenly.

"*Go now, do as I say.*" Neff waved the guard off as he circled the table. He leaned close to Lucia's ear as if to whisper something but instead grabbed her by the nape of the neck and slammed her face down into the table. She cried out as blood dribbled from her nose. He followed with a strike that sent her sprawling to the floor.

She appeared in a daze as he moved to stand over her. "*It's a shame it had to be this way. You're quite pretty, you know.*" He leaned down, taking a fistful of her hair and pressing it to his nose. It was sweet, like the schnapps. "*What a waste.*"

She was less dazed than he'd thought. As he hunched over her, she lashed out with a brutal kick to his groin that sent him stumbling back. The guards didn't have time to intervene before she was on him, clawing and biting and punching as he gasped in pain. One of the guards managed to catch hold of her and yank her back as the other delivered a harsh butt-stroke. It drove the air from her lungs and sent her coughing to the floor. She retreated, slithering against the wall as Neff clutched his bleeding face.

"*You cunt!*" He fumbled with the pistol on his belt until it came loose. "*You stupid whore!*"

She spat at him as he raised it. Without any hesitation or thought, he fired a round through her calf. It was her turn to gasp in pain.

He lined the barrel up with her face. "*I might have taken you back with me. Not now, though. I have no need for a rabid bitch.*"

From somewhere far away in the village, a deep tone cut through the smoke-filled streets. It echoed over the mountains and pierced the thick glass of the windows. It came again and again in long droning waves. It was a horn of some sort, though Neff had never heard any like it.

He eased his finger from the trigger as a devilish smile grew over Lucia's bloodstained face.

"*What is that?*" he demanded.

Her words came from deep in her belly. "*He's come.*"

From outside came a scream and a gunshot. Then another and another until the plaza rang with the symphony of combat. They were not women's screams. They were crackling and deep. The screams of dying men.

Neff kept the pistol trained on her as his vision turned to the windows. The smoke that clouded the plaza before them lit up with the flashes of gunplay. They were under attack — by whom, he had no idea. Were these women, so pathetic and ragged, even capable of such violence? Was anyone? These were elite soldiers, the Jäger at least, yet to his ears it sounded like a massacre.

A dark figure passed by the window, and the door slammed open. All three guns in the room turned on the man that came through. It was the grizzled Oberjäger. Blood coated his uniform, and his arm hung useless and shattered at his side. At its end, his hand was gone, replaced by a bleeding stump. He slumped against the table, gasping and wide-eyed.

Neff's focus zeroed in on the egregious wound. He barely managed to stutter out, "*W-what happened to you?*"

The Oberjäger ignored him, his ghastly face turning to Lucia. "*It caught us outside the village as we left. It's over now. Call it off. We surrender.*"

"What the hell are you talking about! Answer me, dammit!" Neff shouted.

"*They've conjured the devil,*" the Oberjäger muttered, his eyes never leaving the woman.

A single man's voice peeled above the chaos outside. Neff recognized it. It was Hugh, the man he'd just sent off. A man he'd played poker with in the barracks of Rothenspring. A man whose wife he'd met and whose children he'd held. Hugh screamed in terror, repeating the same thing over and over again, "*Neff! Neff! Help me! Help!*"

Neff watched through the window as his silhouette formed through the wall of smoke. He was running toward the tavern. The tank of the flamethrower bounced atop his back, and its nozzle trailed behind him like a forgotten tail. Before he could reach the door, something seized him from behind, and he was yanked violently backward. He kicked and screeched as he disappeared into the haze. Neff's mouth fell open as he stepped closer to the glass, lip trembling. A blinding flash accompanied a plume of flame that bloomed skyward. The shockwave from the flamethrower's explosion washed over the tavern, shattering the windows and knocking Neff to the floor.

As suddenly as they had begun, the last of the dire screams cut away.

Everything had happened so fast that Neff hadn't truly processed any of it. In the sudden silence, he struggled to reorient. Smoke drifted lazily through the windows along with something else — a horde of tiny, flitting insects. They dispersed through the room, landing on tables and crawling along the walls as they filled the air with a fierce buzzing. One landed on his hand, and he looked down at it in shock. It was a honeybee, of all things. It stung the soft flesh between his fingers, and he shook it away angrily.

As reality began to set in, he felt his breath coming hard and fast. He began to hyperventilate and had to lean against the fireplace to keep steady. "*You, and you,*" he gasped out, jabbing his pistol toward the two guards who now quaked in the corner. "*Go, find the others. Find out what is happening.*"

One shook his head, and the other just stared dumbly.

A low chuckle filled the room. It started slow, then built into a deep rhythmic belly laugh. Neff looked in horror to the crazed woman still leaning against the wall. He raised his pistol. "*What have you done?*"

She nodded to the Oberjäger, who had collapsed to the floor and now lay unmoving. "*He already gave you your answer, Herr Neff.*"

He fired a round into the wall beside her. She only laughed harder.

"*What is it, woman? Tell me! Tell me or I will kill you all!*"

Her laughter petered away as her gaze shifted to the top of the stairwell. She smiled warmly. "*Welcome back, my love.*"

The room exploded with the song of gunfire, shrieks of terror, and the raw sound of ripping flesh.

Epilogue

1983

A LONE woman hiked through the mountains of Bavaria.

Her name was Isabella. She had stepped off from Switzerland nearly a week before. Her pack was heavy, but she was young and strong, only twenty-three last September. Among the things she carried were a tent, four sets of clothes, a compass, plenty of food, a small pocket knife, and a yellowed old map with a line of German scrawled across the bottom.

Late spring in the Alps had come with untold beauty. The forests budded with bright green, and flowers filled meadows far beneath the frozen mountain caps. Mushrooms hid in the shadows and birds sang in the sun. She stopped at a curve in the trail to pull her camera from its case. It was a Minolta, an expensive one her parents had gifted her for her graduation. She used the telescopic lens to snap a photo of a reddish-brown hare as it lazed on a hillside. A pair of ravens flew overhead, and the hare scampered away. She adjusted her pack and moved on.

Over the next hill she caught sight of what she had been searching for. It was a village, quaint and antiquated, more so even than she had expected. Then again, she had not really been sure of what to expect at all. It sat nestled between the mountains beneath a frighteningly steep cliff. Atop the cliff, an ancient looking tower looked out over the valley. She sighed in relief. It *was* real. For most of her journey, she had been worried that she was chasing a ghost.

It took her over an hour to reach the freshly sown fields that sprawled on the village outskirts. She saw a girl there and waved. At first, the girl seemed taken aback. Then she smiled warmly and waved back.

"Hi there! Could you tell me where I am?" Isabella called out as she fished for the German dictionary in her pack, unsure if these people would speak English.

"Are you lost?" Though her accent was thick, the girl answered her in perfect English. She was in her late teens with long blonde braids and vibrant green eyes.

"No. I mean, not really. My name is Isabella. I think this is the place I'm looking for."

"Where are you from?"

"New York," Isabella told her, then realized that she was in a foreign land and this girl might not know the States. "America," she added.

The girl laughed. "I know where New York is."

"Sorry." Isabella felt a bit foolish. "I, uh… I wasn't sure if this place actually existed. You know, you're not on any of the atlases I could find."

"Yes, I'm aware. We are a shy people. What brings you here?"

"I'm looking for a woman named Hilde. She's probably quite old at this point."

"Hilde? Do you know her surname?"

"No, I'm sorry." Isabella pulled the old map from her pocket and held it out. She pointed to the line scribbled at the bottom in German:

I will always love you.
–Hilde

The girl looked the map over twice, her eyes thinning. "Where did you get this?"

"My grandfather passed recently. We found this hidden in his things when we cleaned out his house. He was from Italy and was in the first World War, a POW here in Germany. He never talked about his life before he came to America, but I found this, and I…" she drifted off sheepishly. "I don't know. I guess I just wanted to know more about him. He was a hell of a guy — started his own business, raised a big family, was always there when anyone needed him. I guess I just wanted to know more about him." When the girl didn't respond, she waved toward the mountains. "Plus, you know, I've always wanted to see the Alps in spring."

The girl's face lightened back into a smile. "I understand. They are beautiful. However, I'm afraid the Great War was quite a long time ago. I do not know any Hilde. Although…" She paused.

"What is it?"

"Come. Let me introduce you to my grandmother. Perhaps she would know."

The girl led Isabella into the village. The buildings were old but pristine. Some looked as if they'd stood for hundreds of years, while others appeared to have been built shortly after the turn of the century. Flowers adorned doorsteps and vines wove over walls and lattices, making the whole place appear as if it was the setting of a children's fantasy.

They entered one of the newer homes — newer being relative, as it was still older than most of the houses Isabella had seen in New York. The parlor was spartan and the walls displayed a rich mix of tapestries, mounted skulls, and framed photos of smiling faces. The girl, whose name Isabella realized she had not gotten, led her upstairs and knocked on a door.

"Come in," an elderly voice croaked from the other side.

The bedroom was cozy, and at its center a very old woman lay propped up in her bed. The girl went to her side and took her hand.

"Grandmother, we have a visitor. This is Isabella. Isabella, this is my grandmother, Lucia." She motioned between them. "Isabella has come all the way from America to find us."

The old woman, not a day under ninety, raised an eyebrow. Despite her age, her hair was still a silky silver that cascaded over her shoulders. "From America, you say? That is quite a journey just for us."

"Quite a journey indeed." Isabella glanced out the window to the people milling about the street below. "I have to ask, does everyone here speak English?"

"Yes," the old woman said. "My husband taught us."

The girl cut in. "She wants to know about a woman named Hilde."

"Hilde?"

The girl motioned to the map, and Isabella handed it over. The old woman stared at it for some time. "Hilde," she finally muttered. "Yes. Hilde. She was a wonderful girl. Passed away in childbirth many, many years ago. She is young Enzo's great grandmother."

"Enzo?" Isabella interrupted. "I'm sorry. It's… odd, that was my grandfather's name. Enzo Accardi."

"I know." The old woman smiled at her. "I remember him well. Hilde cared for him greatly. As we say, he was the one that got away."

Isabella clapped her hands in excitement. "This is incredible! We really know nothing of what happened to him before he came to America. Do you think you could tell me what he was like? What happened to him here? How was it that he ended up in these mountains?"

The old woman sighed and handed the map to her granddaughter. "My memory is tired, dear. All I can tell you is that he was a strong boy, perhaps sixteen years of age when he passed through here. A brave boy who followed his heart. I'm afraid everything else has been lost to the years. You'll understand someday, I'm sure."

Isabella struggled to conceal her disappointment. The old woman coughed, then coughed again, harsher this time, and the girl rushed to tend to her. Isabella noticed the old woman's cracked lips break apart in a whisper as the girl leaned close.

Afterward as the girl ushered Isabella outside, she seemed reluctant to hand the map back. "You should not have this. As I said, we are a shy people."

"I'll need it to find my way back," Isabella told her, then, "I'm... I'm sorry if I've intruded. I just... I wanted to know what happened to my grandfather before he becomes just another memory."

The girl handed over the map. Isabella folded it gently and returned it to her pocket. As she scanned the plaza, her eyes caught on a darkened inlet in the cliff face. "What is that?"

"Nothing but a cave," the girl said. "You should leave now. A storm is due in the next few days. It would be smart for you to beat it."

Isabella noticed the shift in the girl's voice. The welcoming undertone was gone. "Is there a room here that I could rent for the night? I've been on the trail for days — a hot shower and some real food would do me wonders."

"I'm afraid not."

"Did I... did I do something wrong? I hope I haven't offended you or your grandmother, I just—"

"No, no," the girl reassured her. "Like I said, we are a reclusive community. Outsiders tend to make the old timers a bit uncomfortable."

"I didn't mean to—"

"It's fine, really."

"May I ask you a question?"

"Yes."

"This boy Enzo, do you think it's possible... you know, that he's related to me?"

The girl shrugged. "Anything is possible, I suppose."

"Do you think I could come back here some day? Maybe find out more?"

The girl shook her head. "Isabella, you seem like a nice woman. Please take heed of my words: do not ever return here. When you finish your journey, you will burn that map, just like your grandfather should have. Now go. Go, and be far from here by the time the sun sets."

The sun had grown low in the sky as Isabella trudged between the trees. The trail was thin here and the wilderness thick. She had not been able to shake the eerie feeling that had smoldered inside of her since stepping off from the village, nor forget the way the people there had amassed in the plaza to watch her leave. She attributed the prickling sensation that rose along the back of her neck to this as she plodded along, lost in thought.

Without warning, a man erupted from the brush ahead. He was young, perhaps in his thirties, and bare-chested beneath a patchy bearskin coat. His face bore a thick beard, and he carried the fresh body of a large ibex over his shoulder with ease. Isabella startled at his sight. She had not heard even a whisper of him in the quiet woods. He glared at her from dark eyes, nearly black, and she stared back in surprise.

"Hello?" she ventured, realizing that, despite his odd garb, he was likely a hunter from the village.

He didn't respond, and the longer she stared at him, the more frightened she became. When he finally stepped forward, it was at a brisk pace. He passed by without a word, moving silently in the direction of the village. From beneath his cowl she caught the raised pink of a scar over his left eye.

Acknowledgements

First and foremost, I must thank the strange woman who lurks around my house, bears my children, and edits my books. Though she often calls me by the dogs' names and makes me use silverware, I believe some affection has grown between the two of us. I wouldn't trade her for anything.

Thanks to all those friends and family who have supported me in the endeavour of writing over the past decade, especially to my beta readers Buck and Anne for their valuable insights, and to Suzanne for her keen eye.

Lastly, I want to thank you, the reader. Small time authors like myself face an increasingly difficult series of hurdles these days. Thank you not only for picking up this book, but also for seeing it through to the end. I hope that you enjoyed it.

OTHER WORKS BY

THE NORTH WOODS

Over three million acres of dense woodlands make up the North Maine Woods. There are no major towns. No public roads. Nothing but forest for as far as the eye can see.

When two Marines and their Corpsman reunite after a decade apart, they find themselves caught up in the mystery of their former squad leader's disappearance. With little more to go on than a handful of disturbing charcoal sketches and the whispers of a local legend, they plunge into the depths of one of America's last truly wild places.

But the trees themselves begin to whisper dark secrets. Secrets of trafficking and violence. Of rotten science and blood. Of something else that lurks in the shadows of the pines — something ancient, savage, and hungry.

Praise for The North Woods

"*The North Woods* is both a terrifying horror novel and a sincere and heartfelt story about coming home from war... Hoover throws his hat in the ring with that other Maine horror author, and not only holds his own, but brings something entirely new to the genre. This story made me feel like I would gladly face eldritch horrors in the Maine woods if it meant I could go on one more patrol with the boys."
-Kacy Tellessen, Eugene Sledge Award winning author of *Freaks of a Feather: A Marine Grunt's Memoir*

"*The North Woods* reads like a Stephen King novel that went to war. Hoover writes with the infantryman's sardonic wit — a mixture of wisdom and dark humor only found in fighting holes and smoke pits."
-Mac Caltrider, journalist for *Coffee or Die Magazine* and founder of *Pipes & Pages*

"I love this book, it is at once an exciting character-driven horror novel and a deep conversation about life, evil, and redemption. And perhaps more importantly than anything, it's a window into the very real struggles of combat veterans even after they come home."
-Christopher Packard, author of *Mythical Creatures of Maine*

DOUGLASS HOOVER

THE ACCURSED HUNTSMAN

Haunted by the hunting accident that took both his leg and the life of his best friend, wilderness guide Jack Steward exists on the wooded fringes of society. When an infamously foolhardy millionaire offers Jack the means to reconcile his past wrongs in exchange for participating in a remote archaeological dig along the coast of Nova Scotia, Jack straps on his worn prosthetic and ventures forth into a world of mystery, deceit, and horror. Little does Jack know that the mismatched gang of killers, junkies, has-beens, and frauds he is about to join will uncover an artifact that will shake the very foundation of history, and maybe even grant him the ability to defeat the demons of his past. However, the expedition also unearths a horrific truth – the artifact wasn't the only thing hiding deep under the Nova Scotian cliffs...

Praise for The Accursed Huntsman

"You can feel the skies darkening as you read, swelling with moisture and violence, ready to unleash on those foolish enough to be caught in the open. I rate this book a sturdy four spades and I highly recommend that you pick this up and let it consume you this fall."
   —*OAF Nation*

"Reminiscent of campfire stories, urban myths, and a Stephen King horror story, this chilling tale is the stuff from which nightmares stem. The dynamic plot and spine-chilling storyline kept me on the edge of my seat until the story reached its harrowing conclusion."
   —*Readers' Favorite*

"A rip-roaring adventure through the bloodstained underbrush of the human psyche. I simply couldn't put it down."
   —*Joseph Donnelly*

About the Author

Douglass Hoover is a writer, craftsman, veteran, and an avid outdoorsman. He has written four novels and holds an MFA from Emerson College. When not slaving away over a keyboard, you can find him hunting, blacksmithing, farming, or bushwhacking skinwalkers in the forests of rural Maine with his wife, their little goblin, and the pack of wild dogs that nip at their heels.

Follow their adventures on Instagram
@StripedDogForge
@DouglassHooverAuthor

Find handmade outdoor equipment and signed books at
www.stripeddogforge.com

Perhaps most importantly, sign up for our newsletter at
www.douglasshoover.com for updates on future projects

Made in the USA
Middletown, DE
29 August 2025

13238379R00227